ALIGHT

ALIGHT

BOOK TWO OF THE GENERATIONS TRILOGY

SCOTT SIGLER

DEL REY
NEW YORK

Alight is a work of fiction. Names, places, characters, and incidents either are the product of the author's imagination or are used fictitiously. Any resemblance to actual persons, living or dead, events, or locales is entirely coincidental.

2016 Del Rey Trade Paperback Edition

Published in the United States by Del Rey, an imprint of Random House, a division of Random House LLC, a Penguin Random House Company, New York.

Del Rey and the House colophon are registered trademarks of Random House LLC.

Originally published in hardcover in the United States by Del Rey, an imprint of Random House, a division of Penguin Random House LLC, in 2016.

This book contains an excerpt from the forthcoming book *Alone* by Scott Sigler. This excerpt has been set for this edition only and may not reflect the final content of the forthcoming edition.

Library of Congress Cataloging-in-Publication Data

Names: Sigler, Scott, author.
Title: Alight / Scott Sigler.
Description: First edition. | New York : Del Rey, [2016] | Series: Generations trilogy ; Book 2
Identifiers: LCCN 2015051412 (print) | LCCN 2016014322 (ebook) | ISBN 9780553393170 | ISBN 9780553393163 (ebook)
Subjects: | BISAC: JUVENILE FICTION / Action & Adventure / Survival Stories. JUVENILE FICTION / Science Fiction. | GSAFD: Science fiction.
Classification: LCC PS3619.I4725 A785 2016 (print) | LCC PS3619.I4725 (ebook) | DDC 813/.6—dc23
LC record available at lccn.loc.gov/2015051412

Printed in the United States of America on acid-free paper

randomhousebooks.com

2 4 6 8 9 7 5 3

Book design by Caroline Cunningham

To my nieces, Riley and Sydney.

May you grow to be strong and wise in all things.

I love you.

THE BIRTHDAY CHILDREN

Italics=deceased

Parentheses=missing

	EM'S GROUP
◎	Aramovsky, B.
○	(Bello, K.), Savage, M.
◑	O'Malley, K.
✪	*Yong, J.*
☼	Spingate, T.
⊕	

	BISHOP'S GROUP
◎	
○	Cabral, R., D'souza, M., *Harris, J.*, Ingolfsson, O., Johnson, Y., Okereke, E.
◑	Borjigin, G., Opkick, Q.
✪	Bawden, Y., Bishop, R., Coyotl, U., *El-Saffani, T.*, *El-Saffani, T.*, Farrar, Q., *Latu, S.*, Visca, W.
☼	Beckett, G., Gaston, X.
⊕	Smith, K.

XOLOTL KIDS	
◎	Walezak, B.
○	Abbink, D., Abrams, G., Alves, W., Andreasson, R., Ansel, R., Aucciello, A., Baardwijk, K., Bardsley, M., Bohner, S., Broz, R., Buffone, V., Chowdury, H., Csonka, A., Doyle, D., Esser, L., Grosser, K., Harman, N., Hoffman, M., Howland, P., Jahoda, E., Jepson, K., Kysely, W., Lestrange, E., Marshall, U., Maus, L., McBride, D., Mehmet, G., Pecora, R., Perreault, I., Poole, A., Pope, F., Queen, J., Raske, Y., Rigby, J., Romagnoli, T., Roth, D., Savona, M., Schoettmer, A., Sharman, I., Sherazi, V., Simonis, E., Snider, G., Szwarc, D., Taylor, Z., Tittensor, A., Tosetti, J., Tosto, I., Traverso, M., Van Kane, P., Vincent, G., Wieck, L., York, J.
◑	Abrantes, J., Aeschelman, T., Bariso, L., Bemba, H., Derrickson, N., Schuster, T.
⍟	Abdul, V., Afoyalan, O., Argyris, E., Arkema, T., Blaha, H., Boesch, C., Brankovich, U., Brown, K., Bruhn, P., Cadotte, W., Cody, B., Darzi, I., Değirmenci, P., Derrickson, N., Dreesens, A., Fields, I., Giroux, D., Holub, N., Horn, H., Hornick, D., Horvat, P., Hrabe, C., Krejci, M., Kysely, S., Loncar, E., Marija, B., Metharom, F., Metharom, V., Mohammed, R., Muller, V., Myska, S., Olson, J., Pokorny, C., Radic, S., Resnik, I., Schovajsa, S., Thorn, J., Tosi, C., Uzun, A., Vendi, M., Wakefield, Q., Xanth, S.
⚙	Cathcart, M., Kalle, C., Nevins, A., Peura, N., Zubiri, B.
⊕	Pokano, L., Yilmaz, F.

PART I

BEGINNING AND BELONGING

ONE

A stabbing pain jolts me awake.

I open my eyes to darkness. *Total* darkness.

My head feels thick, my thoughts clogged.

The pain is where my neck meets my shoulder, but it's already fading. I remember a sting just like it, but much worse. That day . . . was it my birthday? Yes, I think so. My *twelfth* birthday.

A chill floods me—this has happened before.

I am in a coffin.

A monster is coming for me, a rot-black thing with one ravaged eye.

Matilda.

No . . . that's not quite right. It's different this time. I can move my hands . . . last time they were held down. My fingers rise up through the darkness. I feel a lid, so close it's almost touching my face and chest. I need to escape before the monster destroys me.

I need a weapon.

The spear . . . where is my spear?

I punch at the lid, I scream and I hammer at it with fists and knees.

A noise, a whir of machinery; I feel the coffin lid start to slide down toward my feet. Light hits me, burning my eyes even through tightly scrunched lids—*I can't see.*

I lash out wildly, blindly, punching and clawing.

Hands grab my wrists.

"Em, it's okay!"

A girl's voice. I recognize it: *Spingate.*

"Calm down," she says. "Everything is fine."

Her hand takes mine. Our fingers clasp tightly. Her skin is warm and soft, her grip strong and confident.

"We've landed," she says. "You're safe."

Safe. That word is an illusion. And yet, I feel my body relax a little. I recall something big and silver, something that gave me hope, but the image evades me.

"Landed? What are you talking about?"

Her other hand strokes my hair. It comforts me, takes away some of my fear.

"You're still groggy from the gas in your coffin," she says. "The effects should wear off pretty fast."

Even as she says this, I feel my head clearing. The fog drifts away. Memories rush back.

Horrible memories.

Waking up in a coffin. The needle driving into my neck. Fighting my way out. Not knowing who or where I was, my entire past gone save for a few wisps of someone else's life.

Saving Spingate. Then O'Malley. Then Bello, Aramovsky and Yong.

The hideous, cracked skull of a little boy, skin dried tight to his bones, clothes too big for his small body.

The skeletons. The dust. The endless dungeon hallways. Our long walk.

My knife sliding into Yong's belly.

Finding Bishop, Gaston, Latu and the rest. The vote, where I became leader—two tribes merging into one.

The pigs. Latu's death. The Garden. That's where I last felt *safe,* when I still believed that childish concept existed.

Bello's terror-wide eyes when the monster's wrinkled black hands dragged her into the Garden's underbrush. Those monsters—the *Grownups*—with their red eyes and spindly limbs, their gnarled skin, fleshy folds hanging where their mouths should have been.

Bello.

The shame of that moment hammers me. I *left* her. For the greater good, my head tells me, but my heart calls me a coward.

Meeting Brewer. Discovering that we weren't underground, that we were on an ancient spaceship called the *Xolotl.* The Grownups were creatures that should have died centuries ago. They wanted to wipe our minds clean and take over our young bodies as easily as someone might change their clothes.

Learning about Omeyocan, the planet we were made for.

Then, my decision to attack. Harris, dying somewhere in the Garden. Capturing Matilda. Finding the big silver shuttle. And when we were almost away, El-Saffani—the boy and girl twins who finished each other's sentences—charged an army of withered, walking corpses and were blown to pieces.

We escaped the *Xolotl,* but at such a price.

"Let's stand you up," Spingate says.

She helps me rise and step out. My legs immediately buckle—Spingate holds me, keeps me from falling. I think of an almost identical moment when *I* was the one comforting *her,* telling her to be calm, helping her out of a coffin.

My eyes don't sting as much. I blink them open, and see the face of my friend. Spingate's curly red hair is a tangled mess. Her green eyes are sunken, ringed by skin so dark it looks bruised. I've never seen her this pale; the black, circular gear symbol on her forehead stands out in stark contrast.

"I think I can stand on my own now."

Spingate kisses me on the cheek, lets me go.

We're in a long, narrow room. Red walls and ceiling, gleaming black floor. Two rows of thin white coffins lined up side by side run the length of the room. Wide aisles run along each wall, as well as one down the middle that leads through a curved opening. Just past that opening and to the right is the door we used to enter the shuttle. Past that door, the strange room of light where Gaston and Spingate glowed like angels.

These coffins are simple and plain. Designed just to let people sleep, I think. They aren't like the big, carved coffins that tended to us while we grew from babies into the bodies we have now.

My coffin is open—the lid rolled down somewhere into the foot of the thing. The other coffins remain sealed tight. The one to the right of mine holds O'Malley; the one to the left, Bishop. I held their hands until the lids closed.

A boy walks through the curved opening, shuffles down the middle aisle toward us. It's Gaston—he's holding my spear.

He's still wearing his red tie, which is embroidered with a yellow and black circle of tiny images, the word MICTLAN in white letters at its center. His white shirt is mostly clean, mostly untorn. I glance at my own too-small shirt, ripped in a dozen places and splattered with blood. My shredded plaid skirt barely covers me.

Gaston offers me the spear. I take it, then he clutches me in a hard hug.

"Em! We did it!"

I return the hug. It feels so good to hold him.

"*You* did it," I say. "You flew us to Omeyocan."

He steps back. His smile—part charm, part arrogance—is as wide as ever: Gaston is impressed with himself.

Despite his joy, it's clear he also has had no rest. His black hair hangs down his face, partially hiding his eyes.

"It was *amazing*," he says. "Once the pilothouse lights hit me, I remembered my creator's training from when I—I mean *he*—was little. Some of my blanked-out areas seemed to clear."

I don't know how that's possible. I have "blanked-out areas," too. We all do. When our brains search for memories we know should be there, they usually return only whispers and echoes. We were never meant to know anything for ourselves. We are *receptacles,* shells, created to house another person.

If he can "remember" how to fly, maybe our blank areas aren't *permanently* blank, like Matilda told me they were.

Gaston and Spingate look exhausted. I'm sore and scratched, bruised and beaten, but I don't feel tired at all.

"How long did I sleep?"

"Only the two hours it took us to land," Spingate says. "The shuttle told us the coffin gas does something to our brains, lets you sleep far deeper than you could on your own. We can take it in the pilothouse, too. You'd still be sleeping if I hadn't told the shuttle to give you the wake-up injection."

That sting in my neck. Not a knife, not a snake, not a bite . . . just a needle. I think about Brewer, how he tried to use a coffin needle to murder me, then I push that thought away. We don't need to worry about him anymore—we're *home*.

"What's it like outside?"

Gaston's little hand reaches over to Spingate's. Their fingers lock.

"We don't know," he says. "It was dark when we landed. The

shuttle had a preprogrammed landing path that took us down a big, circular hole of some kind. Maybe to protect us from wind, I'm not sure. It was nighttime when we flew in, and there was heavy cloud cover."

He says *cloud cover* like he's proud of the words, like it was an obstacle that not just anyone could overcome.

"So you haven't been outside at all?"

Spingate shakes her head. "You deserve to be the first."

They waited for me, out of respect. I don't know what to say.

"I'll go with you," she says. "The shuttle says the air is safe for us."

For *us,* but not for the Grownups who made us. We were designed to be able to survive down here. And in that lies our safety; even if the Grownups could reach Omeyocan—which they can't, because this was the last shuttle—this planet's very air would kill them.

Spingate holds up her left arm. Her forearm is wrapped in a sheet of gold, intricately carved and studded with black jewels. It reminds me of the bracelets the Grownups used to kill El-Saffani, but somehow I know it's not a weapon.

"Gaston found this in storage," she says. "It's called a *bracer*. I can use it to scan for things that could hurt us, things like *microorganisms* or *toxins*."

She speaks those words the same way Gaston said *cloud cover*—new, important words that she is proud of knowing.

There's no reason to wait any longer. We have nowhere else to go. The Birthday Children will survive on Omeyocan, or the Birthday Children will die here.

My stomach lets out a loud growl. An instant later, I wince at the pain—I'm so hungry it *hurts*.

"We have food," Gaston says. "The deck below has storerooms full of tools, clothes and lots of food."

"What's a *deck*?"

"A floor," Spingate answers. "Except on a ship, it's called a deck."

It never occurred to me this shuttle had more floors.

"Show me," I say.

We walk to the rear of the coffin room. The back wall is red, like the side walls. Up close I see the thin, almost invisible outline of a door. In that door is the faint shape of a handprint with a gear symbol in the palm.

Gaston presses his hand to the print. The door silently swings inward, revealing a metal staircase spiraling down. We descend. Ten stairs below is another door—the handprint here is also a gear. Spingate leads us in.

The corridor looks long, perhaps as long as the shuttle itself. There are doors on my left marked STORAGE 1 through STORAGE 6, and on my right labeled LAB 1 through LAB 3. At the end of the corridor is a door marked MEDICAL. The storage rooms have handprints with gears and half-circles. The labs, only gears. Medical's handprint is a circle-cross.

"We didn't have time to look at the labs," Gaston says. "Just the"—an eye-scrunching yawn pauses his words—"just the storage rooms."

The first storage room holds floor-to-ceiling racks of black bins. Gaston opens one: black coveralls made from heavy cloth. I think back to the *Xolotl,* to the hundreds of mutilated, tortured bodies dressed in similar outfits. It would be nice to change out of my torn rags, but the black clothes are some uniform of the Grownups, and right now I don't want to think about the Grownups.

Four rooms hold racks of green bins. Gaston opens one of the bins; it's full of small white packages with black letters that spell out GRAIN BAR. A second bin's packages are labeled CRACKERS.

"All the bins are full," Gaston says. "There's enough food to last us—*all* of us—for about thirty days. Isn't that great?"

He thinks thirty days is a long time? It will go by very quickly.

The final room holds neat racks of tools. One of Matilda's memories rushes up, where she first saw pigs—these are the kind of tools people use on a farm. Other racks hold bins filled with smaller tools, the kind used to fix things, to make things. I see another bracer, like the one Spingate is wearing.

I'm sure there will be a need for all of these tools, but until we know what awaits us outside the shuttle, there is something we need even more.

"What about weapons?"

Spingate shakes her head. "No bracelets. Nothing."

Damn.

"As soon as you get some rest, learn about the labs," I say to her. "Are there more floors? I mean *decks*."

"Two more," Spingate says. "But they have half-circle handprints on the doors. They won't open for us."

A half-circle: the symbol on O'Malley's forehead.

"We asked the shuttle what's down there," Gaston says. "It says it doesn't know."

I can tell it bothers him greatly that he can't access those decks. I heard the shuttle call him *Captain* Xander—how can there be parts of the shuttle that won't open for him?

We can worry about that later. I'm consumed by my need to get outside, see Omeyocan.

"Spingate, wake up the circle-stars. And O'Malley."

She nods. "Right away. Anybody else?"

"Smith," I say. "Tell her to learn all she can about that medical room."

Smith seems to know how to treat cuts and scrapes. I think it has something to do with her forehead mark: a circle-cross. She's the only one our age with that symbol. Two of the younger kids have it, though, so maybe soon Smith will have help healing our sick and wounded.

Gaston and Spingate look like they might pass out at any moment. I will make sure they rest, just not right now.

"I know you're both tired, but I need you a little while longer before you can sleep."

"Whatever it takes," Gaston says instantly.

Spingate simply smiles at me, as if to say, *I will always help you, no matter what.*

I've only been alive for a few days, yet I love these two so much it hurts. Spingate and Gaston—my *friends.*

"Spin, you'll come with me outside. Gaston, while we're gone, wake up everyone else and also prepare a meal. We should all eat together."

I lift the spear slightly, let it fall back to the hard floor with a soft *clomp*.

"It's time to see our new home."

TWO

We gather just inside the shuttle's main door.

My circle-stars: Bishop, Farrar, Visca, Coyotl and Bawden. They wear nothing but filthy cut-off pants. On the *Xolotl,* they covered themselves in a paste that made them all the same color—gray. Now that material is flaking away, showing the different skin tones beneath.

We don't have bracelets like the ones Grownups used to kill El-Saffani, but the rack of farming supplies means we are not completely unarmed. In our hands, tools have once again become weapons.

"Maybe you should stay here, Em," Bishop says. "You could help O'Malley explore the rest of the ship."

He holds a red axe he took from the storage room. I think about him swinging it as hard as he can, powerful muscles driving the sharp blade into a living thing, and I have to suppress a shiver.

"I'm going," I say, adjusting my grip on my spear. "I need to know what's out there."

He wants to protect me. His concern makes me feel warm inside, but I will not sit back while my people face danger.

The flesh around his left eye is swollen and bruised. When he put me in the coffin—trying to save my life—I went crazy and punched him. I feel horrible about that. Such seriousness in his face. I want to reach out and touch his blond curls, but now is not the time. When I first met him, he smiled easily, seemed so happy and confident. Not anymore. He killed two Grownups. Taking those lives changed him. I hope he can find his smile again, but if he feels inside the same way I do, I doubt it.

At the back of the coffin room, I see the door in the red wall open. O'Malley and Spingate step out, walk down the center aisle to join us. He's holding the knife I used to kill Yong. Somehow, that weapon became his.

"I'll take a good look around the shuttle while you go outside," he says. "But . . . are you *sure* I shouldn't come with you?"

Does he want to see the planet, or does he also want to protect me? It doesn't matter; we need to learn all we can as fast as we can. Besides, he's made for *thinking,* not *fighting*.

"I'll be fine. I have Bishop with me."

O'Malley looks down, and I cringe inside. I meant to say *I have the circle-stars with me,* but that's not what came out.

If he's hurt, he recovers quickly, grins at me.

"Just be smart," he says. "We have all the time this world has to offer—don't rush anything."

Our ordeal has affected him, too, but not like it has Bishop. O'Malley's blue eyes are vibrant, filled with excitement for our new adventure. Brittle bits of leaves cling to his brown hair. Dried blood stains his ill-fitting white shirt, especially at the collar below the nasty cut on his left cheek. He suffered that wound in the Garden, during our fight with the Grownups. I wonder what he had to do back there. I wonder if he—like Bishop and I—now knows how it feels to kill.

O'Malley looks at Bishop, then offers the knife, hilt-first.

"Take it," O'Malley says. "If I'm staying here, you need it more than I do."

Back on the *Xolotl,* the two boys came close to killing each other. Will they get along better now that we're on Omeyocan?

Bishop lifts his axe slightly.

"I like this better," he says.

The two boys have been "alive" for only a few days, yet they are both already marked with wounds that will become scars. In that, they aren't alone. My fingertips touch my split upper lip, the bump on my forehead, trace my cuts and scratches and bruises. We earned these badges of bravery.

Our creators designed our bodies. Our faces are theirs—these scars are the only things we can truly call our own.

Bishop isn't the only one with a new weapon.

White-haired, pink-skinned Visca holds a sledgehammer that is almost as tall as Gaston. Farrar chose a long-handled shovel. He is the largest of us save only for Bishop, and I bet the point—or edge—of the thick shovel blade could do horrible damage to flesh and blood. Bawden has an axe just like Bishop's. I find myself wondering how long it takes hair to grow: the first hints are showing on her shaved head, dark-brown skin giving way to stubble. With most of her dust gone, there is no ignoring the fact that she wears nothing but a tattered skirt. Her nakedness makes me want to look away; she doesn't seem to notice it.

Coyotl made the strangest choice of all—he still holds the thighbone he used against the Grownups. His skin has a bright hue, as if he spent far too long in the sun.

I meet Spingate's gaze. Her eyebrows rise in a silent question.

It is time.

"Open it," I say.

The shuttle doors slide apart.

The morning sun is a blinding, reddish ball creeping above the high tree line. I lift a hand to block out the light, feel the sun's heat against my skin.

A breeze caresses us, carrying new scents. My head spins as Matilda's fractured memories rush to the surface, try to put names on what I smell: *damp wood, burned grass* and something like *mint*.

I step onto the shuttle's platform. I don't know where the platform goes when we fly, but it is exactly as it was on the *Xolotl:* a metal rectangle big enough to hold us all. A ramp leads down to flat ground covered in dark-blue vines with wide, pale-yellow leaves. Some of the leaves and vines are burned black; maybe our shuttle did that when it landed.

We're in the center of what looks like a large, round clearing. A dense wall of leaves—the same pale yellow as the vines that cover the ground—towers up from the clearing's curved edge. The sky is a circular patch high above us.

I understand why Gaston thought we flew into a hole.

Bishop walks slowly down the ramp, both hands on his axe. Muscles twitch and flex. He scowls at the trees, at the vines covering the clearing, maybe at the sun itself—he wants this world to know he is ready to fight.

He stops at the ramp's end, reaches one bare foot toward the vines.

"Wait," I say. "Spingate, come with me."

The reddish sun seems to ignite the air around her hair. If anyone was made for this place, it is Theresa Spingate.

We walk down the ramp and join Bishop. I point down at the vines.

"Do you think those plants are safe to step on?"

Spingate kneels at the ramp's edge. Fingers outstretched, she waves her bracer-adorned arm over the leaves. The black jewels come alive, sparkle in many colors.

"The shuttle doesn't detect any known poisons," she says. "None that can go through the skin, anyway. Just don't eat anything."

I glance back at the big silver ship that brought us here, then at her.

"The shuttle told you that?"

She turns her head and pulls back her hair, shows a small black jewel nestled in her ear.

"It can speak to me through this. So can Gaston."

I again look down at the vines. This is it—our moment. I consider letting Bishop go first, or even Spingate, giving one of them the honor of being the first person to set foot on our new world.

But I want that honor for myself. I am the leader, and it is my right.

I step off the ramp. The leaves are soft and cool under my bare feet, except for the ones that were blackened during the landing; those crunch and break. There is something firm beneath the leaves. I turn my spear upside down. Dried red-gray—Matilda's blood—coats the blade's flat metal. I need to clean that up soon; I want to leave all memories of her behind.

I push the spear tip into the plants. It sinks in a little, then clonks against something hard.

"Bishop, come help."

He kneels beside me. His big hands rip at the blue vines and yellow leaves. That minty smell grows stronger. He clears the plants from a small area, leaving only crumbly brown dirt. He wipes that away as well, revealing flat metal.

I walk to a new spot, push the spear tip into the vines: *clonk*. I move to my right, do it again, hear the same sound.

The tree line . . . those leaves go *straight up,* a sheer curved wall of pale yellow surrounding a perfectly circular clearing. That can't be right . . . can it?

Bishop stands. "Farrar, Coyotl, come with me."

The three boys jog toward the wall of trees.

I turn back to Spingate.

"We're standing on metal," I say. "What is this place?"

Wide-eyed, she blinks. "I don't know. The shuttle told us where to land, so we landed. I'll see what Gaston can find out."

Her lips move, but I can't hear what she says. She cocks her head, hearing a voice meant only for her.

She's so exhausted she didn't think to ask about where we landed? Until this moment, neither did I. We were all so focused on escaping the *Xolotl* we didn't give much thought to what awaited us on Omeyocan.

Spingate nods.

"Gaston says the shuttle doesn't know much, but this isn't a clearing—it's a landing pad."

So Omeyocan isn't an unexplored wilderness after all. Did the Grownups build this? If so, *when,* and are those builders still here? This planet *is* ours, but that doesn't mean we won't have to take it away from someone else.

"*Em!*"

Bishop is shouting at me from the tree line. Coyotl and Farrar are leaning to the left and right, respectively, pulling apart the yellow trees. Only they aren't *trees* at all, they are *vines,* the same kind I'm standing on—and in the shadows behind them, a metal wall.

Spingate tugs on my sleeve. "Gaston says he figured out how to make the landing pad rise up."

It takes me a moment to process what she just said. I start to tell her *no,* but before the word comes out, a violent tremor knocks me off-balance, throws me down on the vines. Spingate falls to her hands and knees. The ground beneath me lurches upward, then stops so suddenly it tosses me into the air—I crash back down onto the soft plants. Another vibration shakes my bones, then we rise up, *fast*. Screams of metal hurt my ears.

"Spingate! Tell Gaston to make it *stop*!"

Another shudder knocks her flat, but she isn't afraid. Her eyes are wide with wonder—she's *laughing*.

"Gaston says it's okay. Just hold on!"

The ground presses into me: we're moving faster now.

At the edges of the clearing, the vines seem to pour down the sides, bunching up at the bottom like falling rope, but the vines aren't *falling*—instead, the ground is coming up beneath them. Bishop, Coyotl and Farrar are still on their feet, lithely dancing away from the sprawling mass of plants.

What I first thought was the clearing's edge is actually vine-covered walls, walls that shrink before my eyes. We're rising to the top of this . . . this *tube*.

I suddenly feel lighter. We're slowing.

With a harsh clank of steel and a tooth-rattling shudder, the landing pad stops.

I stand on wobbly legs. The landing pad's edge is still circular, but now it is ringed by a pile of vines three times taller than I am. The sun beats down on us, lights up what looks like pointy, yellow hills rising all around. Not *hills,* but rather *shapes* . . . I almost know what they are. Or rather, *Matilda* knew what those are.

Then Bishop is beside me.

"Em, come on! You've got to see this!"

He takes me by the hand, pulls me so hard my head flops back. I stumble along behind him, still clutching my spear.

In seconds we reach the vine ring. At the top stand Farrar and

Coyotl. Bishop scrambles up, pulling me along behind him. My feet sink into the thick plants, but find enough purchase to let me ascend.

I reach the top and look out.

This can't be . . .

In all directions, as far as I can see, what I thought were pointy hills are not hills at all. They are *buildings,* overgrown with thick yellow vines, bluish trees and other strange plants. Some of the buildings are pyramids, so tall they scrape the sky.

We are standing in the middle of a vast, ruined city.

THREE

I don't know how long the four of us stand atop the vines, staring out. Long enough for Spingate and the other circle-stars to join us.

The *immensity* of it all. The sky is like a dome above us, so big I could never reach the edge even if I walked forever. The buildings, the land, the trees and vines . . . this place is a million times bigger than the *Xolotl,* which was the biggest thing I had ever seen.

It's so overwhelming. I fight an urge to run back to the shuttle's familiar, confined area. I can tell the others feel the same.

"Spin," I say. "What is this place?"

I hear her mumbling, speaking quietly to Gaston back in the shuttle. While I wait, I stare. Tall pyramids block my view in most directions. Where they do not, the city seems to go on and on.

"The shuttle doesn't know," Spingate says.

"But Gaston said the shuttle told him to land here," I say. "How can it know where to go and not know what this city is?"

She has no answer.

Coyotl is on my right. He points toward the horizon. "Are those birds?"

Several somethings fly over the city. Maybe birds, but we're too far from them to make out what they are.

There is no sound save for the breeze sliding past leaves—it sounds like this city is hissing at us.

"No movement on the streets," Bishop says.

Streets seems like a strange term for what we see: wide, straight spaces between the buildings and pyramids, but those spaces are so choked with vines they look like the flat bottom of steep valleys instead of a place where people might walk.

"Abandoned," Farrar says. "Where are the people who made all this?"

Coyotl turns, looks behind us. The thighbone slips from his hands, thumps on the vines and rolls down the inner slope.

I turn, and am just as stunned. The shuttle lies before us, sitting on its bed of yellow leaves in the middle of the vine ring. Beyond the shuttle, towering buildings block a view of the city—far beyond those buildings is a pyramid so massive the sky itself seems to balance on its point. All the buildings are covered in yellow, but not the tip of this pyramid, which is an orange-brown.

"I don't like this," Farrar says. "Should we go back to the shuttle?"

A loud growl answers him. We all look to Bawden—the sound came from her belly.

She shrugs. "I'm hungry."

So am I. We all are. There is so much to explore here it might take us a lifetime. *Don't rush anything,* O'Malley said. We have to carefully think about what we should do next. This place *appears* abandoned, but I have been alive long enough to know that things are not always as they seem.

We return to the shuttle, which gleams beneath the hot sun. I can't believe I once thought of the shuttle as *large*. Nestled in this sprawling city, it is nothing but a toy.

We enter to the sound of laughter and excitement. So many happy voices—music to my ears. Everyone is awake, older kids and twelve-year-olds alike. Some are alert, others are still groggy from the gas.

I have Spingate seal the doors behind us.

In the coffin room, Gaston and Okereke hold green bins, from which they are passing out white food packages. Okereke is a circle, like me, short and thick with muscle. He has the darkest skin of any of us, almost as black as that of the monsters.

Bishop takes the bin from Gaston and pats him on the back. Gaston looks to me for the next job. I tilt my head toward the pilothouse.

"You and Spingate get some sleep," I say. "We'll all stay here until you're rested. I need your input to figure out what we do next."

He grabs a handful of packages from the bin, then he and Spingate stumble their way to the pilothouse and shut the door behind them.

I walk toward my coffin. It's not *my* coffin, not like before, because none of these have our names engraved on them. It's the one I came down in, though, and it seems like the only space in this crowded room that belongs to me.

Everyone gives me smiles. They hug me, give my shoulder a squeeze, pat me on the back. They are happy to be alive, excited to explore their new world.

I lay my spear down in my coffin's white padded fabric, sit cross-legged on the black floor.

So many people in this red-walled coffin room. Not counting Gaston and Spingate, there are seventeen of us with full-grown bodies. And then the kids—108 of them. They are *everywhere,* mostly clean shirts and skirts or pants, red ties still on. They are laughing, eating, playing, sometimes running around madly until someone my age snaps at them to calm down.

My age? That's a funny concept. Am I an "adult"? In body, I suppose, but big or small, we are all twelve years old. We are the Birthday Children. At most, I am a few *days* older than the smaller kids, not a few *years*.

Bishop strides toward me, a green bin under his big arm. His subtle movements carry him over and around people without jostling a one.

He tilts the bin down to me.

"The food is good, Em. Grab some."

I reach in, take a handful, read the black letters: PROTEIN BAR, HARD BISCUIT and GRAIN BAR.

All I've ever eaten was fruit and some pig, and not much of either. I tear open the grain bar's wrapper—inside is what looks like a thin brown brick. I take a bite. The material crumbles between my teeth, and a new flavor explodes across my tongue. I've never tasted this, but I know the right word—it tastes *nutty*.

"Everyone, stop eating!"

It's Aramovsky. He's standing on a closed coffin, arms outstretched. All heads turn to look up at him.

"We must give thanks for this food," he says. His voice is deep and rich. "We must not anger the god who delivered us here."

He is the tallest of us. Standing on the coffin, his head almost reaches the ceiling. He stayed clean for a long time, but now dried blood stands out on his torn white shirt. The damage—both to his dark skin and to the fabric—came when he crashed through a thicket to save me. He stabbed a monster, not knowing it was actually his own progenitor. Our Aramovsky learned that truth just moments before Bishop killed the creature with a broken thighbone.

I think Aramovsky was actually ready to have his mind wiped, maybe even *excited* to become one with his creator. He wanted it because he thinks that's what his religion dictates.

Everyone is watching him, waiting. They have all stopped eating except for one young circle-star. She laughs at Aramovsky as she takes a big bite from her bar.

He points at her, long arm and long finger stretched out like a different kind of spear.

"This god is *watching* you, girl. Do not anger him."

The laugh drains from the girl's face. She lets the food slip from her hand. It drops to the floor.

She's eating and having fun, and he's scaring her? His mysterious invisible gods didn't deliver us here, *I* did. He makes me so angry.

I stand.

"You usually talk about the *gods,*" I say. "Magic beings that don't actually *do* anything for us. Now it's just *one* god? Well, which one is it?"

I hope that, for once, our sparse memories will work in my favor. Forcing him to name something he can't recall will make him look stupid in front of everyone, maybe shut him up.

Aramovsky smiles at me with his big, beautiful, *fake* smile.

"The God of Blood, Em."

That sounds ridiculous. I laugh, look around expecting others to be laughing with me, but only a few are. Most stare at him wide-eyed, like he'd just said something brilliant.

I'd hoped he would leave this nonsense up on the *Xolotl*. Aramovsky is going to be a problem.

"No prayers," I say. "Everyone, eat."

Aramovsky bows to me. "As you say, great leader."

He steps down and sits. People gather around him.

Laughter and talking slowly return. So much hope in this room. Pure joy.

The circle-stars seem happiest of all. Coyotl and the bigger Visca are wrestling. They strike each other so hard I wince at the sound, but they laugh madly at each impact. Bawden has figured out how to belch on command. Every time she does, circle-star kids howl with delight and try to imitate her. Those children are skinny, but they will grow taller, fill out, gain the thick muscle so familiar on the teenage circle-stars.

Farrar is rooting through every green bin as if he's searching for something very important. He looks up, meets my gaze, then runs to me.

"Em, do you have anything *sweet*?" His hopeful expression makes him look like a child. Wide smile, wide nose, dark eyes and that big jaw . . . Farrar is pretty. *Everyone* here is pretty: I wonder if the Grownups somehow modified their "copies" to fit a vision of what they thought they *should* be, rather than what they *are*.

I shake my head. "I don't think *protein bar* and *hard biscuit* sound sweet." I offer him the half-eaten grain bar. "Want to try this? It tastes nutty."

He takes a bite, chews, thinks, hands it back to me, then leans in close.

"It's just . . . well, you're the leader. I thought maybe someone brought you *cookies*."

He says that word the way Gaston said *cloud cover* and Spingate said *microorganism*.

"Sorry. If I had any, I would share them with you."

He snarls, smacks a closed fist against an open palm. I know it's only a gesture of frustration, but it scares me a little.

I notice Bishop is still holding his bin, still walking from person to person, offering more food. He stops in front of Aramovsky, who is sitting at the foot of his coffin, and offers the tall boy a package. Aramovsky takes it and sets it on a pile of unopened packages on the floor—his food, and food from the others around him.

Bishop is making sure everyone has enough, and Aramovsky is hoarding?

I think of when I was first walking down the *Xolotl*'s endless hallway with Bello, O'Malley, Spingate, Aramovsky and Yong. We were starving, talking about the food we dreamed of. Aramovsky wanted cupcakes.

I whisper in Farrar's ear.

"Maybe there's something sweet in Aramovsky's pile, even if it isn't labeled like that. The people who packed the food could have made a mistake."

Farrar runs down the center aisle toward Aramovsky. Children scramble out of his way. Aramovsky sees the big circle-star coming and moves a hand to cover up his collection.

That wasn't nice of me, but it's fun to watch them argue about something unimportant. And it makes me happy to give Aramovsky some grief. It shouldn't, but it does.

Two little girls run up to me and throw themselves down, somehow landing cross-legged. One is Zubiri, the dark-skinned tooth-girl who calmed me when I fought against O'Malley and Bishop putting me in my coffin. There are no leaves in Zubiri's jet-black hair. No blood, no scratches, no bruises, no scars. Like most of the younger kids, she hasn't suffered that much.

The other girl I don't recognize. She's got hair just as black as Zubiri's, but her skin is light and her eyes are so thin I can barely tell they're open. She's also a little chubby. The symbol on her forehead is a circle inside of a circle: a double-ring, the same as Aramovsky's.

"Hi, Em," Zubiri says.

"Hi, Zubiri. Who is your friend?"

"This is B. Walezak," Zubiri says. "Our cradles were next to each other."

I offer my hand. "Nice to meet you, B. Walezak."

The girl stares for a second, then giggles and hides her face behind Zubiri's shoulder.

Zubiri rolls her eyes dramatically. "Oh, Walezak, you have to learn how to talk to people."

I've spoken with Zubiri only a few times. Somehow, she seems older than me. Maybe more *mature* is the right word. That's good, I think. Soon, she will have to do her part. All the kids will.

Like a shadow, O'Malley silently sits down beside me.

"I was able to access the lower decks," he says. "You need to see this."

Farrar and Aramovsky are yelling at each other. Everyone is watching them, laughing at the argument. I quietly follow O'Malley to the back wall and through the stairway door.

"Once a door is unlocked, we can leave it that way if we close it and don't press the handprint or turn the wheel," he says.

We descend past Deck Two to Deck Three. As Gaston told me, the door has a wheel with a half-circle symbol on it.

"Try and open it," O'Malley says.

The pilothouse door has a gear symbol. That door wouldn't open for me, so I doubt this one will, either, but I try. The wheel spins easily—the door unlocks.

"I thought so," O'Malley says. "Locked doors will mostly only open for people who have the matching symbol, but there are a few exceptions. I think you can open some doors because Matilda was in charge of the Grownups—I'm pretty sure the other empties can't open any door that has a handprint lock."

Empties. That word makes me instantly angry and I don't know why. O'Malley seems surprised he said it, embarrassed, but I can tell he's just as clueless to its meaning as I am.

"Anyway," he says, "let me show you what I found."

O'Malley pulls the door open. Inside is a small room with three waist-high white pedestals, the same kind that were in that spherical room where I first saw Brewer and Matilda—the place she called the Crystal Ball.

I instantly want to knock the pedestals over, smash them . . . if Matilda's face appears, or Brewer's, I will do just that. We need to leave the Grownups behind, forever.

O'Malley steps to the middle pedestal. Sparkles flare up above it, just like they did in the Crystal Ball, but instead of Brewer's red-eyed face, I see the words GAMBIT PRIV, and below them, small images: O'Malley's face, and Aramovsky's, and . . . mine?

I've seen myself only once, a brief reflection in the shuttle's polished hull. That reflection showed dirt and blood, dust and damage, all the bruises I suffered in our fight to escape. Messy hair, split lip, black eye, scratches from my fight in the woods and being dragged through the thicket.

The tiny face above the pedestal, though, has no marks. No cuts, no blood. It's me, but older. The last of the girl I am is gone—what I see is all *woman,* striking and confident.

O'Malley's and Aramovsky's images look older, too. So . . . *manly*. The image makes O'Malley look even more handsome than he already is.

"I don't understand," I say. "Is that us?"

"Maybe it's how the Grownups thought we would look in a few years. Or how our progenitors looked when they first designed us, set us to growing in the coffins?"

It's so strange to look at an older version of myself. Glossy black hair hangs in luxurious curls rather than being pulled back into my severe braid. Smooth light-brown skin. Lips a dark shade of red. Eyelids painted pink.

But that face . . . it's not *real.* It is the face of a doll, dressed up the way its owner wanted.

"You're beautiful," O'Malley says.

The word makes my breath catch. I glance at him—he's not looking at me, he's looking at the image. That isn't me, it's *Matilda,* how she would look if she wiped me from existence.

"A picture of me is beautiful, but the real thing isn't?"

His eyes flick to me, widen.

"Well, no . . . that's not what I'm saying."

"That's exactly what you said."

He shakes his head. "You're beautiful, too, Em. When those bruises heal, you'll look amazing."

But I don't look amazing now. I don't want to talk about it anymore, so I change the subject.

"Those words, *gambit priv*. What do they mean?"

"No idea. When I walked up to the pedestal, this is what appeared."

He reaches out and touches the image of my face. Next to it appear two symbols in gold: circle-star, circle-cross. Two symbols in silver: the gear and the half-circle. And one symbol in white: the double-ring.

There are no plain circle symbols at all—no *empties*.

"I think gold means you can access any door with those symbols," O'Malley says. "Silver might mean you can access *some* doors with that symbol."

"And white means I can't access those areas at all?"

He nods. "I think so."

I touch the floating picture of O'Malley's face. The symbols and colors are the same as mine, except for the gear, which for him is white. He can't access anything with a double-ring or a gear.

Then I touch Aramovsky's face: gold for the double-ring, white for everything else.

Why just our three faces? No image of Spingate or Gaston. The shuttle will fly for Gaston, but has areas he can't access? Why? When Grownup Aramovsky died, he was with Matilda. Did they have some connection? And what about Grownup O'Malley—is that monster still alive, too?

The Grownups kept things from each other. They fought, they murdered, they kept themselves divided. I don't want to be anything like them.

"Can we change this, so everyone has access to everything?"

"I tried," O'Malley says. "It won't let me do much of anything."

He faces the pedestals, licks his lips. He's acting so strange. What has him so anxious?

"Shuttle, where are we?" he asks.

A soft voice purrs from the walls.

"Omeyocan."

Black spots form above all three pedestals. The spots fuzz with sparkles of every possible color, then solidify. I'm looking at a planet: blue, green and brown. It spins slowly. It is exactly what I saw up on the *Xolotl.*

"Shuttle," he says, "I need to change access privileges."

"Chancellor, O'Malley, Kevin Patrick, speak the access code to continue."

His first name is *Kevin*? I like that name. But I like *O'Malley* more.

"I think some info is available to anyone," O'Malley says. "But most of the questions I ask, it wants a code that I don't know."

The shuttle obviously recognizes him. It must think he is the Grownup O'Malley, after an overwrite. Maybe it will make the same mistake with me. On the *Xolotl,* Matilda seemed to be in charge.

I face the pedestals.

"Shuttle, do you know who I am?"

"Savage, Matilda Jean, Empress."

Empress?

O'Malley laughs. He rolls his eyes, smiling. "Your *Highness.* Should I bow?"

I punch his shoulder.

"Shuttle," I say, "what do our symbols mean?"

"Speak the access code to continue."

"If I'm the *empress,* I don't need a code. What do our symbols mean? What is this city?"

"Gambit-level information requires verbal confirmation of access code, Empress. Speak the access code to continue."

"Told you," O'Malley says.

"What else is on this deck?"

"Nothing as far as I can tell. I think the rest of this deck's space has machinery . . . maybe to take care of what's below us, on Deck Four."

His voice wavers when he speaks. He sounds anxious, and perhaps a little afraid. Whatever he's afraid of, it's down there.

"All right," I say. "Show me."

His lips press into a flat line. "Come on."

I follow him down to the last deck. There is a wheel-door, just like the others, but this one has a circle-cross in the hub.

"I was able to open it," he says. "According to the symbols in the pedestal room, I think you can, too."

He waits for me to do so. Now I'm a little afraid, as if his anxiety is contagious.

I grip the wheel. It spins easily. I pull the door open and step through.

I am looking into a long space undivided by walls or doors. There is nothing here, in fact, save for what lies on the floor.

Two long columns of brown coffins, clean and shining, covered in carvings of jaguars, pyramids and suns.

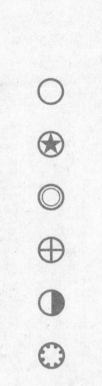

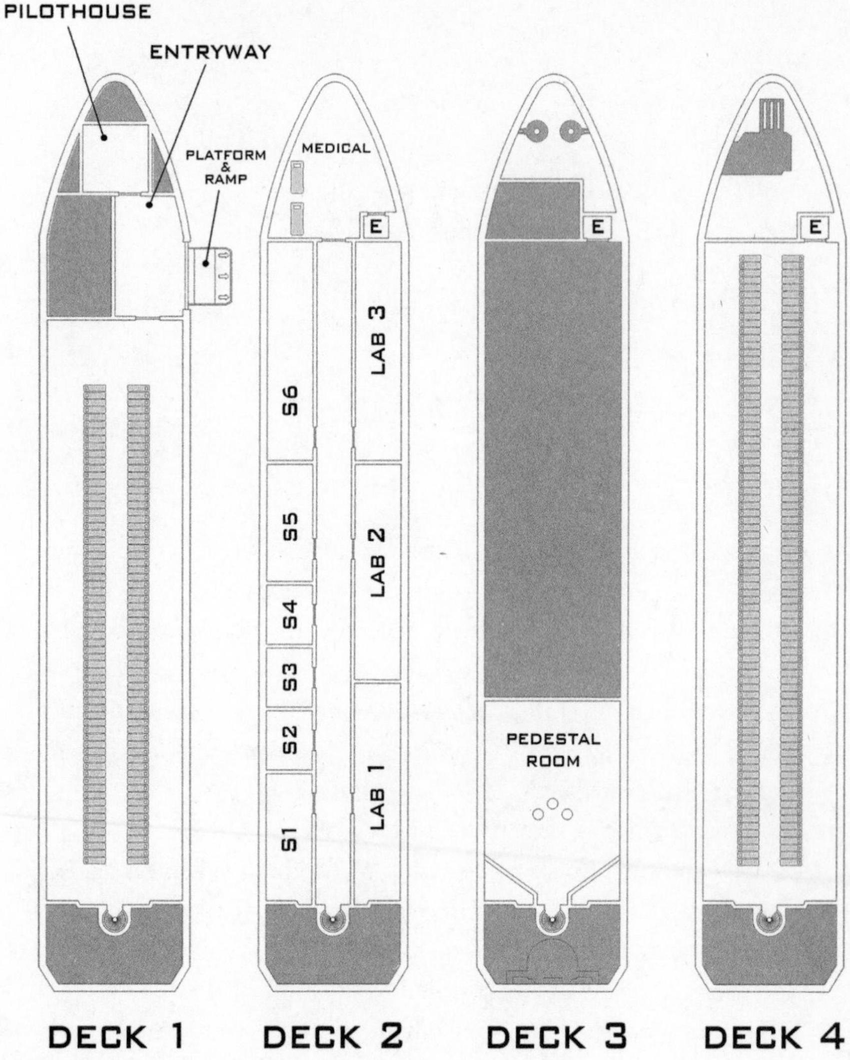

KEY:
S = Storage
E = Elevator
Gray areas are inaccessible (shuttle-specific machinery)

FOUR

O'Malley and I return to the top deck. People are playing, talking, even napping inside the white coffins.

I catch Bishop's eye, tilt my head toward the pilothouse. He nods, picks up his axe and follows us.

Before we reach the pilothouse door, the wheel spins. Gaston and Spingate step out. They don't look as rested as I'd hoped, but they look happy, and that's something.

"Back inside," I say. "I need to talk to you both."

We enter. Bishop starts to swing the door shut behind us, but it stops halfway: smiling Aramovsky is blocking it with his body.

"Are we making plans?" he says. "Good. We need to discuss the spiritual needs of the people."

Bishop glances at me, but when he does, skinny Aramovsky slides through the door and into the room. It would have been one thing to say he couldn't come in—it's entirely another to make him leave. Which, of course, Aramovsky knows.

Bishop shuts the door.

The first time I entered the pilothouse, the walls were black. Now it's as if there are no walls at all. It looks like I'm standing in the middle of the clearing that ends in a tall, circular wall of piled vines. I see the shapes of the strange buildings beyond, and I seem to float high above yellow vines even though the pilothouse floor feels just as solid as it ever did.

Bishop leans the flat of his axe against his hip. He's waiting for me to speak, as are the others.

"O'Malley accessed the shuttle's lower levels," I say.

Gaston glares at O'Malley. O'Malley is expressionless, as he always seems to be during discussions like these.

I don't mention the room with the pedestals. If Aramovsky is going to make everything his business, I don't want him messing around in there. I quickly describe the room we saw on Deck Four, making sure my friends understand these are not simple white coffins, but rather the same kind in which we all first awoke.

Bishop looks angry. Spingate and Gaston seem shocked.

Aramovsky is delighted.

"How *wonderful,*" he says. "Did you open them?"

Bishop huffs. "Of course she didn't. Em wouldn't do something that dangerous without me and the circle-stars there."

"Dangerous," Aramovsky says. "Ah, I see. Those new coffins might hold Grownups instead of people like us. Don't worry, Bishop, I have absolute faith in you—if there are Grownups, I'm sure you'll find a way to kill them all."

Bishop snarls. "I did what I had to do."

"You *had* to murder?" Aramovsky's hands close into fists, open, close into fists. "Is killing the only thing you're good for, Bishop?"

"*Stop it,*" I snap. "Aramovsky, your progenitor would have overwritten you, don't you get that? Bishop saved you."

"I didn't need to be *saved*. I was made to join with my creator. Now he's dead—his thousand years of wisdom and knowledge, lost forever."

Aramovsky makes it sound like we're not as important as the people who wanted to erase us.

"We have the right to survive," I say. "The Grownups think we're property, shells to be filled up. They are *wrong*!"

I realize I'm yelling. I take a deep breath, try to calm myself. Aramovsky is so infuriating.

"We shouldn't open them," O'Malley says, so calmly it makes my yelling seem all the louder.

Aramovsky holds up his hands as if to say, *What choice do we have?* "We must open them. And quickly. We don't know what dangers we'll face on this planet—there is strength in numbers."

"There is *hunger* in numbers," Spingate says. "Our food won't last long as it is. And as far as we know, there could be people in there who look just like us but have already been overwritten—Grownups in young bodies."

If that's the case, would they accept us? Would they try to take over, marginalize us, because they think they know better how to live, how to run things?

Or maybe they would just kill us. We're only receptacles, after all; empty vessels have no rights.

Gaston nods in agreement. "Spingate is right about our food situation. How many coffins were there?"

O'Malley answers. "One hundred and sixty-eight."

The number frightens me. Once upon a time, I led five people. If those coffins open—if the people inside *are* like us—I could be responsible for almost three hundred.

"That would more than double our numbers," Gaston says. "Our food will be gone in half the time."

Spingate frowns. "The Grownups sure seem to like multiples of three. Or maybe twelve. Were any of the coffins cracked open, like back on the *Xolotl*?"

O'Malley shakes his head. "I didn't see any damage. They all looked sealed."

"Leave them that way," Bishop says. "At least until we find more food. Whoever it is, if they're in the coffins they aren't eating anything. And they aren't a threat."

O'Malley picks at the scab on his cheek.

"What if the shuttle decides to wake them up?" he says. "Or what if someone up on the *Xolotl* can do it somehow? Gaston, you've been talking to the shuttle. Ask it about the coffins."

Gaston sighs. "Shuttle, what do you know about the coffins on Deck Four?"

The honey-sweet voice answers from the walls.

"I have no information on Deck Four, Captain Xander. My knowledge of that part of the ship has been erased."

"I figured," Gaston says. "*This* has been erased, *that* has been erased—if I ask about anything other than flying, the shuttle doesn't know anything. It doesn't even know why it picked this place to land."

Like us, the shuttle has blank areas.

There are instant questions of who erased its memories, and why, but those things aren't important right now.

"We have to find food," I say. "We'll eat up what we have very quickly. Finding food is our first objective."

Bishop shakes his head. "First we need to understand our immediate surroundings. Find places from where we could be attacked, and ways to escape if we are. We need to *reconnoiter* the area, Em."

He says that big word the way Spingate said *microorganisms*.

Gaston's sleepy face brightens. "I can help with that. The shuttle has powerful sensors for flying. I bet it can make us a map."

He whispers something. He tilts his head, listening, and I see a black jewel in his ear, just like Spingate's. He raises his hands. Light bathes his skin, making him glow like a god.

The images on the walls around us suddenly flow toward the middle of the pilothouse, shrinking rapidly as they go, the contracting vine ring at the center. In a blur of motion, the entire ruined city seems half the size, a quarter, a tenth, a hundredth. Buildings rush in, transforming from immense blocks of stone to tiny toys lined by tiny streets.

The pilothouse walls are once again black. The city that spread out in all directions is now a circle hovering at waist level. Bishop, Aramovsky, Gaston, Spingate, O'Malley and I stand at the map's edge.

A glowing compass rose points out north, south, east and west. The center of the rose is a circle with the same Mictlan symbol that decorated our ties.

Streets and avenues are laid out in a grid. The two widest streets are perpendicular. Where they would cross each other, they vanish beneath the city's largest building—that towering pyramid I saw when I was standing atop the vine ring.

To the northeast, a river flows into the city, so real I see the water sparkling, moving. The river ends at a tiny waterfall that drops into a wide pool.

I notice something about the vine-covered pyramids: they are flat squares stacked one on top of another, each smaller than the layer below. They look like the ones that were carved into my birth-coffin.

"*Ziggurats,*" I say. The word just pops out; I've remembered something from Matilda's past. The others look at the stepped pyramids, at each other, and nod. They now remember that word, too.

Spingate points to a glowing dot at the map's center. "That's our shuttle."

It seems so small, further emphasizing the vastness of the ruined city.

Gaston gestures to the map's circular edge. "That's as far as the shuttle can see."

Even though it's fairly small on the map, the tallest ziggurat—the one on top of the two intersecting roads—is detailed enough for me to make out a pillar at the very top, where the yellow vines don't grow. Six black symbols run down its length: empty circle, circle-star, double-ring, circle-cross, half-circle and, at the bottom, the tooth-circle or "gear."

About two-thirds of the way up that ziggurat, on a corner, a vine-covered statue of a person faces up toward the peak. I can't tell if it is a man or a woman. The statue must be huge.

This building seems important.

"Gaston," I say, "how long would it take us to reach that tall ziggurat?"

He leans toward it, thinks. "If you walk fast, the better part of a day, most likely."

O'Malley reaches out to touch the buildings near his waist, as if they are tiny things he might pick up. His hand goes right through them, kicking up a small cloud of sparkles.

"These buildings look different from the rest," he says.

I see what he means. The ones near him are more broken down: partially collapsed, many with caved-in roofs and trees growing out of them. Their shapes are different—six sides, not four like most of the buildings on the map. And they are smaller, dwarfed by even the medium-sized ziggurats.

To the northeast a bit past the waterfall, I notice a thick line that intersects the map's circle. The six-sided buildings are all on the far side of that line.

I point at it. "Is that a wall?"

Gaston reaches down with both hands, grabs the air above that section, and stretches his hands apart—the map zooms in. There is less detail now, and the image looks a bit fuzzy, but it is clearly a high, thick wall.

Aramovsky crosses his arms, frowns in thought.

"Four-sided buildings on our side of the wall, six-sided on the other," he says. "Why would that be?"

No one answers.

O'Malley takes in a sharp breath of surprise, points. "Zoom in on that!"

Gaston does. It's a rectangular building, big enough to hold a dozen shuttles, about halfway between us and the waterfall. The building is covered in yellow vines, like all the others, but it has a unique feature: thick, vine-draped poles rising up from the roof's edge, as if there is an army of spear-holders down there, standing guard, weapons held high. The poles taper to a rounded tip with just the hint of a point. I almost recognize that shape.

"Those are statues of corn," O'Malley says. "The building is a warehouse."

We all look at him, doubtful.

O'Malley's steady calm has vanished. His eyes are bright and his smile blazes, a smile so real and beautiful it makes my breathing stop.

"I remember something," he says. "My father—I mean, my *progenitor's* father—worked for a city. Maybe. Anyway, my progenitor saw buildings like this. They're used to store food."

If he's right, that means the Grownups built this city. So where are they? What happened to them?

If that building holds food, it could mean the difference

between life and death. We need to learn what plants we can and can't eat, how to farm and hunt, but mastering those skills will probably take much longer than our supplies will last.

"It's not far," Gaston says. "It would only take a couple of hours to walk there."

Aramovsky points to the glowing dot at the map's center. "Why not just fly the shuttle right to it?"

"I'm not sure there's a place to land," Gaston says. "And besides, the shuttle needs fuel to fly." He pauses, opens his mouth to say something, then closes it.

Spingate finishes for him. "We have barely enough fuel left for one trip to the *Xolotl*. If we fly around for other purposes—for *anything*—we won't be able to go back. Not ever."

Everyone falls silent. I hadn't realized going back was an option. The thought is uncomfortable: if we fail on Omeyocan, our survival might depend on returning to a place where people want to kill us.

Aramovsky waves a hand dismissively. "The God of Blood sent us here. We are destined to succeed. God gave us this shuttle, and we should use it to—"

"We walk," I say sharply, cutting him off. "Like Bishop said, we have to reconnoiter anyway, so we'll do some of that while we go to the warehouse. If we find food there, we have more time to figure out what to do next."

Bishop stands straighter. "I'll take Farrar and Coyotl. We'll move fast, come back and report to you."

"I'll go as well," Spingate says.

Bishop shakes his head. "No, you'll slow us down."

Spingate lifts the arm with the bracer. "If we find food or water, this will tell us if it's poisonous."

"If we find food or water, we'll bring some back," Bishop says. "Then you can tell us if it's safe."

Spingate puts her hands on her hips.

"She's going," I say. "As am I."

Bishop glares at me. So does O'Malley.

"It's dangerous, Em," O'Malley says. "The leader shouldn't go out until we know you won't get hurt."

Once again the boys want to keep me *safe*. Too bad—I'm not the kind to hide away when there is work to be done.

"If I don't face danger, I can't ask others to do the same," I say. "And we don't know what plants or animals we'll find on the way. We have no idea what might be edible here. Spingate will evaluate as we go."

Bishop sighs, shakes his head. O'Malley forces the scowl off his face.

"Let's get ready," I say. "O'Malley, you and Gaston are in charge while I'm gone. We need to know everything that's in this shuttle—and find out who's inside those coffins."

FIVE

We set out from the shuttle: Spingate and I, along with Bishop, Coyotl and Farrar. Everyone sees us off, waving and cheering. O'Malley is staying behind. He can't hide his concern. Is he worried about my safety? That he'll have to keep an eye on Aramovsky? Or is he worried I'll be with Bishop?

Maybe it's all those things.

At least O'Malley wasn't as bad as Gaston. The little pilot looked like he was on the edge of tears because Spingate was leaving. Just before we left, I saw them facing each other, holding hands. He looked at the ground, nodding his head while she spoke softly.

I have the spear. Bishop has his red axe. The heavy shovel rests on Farrar's shoulder. Coyotl still prefers his tried-and-true thighbone.

Spingate carries the jewel-studded tool I found back in the *Xolotl*'s coffin room. Her bag also holds a white case filled with bandages, sharp little knives, pills, needles and thread for stitching wounds, containers of ointments and other things. Smith taught Spingate how to use all of it.

Opkick and Borjigin—teenage half-circles who were originally with Bishop's crew—took it upon themselves to start an inventory of the storerooms. They sent each of us off with a small black bag containing some food, a bottle of water and a flashlight. They also found a handful of knives, with sheaths that strap around our thighs. There aren't many of these, so we only give them to the circle-stars.

We climb the ring of piled vines and descend the other side. Just like that, the shuttle is gone from sight. We're heading into the unknown. Am I frightened? Of course. But I have also grown accustomed to this—the *un*known is all that I have *ever* known.

We walk down a wide, vine-covered street. The sounds of our people quickly fade away. Leaves rattle: the dead city hissing at us. A light breeze brings new smells. I now recognize the minty scent of the vines. Most odors, though, neither I nor Matilda have ever known before.

Buildings rise up on either side of the street. Some are boxy, but most are stepped pyramids. *Ziggurats*. Those remind me of something from my childhood . . . *Matilda's* childhood, I mean. I remember a wedding. I remember staring up at the cake, at four layers, each layer smaller than the one below it. At the top, a little statue of two people. I thought it was a toy. I wanted to play with it, but Mother wouldn't let me.

Some of the pyramids are small, three or four layers, while others are massive, twenty layers or more. The biggest of these have layers so wide that there are smaller ziggurats built upon the flat spaces. Vines cover almost everything, softening shapes, turning the orange-brown stone a pale, fuzzy yellow.

As I walk, I realize I don't feel as anxious about the sprawling sky above. All this open space, it feels like I belong here. I'm beginning to understand that *this* is natural. This is the way things should be—being cramped in a shuttle or packed into narrow hallways is not.

A few buildings have collapsed. Young trees rise up from the street, from rooftops, from the sloped sides of the ziggurats. Trunks of green and brown, leaves a darker yellow than those of the vines. The way tree roots clutch at stone walls makes me think more buildings will collapse as the years roll on.

Birds fly overhead—well, not the *birds* I know from Matilda's memories, but brightly colored animals about the same size. Instead of feathered, flapping wings, these things have two sets of stiff, buzzing membranes. The membranes move so fast they are a blur.

Blurds—that's what I will call these creatures.

Some are small, some big. A large one sweeps its wings back against its long body and dives, then pulls up sharply, extending claws that snatch a smaller blurd right out of the air with a sickening *smack-crunch*.

Death lives here. Death lived on the *Xolotl*. Perhaps death lives everywhere.

Farrar turns in circles as he walks forward, almost tripping, gawking up at the towering pyramids. "Where *is* everyone?"

There should be people. *Lots* of them, yet the only motion comes from blurds and blowing leaves. If O'Malley is right about the warehouse, the Grownups built all of this.

So where did they go?

By the time we reach the warehouse, the red sun is directly overhead. Heat beats down on us, makes my shirt damp. I hope we can go inside and find some shade.

The warehouse is built from the same vine-covered stone that makes up the rest of the city. It's tall and wide, with a peaked roof that faces our street. The vines are so thick they almost obscure two huge stone doors that look like they're designed to slide apart. If those doors opened all the way, the shuttle could roll in with plenty of room to spare on either side.

Cornstalk statues rise up from the roof's edges. This close to them, the vines look like old spiderwebs strung between the posts.

Bishop points to the base of the big doors. "Let's try there."

We walk closer. Through the thick plant cover, I see a person-sized door set into the big sliding one. How did he spot that?

Bishop rips vines, tosses them aside. He exposes a pair of familiar-looking holes in the small door's frame. Spingate looks at me for permission; I nod. She inserts the golden tool and starts pressing jewels, trying to unlock it.

Several minutes pass. The heat pounds down. I'm getting bored, and so are the others.

"Spin, is that going to work or not?"

"Almost got it," she says.

The door clicks, grinds inward. Dirt falls. Dust puffs. A stale smell billows out, carried on a wave of cold air.

Axe in one hand, flashlight in the other, Bishop enters, Coyotl and Farrar at his heels.

I stand alone with Spingate. She seems distracted, as if all of this wonder is lost on her.

"Spin, are you all right?"

She looks at me, forces a smile. "Yes. I just . . . I'm worried about Gaston. Something could happen to him while we're gone."

Not *something could happen to the* OTHERS, but rather, *something could happen to* HIM. I remember the way the two of them wrestled back on the *Xolotl,* laughing and playing. Different from how the others played. I feel awkward and uncomfortable talking about this. I've never kissed a boy—or a girl, for that matter—so I don't know what I'm talking about, but it seems to me she really likes Gaston.

"Are you and he . . . um . . . more than just friends?"

She sniffs. "I think I love him."

Love? I wasn't expecting that. Love is for older people. But then, we *are* older. Aren't we?

Could *I* fall in love?

I feel a surge of happiness. We're starting a new world down here. We need love. We need people to . . . to *make babies*.

A rush of shame. Flashes of people in black uniforms hitting me, calling me *evil* and *blasphemous*. My skin suddenly feels hot, and it's not from the sun. What did Matilda have to go through as a child? For the first time, I feel actual sympathy for her—and I hate myself for it.

"Em, are you okay?"

"Yes, sorry." I wave at myself, trying to cool off my skin. "Gaston . . . does he love you back?"

Her eyes crinkle in a smile that owns every bit of her face. "Well, when we were in the pilothouse, we—"

Bishop's head pops out of the door.

"Em, you have to see this."

No vines in here. Flashlight beams play off tall blue racks that stretch away from us, rise up to the slanted roof far above. White bins pack the racks, bins large enough for me to fit inside if I scrunched tight enough. The floor feels smooth, but is covered in dirt and bumpy spots.

A few blurds zip through the darkness, their presence known only by the buzzing of wings and high-pitched chirps. I try not to think that the bumps under my bare feet are probably blurd poop.

So dim in here, so many places to hide. I think back to the *Xolotl*'s long hallways, the shadowy places where the pigs lurked. I think back to Latu's body, surrounded by bloody hoofprints.

I hate dark places.

Bishop creeps to the closest rack, axe at the ready. Nothing happens. He rests his axe against the rack, slowly pulls out a bin. Flashlight beams catch shimmers of movement: shiny little things scurrying off the bin, scampering away into the darkness. Some kind of insect, maybe.

Bishop places the bin on the dirty floor. On top of the bin is a profile of a jaguar, yellow and black. The jaguar's eye is a clear jewel. Bishop stares at the bin for a moment, hands searching the sides, brushing away dust and dead bugs. He presses the jaguar's eye. A click, then the top of the bin opens, two halves sliding to the sides just like the lids of our birth-coffins back on the *Xolotl*.

We join him. Inside the bin are dark-pink packages, each marked with simple letters. The letters look worn, fuzzy, but we can make out the words: PROTEIN, BREAD, VEGETABLES, VITAMINS.

"That answers that," Spingate says. "The packages are a different color, but other than that, they look exactly like what we found in the shuttle. The Grownups built this place."

Bishop reaches in with his left hand, pulls out a package labeled BISCUITS. He switches the package to his right hand, then looks at his left—red dust on his fingers. The package isn't actually dark pink: there are white spots where his fingers held it.

Spingate frowns. "Bishop, put it down. Let me see if it's still edible."

Bishop sets the package on the floor.

Spingate waves her bracelet over it.

Farrar gives the bin a light kick as if to make sure it's real. He looks up at the endless racks.

"So much," he says. "We can eat forever and ever."

Not *forever,* I know, but there is enough to last us years. This will give us plenty of time to learn farming and hunting. It's hard to control my excitement. I want to dance and shout, I want to celebrate.

Coyotl walks down the long center aisle, craning his head, looking left and right, trying to take it all in.

"The gods provided for us," he says. "Aramovsky speaks the truth."

The mention of that name almost spoils the moment. Of course Aramovsky will attribute this to the gods, when clearly it was *people* who built this city and made this food.

Coyotl pulls a bin from the rack, sets it on the floor and opens it. "Hey, cookies!" He tears open a pink package and pulls out a small black circle. The sight of it makes my mouth water; Matilda had treats like that when she was little. But we don't know if it's safe to eat.

"Coyotl, put it down," I say.

He looks at it wistfully, then sets the cookie and the package back in the bin.

Farrar drops his shovel and sprints to the bin. He pulls out the same cookie that Coyotl held. Farrar's smile is so bright it could light up the entire warehouse.

"Finally—*sweets*!"

Before I can tell him to drop it, he pops the whole thing into his mouth and crunches down.

"The gods provide," he says, chewing and grinning.

Coyotl is frowning. He stares at his fingers like there is something wrong with them, flicks them like he's trying to shake off a bug.

Movement on my left. Bishop, wiping his hand against what's left of his pants, a worried look on his face.

"My fingers are tingling," he says. "They sting a little."

I hear a sharp *beep:* the sound comes from Spingate's bracer. The jewels all flash a bright orange—an obvious color of warning.

She stands quickly. "The red powder is mold. It's *toxic.*"

The word stabs through my chest.

I drop my spear, sprint to Farrar.

"Spit it out! *Spit it out!*"

Still chewing, he looks at me like he doesn't understand what I'm saying—then I realize he's not looking at me at all. His eyes are glassy, unfocused.

"These cookies taste *awful,*" he says in a sleepy voice, then stumbles backward. I try to catch him as he falls, but his weight drags us both down. I scramble to my knees, hearing feet slapping against the floor as the others run our way.

Farrar gags. His eyes roll up, showing only whites that gleam ghostly in the flashlight beams.

Spingate slides down next to me, grabs Farrar's face, jams her fingertips and thumbs into his cheeks, forcing his jaw open.

"Em, get it out of his mouth before he swallows!"

I reach in with my fingers, scoop out half-chewed cookie and throw the black mess aside. I slide fingertips between his lips and gums, under his tongue, fling more poison away—my skin is already tingling.

"Coyotl, *water,*" Spingate barks. She turns Farrar's face to the side. "Wash out his mouth!"

Coyotl aims his container at Farrar's open mouth and

squeezes—a jet of water splashes across Farrar's tongue, dribbles onto the dirty floor.

Farrar starts to twitch. He convulses, body contracting violently—his forehead smashes into Spingate's cheek, sends her sprawling.

Bishop locks his arms around Farrar's upper body, holds him tight.

All our flashlights are on the floor, except for Coyotl's, the beam of which dances madly across Farrar's face.

Spingate is there again, blood coursing down her cheek. She's looking inside the white case Smith gave her, trying to find something specific. She removes a small white device barely bigger than her pinkie, presses it to Farrar's throat.

I hear a small *snikt* sound. She pulls the device away, drawing a thin metal needle with it. She injected him with something.

Farrar's body lurches hard, then relaxes all at once. His eyes flutter open. I can see his irises. His chest heaves.

Spingate holds his face again, but gently this time.

"Farrar, it's Spingate. Can you see me?"

His eyes widen, focus on her. He nods.

I feel my held breath rush out: he's okay.

Farrar looks at me, confused, then at Bishop.

"What happened?"

"You ate the cookies," Bishop says. "Everyone, make sure you do *not* eat the cookies."

Bishop is so solemn and serious—I start laughing. The sound is awkward. I shouldn't be laughing, because there's nothing funny about any of this, but I can't help it.

Spingate examines her twentieth bin. Bishop and Coyotl have been bringing them back from all over the warehouse. Coyotl even climbed up high to grab one, somehow managing to get all the way back down while holding it under one arm.

We watch the bracer on Spingate's wrist as she waves her hand over the bin's contents: a dozen dark-pink boxes that tease us with simple names for food.

The jewels flash orange.

I look over at Farrar. He's sheened with sweat. It's been maybe an hour since he ate the cookie, and he's still breathing hard. Spin thinks he'll be fine, but when we get back to the shuttle I'll make sure Smith takes a look at him.

Spingate closes the bin she just examined. The jaguar's jewel eye sparkles. She looks at Bishop.

"You're sure this was from farther away?"

He points down the warehouse's main aisle. "I got it from the end, next to the far wall. And I looked inside probably a hundred bins along the way—they all have the red powder."

Spingate shakes her head. "The powder is a microorganism so small it can get into the containers, even get through the wrappers and right into the food. If we hadn't acted as fast as we did, Farrar would be dead." She looks up at me. "Once the mold contaminates food, there's nothing we can do to make it edible again."

She looks down, as if it's her fault that we're in a building *full* of food, yet we can't eat any of it.

At least we have the shuttle's supplies. We have time to figure out other answers.

I remember Brewer's strange words back on the *Xolotl*—*Hopefully you can break the mold. If you can't, that was one very long trip for nothing.*

Break the mold. He *knew*. One long trip for nothing . . .

"The mold," I say to Spingate, "how does it spread?"

She stands up, brushes off her hands and shrugs. "My guess

is the microorganisms probably make little eggs. No, that's not quite right . . . they make *spores,* little bits so small they float on the air. They land on things and the process starts over."

If it spreads through the air . . .

I grab her arm. "Could these spores get into the shuttle's stores?"

Spingate's eyes widen. "Yes, they could."

A few minutes ago, we thought we had enough food to last for years. All we have is what's on the shuttle—if that goes bad, we're doomed.

Spingate looks at her water container. She turns it upside down; two drops come out, then nothing. She emptied it—and Coyotl's as well—further cleaning out Farrar's mouth. I emptied mine washing my hands until they stopped stinging. Bishop did the same with his.

Just like that, we're almost out of water.

Spingate stares at the empty container.

"If the water in this city carries the same spores, we can't drink it," she says. "We'll die of dehydration long before we get hungry. We have to find fresh water and test it."

She looks at me, and I know what she's thinking: *the river*. I remember the pilothouse map.

That waterfall isn't far from here.

SIX

We stop and stare. The distant waterfall's soft roar echoes through the streets, but no one is paying attention to that.

Coyotl breaks our silence.

"Those are some big godsdamned doors."

I glance at him, annoyed. Does he need to curse? I can't remember much of school, but Matilda's memories give me the sense that cursing brought discipline. The paddle. Or something even worse . . . I vaguely remember a phrase . . . *the rod*.

He sees me staring, stares back. He raises an eyebrow, daring me to correct him.

In school, he'd be in trouble. But we're not in school anymore. And I have to admit, he's right—those *are* some godsdamned-big doors.

We stand in the middle of a wide street, facing east. The waterfall is somewhere off to our left, to the north. Buildings and ziggurats flank us, reaching up to the sky. Far ahead of us, the street ends at an archway set into a massive, vine-choked wall. The wall is as tall as twenty of us standing on each other's shoulders. Towers spot its length, each of them rising up even higher than the wall itself.

In that archway, metal doors half as high as the wall. They look like they swing outward. No vines on them, although a few dangle down from the arch above. Maybe plants can't grip metal like they can stone.

I see a sliver of yellow between those doors. The door on our right looks slightly open. I remember Gaston's map—that yellow must be the vine-choked ruins that lie beyond.

We'll have to explore that gate soon, but first we have something more important to worry about.

"Let's go," I say. "We need to find the waterfall."

We turn north. We follow a narrower street, moving toward the river's roar.

It looked a lot smaller on the map.

The waterfall soars above us, white froth crashing down into a clear pool. The red sun is just above the waterfall's edge—only a few hours until nightfall. Spray hangs in the air, catching the afternoon light. Brightly colored blurds dart in and out of the hanging mist.

A set of switchback steps carved into dark stone leads up the waterfall's right side: ten steps to the right, sharp turn, ten to the left, and so on, all the way up.

Vine-draped boulders, each as tall as my chest, line the pool's edge. A ring of smaller rocks runs along the outside of the boulders. A second ring—glistening wet from the water that splashes against them—runs along the inside. Vines cover the flat ground. Buildings and ziggurats rise up all around us. Perhaps this place was a plaza of some kind, open and welcome to this lost city's forgotten residents.

Coyotl hops onto a boulder. His covering of caked ash is almost gone. He's more filthy than fierce now, a dirty boy with reddish skin and taut, fluttering muscles. He looks into the pool, then raises his thighbone high and whoops.

"I'm going swimming!"

"No!" I have to shout to be heard over the water's crash. "We don't know if it's safe!"

Coyotl rolls his eyes. "You think because you're in charge you can just boss people around. Aramovsky was right about you."

"Shut up," Bishop says. "Farrar almost died from eating something. That water could be just as poisonous."

Coyotl glances at the water—that commonsense thought hadn't occurred to him. He sighs, sits down on the big rock.

I'm grateful that Bishop supports me, but my thoughts stick on what Coyotl just said. Aramovsky has been talking about me behind my back? I'm the one that got us off the *Xolotl,* I'm the one who got us to Omeyocan—it hurts that Coyotl would think badly of me.

Spingate tries to climb up a boulder. She's not sure how to approach it. Bishop grabs her by the waist and lifts her like she weighs nothing at all. She squeals in delighted surprise as he sets her on top.

She's so much prettier than I am, especially with the sun blazing off her red hair. She makes me so mad my skin prickles, a cascade of tiny needle-pokes washing down my cheeks, my neck. I wonder how pretty she'd be if I punched her in the mouth, gave her a split lip to match the one I got fighting the monsters. Selfish Spingate deserves it—she already has Gaston, and now she wants Bishop, too? My chest tightens, feels solid, like it's made of rock. I'll show that girl, I'll punish her, I'll . . .

I shudder. Where did all of *that* come from? I feel the rage spreading through me, already dissipating but still strong, still vile and repulsive. Theresa Spingate is my friend—I would never hit her. My face flushes hot with embarrassment again, but this time I'm ashamed of my own jealousy. That tightness in my chest, it relaxes, *releases*. My temper . . . it's bad. I have to be careful.

Is that how Matilda took over the Grownups? Did her temper control her, let her control them?

Farrar climbs atop a big boulder, then drops down to the inner ring. He looks much better; the walk did him good. He helps Spingate down, his big hands on the bare skin of her narrow waist.

Does *everyone* want to touch her?

Stop it, Em—she's not doing anything wrong.

Spingate kneels, gets to work examining the water.

Coyotl stands up again, the urge to jump in radiating off him.

"Don't," Bishop says sharply.

Coyotl sighs. "Okay, *Dad*." He sits down. He looks at me. "Okay, *Mom*."

He clearly hates being told what to do. Aramovsky's influence, or Coyotl's normal personality?

Spingate stands, pats her chest as if to still a racing heart.

"No mold," she says with audible relief. "There's some rotten plant material mixed in, though. We could drink from this pool in a pinch, but I wouldn't recommend it." She points up at the waterfall. "Probably cleaner up top. If we can collect it from there, we won't ever have to worry about water."

I breathe out, releasing a tension I hadn't realized I was carrying. This city is so large, there must be a system of pipes to bring water to all the buildings. If that system still works, and we find clean water closer to the shuttle, fine. If not, at least we have this waterfall. I may have to move everyone here. We could live in the buildings surrounding this plaza.

At any rate, we will have to move somewhere—we can't stay in the shuttle forever. We're already packed in there like chickens in a coop, and if we open the coffins on Deck Four, it could be much worse. Eventually people will need their own space.

Coyotl stands atop his boulder, sets his thighbone down.

"Spingate did her testing. Can I do mine?"

I look at her, silently asking if it is safe. She nods.

"Swim away," I say. "But I bet you can't do a perfect dive!"

Coyotl leaps far; his thin body slices into the pool with barely a splash. He stays under for a few seconds. When he pops up, wet dust is running off his skin.

"The water is *great*!" He rubs hard at his face and hair, ducks under, pops up again. Clean, he looks like a different person. On the *Xolotl,* he was an ash-covered gray warrior fighting to keep us alive, fighting to set us free; on Omeyocan, he's a young man barely out of his teens—flawless, perfect, innocent.

I see Farrar help Spingate step into the water. She laughs in surprised, openmouthed shock.

"Coyotl, you liar, this is *freezing*."

She slips on the wet rocks, shrieks, grabs Farrar's round shoulders as she goes down—they splash into the water together. Spingate stands. Her shirt was far too small to begin with. Now it hugs her like a transparent second skin. Either she doesn't know, or it doesn't bother her.

Bishop steps closer to me.

"Em, can we go in, too?"

Dried blood, ash smears and dirt cover him head to toe. More of the same crusts in his blond curls. Coyotl looked beautiful when the water washed away his filth—Bishop will look even more so.

And he's not the only one who could use a bath. I'm still coated in dead-person dust, still caked with grime.

"Sure, let's go."

He reaches halfway toward me, pauses, as if he wanted to take my hand, then didn't know if that was wrong. I could take his, but I don't—the awkward moment hangs there, neither of us knowing what to do, then he turns and sprints toward the boulders. One powerful leg launches him to the top, where the other powerful leg sends him sailing out over the water. He arcs through the air, a dirt-covered mixture of grace and muscle. It looks like he will knife into the water just as Coyotl did, but at the last second Bishop tucks into a tight ball. When he hits, he sends up a big wave that splashes Spingate—she goes rigid and squeals with laughter.

I use my spear like a cane, balancing myself as I climb over a tall boulder to stand on the wet rocks lining the pool. I look into the water. It gets deep fast, but the shallows hide jagged rocks. Are my friends all crazy jumping in like that?

Bishop bursts from the surface. Water cascades down his now-clean skin, sparkling in the sunlight. I flash back to the *Xolotl,* to the talk with Brewer, when I was staring at the gnarled creature and thinking, *I don't know what a god is, exactly, but if gods do exist they don't look like this thing.*

No: if gods exist, they look like Bishop.

I squat down on my heels, cup my hand and fill it with cold water. I rub it on my face; it feels *amazing*. I am so unclean. Should I take off my shirt, be bare-chested like Bishop and Coyotl and Farrar?

The thought of that embarrasses me even more than seeing Spingate in her see-through shirt. I'll keep my clothes on—I don't want these boys to see my body.

At least, not *all* the boys.

I try not to stare at Bishop as I stand and look for a safe place to dive in. My foot suddenly slides off the wet rock and plunges into the water. I cry out in surprise—off-balance, I drop my spear and whirl my arms trying to stay up, but my other foot slips as well and I start to fall.

Bishop catches me before I go all the way under.

His arm is under my back, his hand on my hip. His body feels *solid*, so strong. His arms have the power to crush the life out of anyone, yet he holds me so gently.

He's so close. His skin is so warm.

Bishop opens his mouth to speak, then stops, as if words have escaped him. He lifts me, sets me back on the rock. He's still standing in the water. For once, I am taller than he is.

Water drips from my ripped skirt. The bottom of my shirt is wet—it clings to my ribs, drips down my exposed belly.

Coyotl and Farrar are laughing, splashing, oblivious to anything other than whatever new game they've concocted. Spingate, however, is looking right at me. My eyes meet hers. She smiles slightly, one corner of her mouth ticking up. She turns to Coyotl and Farrar.

"I want to test the water at the top of the waterfall," she says to them. "I'm not sure I can make it up there on my own, can you two help?"

Farrar's wide chest puffs out. "Yes! We'll help you."

Coyotl makes a strange face, then glances at Bishop, who still holds me in his arms. Coyotl's lip curls into a small smile just like Spingate's.

"Sure," he says to her. "Happy to be of assistance."

The stone steps leading up are wide and dry. Spingate doesn't need any help. She's taking the others away so I can be alone with Bishop.

He's still staring at me. He doesn't seem to notice anything *but* me.

Farrar helps Spingate stand on a boulder. He starts up after her, but she pushes him—arms flailing, he splashes back into the pool.

Water dripping from her scraps of clothing, Spingate hops off the boulder and runs for the steps.

"Last one to the top is an ugly Grownup!"

Coyotl and Farrar chase after her, laughing, enjoying the new game. They catch her almost immediately, but don't run past—they're more interested in walking by her side than winning. Up and up they go, talking as they climb. I can't hear them over the waterfall's roar.

Bishop looks down at my foot. "Does it hurt?"

It doesn't hurt at all.

"Yes," I say.

He kneels in the water. His big hands gently grip my ankle. His touch . . . it makes something surge in my stomach and chest. Just like my rage at Spingate was instant and overwhelming, so too is this new sensation of heat, of thoughts lost in a swimming, dizzy whirl.

He leans in, looking closely.

"I don't think it's broken," he says. "I should check your shin and calf . . ."

His hands slide softly up my leg. Fingertips press in; is he really seeing if I'm hurt, or is he pretending just as much as I am?

He glances up at me with those beautiful dark-yellow eyes. A warrior who will snarl and fight and kill, yet he has such pretty eyes?

The waterfall's roar fills my ears.

My heart . . . each beat feels like it's punching my chest.

Bishop's lips, so pink.

He rises slowly, sliding his hands to my hips, then my ribs. I feel weak . . . boneless.

This is the boy who saved my life.

My mouth opens a little, I lean forward and down. My eyes shut . . .

His lips on mine. Soft. Warm. My world is the sound of crashing water and the feel of his mouth, the taste of his breath.

His hands on my face, sliding to the back of my head. Fingers in my hair. My hands shoot out, cup his cheeks, pull him closer. I feel the tip of his tongue touch mine.

Something hits the pool, *boom, boom,* an explosion of water.

Bishop pulls away, looks toward the heavy splash we just heard, putting his body between me and the unknown danger.

Farrar breaks the surface, gasping for air—a second later Spingate does the same. I hear a yell from above, look up in time to see Coyotl leap off the waterfall. His legs kick and his arms flail as he plummets down. He plunges down between Farrar and Spingate, who are already swimming toward us.

They *jumped*?

Bishop launches himself into the pool, heads for Spingate. She swims like a fish, already leaving Farrar behind. She doesn't need help, but Bishop goes to her anyway.

Coyotl pops up, gasping, swims toward me as hard as he can. He's terrified.

I look up at the waterfall, and I see why.

The late afternoon sun silhouettes something, a shape blurred by the nearly blinding light. Long, jointed legs—a segment pointing up connected to one pointing down—Matilda's memories rush forward, flash an almost matching image of that rough, horrifying form.

They aren't that big, they *can't* be that big, but there it is, larger than Bishop and Farrar and Coyotl combined.

A *spider*.

SEVEN

My hand thrusts into the water, my fingers find my spear. I point the metal tip at my new enemy.

Spingate is the first out of the pool. She scrambles over the boulders, out of my line of sight. I can't see her, but I hear her shouting.

"*Run!* That thing is chasing us!"

My feet won't move.

Bishop, Farrar and Coyotl rush out of the water. They snatch up their weapons.

I stare up at the spider, a spindly shape blurred by the shimmering sun. Perfectly still one second, the next it's scurrying along the top of the waterfall, each step kicking up a high splash of water.

We'll never outrun that.

It stops at the stone steps. Long legs reach down, tap at the first switchback step. Reach, tap, pull back, reach, tap . . .

The spider turns away and is instantly gone from sight.

It wouldn't use the steps. Why? Are they too steep for it?

Hands on my waist—Bishop flings me over his shoulder. In an instant he bounds onto the big rocks, then down to the vine-covered street.

"Bishop, let me go!"

He does, fast and firm. He's terrified. As big as he is, that thing, that *nightmare*, is much bigger.

I see the backs of Farrar, Coyotl and Spingate. They're running the way we came, headed for the shuttle or maybe the warehouse. But the warehouse is an hour away, the shuttle even farther. If that thing finds another path down from the cliff, we won't make it—it's far too fast.

There is only one place we can go.

I raise the spear high and scream with the same voice that rallied us in the Garden when we fought the Grownups.

"To me! *To me!*"

They all stop. Spingate and Farrar come running back, instantly trusting me. Coyotl pauses, turns to run away, stops, snarls, then follows Spingate and Farrar.

Bishop grips my shoulder. His touch was tender before; now he forgets his own strength and it hurts.

"Em, what are you doing? Didn't you see that thing? We have to run!"

I whip my arm up, knocking his hand away.

The others reach us. They are on the edge of panic. That shape, the way it moved—it frightens us at a level we can't deny.

I look each of them in the eye as I speak.

"We're going to that gate."

Coyotl shakes his head.

"We should have run," he says. He gestures wildly with his thighbone, left, right, all over. "Now we have to hide in one of these buildings."

"It took Spingate forever to get into the warehouse," I say.

"We can't be caught in the open if that thing comes. The gate is close. If the spider can't handle stone steps, it can't climb the city wall. We shut that gate behind us, we'll be safe."

Farrar clutches his shovel to his chest.

"The door could be stuck," he says. "Will it close?"

I have no idea if it will move at all, but I'm not going to waste a moment second-guessing myself.

"It's our best chance," I say. "Move!"

We run south down the vine-choked street, heading for the larger road that runs east-west. Spingate trips, regains her balance, runs hard at my side. She's so *slow*.

Bishop stays beside me. I'm sprinting all out, yet he looks like he's barely jogging. Farrar and Coyotl could easily run out ahead of us, but they stay a few steps behind, protecting our backs.

We reach the intersection. We turn left—away from the shuttle and the warehouse—and see the gate far off down the road. Tall doors set into a taller archway.

Bishop sprints toward it, red axe gleaming.

We chase after him, running as hard as we can. My lungs burn, my stomach clutches. Spingate stumbles. She's already drained. I hold the spear in one hand, slide my free arm under her shoulder to support her. I have to keep her moving. She gets a burst of energy when we hear Farrar call out from behind us.

"It's coming!"

I don't look back. The door: it is survival, it is life itself. I run, part of me waiting for the spider-thing to bring me down from behind, for the pointy legs to punch through my back and out my chest.

The gate looms closer.

Bishop is already there. He stands half behind the right-hand door, which is slightly open to whatever lies beyond. The wall stretches off to either side—high, impenetrable. He waves us in, desperate for us to move faster.

Spingate and I reach the doors: sheets of metal, as thick as my forearm is long. We rush through the opening. Coyotl and Farrar are right behind us. They drop their weapons, throw themselves against the door alongside Bishop.

I stand there, trying to breathe, as the three boys attack a metal slab that is four times as tall as they are. Their arms shake, their legs tremble, their feet push against vines that slip and slide away.

Over the boys' grunts, I hear a faint grinding sound—the door is closing, but too slowly. As it moves, long vines bunch underneath it, thick stalks jamming between the bottom of the door and the street's flat stone.

I rush back through. I use my spear blade to slice at the vines. Spingate joins me, chopping away with Farrar's sharp shovel. Blue juice splatters and sprays. The smell of mint is everywhere. We cut, we kick, clearing space.

A new sound—a horrid *whine*.

Far down the street, I see it coming. My skin shivers and prickles. Dark yellow, with thin strips of green and brown. Three-jointed legs moving so fast they are blurs, little flecks of torn vine tossed high in their wake. The hungry whine echoes through the streets, bounces off the ziggurat walls. The spider runs with a wobble, a halting hitch—one of the legs is lame, maybe.

If it reaches us, it will tear us to shreds.

I grab Spingate, shove her through the slowly closing door, then squeeze through the narrowing gap myself. On the other side, I stand next to Coyotl, hurl all my strength at the door. Spingate does the same.

The massive hinges screech and howl, seem to fight our desperate effort, but my toes find purchase in the plant-juice-slick stones and I feel the slab of metal moving. The door's grinding grows louder, but so does the spider's whine.

Bishop's extended arms tremble with effort. Sweat pours off his skin. His voice is a roar of command.

"*Everything you've got!* Godsdammit, *push!*"

Coyotl and Farrar groan with effort. Spingate screams, a combination of fear and frustration and rage.

The door picks up speed.

I hear the spider's hard feet clicking against the stone street lying beneath the vines, a harsh, rapid drumbeat of oncoming death.

The hinges give a final, tortured shriek—the door clangs shut with a reverberating *gong* that hangs in the air.

Everyone sags, even Bishop. If the spider can get through these doors, we don't have the strength to run, let alone fight.

The whining sound stops.

I keep my hands pressed against the door. I hear and feel a scraping coming from the other side, hard-shelled legs scratching at thick metal, searching for a way through, a way to get at us.

The scraping stops.

That whine again. Faint . . . then fading . . .

Then nothing.

Is the spider gone? Or is it standing there, motionless, waiting for us?

"We'll rest here for a minute," I say, as if we could do anything else.

Farrar falls to the ground. Coyotl slumps to his butt, his back against the door. Bishop's hands are on his knees, his stomach heaving in and out as he tries to get his breathing under control.

Spingate seems the least winded; her hands are on her hips, her lips are pursed.

"Spin, what happened back there?"

She laces her fingers over her head.

"At the top . . . jungle on either side of the river," she says, forcing words through deep breaths. "Trees . . . *real* trees, not the vines. Coyotl went in . . . for a closer look. I was testing the water. He came sprinting out . . . shouting at us to jump. I saw what was behind him . . . it almost got us. But . . . it wasn't a spider."

"What are you talking about? We all saw it."

She closes her eyes, shudders.

"Five legs . . . not eight."

Her correction angers me. Like the number of legs matters?

Bishop stands straight. He gleams with sweat. "So it attacked?"

Coyotl sees that Bishop is standing, struggles to his feet. "It came after us. Maybe I should have fought it . . . I wasn't afraid, but there was Spingate, and . . . well, I *wasn't* afraid."

Still lying on his back, Farrar raises a hand. "I was. Glad we jumped into the pool, because when I saw that thing I think I peed in my pants a little."

Coyotl glares at him.

Bishop nods. "It scared me, too."

His admission of fear seems to relax Coyotl. If even Bishop is afraid, then running away from the spider couldn't be such a bad thing.

I put my shoulder to the door again, give it a little push to make sure it's really closed. It is. At my feet, I see mashed vines, blue-smeared curving lines on the stone where the door scraped against it.

No way I can relax, not even a bit, but with the door shut I have a moment to think.

I turn and rest my back against the door. In front of me, *trees,* more than I could ever count.

Before us lies a dense jungle, growing up and through and around blackened, burned, crumbling, vine-choked six-sided buildings. Trees also grow out of giant, plant-covered holes in the ground. There are long, open spaces that were maybe once roads, but it's hard to tell with all the holes and trees and the endless yellow vines that cover everything.

When we first landed, I thought the sprawling city was a ruin, taken by the hands of time. What I see now shows me I was wrong. The city we landed in isn't ruined, it is merely abandoned and overgrown: most of those four-sided buildings are still standing.

What I look at now is something else altogether.

These six-sided buildings weren't abandoned.

They were *destroyed*.

PART II

WALLS AND WONDERS

EIGHT

We walk through the jungle.

The curving wall is on our right, tall and constant, covered with layers of thick vines. Following it takes us mostly south and a little east. We hope to run across another gate soon, but we have no way of knowing if we will, or if it will be open. I'm very worried—we've eaten what little food we brought with us, and we're already out of water.

Keeping the wall on our right means the thick jungle is on our left. Tall trees with dark-yellow leaves, green or brown trunks. Plenty of vines there, too, dangling from branches and covering the collapsed buildings. Blurds—some as big as I am—dart in and out of the trees, or fly full speed into the deep canopy where they vanish from sight.

The heat is worse here than it is in the city. It's so humid. It seems that every other step squishes into mud, which hides jagged old sticks and a brown plant that has sharp thorns. Each time we step on one, we have to stop so someone can carefully pull thorns from the soles of our feet. That slows us down, makes me hate the Grownups anew—they dressed us up like dolls, so couldn't they have given us shoes?

The sun is descending on the far side of the city. The wall casts a growing shadow upon us. I don't want to be outside when night falls, but it looks like we can't avoid that. Animal noises reach out to us from deep in the jungle, the cries and howls of creatures that might be waking up from a day's sleep to hunt when darkness fully sets in.

So many questions. These six-sided buildings, scored and gutted, covered by the undying jungle—how far do they reach? Does this massive wall go all the way around our ziggurat city?

Spingate gestures to the sprawling ruins on our left.

"Maybe a big fire burned them all," she says. "Or it could have been a meteor shower, rocks hitting so hard they made craters, caused explosions that started fires."

Bishop laughs at this. "Spingate, are you joking?"

"Not at all," she says, bristling that he would doubt her. "Rocks can come from space at high speeds, partially burning up as they hit the atmosphere, and—"

He holds up a fist, which means we're supposed to stop. We do. He faces her.

"You really don't know what caused all of this?"

She seems defensive. "No. Do you?"

Bishop nods. "War."

One word. So simple. And from looking at the devastation around us, so *horrible*.

We start walking again. It seems so obvious now—how could I have thought so much damage came from anything *but* war? Destruction, killing . . . just like on the *Xolotl,* but at a scale that is hard to conceive. How many people died? Thousands? *Millions?*

On one side of this wall lie endless ruins and carnage. On the other, untouched buildings damaged only by plants, only by time and neglect. It doesn't take a genius like Spingate or Gaston to figure out what happened. My kind destroyed a city so they could build their own in the same place. Even down here, we can't escape the Grownups' violent touch.

Bishop raises a fist. We stop.

He crouches down, stares off into the darkening ruins.

"Em, come here," he whispers.

I squat beside him. He points to a ruined building. Three of its six vine-choked walls have collapsed. There is no roof to stop the young trees growing tall from within.

Bishop leans close to me. "Do you see it?"

I look, but see nothing that should cause concern. "It's a ruined building. We've passed hundreds of them."

His eyes narrow, like he's disappointed. My heart plummets—I can't stand the idea that he thinks poorly of me.

"Not the building itself," he says. "Look just above it."

Now I see it: against the barely lit sky, a thin column of smoke rises up from somewhere beyond that building.

"A campfire," he says. "Someone is out there."

People. People who are not *us*. We're not alone after all.

Bishop looks at me. Once again we're close enough to kiss, but this isn't the time for that.

"I'll go look," he says. "See what's there."

"No, it's too dangerous. What if it's another spider?"

He considers this carefully, then shakes his head. "The spider didn't try to open the door. It easily outweighs all of us combined. All it had to do was *push,* but it didn't even try. If it's not smart enough to open a door, it's not smart enough to build a fire."

He's right. It's an animal—an animal that attacked us.

"The spider is inside the city walls, where the rest of our people are," I say. "We need to get back to the shuttle as fast as possible. And besides, it's almost dark. There could be more spiders in the jungle."

Bishop considers this, bites at his lower lip. He used to just *act*. Now, he *thinks* first. It's definitely an improvement.

"The fire means someone lives out there," he says. "Doesn't that mean they must have food that isn't poisoned by the mold?"

From behind me, Spingate lets out a cough of surprise.

"He's right," she says. "I mean, they could be immune to the toxin somehow, but however they beat it, we need to know."

Bishop has a good point. And looking for food was the whole purpose of this trip.

"All right," I say. "We'll check it out."

He smiles, starts to rise.

"I said *we,* Bishop. You're not going alone."

He wasn't expecting that. "Then I'll take Farrar."

I touch the back of his hand. "No, all of us, together. We shouldn't have split up before."

He pauses, then pulls his hand away, his eyes cast down.

Together, he and I made the choice to abandon Bello, and did we learn from our mistake? No. At the waterfall, we let Spingate, Farrar and Coyotl go off by themselves so we could be alone together. The spider could have hurt them, and that's our fault.

Bishop turns his head, speaks just loud enough for everyone to hear him.

"Farrar, stay on my right. Coyotl, on my left. Em and Spingate, stay close behind, but far enough back so you can run if something attacks."

We are new to this planet, to this city, but it seems we have neighbors. In a moment, we will find out if they are friend . . . or foe.

Bishop silently leads us into the jungle ruins.

NINE

We find the fire. Whoever made it is gone.

Glowing coals cast tendrils of smoke into the darkening night. Someone built a fire pit in the middle of this six-sided ruin. With no roof and one wall collapsed, the fire-builders had protection from five sides. Maybe they cooked bread—I faintly smell burned toast.

The sun finally slides behind the city wall. The sky burns a molten-sunset red. Jungle shadows thicken. Strange, new noises rise—animal screeches, echoing hoots, beastly bellows, all completely alien to anything hiding in Matilda's memories.

Bishop, Farrar and Coyotl move silently through the ruin, weapons at the ready. Bishop kneels by the fire pit. He pokes at the mostly black coals, careful not to touch those that still shimmer with soft waves of orange. From the pit's edge, he pulls out a fist-sized chunk of half-burned wood. He tosses it to Coyotl, throws another to Farrar, then pulls out a third for himself.

The boys set down their weapons. They rub the charcoal on arms, legs, faces. Farrar uses his shovel to cut free several long vines, which the boys wrap around themselves, coiling them over shoulders, across chests, around waists, tying them off here and there. Finally, the circle-stars scoop up mud and grind it into their hair.

Just like that, they are transformed. For a few hours, they were boys again—clean and beautiful. Now they are the jungle.

Coyotl moves to the inside walls, checking them carefully, his thighbone held in front of him. Farrar takes the outside.

Bishop remains at the fire pit, fingers drumming an absent pattern on the head of his axe.

I kneel next to him. "Could they have heard us coming?"

"No, we were very quiet. Even you and Spingate."

He sounds surprised by that. I take it as a compliment.

I am both afraid and excited. We couldn't have missed the fire-makers by much. They could be close. They might come back.

Spingate joins us. She pokes at the ground next to the pit, pinches her fingers around something small and black—it's a bone.

"There's a little bit of flesh on here," she says. "This animal was *cooked*."

She waves her bracelet over the tiny bone. I wait for the jewels to give off the orange warning color, but they do not. Instead, they flash with a mixture of blues, greens, purples.

Spingate smiles.

"Edible," she says. "No sign of the red mold's toxin."

That food in the warehouse—if all we need to do is cook it, we'll be fine.

"Did the fire burn it off?"

"It doesn't work like that," she says. "Fire kills the mold, but won't neutralize the toxin secreted by the mold."

Dammit.

Spingate turns the bone, looks at it from a different angle.

"Maybe the mold can't grow on live animals," she says. "Or maybe this particular animal is resistant to it. We need to catch one to find out."

She doesn't have answers, but at least there's hope. We have to find the people who built this fire, befriend them if we can, learn their secrets.

"Em, Bishop," Farrar calls out softly. "Come see."

We join him at the collapsed wall. He taps the tip of his shovel against the rubble.

"The broken edges are clean," he says. "No moss or dirt on them. Something knocked this wall in, and very recently."

In the fading light, a spot on the ground just past the collapsed wall catches my eye. A patch of blackness. I walk to it, careful not to trip on the loose rubble. The spot is a neat hole, from something long and pointed punching into the dirt.

Long and pointed . . . like the feet of the creature that chased us out of the city.

"I think a spider knocked down this wall," I say. "Maybe to get at the people who were inside."

Is that why the fire was abandoned? Whoever the fire-makers are, I hope they got away.

We are all suddenly aware that danger could be close by. Our eyes flick to every growing shadow, to every dark spot in this tangled mass of yellow, green and brown.

Those colors . . . the spider's shell matches them. *Exactly*.

I glance at Bishop, Farrar, Coyotl. Their charcoal and vines and mud . . . camouflage that lets them blend in to the jungle.

"We have to get out of here," I say.

Bishop nods, his mud-smeared face turning this way, then that, white eyes wide and darting.

"Back to the city wall," he says. "And move *quietly*."

Darkness falls. For only the second time in my short life, I see stars.

We walk along the city wall, quiet as can be. We don't use the flashlights for fear they might draw attention from the animals screaming in the night, or from the dreaded spider.

Bishop leads us; Farrar and Coyotl stay a few paces behind. I can't help but look up through the thick jungle canopy. Countless pinpricks of bright light, like sparkling jewels, impossibly distant and immensely beautiful. There are two big circles up there as well: one bluish, the other maroon. Spingate says the circles are *moons*—small planets that orbit Omeyocan. That sounds impossible to me, but if Spingate says it, I believe her.

City wall on our right, dark jungle ruins on our left. The spider could be anywhere. At night it would be almost invisible in the trees, even if it was only a few steps away. But there was that whine—if it comes, hopefully we'll hear it before it sees us. If so, maybe we can hide.

Spingate says the spider isn't alone, that there have to be enough of them to support a "breeding population." Sometimes I wish she wasn't so smart. It might be better *not* to know some things.

Bishop raises a fist. We stop instantly. He's staring down at his feet. No, at the wall near his feet. He waves us forward.

He kneels, points to the base of the wall and looks up at me. Moonlight shines off his wide eyes.

I look, but once again, I don't see anything.

He reaches down and pulls the vines aside.

There is a hole in the wall.

I drop to my knees and look in. It's rough and uneven. The

city walls are thick, as thick as two Bishops lying head-to-toe, but past the far end I see the moonlit base of a ziggurat.

This hole goes all the way through.

Someone spent a long time making this, chipping away bit by bit. It's *narrow*—I could crawl in easily, but I'm much smaller than the others.

A scent . . . burned toast again. There one second, then gone.

I look up at Bishop. "Are you sure you can fit through?"

He shrugs. "I know *you* can."

I don't like the sound of that. Does he think I would leave without him?

"Even if we get inside, we're probably way past the edge of the map Gaston showed us," I say. "We'll still be lost."

Spingate kneels next to us. She taps the black jewel nestled in her ear.

"I can get us back with this," she says. "It's out of range now, but if we get inside the wall and keep heading west, I think I'll be able to reach Gaston soon enough. Then he can guide us back."

Bishop tilts his head toward the hole.

"Coyotl, go through, make sure it's safe."

Coyotl is muscular, yes, but his muscles are long and lean. Compared to Farrar and Bishop, he's skinny. He crawls into the hole, pushing his thighbone and black bag before him.

Bishop looks at me. "You next, then Spingate, then Farrar."

"Then you?"

He looks at the hole. He shrugs again. He doesn't think he'll fit.

"Then we keep looking for another way in," I say. "There has to be another gate farther up."

Bishop shakes his head. "We don't know that. Even if there is one, it could be closed, locked. You have to get back to the shuttle. Our people need you."

The tunnel makes Coyotl's voice sound strange: "Nothing on this side. Come on through."

Spingate crawls in, not waiting for permission.

"Bishop, you have to try," I say. "We can't be separated, remember?"

"Farrar, go," is his only response.

Farrar throws his bag and shovel into the tunnel. He isn't quite as big as Bishop, but he's thicker than Coyotl—he crawls in carefully, pushing the shovel before him. His grime-coated skin scrapes against the craggy surface, leaving little dirt smudges behind. If it's hard for Farrar, it's going to be very difficult for Bishop.

Bishop points to the hole. "Your turn, Em."

"And you'll follow me?"

His nostrils widen. He blinks rapidly. "Yes, I'll follow you in."

He's lying. This is the first time he's done that to me. He's terrible at it.

"You first," I say.

Bishop looks out to the jungle, scanning for threats. "Don't play games. Get back to the shuttle."

Out in the solid darkness of trees, I hear something rustle. Something *big*.

Bishop grabs my shoulder. "Em, get into that tunnel, *now*."

I stand firm. *"You first."*

A loud crack, the whoosh of leaves and branches. I see a young tree fall, moonlight playing off spinning leaves. Before it even hits the ground, a shadowy something scrambles over it.

The spider, coming fast—it will reach us in a minute, maybe less.

Bishop shakes me so hard my head rattles. *"Get into the godsdamned tunnel!"*

He's hurting me again. He doesn't know his own strength, but I know mine.

I slap him so hard my palm stings.

Bishop stares at me, shocked.

"*I* am the leader," I say. "I'm *ordering* you into that tunnel!"

He blinks, glances to the jungle. The spider is closing in, a moving shadow-blur scuttling over rubble and fallen walls, down the far side of craters and up the near, knocking over any thin trees in its way.

Bishop throws his axe into the tunnel so hard I bet it sails all the way through. He dives for the hole and gets stuck almost immediately, thick shoulders wedging against the rough surface.

I look back at the rushing monster. It's too dark to see much, but Spingate was right—five spindly legs. A Matilda memory pops into my head: *five legs, like a starfish*.

My body goes cold. Fear vanishes. If I'm going to die, that is the way of things, but with my last breath I will make sure Bishop survives.

I kneel.

"Bishop, slow down. Breathe. Put your right arm in first, stretch as far as you can."

He's still thrashing. His big frame holds so much power, but right now his size hurts him.

I place a hand on the small of his back. At my touch, his body stills.

"Listen to me," I say. "Right arm first."

His left shoulder scoots back toward me as he reaches his right hand far in front. I feel his muscles flex, see his knees bend, his toes dig: his shoulders slide through.

"That's it. Keep your shoulders angled, use your toes to push."

He goes in farther. Now only his feet and ankles are visible.

I look up, and that icy feeling explodes into hot fear—the spider is only ten steps away, a crawling nightmare barely visible in the darkness, *coming* to rip me apart.

Quickly but carefully, I slide my spear past Bishop, then dive in after him so fast I bang my head on the tunnel's edge. Brain ringing, I wriggle forward until my face presses against Bishop's filthy feet.

He's blocking the way—my legs are still exposed.

My chest is on the damp ground, and through it I feel the vibrations of the spider's pounding feet. It should be on me already . . .

"Bishop, move move move!"

Pain explodes through my calf.

My body acts on its own, curling me into a ball, pulling my feet and legs away from the opening. I grab my spear—it's too long to turn around and use point-first, so I jam the butt backward, feel it smash into something solid.

Bishop crawls forward, slow but steady.

My leg is on fire.

What if the spider comes in after me?

I turn slightly, just enough to look back down the tunnel. A patch of blackness blocks the opening—the creature is too big to fit inside.

My leg *screams*. Is the spider's poison already spreading through me?

A strange thought: *Why didn't I hear that whine?*

I face forward and crawl. Someone pulls my spear out first, then strong hands grab my wrists and drag me free.

The others pack in around me. Bishop's face is a mask of fear and concern.

"Are you hurt?"

I look at my leg. The moonlight plays off the glistening wetness coursing down my calf.

"It bit me," I say. "Why are things always biting me?"

My calf seems to blur. The moonlight fades.

Blackness drags me down.

TEN

My brain buzzes. Am I sliding into a dream or coming out of one? Strong arms carry me. My head rests against a warm chest. For once, I actually feel *safe*.

My eyes open. Blackness and bright stars high above. Bishop is carrying me.

"She's awake." Spingate's voice. "Em, can you stand?"

"I'm not sure. Let me try."

Bishop sets me down. The moment I put weight on my right foot, my calf sparks with agony. He bends to pick me up again.

"No, I can make it on my own."

He looks doubtful, concerned, but he takes a step back.

Farrar hands me my spear. I lean on it, take a few painful steps. Not the best solution, but it will do for now.

Towering ziggurats rise up all around us. Shadow drapes everything, resistant to light from the double moons. Up ahead, there is a glow coming from behind a thick, curving wall of vines. We're back at the shuttle.

My leg *hurts*. My calf is wrapped in a purple bandage that

must have come from Spingate's medical kit. Spots of blood look black.

"Did the spider poison me?"

Spingate shakes her head. "It doesn't look like a bite or a puncture wound. I think you tore it on a sharp rock."

I not only banged my head against the tunnel entrance, I hurt my leg on it as well? I thought the spider was right on top of me . . . in my desperation to escape, I must have flailed about too much, caught my calf on a jagged edge.

The fear of that moment comes rushing back. My body starts to shiver. Spingate holds me tight.

"You made it through," she says, gently stroking my hair. "That's all that matters." She lets me go, rubs my back as she guides me down the street. "We're almost there. Smith is waiting to look at you and Bishop both."

Bishop has purple bandages wrapped around one shoulder. The other shoulder is tied with strips of blood-streaked white cloth.

I realize that most of Spingate's shirt is gone, shredded into strips. The fabric that remains barely covers her breasts.

"We ran out of bandages," she says. "Bishop insisted I use what I had on you first. I improvised for his wounds."

We climb up the wall of vines. Coyotl stays close to me, helping me when I stumble. I feel weak. Weak and dizzy.

At the top, I pause, look out at our shuttle. Lights on the tail, the wing tips, the top, all gleaming in welcome.

We made it.

Coyotl helps me descend the ring of vines. I'm almost to the bottom when I freeze, that now all-too-familiar blast of paralyzing fear driving straight through me—two Grownups, sprinting toward us.

"It's all right," Coyotl says. "That's Visca and Bawden."

As soon as he says that, I see it. Visca and Bawden, yes, but dressed all in black. The coveralls in the storeroom. My pulse is racing. I can barely see straight. I need to lie down.

The two circle-stars sprint to the top of the vine ring, scouting for danger in case we were followed here. The rest of us shuffle to the shuttle.

Farrar, Spingate and Coyotl start up the ramp. Bishop stops at the base. So do I.

Spingate turns. She's beyond exhausted.

"Em, come on—you need to see Smith."

"In a minute," I say. "Just go."

She doesn't need to be told twice. She drags herself through the door.

Bawden and Visca return. I send them into the shuttle, leaving Bishop and me alone once again.

He can barely meet my eyes—he's ashamed. At the hole in the wall, he panicked and he knows it. He wanted to protect me, but I sent him into the tunnel first, exposing myself to danger so he could get away.

He tilts his head toward the shuttle door. He wants me to go inside. He needs to be the last one out here.

"Bishop, we should talk about what happened at the waterfall."

"What happened is we were stupid," he says. "We were selfish, only worrying about ourselves. People could have been hurt."

As if I didn't feel guilty enough about that already.

In at least one way, Bishop and I are the same: we have a need, an *urge* to protect everyone. I don't understand why sometimes I can't think straight when I'm around him—or O'Malley, for that matter. What I *do* know is that my selfish actions almost got our friends killed.

I glance up at the shuttle, out to the vine ring—no one else is here. I reach out and take his hand.

"We just have to be smarter," I say. I think about him kissing me. I want him to do it again. "We won't do anything like that around other people."

He stares at our hands for a moment, fingers intertwined. He gives me one short, firm squeeze, then pulls away.

"We won't do anything like that, *period,*" he says. "We're fighting to keep everyone alive, Em. I can't lose sight of that, not even for a second."

When we kissed, there was this look in his eyes—he couldn't get enough of me. That look is gone. I feel like everything is ruined.

I trudge up the ramp.

This is what happens when you let your emotions control you? Well, never again.

At the shuttle door, O'Malley is waiting for me. He's wearing black coveralls. A scabbard hangs from his waist, the jeweled handle of his knife sticking out. And . . . he has *boots*. My leg hurts so much I'd almost forgotten about my poor feet, beat up from the long hike, punctured by dozens of thorns. A Mictlan patch—just like the symbol on our ties—is stitched in metallic thread on O'Malley's left breast. He's holding a black blanket. When I stumble in, he wraps it around me.

"Welcome home, Em."

He's clean. His hair is combed, glossy black and perfect. It surprises me how good it feels to see his face.

I glance back down the ramp at Bishop, notice the contrast between the two boys: one scrubbed and neatly dressed, as if our living nightmare never happened, the other shirtless, bloody and bandaged, a walking testament to what we just endured.

O'Malley's smile fades. "Bad news. Aramovsky got into Deck Four."

His arm around my shoulders, he guides me into the coffin room. I see the familiar faces of Gaston, Beckett, Smith, Visca and the others. I see Zubiri, Walezak and the kids we found wandering the halls of the *Xolotl*.

I also see faces I don't recognize. *Hundreds* of them. No, not hundreds, I already know the exact number—168.

Aramovsky, godsdamn him . . . he opened the coffins.

Little faces on little bodies. Kids dressed in clean, perfectly fitting white shirts, red ties, and black pants or red and black plaid skirts.

More mouths to feed.

Everything catches up with me in a crashing wave of despair that washes away the last of my strength. The room spins. I'm tired, *so* tired.

"O'Malley, get me out of here. Take me to Smith."

I don't care what she does to me, as long as she gives me more of that gas and puts me under.

ELEVEN

My eyes flutter open. I'm lying on firm padding. I see something white, close above my face . . . too close—I'm in a coffin again.

I am *trapped*. Someone put me in here Matilda put me in here she won't take me she *won't* I'll fight and have to get out *have to get* . . .

No. It's not like that. I think I remember people putting me in here. O'Malley. Yes, that was it. And Smith. I'm not trapped, but this tiny space is squeezing in on me.

"Um . . . can I get out?"

"Yes, hold on."

Someone is nearby. Such a relief. I close my eyes and take deep breaths, try to control myself. So confined in here, so *tight*.

The white above my face splits down the middle, slides away to the sides. Spingate grins down at me. She's dressed in black, just like O'Malley.

"Hello there, Sleeping Beauty!"

Someone else leans in next to her, smiling at me. It's Smith, the skinny circle-cross girl with the short brown hair who was in Bishop's group back on the *Xolotl*. She's also wearing the black coveralls. Her gray eyes are so pretty.

"Your leg was badly wounded," she says. "Spingate did a good job binding it, but there was only so much she could do in the field. You lost enough blood to make you dizzy. Or maybe you were just exhausted and stressed."

"Leaders don't get stressed," I say.

Smith sighs. "As you like. How do you feel now? Better?"

I do. I take a deep breath. I don't just feel *better* . . . I feel *great*. They help me sit up.

Cloth against my skin—I'm wearing black coveralls. I stretch my arms out, look myself up and down. The coveralls have long sleeves and many pockets. New black socks on my feet. Except for my face and hands, I'm completely covered. For the first time in my few days of life, I'm wearing clothes that fit. My hands are clean. I touch my face: also clean. And the big bump on my head . . . it's almost gone. I tenderly try out my split lip—healed.

Smith and Spingate steady me as I step onto the floor. The room marked MEDICAL is small and white. There is a second coffin, open and empty. Both coffins are dark brown, glossy and clean. They are free of intricate carvings, but other than that, they look just like the one I fought my way out of on the *Xolotl*.

Off to the right, a single white pedestal with a red circle-cross engraved on the stem.

Smith taps the coffin's edge. "Put your foot up here."

She sounds as confident as Gaston does in the pilothouse. I do as I'm told.

She slides my pant leg up to my knee, touches my calf. She leans in, checks the area that was wounded. She squeezes the muscle and I wince.

Smith's smile is full of pride.

"All better, Em. See for yourself."

My calf is slightly bruised. There's a thin pink line that shows me where the tear was, but it looks like the wound happened years ago.

"That's amazing," I say. "How did you know what to do?"

"Gaston said you wanted me to come in here and learn all I could. As soon as I started, some of those blank areas in my head filled in. I remembered medical classes, people teaching me things, and how to use the medical system. The machines perform most of the work, I just use the pedestal to ask questions and make a decision as to what needs to be done."

Another person with recovered memories. Some, anyway, and these particular memories are critical to our survival. It feels good knowing that Smith is ready to take care of us.

She opens a cabinet, hands me a pair of black boots. It's all I can do not to squeal with delight. As I put them on and start tying them, I look up at Spingate.

"Was I asleep long?"

"All night and half the day."

That's a long time. Too long.

"Has the spider shown up?"

Spin shakes her head. "Not yet, anyway. O'Malley made everyone stay inside the shuttle. He said that if it can stop attacks from the Grownups, it can probably stop the spiders."

I finish tying my boots. I stand, put weight on my leg, bounce on it. My calf is sore, but feels so much better.

"Smith, you're amazing."

She blushes. She can be as modest as she likes, as long as she keeps fixing us up.

"Hey, where are my old clothes?"

Spingate's face wrinkles. "Incinerated, I hope. Em, we *stank*."

O'Malley brought me down here. My face flushes hot as I think of him seeing me naked.

"Who, um . . . who undressed me?"

"Don't worry, the med-chamber did it," Smith says, gesturing to the gleaming coffin. "It removed your old clothes, cleaned you up, treated your wounds, fed you intravenously, handled your waste and fixed your hair. It even put on your new clothes for you."

She calls it a *med-chamber*? I like that, although I suspect she'll be the only person to use that term. This thing "handled my waste." Disgusting, but it explains a lot. I was in my original coffin for years—*centuries,* according to Brewer. The coffin took care of me.

Some of the *Xolotl*'s coffins broke down. The kids inside of those died.

If things break down here, what will happen? Smith can use this equipment, but can she fix it if it stops working? Same thing with Gaston and flying the shuttle, or Spingate and the bracer. Knowing how to *use* technology is not the same as knowing how to *make* it, or how to *repair* it.

Spingate puts a hand on my shoulder. "Time to go up. Everyone is waiting for you on Deck One."

"Why?"

"The meeting," she says. "O'Malley said when he brought you down here, you told him as soon as you woke up you wanted a meeting about the food situation."

Other than O'Malley putting that blanket around me and showing me the new kids, I barely remember talking to him. I must have really been out of it. Still, a meeting is exactly what we need.

"So many people to feed now," I say. "Aramovsky's stupid act might mean we starve. Gods*damn* him."

Smith's eyes narrow. "Because you're in charge, you think you can curse like that?"

Because you're in charge . . . so close to what Coyotl said at the waterfall. Do people think I'm abusing my position as leader? Well, someone has to make decisions, and I have every right to be angry at Aramovsky.

"He shouldn't have woken them," I say. "They were in those coffins for centuries. A few more days wouldn't have hurt. How did he wake them up, anyway? Did his progenitor know how to operate the coffins?"

Spingate looks down, takes a small step away from Smith.

Smith glares at me defiantly.

"*You,*" I say to her. "You opened the coffins."

She crosses her arms. "Aramovsky asked for my help. He said the gods willed it. The pedestal had instructions for waking them, just like it had instructions for healing you."

I remember Spingate's words in the pilothouse, her worry that the kids might already be overwritten.

"Spin . . . are they like us?"

She nods quickly, instantly understanding my concern.

"O'Malley and Gaston said the new kids didn't know who they were or where they were, just like when we woke up. The kids were terrified."

There is anger in her voice. Like me, she understands how much trouble we're in now that our numbers have doubled but our food has not.

I wish I had my spear. I'm so mad I could almost use it on Smith. I'm hot in the face and chest. It feels the same as when I lost my temper with Spingate—the difference is Smith *did* do something to deserve it.

"You woke them up, Smith," I say. "Can you put them back to sleep?"

She juts out her chin. "You don't have the right to do that, you—"

"Answer my question."

Something in my voice makes her take a step back.

"It's not safe for them," she says. "Once someone comes out of a coffin for the first time, they're *alive*. Putting them back into deep sleep could kill them."

Her words, or Aramovsky's?

"You're lying," I say.

I have no idea if she is, or if she's telling the truth. I'm just so *frustrated*.

Smith sneers. "You think you know everything. Well, you don't know *anything* about this. If you're smart, you'll believe me."

I want to hit something. We've worked so hard, sacrificed so much, and now everything is at risk. My fury isn't going to fix anything, though, not when our survival is at stake. Calm plans can keep us alive—decisions driven by anger could move us closer to death.

A knock on the room's metal door.

Smith walks to it. The handprint there—of course—has a circle-cross in the palm. She presses it and the door slides open.

O'Malley. Holding my spear.

He enters, smiling that lovely smile of his. He hands me the spear.

"Em, you look *much* better."

He glances at Smith and Spingate.

"Can Em and I have a quick moment alone?"

"Sure," Spingate says. "I have to test some of the shuttle's food stores before the meeting anyway, make sure the mold hasn't gotten in. Smith, come help me."

Smith looks like she would rather go anywhere than with Spingate, but follows her out.

O'Malley waits a moment to make sure they're too far away to overhear.

"Everyone knows about the spider, the food warehouse and the mold," he says. "They are afraid. They need to hear from their leader that we'll find a solution."

I'm sure people are scared. I'll do what I can to make them feel better.

"Thank you," I say. "But . . . I don't remember asking for a meeting. Did I?"

He shrugs. "I figured you would want to talk when you woke up, so I told everyone you called a meeting."

That seems like odd behavior.

"Why didn't you just say it was your idea?"

"Because people listen to *you*. You're the leader. Ready?"

I'm not happy he lied. I'm also not happy that I left him in charge, and came back to chaos.

"We'll go in a minute," I say. "First, what happened while I was gone? How could you let Aramovsky open up the coffins?"

The question angers him.

"I didn't *let* him do anything. Gaston never left the pilothouse. I had to control the kids from the *Xolotl*. They were getting into the food, going outside, running around. While I was busy watching them, Aramovsky slipped away."

I notice the cut on O'Malley's cheek is almost gone. It's just a pink line, barely even a scar.

Smith healed him, too.

I point to the coffins. "Did Aramovsky and Smith let the new kids out while you were in one of those?"

He reactively touches his cheek. I've caught him in a second lie.

"Yes," he says. "I didn't think Aramovsky would try something while I was in there. How could I have known he would?"

It makes sense now. With me, Spingate and Bishop gone, with O'Malley unconscious, with Gaston learning about the shuttle, no one was watching Aramovsky. Someone *always* needs to be watching him.

"Em, I made a mistake. I'm sorry."

He did. I'm so angry at O'Malley. He always seems to think things through, but this time he didn't.

"*Sorry* won't keep us alive. The next time I tell you to do something, *do* it. Do you understand what this does to us?"

That familiar, blank expression settles over him.

"I get it," he says. His voice is thin, his words clipped. "Are you finished yelling at me?"

I can only hope I've made my point.

"I'm finished. Let's go."

TWELVE

Deck One's coffin room is packed. People sit or stand on closed coffins, sit on the black floor in the aisles, lean against the red walls. Almost three hundred faces—most of which I've never seen before—stare back at me. White-shirted little kids whisper to each other, pointing at me as if I'm an ancient myth come to life.

Everyone my age is dressed in coveralls and boots. Okereke and Johnson, Borjigin and Beckett, Bawden and Farrar. Even Bishop, who stands by the shuttle door, red axe at his side. They all wear black. I can't help but think of the Grownups we left back on the *Xolotl*.

Gaston is standing on a small stage made from empty food bins. He sees me and steps down.

As I walk toward it, people close in behind me. I'm surrounded. I step up on the stage. For once, I am taller than most of the people here.

I look out at the mass of faces. They're waiting for me to tell them what happens next, that everything will be fine. I see everyone except Spingate. Where is she? I'd feel better if she was here.

"Uh . . . thank you all for coming."

First thing out of my mouth and it's so stupid. Where else would they be? Silence makes me nervous, so I fill it.

"Hello to you new kids. I know this is scary, but I was just like you not long ago—frightened, confused, no idea of what was happening. Try to relax, you're with us now. See the people in black? They've been through far worse than this. We—"

A little hand goes up: Zubiri's.

"Yes?"

"Food," she says. She puts her arm down, stands. No smile this time. She's as serious as Bishop. "What are we going to do about food?"

That's something we'd all like to know.

"We're working on it. There are animals here we can eat, it's just a matter of figuring out how to catch them. And we haven't even started looking at plants yet. It might be—"

Aramovsky raises his hand. I know he's going to try and cause trouble, but I just answered Zubiri's question—I can't have people think I'm ignoring only him.

"Yes, Aramovsky?"

"Who built the fire? Other than having us cower in the shuttle, what have you done to protect us from this threat?"

He's doing it again, asking me questions to which he knows there are no answers. He's trying to make me look bad.

"We don't know they're a threat."

"You didn't find any food," he says, not hiding his disgust. "Now the fire-builders—whoever they are—probably know we're here. Sounds like your trip was a failure."

"We found *water,*" I say. "Without fresh water we'd all die. Does *that* sound like a failure?"

"Water we can't get to is the same as no water at all. How are you going to kill the spiders that guard it, Em?"

Why does he have to be so difficult? I hate him.

"We don't know yet," I say. "We will find a way. Now, about our food situation. Gaston, assuming we eat small meals, how long will the shuttle's supplies last?"

Gaston glances across the room, at Borjigin, the half-circle wisp of a boy with big teeth and straight hair as black as his coveralls. When I left for the warehouse, he and Opkick were doing inventory on the storerooms.

"Twelve days," Borjigin says. "If we stretch it."

I feel some of the pressure ease out of the room. A bubble of calm sets in: we're in bad shape, but we're not going to die tomorrow.

Then, that bubble bursts.

"It's worse than that."

Spingate. She's standing in the back wall's open door. She must have been on Deck Two, maybe in one of the labs. She holds up a white package: CRACKERS.

"This came from a bin we opened when we landed, not even two days ago."

She waves her bracer above the package.

The jewels flash orange.

"Contaminated," she says. "Enough to make us sick. Maybe even enough to kill us. Everything in the open bins is contaminated. We have to assume the only safe food is in bins that are still sealed. Even those might go bad."

I look at Gaston.

"How many bins did we already open?"

He hesitates before answering. "About half of them."

We have, at most, seven days' worth of food left. Not enough time to farm. Maybe enough to learn to trap those small animals, but how many of those would we need—every single *day*—to feed three hundred people?

Gaston looks nervous, like he thinks the crowd is about to attack him.

"Not my fault," he says. "We didn't know about the mold."

Beckett stands up. The tan-skinned redhead has said almost nothing since my group merged with Bishop's, but he's suddenly so mad he can't help himself.

"Why did you open so many bins, Gaston?" Beckett points to the gear symbol on his own forehead. "A *real* scientist would have tested first, made sure there was no reaction from the environment!"

Gaston huffs. "You're a *real scientist*?"

"I wouldn't have ruined half our food!"

Grumbles of agreement, even a few shouts—Gaston couldn't have known, yet people blame him anyway.

This room is growing angry, fast.

Bawden points at some of the new kids. "The food would last longer if it wasn't for all of these new *empties*."

The coffin room falls quiet.

That word again.

O'Malley was embarrassed he said it. Bawden is not.

I don't know the names of all the *Xolotl* kids, but I recognize their faces. On their foreheads, symbols: circles, yes, but also circle-stars, half-circles, gears, circle-crosses and a double-ring. On the foreheads of the new faces, though, I see only one symbol.

The empty circle. Like mine.

I scan the crowd, find O'Malley. I know full well he already counted.

"Are all of the new kids circles?"

He nods.

What does that mean? An entire shuttle full of my people? No, *everyone* here is "my people." In only one other place were all the symbols circles: the countless massacred bodies in Bishop's section of the *Xolotl.*

I see some people my age glaring at the new kids. The children sense this sudden hostility. They lean into each other, hold each other, eyes flicking from one black-clad person to the next.

Can we really be capable of turning on each other this fast? We're not even hungry yet—what will happen when we are?

"Bawden, that word is off-limits," I say. "Don't use it again."

She sneers. "It doesn't mean anything. Their circles *are* empty. And you can't tell me what to do."

A metal-on-metal *gong* reverberates through the room, makes everyone jump. All heads turn toward Bishop: he has smashed the flat of his red axe against the red wall. He stares straight at Bawden.

"Em is our leader," Bishop says. His voice is calm, but unforgiving. "That means she *can* tell you what to do. She got us this far, didn't she?"

Bawden stares at Bishop as if she's ready to fight him, but he isn't being aggressive. He's *asking* her to cooperate, not ordering her. That seems to make a difference.

She looks at me. "Fine. I won't use that word anymore."

Not an apology, but it's something.

How can we know a word is bad, but not know *why* it's bad?

Aramovsky stands on a closed coffin.

"We shouldn't fight each other," he says. "The mold is our biggest threat. And its red color is no coincidence. It is punishment from the God of Blood, because not enough of us have accepted his divine way."

Spingate shakes her head. "It isn't a *punishment,* you idiot. It's biological."

"I see," Aramovsky says. "Well, since it's *biology,* I'm sure you already have a cure." He smiles. "You'll cure this before we run out of food, right, Spingate?"

Her face wrinkles with rage. She rightfully blames him for waking these kids up in the first place.

"Science doesn't work that way," she says. "It's a process."

Aramovsky looks around the room, playing to the crowd.

"She can't promise us when she'll find a cure, or if there even *is* a cure. See what happens if you put science over faith?"

The package of crackers smacks into his head, making him wince in surprise.

She puts her hands on her hips.

"When you put science over faith, you *save lives,*" she says. "Those crackers that just bounced off your thick skull? If you had eaten those, you'd be dead. My *science* revealed that before anyone got hurt. Why didn't your *god* tell Farrar not to eat the contaminated food? Does your god want everyone to die?"

Aramovsky's eyes narrow. "Not everyone, Spingate." He stretches out his long arm and points a finger at her. "Just those who deserve it."

Around the room, roars of outrage—and some of approval.

I slam the butt of the spear down on the makeshift stage. The plastic *thonk* isn't as impressive as Bishop cracking his axe against the wall, but it quiets the room.

Spear in hand, I step off the stage and stride toward Aramovsky. People scramble out of my way. I stand in front of him, not hiding my anger.

"Did you just threaten Spingate's life?"

"Of course not," he says. "I was merely answering her question."

"You pointed at her when you said it."

He speaks loudly, making sure everyone can hear him: "My

apologies. I see how that might have looked." He faces Spingate, bows. "I would never threaten your life. Only the God of Blood can decide who lives and who dies."

He stands straight again, looks down at me. "Just like only the gods can decide who leads."

My skin prickles. Is he challenging my leadership? That thickness in my chest again . . . my temper, surging. I control it, but barely. I lean close to him, whisper so quietly he has to bend forward to hear.

"If anything happens to Spingate, I'll hold *you* responsible."

Aramovsky glances at my spear. The blade is only inches from his face. He wants it, wants to stab me with it.

Bishop clears his throat. "Aramovsky, let's take a walk."

The tall boy's face goes blank. He looks around the room, as if searching for someone who will help him. Everywhere he looks, people stare at the ground. No one wants to cross Bishop.

First Bawden, now Aramovsky—Bishop is making things worse. People will think I can't handle problems on my own. I want to tell Bishop to be quiet, but if I say something now it will just cause more confusion.

"Now, Aramovsky," Bishop says. "A word, please?"

Aramovsky swallows, smooths out his new black coveralls. He walks to the door, trying to look like this doesn't bother him. He and Bishop exit the shuttle.

The coffin room is quiet, tense. No one knows what to say. How did things get out of control so fast? The only noise comes from Spingate. She's crying a little—because she's so angry, I think. Gaston stands next to her, rubbing her back. Some people are looking at her like *she* did something wrong.

O'Malley steps onto the stage.

"That's all for now, everyone," he says. "As soon as we have more information, we'll share it." He steps down, walks to me, whispers: "Can I see you in the pilothouse?"

O'Malley is better at these situations than I am. Maybe he can help me figure out what to do next. I follow him to the pilothouse. He closes the door behind us.

THIRTEEN

The pilothouse walls are solid black. Perhaps this place only comes to life for Spingate or Gaston. It hits me that if anything happens to them, we won't be able to take the shuttle anywhere. Beckett is a gear . . . could he fly it?

O'Malley leans against a wall. "Aramovsky is a problem."

"Wow, *Chancellor,* you're really observant."

He says nothing. His expression remains blank.

I take a slow breath. I'm so mad at Aramovsky I want to attack everything and everyone.

"Sorry," I say. "I can't believe he threatened Spingate."

"While you were gone, he was talking to people. He wants everyone to follow his religion."

I feel my teeth grinding. "He doesn't even know what the religion is. The *God of Blood*? Doesn't sound familiar to me, at all. I think he's making it up as he goes along."

"He doesn't care about truth, Em—he cares about *power*. *Your* power."

"I don't *have* any power."

O'Malley shakes his head. "You do. That's why you're the only leader for us. That's why you're the only leader for *me*."

"Watch him," I say. "*Really* watch him this time. We can't let him do something else to make things even worse."

O'Malley comes closer. There is a hunger in his eyes. I see his gaze flicking all over my face, like he's trying to take in every part of me all at once. He reaches out, gently holds my shoulders. Even through the coveralls, his touch sends a tingle through my body. He smiles, which chases away my thoughts of anything *but* that smile.

My breath gets short. What is he doing? I try to tell him to stop, but the words won't come out.

He pulls me closer.

"Em, you're so beautiful."

He said the same thing on Deck Three, when he was looking at Matilda's face.

"Because my bruises have healed, right? *Now* I'm pretty enough for you, is that it, O'Malley?"

"When we're alone, you can call me Kevin." He leans closer. "You were the first thing I saw when I woke up. You'll *always* be pretty to me."

I want to be mad, but I can't. So I'm healed up now, so what? This isn't Matilda's face—it's *mine*.

O'Malley is so sure, so confident, but I'm confused. Bishop likes me. I know he does; he kissed me. Now, though, it's like he doesn't want to be near me. O'Malley leans in. He's moving slowly, giving me plenty of chances to pull away if I want to.

I don't.

His lips meet mine. It feels . . . delicious. As good as it felt with Bishop, but different. Does every boy kiss different?

O'Malley's fingertips caress the back of my neck. I can't think of anything but him, his lips, the way he smells, the feel of his hands on my body.

Unlike Bishop, O'Malley wants me and he's not shy about it.

Bishop . . .

Our kiss almost got Spingate killed.

I shove O'Malley. He stumbles back, surprised.

"Don't ever kiss me again." I try to sound hard, but my words come out as a cracked plea.

He smiles. "I won't. Until you ask me to."

Anger floods in, washing away the confused feelings.

"That's not going to happen," I say. "Now get out."

His smile widens. So stunning, and yet there is something off about it.

"As you wish, *Empress*."

He leaves the pilothouse.

I close my eyes, try to calm myself. I didn't want him to stop, I admit it, but who does he think he is?

I don't know. But I know what he *doesn't* think he is—he doesn't think he's a leader. He's not like Aramovsky in that way, or even Bishop. O'Malley is comfortable being at my side, giving me counsel, providing the information I need. Not once has he challenged my leadership. Not once has he stepped in because he thought I couldn't handle something.

But just now he was so . . . *aggressive*. Not physically, he was *emotionally* aggressive.

When I opened his coffin and looked at his face for the first time, I had never seen anything so beautiful. Since then, I've experienced so much more: spaceships, cities, ruins, stars and moons, blood and death, love and tenderness . . .

. . . and through all of that, Kevin O'Malley is *still* the most beautiful thing I have ever known.

He kissed me.

He *wants* me.

I don't know if I can be mad at him. I don't know if I can be mad at Bishop, either. I don't know what to think about any of this.

A shake of my head, a rub of my face. *Push those thoughts away, Em—there are more important things to worry about.* We need food. There are people who survive in Omeyocan's jungle, who obviously know what to eat. For us to survive, I have to find them.

And that means tomorrow, as soon as it's light, we have to go outside the walls again.

FOURTEEN

The sun is about to rise. Most everyone is still asleep. I am in the pilothouse with my friends: Spingate, Gaston, O'Malley and Bishop. And, unfortunately, Aramovsky.

I don't want him here, but what choice do I have? If he's with me, he's not talking behind my back. And as much as I hate to admit it, he's *smart*. I won't ignore good ideas just because they come from someone I don't like.

We stand around Gaston's map. Somehow, the area shown seems smaller than before.

"We all know how much trouble we're in," I say, concentrating on not looking at Aramovsky when I do. "You are the people I trust to help me make decisions. I think we need to send a party to the fire pit."

"But a spider was in the jungle," O'Malley says.

I nod. "It was also inside the city walls. If it's a threat no matter where we go, we might as well try to find the people who know what food is safe to eat."

Spingate hugs her shoulders. Everyone else looks rested. She looks like she hasn't slept at all.

"It's not just the spider," she says. "We heard many animals. And the people who made that fire might be hostile."

We're desperate. If they are hostile, can we *take* food from them? How far are we willing to go to survive?

"We should focus on the mold," Spingate says. "The labs on Deck Two have scientific equipment, and pedestals with instructions on how to use it. I'm studying the mold, trying to find a way to neutralize the toxin. I worked on it all night."

No wonder she's so tired.

"Brewer knew about the mold," I say. "Is there any information about it in the pedestal's memory?"

She shakes her head.

"How convenient," Aramovsky says.

I shoot him a glare, but he ignores it, continues.

"You and your *cure*, Spingate. How long will it take?"

She shrugs. "Maybe ten days. Maybe twenty. Maybe never."

"Keep working on it," I say. "You can do that while the rest of us look for other solutions."

Gaston gestures to the countless buildings laid out on the map. "We've only looked in the warehouse, right? Other buildings could have uncontaminated food. We need to search them. And as far as we know, there *are* people in this city, we just haven't seen them yet."

He drags his fingertip through the map, leaving a glowing line from the dot that represents the shuttle, through the streets we used to reach the warehouse, then to the waterfall. I see his point—we've explored only a tiny portion of this city.

"The warehouse bins were sealed," O'Malley says. "The

mold got in anyway. If we find more food, odds are it will be in the same condition."

"Still worth a try," Gaston says. "We should explore."

Maybe that's dangerous, too, but there are a lot of us. And Gaston is right—we have to try everything.

"We'll send teams to search buildings around the landing pad," I say. "We'll assign lookouts, keep the teams close enough that they can run to the shuttle if the spider is spotted. We can do that in addition to sending a team to the fire pit."

O'Malley crosses his arms, purses his lips in thought. "There are thousands of buildings. If only there was a way to see if some were more important than others. Gaston, the landing pad had to have power to rise up, right?"

Gaston nods. "I think it has its own small power plant. Nuclear, probably. When the shuttle came in range, I think the power plant activated."

O'Malley opens his mouth to speak, but Gaston cuts him off.

"Before you throw out your genius idea, O'Malley, I already asked the shuttle if it could detect other buildings with power. It said that capability had been erased—like almost everything else I've asked it."

O'Malley puts his hands on his knees, bends so he's looking down the north-south street at eye level. "Maybe the shuttle has bad memories like us. Maybe it's recovering them, just like we are. Ask it again."

Gaston rolls his eyes. "All right, *fine,* O'Malley. Let's do it one more time, just for you. Shuttle?"

"Yes, Captain Xander?"

"Highlight any buildings or areas that have power."

A small circle lights up below the shuttle icon, and so does one other spot—the massive ziggurat at the city center.

"But . . . wow, it *worked,*" Gaston says. "O'Malley, I take back half the bad things I've ever said about you."

This seems strange to me. It was almost like O'Malley already knew what the shuttle would find. Did he remember an access code for the pedestals on Deck Three? No, that can't be—he would have told me right away if he had.

"Let's test our luck," Gaston says. Then, in an overly sweet voice: "Shuttle, love of my life, my true north, do you know what that building is?"

"Yes, Captain Xander. That is the Observatory."

Bishop's face wrinkles. "What's an *observatory*?"

"A place to see stars," Gaston says.

Bishop points up. "We can see them at night. We don't need a building for that."

"It still has power," Spingate says, ignoring him. "We *have* to go there. If the city builders wanted to make sure their knowledge was preserved—science, engineering, maybe even *history*—they would store that knowledge in a database of some kind. It makes sense they'd keep that database in a building that maintained power no matter what happened."

"History," Aramovsky says, his voice full of longing. "We might finally learn what our symbols mean."

O'Malley's eyes flick to me, then instantly back to the map. He looks . . . *guilty*. Almost as if he already knows what the symbols mean and isn't telling us.

Spingate leans over the map, squints at the towering ziggurat. "The city builders must have encountered the red mold. Maybe they found a way to beat it."

Bishop grunts. "If they beat it, why would people leave?"

Spingate throws up her hands. "I *don't know*! Why do you people think I already know everything? Look, if the Observatory holds any data on the red mold, I *have* to have it."

She stops. She's breathing hard. A heavy lock of curly red hair hangs in front of her face.

Bishop's point disturbs me. Is the red mold the reason the city is empty? Did it drive people out? Did it kill them all? If so, what chance do we have of surviving here?

I stare at the ziggurat's image. At this scale, where most buildings are the size of my thumb, that one is as big as my head. It's so real I could almost reach out and brush the vines away from the stone.

O'Malley clears his throat.

"The Observatory isn't far from here," he says. "Someone could leave now, be there about midday and take a look. They'd be back just after sunset. I know we're short on time and food, but one day isn't much to sacrifice if it saves us the risk of sending people into the jungle. Also, Em, you were saying earlier that we need to know if there are any spiders close to the shuttle. Whoever goes to the Observatory could also reconnoiter our area."

Bishop's head snaps up at the word *reconnoiter*. He nods in wholehearted agreement. He uses his fingertip to trace a glowing path down the streets, moving from the shuttle to the towering ziggurat. He traces another path back, using different streets.

"I could take two circle-stars with me," he says. "We'd be able to check a large area of the extended perimeter for spiders, *and* recon the big ziggurat. Great idea, Em."

It *is* a great idea—but did I come up with it? Maybe. There's so much going on I can't remember everything I've said. Or did O'Malley once again pretend his idea was mine? Either way, it's a good plan, but not one without risks.

"It might be too dangerous," I say. "That's a long time to be gone with the spider out there somewhere."

Bishop stands tall and rigid, holds his axe against his chest. He seems to be staring at something that isn't there.

"We are shadows." His voice sounds different, quiet and soft. "We are the wind. We are *death*."

The rest of us glance at each other, not knowing what to say. Bishop's blank stare is creepy. What just happened to him?

I gently put a hand on his arm. "Bishop, what does that mean?"

His trance breaks. His face flushes red.

"It means circle-stars can move quietly, that's all. I think some of my memories came back. I was taught to say that phrase when I was little. We were instructed on how to move without a sound, how to track people and animals, how to sneak up on anyone, how to . . ."

His voice trails off, but I know what he was going to say: *how to kill.*

"Like how I was taught math and science," Spingate says. "They trained me early. I mean, they trained my progenitor."

"Like I was taught how to pray," Aramovsky says.

"Or fly," Gaston says.

Flying, fighting, science, even *religion*—there seems to be a specialized area of knowledge for each symbol. My friends were all taught something *important*. What was *I* taught? I am a circle, there are more of us than any other group—what is it that *we* were born to do?

"I could take Visca and Bawden," Bishop says. "They're fast, like me. If we see the spider, we come back. Even if the spider catches one of us, two will return and share what we've learned."

He wants to take three because he knows a single person might not make it back. Is information more important than lives? I wonder what else the circle-stars were taught when they were little.

"Why not Coyotl and Farrar?" O'Malley asks. "They went out before and made it back. Wouldn't you rather have their experience?"

Bishop winces. "Farrar didn't follow orders. And Coyotl is . . . noisy." He looks at me. "You could move quieter than him, Em. I could teach you."

That's something I'd like to learn.

For now, though, if I agree to Bishop's plan, that's three circle-stars gone for a whole day. Spingate is right—a building with power is more important than the fire pit. I don't think we can risk sending additional people into the jungle. That will have to wait for tomorrow.

"Go now," I say to Bishop. "Be back by nightfall."

He turns and walks out.

"I have work waiting in the lab," Spingate says.

Aramovsky snorts. "*Work*. Is that what you call it?"

That's it—I've had enough of his crap.

"Everyone, out," I say. "Except you, Aramovsky. I want to talk to you."

O'Malley's eyes widen. He wants to stay. He clearly thinks I need his help with this. I ignore his unspoken warning; I can take care of this myself.

Spingate grabs Gaston's hand. "Come on," she says. "I need your help in the lab."

Aramovsky crosses his arms, waits.

O'Malley is still standing there.

"I asked you to leave," I say.

He flashes Aramovsky a clear look of warning. Aramovsky pretends to yawn.

O'Malley storms out.

I follow him into the corridor, stop him at the shuttle door.

"Wait," I say. "You're acting strange. Is there something I should know?"

We're alone. This is his chance to tell me that he already knew the Observatory would have power, to tell me he knows about the symbols.

He shakes his head. "No. Just be careful with Aramovsky. He's tricky."

O'Malley turns and walks into the coffin room.

Is he hiding information from me? I'll have to find out soon.

But first things first—it's time to deal with Aramovsky.

FIFTEEN

I shut the pilothouse door. I don't have the ability to lock it, but the others had to see how angry I am—Aramovsky and I won't be bothered.

He smiles his fake smile. "Decided to do your own talking instead of having Bishop do it for you?"

"He doesn't talk for me."

Aramovsky looks at his fingernails, checking them for dirt. "Bishop told me that I needed to stop arguing with you"—he looks me in the eyes—"or he would *hurt* me."

Is that true? I can't have Bishop threatening people, and I can't have him thinking he needs to fight my battles for me.

"I'll talk to him about it. No one is allowed to threaten you for speaking your mind. We need everyone's ideas."

"Funny, I was speaking my mind in the coffin room when I said the red mold is a punishment from the gods. You got in my face, brandishing your spear. Tell me, Em, if Bishop hadn't taken me outside, would *you* have threatened me?"

I don't think I would have, but I can't say for sure—I was furious.

"If you want to talk about threats, let's talk about how you threatened Spingate."

"I told you, all I did was repeat what the gods told me."

Now he's pretending the gods speak directly to him?

"The others might believe your lies, but not me. I know what you said to Spingate, and I know what you're trying to do."

"And what is that?"

"You want to be the leader."

He smiles again. This time it feels genuine—but also dismissive, the smile of an adult dealing with a child.

"I want no such thing," he says. "I merely want to give people guidance. I want us to be right with the gods."

"You're going to stop doing things that hurt us." I keep my tone level, but I know he hears me. This is his warning. "That includes you stopping all this religion nonsense."

I expected that to rattle him, perhaps make him mad, but he seems more exhausted with me than angry.

"You called it *nonsense* when we spoke at Latu's grave. Think of all the miracles we've seen since then, and yet you still don't believe in our destiny?"

"There are no miracles. We make our own destiny."

Aramovsky sighs and crosses his arms. "You shouldn't fight religion. Religion helps guide your decisions, helps people *follow* those decisions. We're almost three hundred souls now—you're struggling to make everyone obey."

"The only people who don't *obey* are the ones listening to you. And we're *almost three hundred* because you let those kids out."

He nods. "I did, because it was the right thing to do. Keeping them in their coffins because it is convenient for us would make us no better than the Grownups."

That takes me by surprise, crushes my anger. I hadn't thought about it that way. I never, *ever* want to be compared to Matilda and her kind.

"Maybe you have a point."

"Thank you," he says. "But I didn't come to that decision on my own. I was guided to it." He pauses, thinking carefully about his next words. "Let me *help* you, Em. The gods want to guide you—I can be their voice."

Of course. With Aramovsky, it always comes back to power.

"I don't need anyone's voice to guide me."

His eyebrows rise. "Oh? Then maybe I don't understand what O'Malley is doing when he whispers in your ear."

My face flushes hot. "O'Malley is not *whispering,*" I say, even though I know that's exactly what O'Malley does. "I listen to everyone. He has good advice."

"Oh? So was it really *your* idea to have Bishop reconnoiter for spiders?"

He noticed the same thing I did. Is he saying O'Malley *manipulates* me? That's ridiculous . . . isn't it?

I shake my head. "*I* make the final decisions"—I hold up the spear—"because I have this."

"Yes, you have the spear. The spear that the God of Blood guided into your hands."

He wants to pretend it wasn't the people who voted me leader, but rather the will of his invisible friends? I will never get through to this boy. He is a danger to us, a wedge that can divide us all.

"I'm sick of your God-talk. Where exactly *are* your gods, anyway? Why don't they just show themselves and help us?"

Aramovsky's expression is so condescending I want to slice it off his face.

"Em, how can you be so blind? We traveled on a ship that moved between planets. We were *created* in that ship, designed to live on Omeyocan when those that designed us cannot. We are standing in a city that was made for us. If you need more evidence of the gods, Little Matilda, then—"

My spearpoint at his throat, a blur of motion that my hands perform before my brain even engages.

"Don't call me that," I say, my words low and growling. "Don't you *ever* call me that."

Aramovsky stays very still. He tries to appear unafraid, but the point of my spear is just below his Adam's apple. I could push forward (*it would be so easy and you'd be forever free*) and shut him up for good.

The same way Bishop shut up Aramovsky's progenitor.

I remember the black body crawling, the broken thighbone plunging into its back. That sickened me, made me want to run . . .

A hard shudder shakes me. What am I doing? My temper again. I almost killed this boy. I pull the spear away, set the butt on the floor.

Aramovsky rubs at his throat. "Unless you intend to stab me again, may I go?"

"I didn't *stab* you." I say it sharply, defensively. I feel stupid, clumsy and out of control.

He lifts his fingers from his throat: they are traced with a thin smear of red. "The God of Blood approves, Em."

"Get out."

Aramovsky leaves.

I'm sure of it now—he wants to lead. On his own if he can, or by controlling me.

Be careful with Aramovsky, O'Malley had said. *He's tricky.*

O'Malley was right about that. But is O'Malley trying to

control me just like Aramovsky is? Am I really in charge, or is O'Malley shaping the way I think?

Spingate seemed so upset in the meeting. I'm going to check in on her first, then I'll find O'Malley. I have to know if he's hiding information from me.

SIXTEEN

There are little kids *everywhere*. Running around, goofing off and generally getting in the way. The shuttle is big, but we have far too many bodies in here. I'll find a way to put them all to work.

They are even on Deck Two, where the labs are. The lab doors are closed. I heard Spingate's voice coming from behind the door of Lab One. She's yelling at someone.

I knock.

"Go *away,*" she shouts.

"Spin, it's Em."

A pause. The door slides open. Gaston steps out. He's wide-eyed, frazzled. He closes the door behind him.

"Em, save me," he says quietly. "She wants help, but the work she's doing is way beyond me. I was trained to fly, not to do biology research. I need to be in the pilothouse—I think I've found weapons systems."

My heart surges at this good news. "You mean like bracelets?"

He shakes his head. "No, weapons that are part of the shuttle, that it can use on outside targets. Like missiles."

I vaguely know what a missile is. I can't see how it will help us unless he can aim it at a spider.

He takes my hand. "Come on, talk to Spingate"—his voice lowers—"and *watch out.*"

Before I can ask him what he means, he pulls me into the lab. The narrow room is white, like Smith's medical room. Cabinets, gear and devices I don't recognize line the walls. Spingate is staring at something floating above a white pedestal marked with a golden gear symbol.

"Hi, Spin," I say. "I came to see if there's anything I can do to help."

"I doubt it," she says without looking up from her work. "Gaston is already helping me."

The image on the pedestal before her looks like some kind of twisting ladder, rungs made of different colors. I don't know what it's supposed to be.

Until now, every time a puzzle presented itself, Spingate was excited to solve it. Not now. No smile, no giggle. Eyes sunken, hair askew—she's frustrated.

She stares at the twisted ladder, seems to have already forgotten I'm here.

I glance at Gaston. His eyes plead with me—he wants to leave. Partially because he wants to learn more about the shuttle, I know, but more so because of the angry mood that radiates from Spingate.

That reminds me: he's the only one who knows how to fly—maybe I can solve two problems at once.

"Gaston, can you teach Beckett to fly the shuttle?"

He frowns. "Why? I know how to do it."

Maybe he's still mad that Beckett yelled at him about the food contamination. Or maybe Gaston doesn't want anyone else to know what he knows, so that he continues to be special.

"Because if something happens to you," I say, "we could be stranded."

He gestures to Spingate. "She could fly it herself, with a few more lessons. I could teach—"

Spingate's eyes snap up, her lip curls into a sneer.

"In case you couldn't tell, I'm *busy*. Of course I could fly the shuttle, but it would take time to learn. Does it look like I have time?"

Gaston backs toward the lab door.

"I'll go find Beckett," he says. "Orders received and believed, Fearless Leader."

With that, he's gone.

Spingate glares at me.

"Gaston needs to be focused on what he's good at," I say. "I'll have Okereke and Johnson help you. I'll make it their only job."

She throws up her hands in exasperation. "Okereke and Johnson? Em, they're not gears, they're *empties,* they're not smart . . ."

Spingate's words trail off. Her glare fades.

I can't believe she just said that.

"They're *not smart enough,*" I finish for her. "Because they're circles. Like me. Right?"

We made it this far without the symbols affecting us, and the first real division doesn't come from Aramovsky, it comes from Spingate—my *friend*. Has she *always* thought of me as stupid?

"Em, I . . . I didn't mean it like that." Her face is bright red. Her words rush out. "We all have some pre-existing training. Gaston knows how to fly, Bishop knows how to fight. I already know a lot of math and science that only other gears will know. There isn't time to teach these things to someone who doesn't already understand them."

Her excuses fall short. I should have known. I probably knew it all along. Spingate is a tooth-girl; at her core she looks down on me because of my symbol, even though she doesn't know why. Maybe that explains my dim memories of school, of the tooth-girls making my life miserable.

My feelings are hurt, but my feelings don't matter, because she's right—reality is what it is whether we like it or not.

"You need someone who can understand what you're doing," I say. "We had the knowledge of a twelve-year-old when we woke up. The kids from the *Xolotl* do, too, right?"

She nods slowly.

"Zubiri is smart," I say. "Have you met her?"

"I talked to her a little."

"Good. She and M. Cathcart will assist you with your research. Don't worry—Cathcart is a gear, so I'm sure he won't be too stupid to help."

Spingate blinks. "Em, I was angry before you even came in. I haven't had any sleep. About what I said, I—"

"It doesn't matter."

My eyes sting. I leave before she can see me cry.

I've had it with all of this. Our symbols are a simmering poison that will corrupt what we've worked so hard to build.

O'Malley knows something about them, and he's going to tell me.

SEVENTEEN

I turn the wheel. I open the door.

O'Malley pivots to see who has joined him—the image above the pedestals suddenly changes. I don't know what was there a moment ago, but now it's the same thing I saw the last time I was here: little heads of Aramovsky, O'Malley and Matilda.

O'Malley seems pleased—he probably thinks I came to take him up on that kiss—but only for a moment. The look on my face tells him otherwise.

"Em, what's wrong?"

I think he's hiding something, but I'm not sure. My father's voice echoes through my head: *Attack, attack, always attack.*

"You lied in the meeting," I say, letting him hear the anger in my soul even while I hope I'm wrong. "You already knew the Observatory had power."

His mouth twitches, just once.

"I did," he says.

I was right. I don't want to be. I wanted to trust him.

"Did you remember your access code?"

He stares for a few seconds, his expression blank and impenetrable. He's weighing his options: lie and see if he can get away with it, or tell the truth.

"I didn't remember it, but I figured it out," he says. "I thought maybe my progenitor picked a code of something important from his childhood. I've been working on it since I first found this room."

I wait. There is more and he *will* tell me.

His stone-face cracks, shifts to sadness. He looks away.

"When I was little, I had a kitten," he says. "I mean, *he* had a kitten. White, with a black spot on its face. They made him kill it. The kitten's name was Chromium."

I have no idea what to say. I'm excited and jealous that he recalls something from the past. I also feel for him, because it's clear that—although the cat has been dead for a thousand years and was never really *his* to begin with—this is a hard thing to remember.

"Why did they make your creator kill it?"

He stares at the floor for a moment, then shrugs.

"I'm not sure," he says. "I think they were trying to teach my progenitor something about emotions."

What kind of lesson on emotions could be gained from making a little boy kill a kitten? Then I remember who we're talking about—the Grownups. Compared to what we've seen, making a child murder his pet is nothing.

"So that was your access code? Chromium?"

"That and some other numbers and letters," he says. "I'm not sure what they mean, or if they are just random stuff."

The pig I killed in the garden—it was so hard to take that animal's life. I can't imagine what it must be like to do the same to something you love. How unfair that O'Malley remembers that act when it wasn't even him that did it.

Maybe this is something he needs to talk about. If he wants to talk to me, I will listen, but not now. There are more important things than a dead cat.

"We need to know more," I say. "Can the pedestals tell us about the city? The mold?"

He shakes his head. "It looks like most of the information was permanently erased. The Grownups did that, I think. I don't know why. I was able to see some organizational information. That's how I learned the Observatory has power."

The Observatory. All he had to do was come out and tell us about it. Instead, he wanted us to think that going there was someone else's idea.

Attack, attack . . .

"What do the symbols mean, O'Malley?"

His stone-face returns. "You don't want to know."

"Oh, don't I? Now you know what I want?"

"I know what you *need*."

How arrogant. My sympathy for the hurt he feels over the cat is fading fast.

"Out with it. Right now."

He pauses.

"You've been telling us that we can't afford to be divided against each other," he says. "You're correct. So, if I found something the Grownups did that doesn't apply to us, and would upset people, then you're right to say it's best if we leave it alone."

Arguing with each other, splitting into factions, that's the fastest way to failure, to disaster. Do we really need things that could divide us? I want all the information I can get, but . . .

. . . wait.

Wait.

I know we can't afford to be divided—but I never *said* that. Just like I didn't say anything about looking near the shuttle to see if spiders were close.

O'Malley said those things, not me.

My anger spikes, but this time I'm ready for it. I shove it down. I set my spear against the wall, reach out and take his hand. He stares at our linked fingers, somewhat surprised. Maybe he's only comfortable with contact if he's the one initiating it.

"You want people to think your ideas are mine," I say. "Why?"

His eyes go wide. He's been caught and he knows it. Did he think I wouldn't notice? Does he think I'm stupid, *just an empty*?

"My training," he says. "I know ways to . . . to *convince* people to do things. Ways to make sure everyone thinks the leader knows exactly what's going on. It's bad for people to doubt the leader. As soon as I started helping you, back on the *Xolotl,* I remembered some of what I learned in school."

He had a flashfire of memories. The same thing happened to Gaston, to Aramovsky, to Bishop and Spingate. I've yet to have mine.

"What you did was wrong," I say. "Just because you know how to do something doesn't mean you have to do it."

He shrugs. "It's how I was trained."

"That wasn't you. That was your creator."

He huffs. "Is there really a difference? I *remember* that kitten. I remember holding it, petting it. I remember how it purred, loving me, *trusting* me, right before my hands closed around its tiny neck. I remember it scratching me . . ."

O'Malley seems confused. He slides up the sleeve of his black coveralls, stares at his forearm. He turns his arm this way and that, looking for something.

"It scratched me," he says. "Really bad. There were scars."

I take his forearm in my hands. My thumbs make slow circles on his skin.

"Your progenitor had scars. You are *not* him. You asked if there was a difference. There is—you don't have to do things like he would have done them. You have a choice. *We* have a choice. I don't need you to lie for me. We're not going to make the same mistakes our creators made. If people doubt me, that's fine."

"You're wrong," he says. "If people don't think you know exactly what needs to be done, they'll look for someone who does."

I shrug. "Then we'll have another vote and pick another leader. We can't keep secrets from each other."

He laughs, looks away. "That's what you say now."

I cup his face, force him to look at me. "We *will not* keep secrets. Tell me what the symbols mean."

His eyes plead with me. "Leave it be. This will change everything."

I nod. "And we'll handle it."

O'Malley closes his eyes. He slowly tilts forward until his forehead presses against mine. That tiny spot of contact sends a tingle through me. It isn't aggressive, like his kiss, yet this gentle touch reaches me in a way that kiss never could.

He straightens, faces the pedestals.

"Shuttle, show her the wheel."

The invisible voice speaks: *"Yes, Chancellor."*

The little heads above the pedestal blur, then fuzz out. A circle forms, dotted with tiny images around the outer edge. In the circle's center there is a flat, fat-cheeked cartoonish face that looks like it was carved into flat stone. Its tongue sticks out. The style of art reminds me of my birth-coffin's carvings.

That circle of images . . .

I look at the red circle embroidered on the left breast of O'Malley's coveralls.

"Our ties," I say. "That face with the symbols, it matches what was on our ties."

O'Malley nods. "It does. But before you ask, I don't know what it means."

He sees my doubtful expression.

"I told you information was erased. I know it's hard for you to believe me right now, but that's the truth. Shuttle, show her the symbols."

Above the pedestal, three glowing dots appear around the circle. At the very top, the dot turns black, spreads out and becomes a symbol: Spingate's gear. The other two form near the bottom, connected to the gear and each other by straight lines that form a perfect triangle. On the left, O'Malley's half-circle; on the right, Aramovsky's double-ring.

Words appear by each symbol: SPIRIT by the double-ring, MIND by the gear, and STRUCTURE by the half-circle.

"The double-ring is obviously religion," O'Malley says. "The gear is for scientists and engineers. My symbol represents administration—helping leaders, organizing, managing other people who do actual labor. As far as I can tell, people who had these three symbols worked together to rule. Whatever type of culture there was back on the *Xolotl*—I mean before they started slaughtering each other—those three symbols were in charge."

"But Matilda was the leader. If I'm a circle, wasn't she one, too? Circles would have to be in the leadership group, wouldn't they?"

He doesn't answer. He doesn't want to go on.

"Tell me the rest of it," I say.

He clears his throat, speaks loud. "Show the secondary symbols."

Three more dots appear, one each in the spaces between the existing symbols. The dots take shape . . .

Top left: Bishop's circle-star.

Top right: Smith's circle-cross.

And at the bottom, finally, my symbol—the empty circle.

Words appear: MIGHT next to the circle-star, HEALTH next to the circle-cross. By mine, the word SERVICE.

O'Malley points to the circle-star. "*Might* means military. Soldiers or police. People who protect the order of things."

I think of Bishop and the others, of how they are always the first to face any danger, of how without them we would all have been overwritten by now.

"Soldiers help keep people safe," I say. "People who keep us safe would be part of the ruling class."

"They weren't." No hesitation in O'Malley's voice, no doubts. "They did the bidding of the primary symbols."

So Grownup O'Malley would have been in charge of Grownup Bishop? Interesting.

O'Malley points to the circle-cross. "That symbol was for doctors, nurses, people involved in the health of others."

The dead Brewer boy in the coffin, he had the circle-cross on his forehead. Is Brewer a doctor? Perhaps he was in charge of the *receptacles*. That might explain how he had control over our coffins, how he was able to wake us up, to lock out Matilda and the others for all those centuries.

I wait for O'Malley to continue. He doesn't. He looks down, unable to meet my eyes.

"Stop stalling," I say. "Explain my symbol. What was my role in their society? What special skills am I supposed to have?"

He lets out a slow breath. His blue eyes shimmer with tears. Maybe he fakes emotions at will, but he isn't faking this.

"Circles don't have special skills," he says. "Your role was to do whatever the other symbols told you to do. Em . . . the circles were *slaves*."

Like a key sliding into a lock, that word destroys barriers in my mind. Matilda's memories—fractured, distorted, but still *real*—flood in. I am in school, carrying a tooth-girl's things for her while she walks five steps ahead of me, laughing with other tooth-girls . . .

. . . I am in class—no, waiting *outside* of class, with other circles, being taught basic math by an old woman while my tooth-girl—my *owner*—is in the classroom learning physics . . .

. . . I am in the cafeteria, on my knees, wiping food off the floor, food that my owner knocked over just so she could see me pick it up while she and her tooth-girl friends laugh at me, call me a *stupid empty* over and over again . . .

. . . I am in a small room in a church where every person I see is a circle, except for the pastor, a woman in red robes with a double-ring on her forehead, who is saying that *service* is the life the gods planned for us and that if we do it well, if we serve, if we *obey,* then we will be rewarded after death when we go to the Black Mountain . . .

. . . I am outside the church, talking to an older circle-boy while I wait for my owner to finish her own service in a church that is far more beautiful than mine, and the boy looks around carefully before he asks if I've ever heard of the god called Tlaloc, the one who can empower the soldiers and doctors and workers to rise up against the rulers . . .

. . . the feeling of anger, of humiliation, of *hatred* at belonging to someone else, at having no rights, the need to do something about it, *anything,* no matter what the cost . . .

"Em?"

O'Malley is staring at me.

"Em, are you all right?"

No. I'm not. I finally had that moment I wanted, that *flashfire,* just like my friends had. Gaston gets to fly, and I get this?

I share my creator's memories. For the most part, I *am* those memories. Matilda didn't wear chains, she didn't live in squalor, but she was a slave nonetheless. She was *property*.

"On the *Xolotl,* it seemed like Matilda was in charge," I say. "How could a slave be in charge?"

"Because she led a rebellion. The details of it are erased, but I'm pretty sure she started the war on that ship."

I thought she was a monster, inside and out. Maybe things aren't so simple, so cut-and-dried. All those mutilated bodies, the butchered babies . . . only someone who is pure evil could do that. And yet, a part of me—the part of me that is her, perhaps—understands why she would start that war.

"She didn't want to be a slave," I say. "She didn't want *anyone* to be a slave."

For the first time, I truly understand my creator.

O'Malley gently grips my shoulders. "Now you know why we can't tell the others."

"We *have* to." My voice is thin, drained of life. "Everyone wants to know what the symbols mean."

He cups my face in his hands, doing to me what I did to him only moments ago.

"Em, *please*. I was trained to counsel leaders, how to know what people are thinking and how to make sure the leaders say the right thing at the right time. If we share the meaning of the symbols now, it will destroy everything we've accomplished."

I know I should tell everyone, but I don't *want* to. A slave?

That's all I was? But no, that wasn't me, it was Matilda. Omeyocan is a new world. It is *our* world—we can make it whatever we want it to be. My people can handle this news. They can make the right decision and not be ruled by the structures of our history.

"They need to know," I say. "We have to be honest."

O'Malley shakes his head in exasperation. "All right, they need to know, *fine,* but not *now*. Aramovsky is just waiting for the right opportunity to call a new election. Do you want to take the chance that he'll win?"

I think of Aramovsky talking about his God of Blood. So many young minds on this shuttle now. If he could say whatever he wanted, he might corrupt them all.

O'Malley is right—Aramovsky can't be in charge now, it would be a disaster.

"But we *will* tell them, right?" Now I am the one with the pleading tone in my voice. I have never sounded less like a leader. "We'll tell them soon?"

O'Malley pulls me in and holds me tight. I let him.

"We will, Em, I promise. We'll tell everyone about our past, but after we've secured our *future*."

There is nothing arrogant about him now, nothing expected from this hug—I need him to hold me, so he does.

I will tell everyone. I *will*.

Just not now.

EIGHTEEN

The sun hangs low in the sky. Bishop has not returned.

I sit alone atop the pile of vines at the landing pad's edge. The pad is alive with activity, as I have put everyone to work. Under the direction of Opkick, kids are chopping vines and clearing them away from the pad's metal deck. They toss the cut pieces onto the vine wall, making it thicker and taller. If the spiders stay at street level, they can't see the shuttle. Maybe they have other ways of detecting us—sound or smell, perhaps—but we're out of sight, and that's something.

The kids doing the clearing work are mostly circles. That's because most of *us* are circles. Six teenagers have that symbol. Fifty-two of the *Xolotl* kids. All 168 kids that were stored on the shuttle. In total, circles make up three-quarters of our population. I watch them, and I can't stop thinking: clearing away unwanted plants is the kind of work a slave would do.

From here I can see so much of the city—not far enough to spot Bishop somewhere off to the east, but if a spider tries to come this way I'll have plenty of time to call out a warning and get everyone back inside the shuttle.

I'm worried about Bishop, Bawden and Visca. There is nothing I can do to help them. The Observatory has power—does that mean people are there? People who could hurt my friends?

I need to see Bishop again, if only just to lay eyes on him. Spingate has shown her true feelings, O'Malley plays mind games, Gaston is busy teaching Beckett how to fly and Aramovsky is a constant threat . . . Bishop is the only person I can count on.

The city is still. Hot. No breeze. Sweat mats my hair to my head, yet the black suit keeps the rest of my body perfectly cool. I don't know how that's possible. The Grownups knew so much about so many things. If we solve the food problem, rediscovering their knowledge will be a high priority.

I wait. I stare. I don't see Bishop. I don't see our exploring teams, either. Coyotl, Okereke, Cabral and Aramovsky each lead three circle-star kids, searching nearby buildings. They are all close enough to come running if I sound an alarm. So far, they have found only empty buildings.

Borjigin, Ingolfsson and D'souza are moving contaminated food into a single storage room. Easier to guard that way. I didn't want to risk the younger kids doing that job, for fear they might ignore my warnings and sneak some of the bad food for themselves. Borjigin is a half, like Opkick, like O'Malley, and naturally took charge of the operation. Part of me waited for Ingolfsson or D'souza—both circles—to push back, to tell Borjigin to stop being so bossy, but they didn't. Are they working hard because that's what has to be done, or because they were created to follow orders?

I just can't get it out of my head. I wish I could deny it, but O'Malley's information opened up just enough of Matilda's memories for me to know the truth. She was born a slave. Is that why she led the rebellion on the *Xolotl*? To free herself, to free her kind? But if so, then why did all the dead people we saw have the same symbol as her? The same symbol as *me*?

The setting sun casts a warm light on Farrar and the thirty-odd young circle-stars that aren't exploring. They are arranged in formation, Farrar facing them. He squats, yells and punches a big fist straight out into the air while tucking his other tight against his body. He yells again, the fists change position, over and over. The children match his sounds and motions.

While the slaves cut and haul, while the halves organize and the gears study, the soldiers drill. Something tells me this is the way things were for a long time, even before the *Xolotl* left whatever planet it came from.

All the buildings cast lengthening shadows, but one shadow stretches farther and faster, gobbling up the buildings before it—the big ziggurat blocks out the light long before night completely falls. Bishop is somewhere in that shadow. Is he injured? Is he *dead*? My chest hurts when I think about that. What if he needs help?

Omeyocan's two moons slowly reveal themselves. The explorer teams stop searching. Cabral and Okereke smile and wave at me as they return to the shuttle with their young circle-star helpers. Aramovsky completely ignores me, as do the kids on his team. Coyotl sends his kids into the shuttle, then sits down next to me. He's filthy. In addition to his thighbone, he carries a crowbar he got from the storeroom.

"We didn't find anything," he says. "We searched twenty buildings, total. A few were open, but most"—he wiggles the crowbar—"we had to break into. Nothing in any of them. No people, no furniture, no power . . . nothing. Sorry, Em."

"Why are you apologizing? You looked, and now we know more than we did before."

He thinks on this, shrugs.

"We should at least go back to the ramp," he says. "I'll sit with you if you want."

I would like that. The landing pad was full of activity; now it is empty, the newly cleared metal dully reflecting the light of two moons. We climb the ramp, then sit on the metal platform, our legs dangling off the edge.

Together, Coyotl and I watch darkness claim the city. The smell of mint is strong from all the cut vines. We watch the stars come out. I wonder if one of them is the *Xolotl*.

I notice him looking at me.

Oh, no, not him, too.

"Coyotl, you're not going to try to kiss me, are you?"

The redhead gives me a wry smile. "You're very nice, Em, but you're not really my type. I was looking at your spear."

My grip tightens on my weapon. "Why?"

"Because it looks dull."

He reaches into one of his coveralls' many pockets and pulls out a rectangular gray stone. He raises it up to show me, then draws his knife from its sheath and holds it flat against his thigh. He slides the stone against the blade, slowly, methodically, again and again.

After a time, he holds the knife up so I can see it; moonlight plays brightly along the silvery edge.

"Feel how sharp this is, but don't slide your hand down it," he says. "Drag your thumb *against* it, like this." He gently pulls the pad of his thumb perpendicular against the blade, then offers the knife to me, hilt-first.

I use my thumb as he did. The blade feels very sharp. I hand him back the knife. He reaches into his bag and produces a second stone, which he passes to me.

It takes me a few tries to position the long spear in a way

where I can slide the stone against the blade. It makes a small grinding noise when I do.

Coyotl smiles and nods. "That's it."

He didn't want to kiss me, he didn't want my spear—he just wanted my spear to be sharp. Together, we slide stones across steel. Ten strokes. A hundred. Slow and steady. My world narrows to the stone, the metal.

He stops. "I know you and Aramovsky are fighting."

His words pull me out of it. I realize that when I sharpen the spear, I'm not thinking of anything else. In a way, I guess doing this gave my mind a break. I feel more relaxed now.

"We're not fighting," I say. "We have different ideas. We're trying to figure out the best way to take care of everyone."

Coyotl thinks on this for a minute. He nods, goes back to sharpening.

"That's good," he says. "Because this place . . . I love Omeyocan, but it's—" he stops and looks at me "—it's *scary.*"

It is at that. I nod.

He smiles wide, like I have just helped him with a big problem.

"Aramovsky helps me not be afraid," he says. "There's a lot of us who are afraid. He talks to us, tells us that the gods will protect us."

I again put the stone to my spear. I sharpen. I think.

Aramovsky is helping people? He's trying to turn people against me. Could it be both things at once? I think of what he said to me in the pilothouse. He seemed so genuine, so sincere. Maybe he's talking nonsense, but he *believes* that nonsense.

The scrape of stone on metal chases away my thoughts. I lose myself in the task. I don't know how much time has gone by when Coyotl stands suddenly, staring out toward the vine wall.

I look and see nothing. The only light comes from the shuttle behind us. My imagination turns the city's deep shadows into creeping spiders.

"What is it?" I ask quietly. "Do you see—"

"Shhh."

He leans forward slightly, peering—he smiles.

"They've returned."

The shadows move, take shape: Bishop, Visca, Bawden. Long vines are wrapped around their black coveralls. They look like part of the landscape, even though they're running. Standing still, they would be invisible. As they draw closer, I see their faces: covered in plant juice and dirt.

Coyotl runs down the ramp, feet hammering on the metal. Bishop is right—he *is* noisy.

Coyotl meets them halfway. His left hand goes to Bishop's right shoulder, Bishop's left hand goes to Coyotl's right. Coyotl repeats the greeting with the other circle-stars. There is something formal about the motion, and also something deeply emotional. None of the other symbols do that. In many ways, the circle-stars are a people unto themselves.

Coyotl and Bawden enter the shuttle, leaving me with Bishop and Visca.

"Welcome back," I say to them.

I was so worried about Bishop. Now that he's back, I feel exhausted. I just want to sleep.

"We saw spiders," he says. "They stay still and hidden, mostly. We couldn't get a good look at them. We saw some lurking around a strange building near the Observatory. I think it's their nest. We had to go all the way around so the spiders couldn't see us, and approach the Observatory from the far side."

Visca shifts from foot to foot, so excited he can't stand still.

Even with the coating of dirt and gunk, his skin is so much paler than Bishop's.

"Some of my training came back to me," Visca says. "I know tracking, even better than Bishop does."

I remember how Bishop tracked the pig back on the *Xolotl.*

"I don't think the spiders hear very well," Visca says. "When we decided to take the long way around, we didn't see any sign of them. No tracks, no broken vines—nothing. We can take that same path tomorrow and avoid the spiders completely, I bet."

I look at Bishop. He nods in agreement.

"The Observatory is big," he says. "It's cold at the top. We could see the entire city. The landing pad, the shuttle, the city wall, the jungle and the ruins . . . everything looked so *small.*"

"What about other people? Anything moving?"

"No," Bishop says. "We saw maybe four different spiders inside the city limits. When we got up high on the Observatory, we could see over the city walls. We saw more spiders moving through the ruins."

Four of them inside the walls? And more in the jungle? I had held out hope there was just one spider. So many . . . we could never stand up to that many.

"Gaston thinks the wall goes all around the city," I say. "Does it?"

Bishop nods. "Except for the river that leads to the waterfall. There is a gap in the wall where the river flows in from the jungle. Past the wall, there's nothing but ruins and jungle. In all directions."

I'm not sure what I was hoping for. Valleys and fields? Forests? Maybe another city like ours, far off, a city that *wasn't* abandoned?

Bishop seems uncomfortable. He has more bad news.

"Tell me," I say. "What else did you see?"

Visca stops shuffling. He looks down. Whatever he saw disturbed him.

Bishop takes in a slow breath, lets it out even slower.

"There were pictures carved into the Observatory walls," he says. "They showed people who looked so real I would have thought they could talk to us. Some of the carvings were of people killing each other. It reminded me of all the bodies on the *Xolotl*."

If the images disturb Bishop this much, they must be awful.

"You didn't get inside, though?"

He shakes his head.

"At the very top, there were lights," he says. "Small lights, so small you can't see them from here. Gaston is right—the building has power."

It's not Gaston who is right, it's O'Malley. No use in explaining that now.

"I don't know what good that does us," I say. "If we can't get in, what's the point?"

Bishop's jaw muscles twitch. "I think we can. There's a pillar at the top, with all the symbols on it. Each symbol is big, taller than I am. The gear symbol is at the bottom. In the empty space inside the gear, there's a handprint—and on the palm, a golden double-circle."

Damn.

If we want to enter the Observatory, we'll need Aramovsky to get us in.

PART III

LEGACIES AND LANGUAGE

NINETEEN

The Observatory is *massive*.

The vine-covered ziggurat rises into the afternoon sky, enormous layers of stacked stone, one on top of the next. If a giant hand turned it upside down, I bet most of the city could fit inside it as if the other buildings were nothing more than a collection of pebbles. The *Xolotl* was huge, so large I couldn't really process it, but this is different. That was in space. That was . . . well, it wasn't *real*. The Observatory sits on solid ground.

If this is a testimony to what the Grownups can do, I am so grateful they are not here.

Bishop, O'Malley, Aramovsky, Spingate, Visca and I made good time. We left at sunrise. It is now a few hours past midday. Visca's roundabout path took us south, then west, then south again, then west again, adding several hours to the trip—but we saw no sign of spiders. We'll follow that same path back, which means we'll get home well after sunset. Once we enter the

Observatory—if we *can* enter—every minute we spend inside is another minute of darkness on our return.

I brought O'Malley because I need him. Manipulator or not, the shuttle recognizes him as a "Chancellor." Any systems still working in the Observatory might do the same.

Spingate insisted on coming, saying she had exhausted the capabilities of the shuttle's tiny lab. Either she gets more information somewhere else, or she won't be able to stop the red mold. We think we need Aramovsky to get in. As for Bishop, I wouldn't even consider making this trip without him. That left Gaston as the main person I could trust. He's in charge of the shuttle while we're gone. Borjigin and Opkick are helping him.

The towering Observatory is so big it hurts to think about it. We count thirty layers, one on top of the other. The base layer itself is taller than most of the city's buildings, and so wide and long a hundred smaller pyramids could easily fit on it. There is something solemn about this monument that touches the sky, something . . . *frightening*.

I wonder if Aramovsky can comfort me and take away my fears the way he comforts Coyotl.

If this place doesn't have answers, we have no choice but to go beyond the wall. Somewhere on this planet there is food for my people—I will find it. If I have to track down the fire-builders and take food away from them, I will.

Wide steps run up the ziggurat's south face. At the top, faint and faded at this distance, I see the last layer and its pillar of six symbols glimmering in the sunlight. Twenty-five layers up, I can just make out that big vine-covered statue we saw on the pilot-house map.

Spingate's head is tilted so far back she seems to be staring straight up.

"I can't believe this," she says. "To build such a thing . . . the Grownups are amazing."

Aramovsky nods. Before he can mutter some nonsense about gods, I speak.

"We can believe it, because it's right there in front of us," I say. "Save your disbelief for things we can't see."

I meant that as a dig on Aramovsky. He doesn't seem to notice.

So many vine-choked steps. My legs ache just *looking* at them. It will take us hours to reach the top.

"We're wasting daylight," Aramovsky says.

He's right. I take a last, deep breath, resigning myself to the work that lies before us.

"Bishop," I say, "take us up."

He and Visca lead the way. With vines wrapped around their black uniforms, they look like shadows moving across the yellow leaves that blanket the ziggurat's orange-brown stone. Spingate, O'Malley, Aramovsky and I stand out more. We should wrap ourselves in vines, too. Maybe later—vines would add weight, and this damn spear will be heavy enough by the time we're done.

The steps are wide but thin, and painfully steep. I have to raise my knee almost parallel to the ground to move from one to the next. I'm careful, as more often than not my foot lands on leaves and vines that want to squish out from under when I put my weight on them. The stone beneath is unforgiving—even a short fall could break bones.

I count as I climb: the ziggurat's bottom layer has *one hundred* steps. By the time I reach the first plateau, my legs are already screaming.

Twenty-nine layers to go.

My eyes trace the steps that lead to the second plateau—yep, another hundred. At the ninety-fifth, Bishop stops and turns to me.

"Em, don't be afraid of what you'll see next—the woman is just a carving."

We take the last five steps side by side.

I reach the second plateau and am grateful for his warning. A snarling woman in red robes is carved into the wall at the base of the ziggurat's third layer, vines on either side of her held apart like drawn curtains. Bishop must have tied them off. A vine-covered block of stone sits in front of her. She's plunging a knife down. She looks so *real*.

Bishop nods toward the woman. "When we came up, we thought we saw something behind the vines. It was her."

Some of her color has chipped or flaked away, but if I had just glanced I would have thought she was moving, thought she was alive.

The woman has a double-ring on her forehead.

I walk to the block. Through the vines covering it, I see a carved man, on his back, hands chained to the block's sides. The two images are meant to be viewed together—the red-robed woman driving a knife into his chest. The man's face is forever frozen into a twisted mask of pain and terror.

A vine covers his forehead. I push it aside. His symbol is a half-circle.

"There's more carvings," Bishop says. "All the way up, on every plateau. We didn't look at many. After the first few, well . . . we stopped looking at anything but our feet."

Aramovsky walks to the carving. He runs his fingers down the woman's robes, as if they were cloth instead of stone.

"This is important," he says.

He closes his eyes. His brow furrows. I think back to when

O'Malley told me I was a slave, how it felt to have blocked memories suddenly flare to life.

Aramovsky's eyes open wide.

"Ritual," he says. "The God of Blood demands *ritual*."

That is Aramovsky's important word, his *cloud cover,* his *microorganisms*.

I feel O'Malley looking at me. He stares hard, his message clear: *I told you Aramovsky is a problem—now he's going to be even worse.*

"Let's go," I say. "We don't have time to look at stupid art. Let's climb."

At the tenth plateau, we are already exhausted. We're higher than most of the surrounding buildings, yet there are still twenty plateaus before we reach the top. And we thought walking "uphill" on the *Xolotl* was bad.

Every level has more images, all somehow worse than the level below:

. . . red-robed, double-ring priests cutting hearts from the chests of living people, throwing the bodies down the Observatory steps . . .

. . . severed limbs arranged into patterns, like the pinwheel of arms we saw up on the *Xolotl* . . .

. . . people with their hands chained above their heads, shot repeatedly with arrows, their blood draining into troughs that channel it to stone bowls carved into the terrace. Those images alone are disturbing enough, then I notice actual stone bowls beneath the vines at our feet, waiting to be filled with blood . . .

. . . scenes of two people fighting, one armed with a sword and protected by brightly colored armor, while the other is naked, holding only a small knife—or sometimes just a pointed stick . . .

. . . people pinned on their backs by bars like the ones that held me in my birth-coffin, one robed priest holding their jaws open, another pouring liquid down their throat . . .

. . . people being burned alive . . .

. . . people being *skinned* . . .

Every level holds images of torture, terror and death.

Was this what the Grownups wanted? A world of murder and human sacrifice?

We are all horrified. All, except Aramovsky.

We reach the twenty-fifth plateau. The tall statue is there, still looking up toward the ziggurat peak. Even this close I can't make out if it's a man or a woman, not with so many vines hanging all over it.

We need a rest. I tell everyone to sit in the statue's shade.

My legs tremble. They moved past simple pain three or four levels back. Now they are numb. I can only imagine how badly they will ache tomorrow. O'Malley, Spingate and I are drained to the point I'm not sure we can make it the last five levels. Visca and Bishop look tired, but can clearly keep going. Where does their strength and endurance come from?

Spingate and I rest with our backs against the base of the statue. O'Malley lies flat on his stomach. Aramovsky, somehow, is still moving, looking at carvings with wonder. Bishop and Visca sit on the steps, staring out across the city. They don't want to see any more of the horrors.

These top layers are just as thick as those on the bottom—a hundred steps each—but are increasingly smaller in width. It would have taken us hours to walk all the way around the base.

We could walk around the twenty-fifth layer's thin plateau in only a couple of minutes.

Everyone is still except for Aramovsky. He's just as exhausted as I am, I'm sure of it, but you'd never know by his expression. Every new image makes his face blaze with reverence. He's running his hands over a carving that shows two red-robed people—a man and a woman—using stone blades to scrape the skin off a little girl. The child's agonized, terrified face is so real I can almost hear her screams.

For a moment I think, *I shouldn't have brought him.* But we probably can't get inside without him. I had no choice.

I notice that Spingate is watching him. She's getting angry. She stands, walks over to him.

"You like that?" she says.

I hear the threat in her voice. Aramovsky doesn't. He answers without turning around.

"It's beautiful. This had to be carved by hand. And how did the artists make the rock different colors?"

"*Artists,*" Spin says, spitting the word out like it's made of poison. "There's something wrong with you, Aramovsky. I always knew there was, but this proves it."

He turns to face her. If he didn't hear her tone, he can see her body language—fists clenched at her sides, shoulders forward. I'm behind her, I can't see her eyes, but I know they are narrowed to slits.

"There's nothing wrong with me," he says. "I don't know why you'd say that."

She points at the image of the girl, at the girl's forehead. "That's a *tooth-girl* being butchered. Is that why you like it? Or because the two people *skinning her* are double-rings, like you?"

I glance at the forehead symbols of the carved people, see that she's right.

Spingate takes a step toward him. I see Bishop and Visca rise, watching carefully.

O'Malley lifts up on one elbow.

"Give it a rest, Spin," he says. "Aramovsky didn't make this place."

She takes another step closer. Aramovsky takes a step away, unsure of what's happening. A second step away puts his back up against the very carving he so admires.

Spingate closes the distance.

I realize all at once that she's going to hit him. He could crush her if he wanted to, but that doesn't matter—a fight could easily result in someone tumbling down the steps or, worse, rolling off the edge to the hard stone below.

I scramble to my feet and run to them.

"Spin, take it easy," I say. "Like O'Malley said, Aramovsky had nothing to do with making these carvings."

She whirls, fists clenched, eyes blazing with hatred. She hoped this building might bring answers, but it is nothing more than a temple of nightmares.

"He'll do the same to us," she says. "Mark my words, Em, Aramovsky will . . ."

She glances above me as her voice trails off. Then she looks at me again. The expression on her face, it's like a dagger through my heart—she's *terrified*.

I reach out for her. She flinches. I let my hand drop to my side.

"Spin, what's wrong? You don't think I'd let Aramovsky do something to you, do you? I wouldn't let anyone hurt you."

Aramovsky starts to laugh. The deep sound makes my skin crawl. He slowly claps his hands, absolutely delighted.

"Some things you let happen, Em," he says. "Some things you can't stop, because they are your destiny."

He points up at the statue.

I turn and look up, raising a hand to block the sun.

And then I see why Spingate is so afraid.

There are only a few vines hanging from the statue's head. I can see the face—a face that is unmistakable.

Because it is *mine*.

TWENTY

I stare until my eyes water.

It's me. *Me.*

No, it's Matilda, or it would be if she took over my body. All the horror that decorates this monstrosity of a building, all the promises of death and carnage and hearts ripped from chests and tossed down steep stone steps . . . the statue means all of this was her doing.

Being the leader wasn't enough for Matilda.

She wanted to be *worshipped*.

Aramovsky is at my side.

"Our two Grownups were together when we found them." His voice is smooth, calm and low, the hiss of a smiling snake. "The circles and the double-rings working together. *You and I*, working together. This was meant to be. Remember how I told you I wanted to help you lead? This is a sign, Em—a sign that can't be ignored."

He doesn't even know the proper terms. He means *Spirit* and

Service working together. Did my progenitor and his cooperate to create this nightmare?

I feel ill. Aramovsky makes me sick. This place makes me sick. This entire *planet* makes me sick. We woke up in coffins and fought our way off an orbiting tomb only to inherit a city of death.

O'Malley approaches. "Get away from her, Aramovsky. She doesn't need your whispered lies."

The tall boy grins. "Because whispering in her ear is your job?"

O'Malley's right hand flexes, fingers opening and curling. Like a crawling animal, the hand drifts toward the jeweled handle of his knife.

Bishop moves in, his steps noisy only because he wants us to hear him coming.

"The sun will set soon," he says. "We should continue on—I don't like the idea of being on these steps at night."

Neither do I, but *should* we continue? This place is evil, and we're not even inside yet. O'Malley is ready to attack Aramovsky. Aramovsky suddenly thinks he and I are destined to rule together. And the look on Spingate's face—she's scared of me, scared and disgusted.

I stare at her until she looks away.

Arrogant tooth-girl. I wonder what she thinks of "stupid empties" now? Special girl, *rich* girl. I remember people like her laughing at me. One of her kind *owned* me. I remember being afraid to say anything, knowing that my owner could punish me, beat me if she wanted to, that I had no rights. Girls like Spingate liked having power. Now the power has changed hands—of course she's scared. She *should* be.

My thoughts pause. A moment of blankness, of floundering

confusion. What am I thinking? Am I taking *joy* in Spin's fear? Hatred of her and her kind bubbles and boils, but that hatred isn't mine—it's Matilda's. Spingate has done nothing to me.

Those things she said to me in the lab . . . is she suffering the same turmoil as I am? Is her sudden prejudice against my kind actually from *her* progenitor? If I have legacy memories, then Spingate probably does, too.

These emotions aren't *ours*.

"Spin, that statue isn't me. It will never be me."

She sniffs. I can tell she wants to believe me, but it must be hard while seeing these images of her kind being tortured, skinned, *slaughtered,* and with my oh-so-heroic face lording down from above.

"In a way, it *is* you," she says. "Matilda was your age once. You have her mind." Spingate points to the statue. "Like it or not, that's what you could become. This search isn't just about food or the mold, not anymore. If this building can tell us about our past, help us understand how Matilda turned into a monster that sacrifices gears and halves, that's information we need."

Alone, she starts up the thin steps.

Five more steep flights to go.

We follow her up.

At the twenty-seventh plateau, the lush vines start to thin. By the twenty-eighth, they don't grow at all, leaving the orange-brown stone exposed. It's colder up here. The wind whips at us. I see heavy clouds coming in from the north, but for now the skies above remain clear.

The lack of vines means we see all the images. We can't even look away, because many are carved into the flat fronts of the stairs themselves.

We wobble and shudder as we finish the climb. I think I make it up the final steps on willpower alone, because my body gave up on me about three layers ago.

My legs feel like boiling goo. They burn, they sting. O'Malley is grunting and wheezing—I wonder if he's going to throw up. Aramovsky is worse off: he looks like he might keel over and die at any moment, but that horrid glow remains in his eyes. Even Bishop and Visca are tired, trails of sweat cutting skin-toned streaks through the plant juice on their faces. They have made this climb twice in two days—too much for anyone, even a tireless circle-star.

Up here we are no longer sheltered from the wind. It whips us, snaps at our black coveralls. The sun is already heading down to the horizon—the climb took us longer than we had hoped. The fabric that kept us cool now keeps us warm, but our hands and faces feel the wind's biting chill.

The last layer is the smallest one, of course. We stand upon a plateau, a square as long as ten of us lying head to feet. In the center is a stone slab, and, rising up from it, a tall, smooth stone pillar. On it, the six gold symbols, each taller than Bishop. From top to bottom: circle, circle-star, double-ring, circle-cross, half-circle and gear.

Inside the empty space of the gear, a plaque with a red handprint. In the palm, a golden double-ring.

All around us, the city seems tiny. Insignificant. At ten layers up, the tops of the tallest pyramids were at eye level. At twenty, everything looked small and we could see a long, long way. Here at the top, thirty layers above the streets, the city below no longer looks real. The Observatory is more like a mountain than a building.

I can see well past the city walls. Trees, vines and the ruins of six-sided buildings blend together, a broken yellow jungle that stretches out and out and out. To the west, far off, mountains rise up. To the north, a sparkling lake with steep cliffs all around. To the northeast is a wide clearing, crescent-shaped like a quarter moon. Maybe someday soon that clearing will be farmland for us, giving us a place to grow crops where we don't have to clear the jungle.

The same wind that whips at us is driving those dark clouds toward us. Hidden flashes of lightning flicker within. I hope it doesn't rain.

Aramovsky fights away his fatigue, stands to his full height. Atop the city's tallest building, our tallest boy looks important . . . *regal.*

"The gods have called to us," he says, almost yelling so that we can hear him over the wind. "They paint a picture of what has been, and what is to come. They will—"

"Hold on," O'Malley says. He's at the layer's edge, looking down at his feet. "What do you all make of this?"

He's standing on a black line, so faded none of us noticed it. It's a curve. We all glance around the plateau and see it: the curve is a circle that goes all the way around, touching the edges of the square plateau. And inside it, a second circle.

At first I think it's Aramovsky's double-ring, but then I see a dot on the outer circle. The dot is also black. There are four of them. If I were to draw lines from plateau corner to plateau corner, the dots are where those lines would intersect the outer circle.

And on the middle ring, there are two dots, one on either side of the stone pillar.

Two rings: four dots on the outer ring, two on the inner.

I look at Aramovsky. "Do you know what it means?"

He walks around, staring down. "This entire building *has* to be a religious place, some kind of temple, so this symbol is clearly related to mine."

He sounds like he's trying to convince himself, and failing at it. He has no idea.

The wind bites into me.

"Try the handprint," I say to him. "I want to get out of here."

He walks to the pillar, but doesn't press the handprint. Instead, he tilts his head back and raises his arms to the sky.

"Oh gods, you have chosen for us to be here in this divine place, so that we may live out your plans and—"

Bishop grabs Aramovsky and shakes him.

"Just *press the damn thing* already!"

Aramovsky's grand moment is ruined. He's far more worried about his safety than his speech. He presses his hand against the plaque.

Nothing happens.

A wave of relief washes through me. This entrance, if that's what it is, is broken, or Aramovsky is the wrong kind of person. Whatever the reason, we can't get in. I don't have to learn what horrors Matilda planned on committing once she took over my body.

A grinding sound. It stops and starts. Silence. We listen for more, but hear only the wind's lonely howl.

The plateau trembles beneath us. We are so high up. If the Observatory collapses . . .

The pillar shudders. The rectangular slab beneath it rises up, each corner supported by a golden column that reflects the red sun's final light. The bottom of the slab reaches eye level, then shudders to a stop.

At our feet, in the space below where the slab was, an intricate metal staircase spirals down into the darkness.

If I never see steps again, it will be too soon.

As we descend, the dark stone walls start to glow. Dimly, but enough that we don't need our flashlights. The sound of the wind fades away. Soon we hear only our breathing and our boots stepping on metal stairs.

At least there's no "art" on these walls.

Down and down we go. Bishop first, then Visca, then me, Spingate, Aramovsky and finally O'Malley. We hold our weapons at the ready. I don't know how long we descend. Long enough that I'm sure the sun has set, that the Observatory's long shadow has once again engulfed the shuttle.

Finally, the stairs end at a small room with a stone floor. In one wall, a door made of vertical metal bars. Some kind of metallic mesh hangs behind the bars. Next to the door is a plaque with a red handprint: a gold double-ring marks the palm.

This place has a stale odor. It smells like my coffin room did when I first woke up.

I point to the plaque. "Aramovsky, open it."

He glances at Bishop, then quickly presses his hand to the print.

We again hear that sound of struggling machinery, then the bars and mesh rattle, kicking off a brief cascade of rust as they slide to the right, revealing a small room.

"It's an elevator," O'Malley says.

I remember those. My heart pounds at the sight of it. I don't want to be sealed up in that tiny space, but what choice do I have? We came here to find answers. If that means getting into a cramped elevator, I have to do it.

"Everyone, inside," I say.

It's a tight fit. Bishop keeps his axe close to his chest so as not to accidentally cut anyone. Visca stands his sledgehammer in the corner. Aramovsky and Spingate are armed only with the knives strapped to their thighs, although they have to adjust their black bags to make room. My spear is a bit too tall for the low ceiling; I have to hold it at an angle.

O'Malley slides the bars back into place, shutting us in. No plaque in here. No controls that I can see.

Without warning, the cage *drops*. We grab each other out of fear. We're dropping fast. I shut my eyes tight, stifle a scream. My insides feel like they're floating, rising up.

We're going to smash into the ground. I should have never got in here, *never,* we're going to die I'm going to die trapped in this tiny box.

Spingate's fingers intertwine with mine, clasp tight.

"Breathe, Em," she says softly. "We're fine."

I suddenly feel heavier.

"We're slowing down," she says.

Heavier still . . .

The cage bounces slightly. It has stopped.

Spingate all but collapses on me, hangs on me, laughing. I don't know how to react—a little while ago she thought I might kill her because of her symbol.

She shakes her head, then kisses me on the cheek.

"I'm sorry, Em. I said awful things in the lab. I barely even know where to start with the red mold, and there just isn't enough time. And then all the horrible pictures and carvings on the way up here . . . it made me so upset. So many images of people killing my kind."

I nod. I understand, and also, I don't. I've used the phrase *my kind,* too, so I can't hold that against her, but aren't we *all* the same kind?

She kisses my cheek again, hugs me tight. "I know that statue isn't you. You're not like Matilda. You would never do anything like that."

The elevator door slides open to darkness.

As one, we reach into our bags for our flashlights.

Bishop and Visca go first, as always, axe and hammer at the ready, flashlight beams probing the darkness. The rest of us follow. Our lights play off a curved ceiling made of large stone blocks. Carvings cover the stone walls. These images we've seen before: ziggurats, cartoonish people, jaguars, suns.

Not that far from the elevator, our flashlights light up the soft gleam of dusty metal—golden coffins. Four of them, on golden risers so their closed lids are waist high. Laid out side by side, their surfaces are richly detailed with gemstones and the same images we see on the walls. The dust here is thin, not like the thick stuff that coated everything back on the *Xolotl*.

These coffins have no nameplates.

Past the coffins is a raised platform with five white pedestals. To our left, a tall black "X" mounted into the floor. Thick shackles dangle from the top of each arm. A bar runs between the tops of those arms—hanging from that bar, some kind of ornate, black crown. On the wall just behind the X, a colorful, carved mural: an old man shackled to that same X, wearing that same crown, a young man in red robes before him, driving a knife into the old man's chest. To our right, deep shadows filled with racks of bins similar to what we saw in the food warehouse, except these bins all look empty and many are scattered about.

In the room's center, there is a hole about as wide as I am tall. A waist-high, red metal wall surrounds it. A flexible black tube—as thick as my arm—runs from inside that hole, over the wall and under the pedestal platform.

Visca and Bishop move through the room, flashlights in one

hand, weapons in the other. We give them a few minutes, then everyone starts exploring.

I walk to the red wall. Engraved in the metal is a large black symbol. It's like the one from the plateau on top of this building, but slightly different. Two rings, four dots on the outer ring, two in the middle ring, but there is also a thick dot in the middle—right where the stone pillar was.

"Aramovsky, take a look at this."

Maybe with the center dot, he'll recognize it.

He stands at my side, staring at it. He shakes his head—he doesn't know what it is. At least now he admits it.

Spingate joins us. Her eyes squint, like a memory is working its way up from the depths.

"I . . . I think it's a representation of something," she says. "An atom. It's . . . I think this represents a carbon atom."

She points to the six dots on the rungs, one at a time.

"These are electrons, I think. And that dot in the middle, that's the nucleus."

I look around the room, my flashlight beam seeking out this symbol on the ceiling, the walls, the coffins. I don't find it.

"All right," I say, "so what does it mean?" I ask her.

She shrugs. "I have no idea."

Another useless symbol of the Grownups.

Aramovsky walks to the black X. He seems mesmerized by it.

I look down into the hole. The shaft's round wall is nothing but dirt, packed with stones that show white cracks and scrapes from when this hole was dug. Far below, I think I see the bottom: something metal. A machine, perhaps. The black cable runs into the center of it.

Spingate steps onto the pedestal platform. The moment she does, I hear a hum. It's coming from the black cable.

The five pedestals begin to glow.

"Welcome, Grandmaster Spingate."

The voice comes from nowhere, from everywhere. Just like in the shuttle's pilothouse, lights suddenly play off Spingate's skin. Her face glows like that of a goddess. She smiles wide: a new puzzle for her, a new problem to solve. Her frustration, fear and anger are gone—or at least temporarily forgotten.

"Do you have a name?" she asks.

"Much of my memory has been erased. I believe I was referred to as Ometeotl."

"Good enough," she says. "Can you show me a diagram of this building?"

Lights flash. In the space above the hole, a glowing version of the Observatory appears. The building spins slowly, giving us a look at all four sides.

"Thank you," Spingate says. "This place is called the Observatory, is that correct?"

"Yes, Grandmaster."

Spingate nods. That title, *Grandmaster,* doesn't surprise her. Maybe her lab referred to her by that name, just like the Deck Three pedestals called O'Malley *Chancellor*.

"Observatories are for telescopes," Spingate says. "Is there a telescope?"

The fake ziggurat flashes. The sloping sides become transparent. We see hundreds of rooms and intersecting corridors, but the main feature is a long cylinder that starts at the building's base and rises up at an angle to end just inside one of the sloping walls.

The cylinder glows brightly. It is enormous. So big, in fact, I can only come to one conclusion—this Observatory was built specifically to house it.

Spingate steps off the platform and walks to the glowing ziggurat. She continues to shine, lit up so brightly our flashlights are almost useless. She leans on the red metal wall, her eyes tracing the cylinder's length.

"I've seen an image like this before," she says. "It's hard to remember but . . . someone I knew was trained to use this telescope. Someone I went to school with."

Spingate rubs at her face. We all watch, we all wait, because we all know what she's going through—bits of memories are pushing their way to the surface.

She stops rubbing. Hands still pressed against her face, she slides her fingers apart slightly. One eye looks at me.

"Em, our school. We were all being trained to live and work on the *Xolotl.*" She points at the image of the telescope. "Some people were trained specifically for that. The girl . . . she was a gear . . . what was her name?"

Spingate makes fists, grinds them into her temples.

She stops—she has it.

"Okadigbo," she says. "One of the dead kids in our original coffin room on the *Xolotl.*"

I also know that name, because Brewer mentioned her: *Where is Okadigbo? Is she still alive, or did you kill her again?*

"She trained for years," Spingate says. "I can't remember what her classes were, exactly, but it was all she worked on."

The few memories any of us have end at the age of twelve. If Okadigbo had been studying for years, when did she start?

The Observatory, built to house a telescope.

This city, built to support the Observatory?

If these things are true, everything we've seen is dedicated to one thing: the telescope. Why? What does it mean? What does it do?

Spingate reaches out with shaking hands. Her fingertips sink into the glowing ziggurat. She turns it this way, then that, tilting, looking.

"The telescope has a name," she says. "I can't quite . . . dammit, what was it called?"

O'Malley walks to stand next to her. He reaches a fingertip out, traces it down the length of the cylinder.

"It's called . . . ," he says, searching for the word, ". . . it's called . . . is it the *Goffspear*?"

That word is a hammer smashing into my brain. A word of power. *Beyond* power. It might be the most important word there is. Looking at the faces of my friends, I know it hits them just as hard.

"Chancellor, is Adept Okadigbo present?"

"She's not," I say, answering before O'Malley can. I don't know what an *adept* is. Right now I don't care. This building, or system or computer, or whatever it is, is expecting Okadigbo. If it knows she's dead, it might shut down.

The image of the Observatory blinks out. So do Spingate's lights, leaving her again in the darkness.

She's staring at me. So are the others.

Something on my right hand, the hand that holds the spear. Tiny, brightly glowing dots, red and blue and yellow, coating my skin.

"Welcome, Empress Savage."

My friends exchange glances, gawk at me. O'Malley stands quietly, saying nothing.

Spingate's eyes narrow. Her expression clouds over with the same distrust she showed when we were at the statue.

I don't have time to worry about her. Ometeotl hasn't asked for my access code. Maybe we can finally get answers. First, though, I need to see what dangers lie in this very room.

"I am the Empress, so you have to do what I say?"

"Of course, Empress Savage."

"Good. Who is in these coffins?"

"This servant does not understand the query," Ometeotl says. *"There are no coffins here."*

I think of Brewer again, and a word pops into my head.

"The four *husks* in this room," I say. "Who is in them?"

"No one, Empress."

"Open them. Now."

Four coffin lids open simultaneously, splitting vertically down the middle, the halves sliding neatly to the sides.

All empty.

The white fabric inside looks perfect, like it has never been touched.

Goosebumps, cascading up my arms, down my body: something about this place is *wrong*. I look to Bishop to see if he notices anything, but he doesn't seem alarmed.

I push the feeling away. I have so many questions.

"What is this place? What is this city?"

"This is the city of Uchmal. Built for the free peoples of the rebellion."

That word again, *rebellion*. I think of Brewer's warning, that we can make a new future if we don't know the past. This world is ours to do with as we wish.

But only if we survive, and to survive, we have to eat.

"How do we kill the red mold?"

A pause.

"Empress Savage, this servant has no information on red mold."

It has to know. We can't have come this far for nothing.

"We found a warehouse," I say. "Full of food that was contaminated with a toxin. How did the people who came before us deal with it? What did they eat? And where did those people go?"

"As you commanded, there have been no people before you, Empress. You are the first to set foot on Omeyocan."

That makes no sense. I look at O'Malley. He doesn't understand, either. Of course there were people here before us—this city didn't build itself.

"The rebellion," Spingate says to the ceiling. "The slaughter on the *Xolotl*"—she turns her head to stare at me, her gaze malevolent—"why were those people *murdered*?"

I freeze. They died because Matilda led an uprising, but only O'Malley and I know she was a slave, that *all* the circles are slaves. I should have told everyone right away, I knew it. Now it's going to come out.

O'Malley is staring at Spingate, mouth hanging open. His eyes flick to me, and all he does is blink—the whisperer has no idea what to do now.

"I have limited information on the Xolotl*,"* Ometeotl says. *"Empress Savage's valiant efforts stopped a horrible slaughter. She led a rebellion that saved thousands of lives, then she took control of the* Xolotl *and created Uchmal."*

The answer leaves Spingate speechless; that wasn't what she was expecting. I'm at a loss for words, too, but for different reasons—was my creator actually *protecting* people?

I shake my head, try to focus. Even if Matilda was protecting people, it doesn't justify the carvings on the Observatory walls, and it doesn't come *close* to justifying the slaughter up on the *Xolotl*. We saw dead circles, not dead halves and gears.

Wait . . . we're being told this story by the same source that says we are the first ones here, *ever,* when we are standing in a building it must have taken *thousands* of people to create.

And then it hits me, a knife through my heart. Ometeotl just said that Matilda created this city. If that's true, then she created this building—which means she created Ometeotl.

My father's voice, echoing: *History is written by the victors.* The "history" I'm hearing now . . . was that written *about* Matilda, or *by* her?

Frustration claws at me. I can't trust anything Ometeotl says. This computer, or whatever it is, it lies. Everyone lies. This place held our only hope to find out the truth, and now that hope is gone.

More goosebumps; that odd feeling returns, and I suddenly know what it is—I feel like I'm being watched.

Visca's focus snaps to a shadowy corner, then another. He feels it, too.

"Something's wrong," he says.

Bishop's brow furrows as if he agrees but he can't define why.

I smell something, a faint wisp that seems familiar.

The slightest rattle of plastic: five flashlight beams sweep to the racks. The same bins, clearly empty, but one is rocking, just a little.

Something is down here with us, something lurking in the deep shadows. The bin stops rocking—beams dance across the racks, but there is no movement to be seen.

The smell connects: *burned toast,* the same thing I smelled at the fire pit, and at the tunnel beneath the wall. We're not alone—the people from the jungle are here.

I hesitate. We can confront them, but they could be violent and Spingate is with us. If anything happens to her, we have no hope of beating the mold. *Attack, attack, always attack*. My father's voice again, but this time he's wrong. We don't know how many enemies we face . . . and we don't know what weapons they have.

"Bishop," I say, keeping my voice low, "get us out of here."

He moves halfway to the racks, putting himself between us and the unknown danger. He crouches, axe in one hand, flashlight in the other.

Visca at my side, his voice calm but insistent: "Em, get in the elevator."

I do as I'm told, watching the shadows all the way, waiting for someone to come rushing out of them. I enter the elevator as quietly as I can. Aramovsky, O'Malley and Spingate follow. I can feel their fear.

Visca silently walks up to Bishop, taps his big shoulder. Without either of them looking away from the racks, they walk backward right into the elevator.

Bishop shuts the door.

The cage rises.

"All I saw was that bin," Spingate says. "Did anyone see anything else move?"

"I didn't," Bishop says. "But it seems like this cage is the only way in and out." He glances up. "Whoever was down there, if they weren't alone, they could have friends waiting for us to step out—everyone be ready to fight. We need to stay together, get off this building and then back to the shuttle as fast as we can."

Aramovsky shakes his head. "We can't leave. We have to go back down, finally learn who we are. This building, this temple . . . we need to bring everyone here. We need to *live* here."

Live in a building covered in images of human sacrifice? Get answers from a machine voice that is either wrong or lying? And then there's the obvious—someone was down there, someone who was watching us.

The fire-builders.

Aramovsky is almost right. We might have to come back, but not for the reasons he thinks. We have five days of rations left. If we don't find food soon, if Spingate can't beat the mold, then we will capture the people in the Observatory and force them to tell us what they know. I will come back here with *all* the circle-stars.

"We return to the shuttle," I say. "The Observatory isn't safe."

Aramovsky starts to protest, but I *thonk* the spear down on the cage floor.

"No one is allowed to come here," I say. *"No one."*

Heads nod. Even Aramovsky's.

The cage's rise slows. I feel lighter. Then it stops. The doors open. We see the stairs leading up.

TWENTY-ONE

Wind roars down the wide streets, channeled by the buildings on either side. Rain blasts us from all directions, but we dare not stop.

We are being hunted.

Visca carries Spingate in his arms. O'Malley stumbles more than runs, the last of his energy long since spent.

Up ahead, Bishop waves madly for us to come his way. He's at the street corner, half-hidden by the base layer of a small ziggurat. He can't call to us, because the spider is so close it might hear even over the wind-driven rustle of a million leaves.

Visca reaches him first, Aramovsky right on his heels. O'Malley falls hard. I drag him to his feet, shove him on. Then Bishop is there, tosses O'Malley over one big shoulder, grabs my hand and yanks me around the corner.

I'm thrown to the ground next to Spingate, who silently sobs, her elbow clutched to her chest. Before I can get up, O'Malley lands hard next to me. Visca covers us with a thick sheet of vines.

"Stay *still,*" Bishop hisses. "Be silent."

Seconds pass. I stare through the vines out to the dark street. Clouds transform Omeyocan's twin moons into hazy, glowing spots of blue and maroon. The few trees growing up from ziggurat plateaus bend beneath the stiff wind. Our coveralls keep our bodies mostly dry, but the rain runs down our faces and under our collars.

No one was waiting for us atop the Observatory. It was pitch-black, the stars blocked by heavy clouds. Halfway down, the skies opened up. Steep steps were treacherous enough before rain made the vines slick, before high winds blasted us. We only had two layers left when Spingate fell and cracked her elbow on the stone. She thinks it's broken.

We followed Visca's route back from the Observatory, but this time we weren't alone. Over the wind, we heard a whine—the sound of the spider that almost caught us at the city gate. It's looking for us, and it's getting closer.

The whine is much louder now.

"What are we doing?" Aramovsky whispers from behind me. "We need to get to the shuttle!"

Bishop's hand shoots through the vines, grabs him by the throat.

"Be . . . quiet."

We've changed directions so many times I have no idea where we are, but Visca says we're not far from the shuttle. If we can lose the spider, we'll soon be safe.

The deluge pours down, unstoppable. I stare out at the dark intersection as the whine grows louder still, and wonder if maybe—just this once—I should pray to Aramovsky's gods.

A flash of movement: the spider is visible for only a moment as it rushes down the street we were just on, and then is gone from sight.

Seconds pass. We wait for it to come back and kill us.

The seconds become minutes.

Bishop finally releases Aramovsky, then steps to the corner and peeks out. I'm watching him, but as soon as he stops moving, his camouflage soaks him into the night's shadows like water vanishing into a sponge.

He waves us forward.

We crest the vine wall, look down at our shuttle. We made it. Circle-stars rush out to help. Gaston beats them to us, goes straight to Spingate. Someone carries O'Malley. Hands help me, I'm not sure whose.

The shuttle's warmth welcomes me. Someone lays me down in my coffin. Then Smith is there, asking me questions in a harsh, clipped tone. I answer as best I can: *no, I'm not hurt; you're holding up three fingers, now two; yes, I just want to sleep*. Then she's gone, saying she has to operate on Spingate's elbow.

Just like before, O'Malley is in the coffin to my right, Bishop in the one to my left. They're both already asleep. I lie back in mine.

My lid closes. It's dark, cramped, but this time I don't care. As the world around me goes quiet, the questions in my head roar out loud.

Who were the people in the Observatory? Are they Grown-ups? Or are they young people like us, blank kids who somehow found a way down here before we did? Could they be a group that has nothing to do with the *Xolotl* at all, perhaps people who were here before that ship's thousand-year journey even began?

Ometeotl said Matilda was a hero, that she saved lives. That's a lie . . . isn't it? Was Matilda fighting against evil, at least in the beginning? Part of me desperately wants to believe that. A bigger part of me wants to block out the thoughts of something even more disturbing—what if Matilda started out doing the right thing, protecting people, then power *changed* her, made her into a monster?

If power changed her, power could change me.

I try to push the thought away but it refuses to let go, right up until exhaustion finally drags me into darkness.

TWENTY-TWO

I wake to bad news, and from an unexpected source.

"Get up, Em," Zubiri says. "The mold has spread."

I roll over, nestle my face into my coffin's padding. If I ignore her, maybe I can sleep for another fifteen minutes.

A hand on my shoulder, shaking me.

"Em, it's serious." Gaston's voice.

I groan. I roll to my back, blink against the shuttle's bright lights. Gaston and Zubiri are leaning in over me. So is skinny Borjigin. I notice that his face is smooth, hairless. All the other boys my age are showing some stubble—even little Gaston—but not Borjigin. I wonder if that's the way his creator made him.

The two boys look worried. Their eyes are flicking around the room, as if to watch out for anyone listening too close. Zubiri is as calm as can be. Few other people are up; it must be early in the morning.

"How serious?" I ask.

Borjigin looks at his inner forearm. His sleeves are rolled up—he's written numbers on his skin.

"We have one day's worth of food left," he says. "Maybe. And that's if we cut everyone's rations in half."

One day?

I try to sit up. Thunderous aches in my legs stop me. My thighs feel like they're made of bricks—I'm so sore from the Observatory climb. Gaston grips my shoulders, helps me rise.

"You're counting wrong," I say to Borjigin. "We have to have more than that."

Gaston shakes his head. "He has a full inventory of everything on the shuttle. He knows our food situation down to the calorie."

I don't care. Borjigin hasn't been part of the decision-making process. It's been me, O'Malley, Bishop, Gaston and . . .

I notice Zubiri is wearing a golden bracer.

"Where's Spingate?" I ask.

"Medical," Gaston says. "Her elbow will be fine. Smith wants her to rest a little longer, though."

It's one thing after another. Why can't someone bring me good news for a change?

"We had *five* days left," I say. "What happened?"

"I told you, the mold," Zubiri says, her tone matter-of-fact. She runs her hand over the bracer. "Spingate was hurt, so I asked Gaston if I could use this. I adjusted the sensitivity levels so I could scan food that was still inside sealed containers."

Her little face . . . so innocent. She can't be right—she's just a child.

"Zubiri surprised me, too," Gaston says. "She knows how to use the bracer better than Spingate does."

We're all the same age, basically, but I guess I assumed that because we *looked* older, we were smarter. That was stupid. I need to trust that the younger kids are just as capable as I am.

"I think the mold is a weapon," Zubiri says. "Bioengineered

to destroy food stores. It secretes a chemical that makes microscopic holes in the bins so it can get at the food."

A weapon? If Zubiri is right, that explains why all the food in the warehouse was bad. And come tomorrow, I'll have hundreds of hungry people on my hands.

I think we only have three options: defeat the mold ourselves, find safe food, or find the fire-builders.

Spingate and Zubiri should keep working in the lab. Maybe they can figure it out. The jungle is full of life—if we search, we might discover plants or animals that are safe to eat. And, while doing that, we can return to the fire pit. Visca is a tracker . . . maybe he can track the fire-builders.

If those three efforts fail, a return trip to the Observatory will be our last chance.

"Gaston, wake up Bishop and Visca," I say. "We're going back to the jungle."

We head out beneath a sky that glows yellow-orange with morning light. My group consists of Bishop, Visca, Coyotl, Borjigin and a young tooth-girl named C. Kalle. Kalle has the second bracer and knows how to use it—she'll check any food we find.

I'd rather have Spingate, but her arm will be in a sling for another day, and it makes more sense for her to continue the mold research. Zubiri will assist her. Or is Spingate now assisting Zubiri?

O'Malley stays behind as well. He's wiped out from the Observatory climb. We all are, but he's worse off than the rest of us. I leave him in charge of organizing a larger search of surrounding buildings. We're out of time and can't afford to play it safe; everyone will be involved. I'll also have him put Aramovsky to work, make the tall boy so busy he doesn't have time to spread lies.

My food ration is so small it easily fits in my coverall pockets along with some bandages, a water bottle, a few medical supplies and my flashlight. I don't even need a bag. One small grain bar and a cube of protein—perhaps my last meal. At least the last one that isn't full of poison.

Moving as silently as we can, we head for the city gate. The rain has dropped off to a drizzle. The sun is out again, making this city of vine-covered pyramids gleam as if it is sweating from the heat.

We stay close to buildings, ready to hide under vines at the first sign of a spider. Bishop, Visca and Coyotl are far out in front, scanning for threats, leaving me with Borjigin and Kalle. She keeps sliding the loose bracer back up her forearm—it clearly wasn't intended for a small, rail-thin twelve-year-old. She and Borjigin each carry a knife sheathed on their thighs.

"I don't understand why I have to go," Borjigin says.

It's the fourth time he's said that. I try to stay patient.

"You know our food situation better than anyone," I say. "If we find any, you'll figure out how far it will go, how many people we'll need to carry it back to the others, stuff like that."

"I can do logistics from the shuttle—someone could just report back to me. It's dangerous out here."

"Shut *up,*" Kalle says without looking at him, without breaking stride. "I'm half your size and you don't hear me complaining about the danger. We do this or we die. Stop being a godsdamned baby."

Borjigin glares at her. Kalle ignores him.

I'm not happy this little girl curses, but I like her already. She has curly blond hair that sticks up more than it hangs down. It reminds me of Latu's hair, so I try not to look at it.

"Just listen to the circle-stars," I say. "If you want to survive, do exactly what they tell you."

Kalle says, "Yes, ma'am," but Borjigin blanches. Maybe his definition of "dangerous" didn't include the possibility of him dying.

We walk on in silence. It takes us four or five hours to reach the city wall. We join the circle-stars at the gate. The tall doors are closed, just as we left them a few nights ago.

"Still no sign of spiders," Bishop says. "Everyone, on the door. Together now—*push*."

The six of us lean against the thick metal slab. The hinges screech, and the solid door slowly opens a crack. We slide through. Best to leave it open a little, as we don't know if we'll have to come back this way again.

The jungle ruins lie before us. I'd hoped I might see a smoke column snaking into the sky, but no such luck. Of course it can't be that easy.

Bishop scans the tree line. I do the same, but I know he will see any danger long before I do, even danger I would never see at all.

"Looks clear," he says. "Visca, go."

Visca moves out, the vine-choked wall on his right, his eyes fixed on the ground. He thinks he can follow the trail we left a few nights back, which should lead straight to the fire pit. That saves Bishop and me the time of trying to remember where we were when we first found it. From there, Visca will look for signs of the fire-builders.

Bishop gives Visca a head start, then follows. I'm next, then Kalle, then Borjigin, with Coyotl guarding our rear.

"I still don't like this," Borjigin says. "I hear animals in the jungle. What if they attack us?"

Kalle sighs and shakes her head.

Coyotl pats his thighbone against his open palm.

"Don't worry, Borjigin," he says, smiling wide. "If anything happens, I'll protect you."

Bishop stops, turns, waves me forward—Visca has found our trail.

The midday sun beats down, hot on my hair and face whenever it punches through the canopy. Mist curls up from the muddy ground, from water beaded on yellow leaves. The jungle simmers in a low-hanging mist. Despite this steamy heat, despite scratching branches, the jungle's natural beauty grips me. Brightly colored blurds whiz through the air. We hear small animals scurrying in the underbrush. Maybe those animals are what the mystery people cooked in their fire.

Kalle stops every time she sees a new plant, waves the bracer over it. And every time, she says the same thing: *non-edible*.

Finally, Visca leads us to the fire pit. It's now a puddle of black water filled with wet charcoal. The five-walled building shows no sign of anyone having been here since we left.

"I'll start a sweep," Visca says, and creeps off into the jungle.

"Let's rest," Bishop says. "Stay inside the walls, out of sight. Spiders could be out here."

Borjigin is only too happy to sit. Kalle waves her bracer over moss on the walls. At first I think she's being ridiculous, then my stomach rumbles, and I wonder if moss is tasty. The bracer jewels flash orange; looks like I don't have to worry about that.

I find a place to sit and rub at my sore thighs. They've loosened up some, but still ache plenty.

Bishop drops down next to me. He takes a drink from his water bottle, then offers it to me. That's so nice of him. I take a swig, hand it back.

"Do you think Visca will find a trail?"

He shrugs. "Maybe, but don't get your hopes up. He's way better at it than I am, though. Perhaps—"

"I found a path," Visca calls out.

Bishop is up instantly. In moments, we are on the move again.

At first I couldn't see the path, I just kept following Bishop, who was following Visca. After two hours of marching through the jungle, though, I recognize it, could easily follow it on my own.

At eye level, I see it as a narrow gap winding through the underbrush. At my feet, it is a wet, irregular strip of brown notched in among the creepers and ground cover. Shallow depressions filled with water might be footprints, although there is no way to tell how big the feet were. On either side of the path, branches scrape at us, vines smear us with juice.

The going is tiring and messy, and I don't care. The firebuilders made this path. It has to lead us to them.

I hear my footsteps, the rustle of vines and fronds being pushed aside before flapping back into place. As usual, the circle-stars don't make a sound. Except for Coyotl far behind us—I can hear his movements. Kalle makes very little noise, perhaps because she's tiny, but Borjigin is so loud he might as well be shouting.

Bishop raises a fist. Kalle and I stop instantly. Borjigin stumbles into us, making all kinds of noise.

"Sorry," he says.

Bishop strides toward us.

"Borjigin, please be quiet," he says, making a visible effort to control his annoyance. "Watch where you step. Put your heel down first, then let your weight roll forward to the ball of your foot."

Borjigin nods quickly, intimidated.

"Good," Bishop says. "You're behind Em, so just watch how she does it."

Bishop slides silently forward to join Visca, and we're moving again.

Borjigin glances at me, nervous and awkward.

Despite the heat of the jungle, my face feels even hotter than it did a few moments ago. Bishop pointed *me* out as an example of how to move quietly? I'm stunned, embarrassed in a good way. I can't even get my head around it. He's impressed by what I can *do,* not just by the way I look or my position as leader. In my short memory, in everything I can recall from Matilda's childhood, what Bishop just said is the best thing anyone has ever said to me.

I walk, Kalle right behind me. Borjigin isn't as loud as before, but he sure isn't quiet. I make each step a careful thing—I don't want to let Bishop down.

The jungle's animal noises fade, then die out. Save for the buzzing of the blurds, everything is silent. Neither Bishop nor Visca raise a fist, but they don't have to—we all stop walking.

Something is coming, something that the animals fear.

A new sound: a rustling, a fast scurrying across dead leaves and past soft vines.

Bishop looks at me, makes a motion for me to hide. I kneel, look back down the trail: Kalle is already out of sight, but Borjigin is standing there like an idiot.

"Borjigin," I whisper, "*get down.*"

He looks at me, dumbstruck and afraid, then slips under a yellowish-green plant with leaves bigger than he is.

The rustling increases. I hear it from several areas at once, all to my right. Something is coming our way.

A creature runs across the trail—brown with yellowish spots, four legs, about the size of the pigs we saw on the *Xolotl*. It doesn't have eyes like us, but rather a line of three shiny black dots down each side of its strange head. The creature vanishes into the underbrush on the other side of the trail.

Could we kill that, eat it?

I remember how good the pig tasted.

On my side of the trail, rattling and rustling; more of the odd brown creatures, following the first. And behind them, something strange—it looks like a big snake, dirty-yellow and as thick as my thigh, silently rising up from the underbrush. Long, wicked-looking barbed pincers spread wide, ready to strike.

A second brown animal scurries across the trail, then another, and another. A chubby little one scrambles between Borjigin and me. Smaller than the rest . . . it must be a baby. Its foot catches on a root; it tumbles forward, rolling, splashing up mud.

It is so close I could reach out and grab it.

The snake-thing shoots forward: pincers snap together, punching through the little animal's flesh. The baby squeals in pain and terror. The snake rises up, its prey held between the pincers. Short legs kick helplessly. Pinkish blood pours down.

The underbrush shudders and parts as something big rises up—the snake is only *part* of this predator, some kind of elongated nose. The beast stands on four long legs. Tawny fur splotched with brown stripes. Below where the thick snake meets the head, a wide mouth filled with white teeth as long as my fingers. Powerful shoulders and chest slim to narrower hips and muscular legs. Just like with the pig-creatures, the three glistening black dots on either side of the head must be its eyes.

The baby's squeals, so *loud*.

The snake-trunk suddenly whips down, smashing the baby into the trail so hard I feel the impact through the ground.

The squeals change to wet grunts.

The snake lifts it again—the baby is still twitching—then slams it down again.

No more grunts. No more movement.

The snake-trunk curls inward, placing the dead animal into the long-toothed maw. Close, chew, crunch.

Swallow.

The snake-trunk suddenly rises up, stops. I see four little flesh spots on the end, above the pincers. They open, draw in air, close, open.

My blood runs cold: *Does it smell me?*

The snake-trunk twists this way and that, sniffing.

The monster's head is heavy, bony. Beneath the dirty fur, I see twitching muscle and shapes of ribs so flat and thick they make me think of armor. Its chest is a solid plate of curved bone, a shade darker than its fur. My hands tighten on my spear—if this thing attacks, I don't even know where to stab it.

Sniff-sniff . . .

Without a sound, Bishop is crouching next to me, axe clutched in his hands.

The snake swings to Borjigin's plant. The only thing between him and those gore-smeared pincers is a single wide, thin leaf.

Sniff-sniff . . .

The yellow-furred animal takes a step back. The trunk contorts, the pincers lurch up and away—a stream of goo shoots from each of the nostrils.

Did it just *sneeze*?

The beast turns and runs into the jungle. As big as it is, it instantly vanishes into the underbrush.

A few moments pass. Then, almost as if someone slowly turns a hidden dial, noise returns to the jungle.

Coyotl slides out of the jungle onto the trail, runs past us, straight to Borjigin's plant. Coyotl rips the leaf away, revealing a shaking, terrified boy, then kneels, puts his arm around Borjigin and speaks so softly I can't hear.

Bishop and I stand. I feel wobbly, like I was just in a fight, even though nothing touched me.

"I don't understand," I say. "Why didn't it attack? That little animal couldn't have been more than a mouthful."

Visca appears as unexpectedly as Bishop did. I will never get used to how the circle-stars move with such silence.

"We didn't smell right," Visca says. "We must not smell like food."

Kalle steps out of the underbrush.

"An allergic reaction, perhaps," she says. "Maybe it has never smelled anything like us before."

Bishop shakes his head. "I doubt that. Someone built the fire pit, someone built the city. There are people on Omeyocan."

Visca shrugs. "Then our clothes, maybe? Could be a smell on those?"

More questions for which we do not have answers.

"We keep moving," Bishop says. "The next animal might like the way we smell. Visca, move out."

Visca turns and walks down the trail, barely making a sound.

I'm supposed to be in charge, but out here, Bishop is giving the orders. That's fine for now—my pounding heart is crushing my chest and lungs. I don't think I could focus on anything other than staying on the trail.

Bishop points at Borjigin. "And you need to be *quiet*."

Coyotl steps between them.

"Leave him alone, Bishop. He's doing the best he can."

Borjigin says nothing, just stands there, shivering.

Bishop glares at Borjigin, then at Coyotl, then turns and heads down the trail.

We walk through the jungle. Tiny bugs are starting to land on me, but they don't bite. It's more annoying than anything else.

That big predator scared the hell out of me. An hour later and I'm still not feeling right. It was like a bear or a giant wolf, with an elephant's trunk that ended in ant pincers. What do we even call it? Snake-wolf? Bear-bug? Hard to think of a name, because there are no easy comparisons to Matilda's memories.

The buzzing of the blurds. The hoots of unseen animals echoing through the canopy. The heat. The humidity. The red sun blazing off yellow leaves. We are in so much trouble right now, yet my love for Omeyocan overwhelms me. This is my *home*. It was my home before I ever set foot here. I don't want to be anyplace else. Not ever.

Up ahead, Visca stops. He holds up a fist.

Bishop jogs back to us. The leaves seem to part for him, he seems to slide *through* them as if he has no substance at all.

He puts one arm around Kalle, the other around me, nods toward a tree trunk on the right side of the path. He wants us to hide.

The three of us kneel behind the tree trunk. I look around: Visca has vanished. Borjigin is on the other side of the trail, hiding behind a fallen log. Coyotl is with him, vine-wrapped and nearly invisible.

The wind changes slightly—I catch a faint wisp of burned toast.

Then I hear it. A noise, soft, regular . . . branches sliding off something . . . a faint crackle of twigs snapping underfoot . . .

This is it—we've found the fire-builders. My breathing sounds so loud. My heart hammers.

Will they accept us? Teach us how to hunt and prepare food? Can our two cultures live side by side? Or will this go the other way—will we have to *force* them to tell us how to survive?

I see movement down the path. Through the yellow leaves, I glimpse a flash of red and green.

Will they be young, like us, or old, like the Grownups?

The fire-builder comes around a thick tree trunk, into view.

My stomach drops.

The fire-builders, who lurked in the Observatory's shadows, who smell like burned toast . . .

They aren't like us.

They aren't Grownups.

They aren't *people* at all.

TWENTY-THREE

Borjigin's hiss of fear slices through the jungle.

The fire-builder stops.

Underbrush and dangling vines partially obscure it. It's not an animal—animals don't carry tools. Is that a club it's holding?

I feel numb. Not the "blanked-out" sensation I've grown used to, this is something else . . . a feeling of *nothingness*.

It wears rags for clothing, frayed strips of yellow, green and blue—the colors of the jungle—tied around long, thin, strong arms. Between the strips of cloth, I see wrinkled, dark-blue skin.

It is almost my height. Head wider and longer than mine. Eyes, *three of them,* middle one set slightly above the bottom two, a shallow triangle of eyes that flick about, searching. Even from a distance, their color jumps out: bright blue, like O'Malley's. Below the eyes, a wide mouth: purple lips curve downward in an exaggerated frown.

Matilda's memories struggle to define what I see. A flashfire of images: *toad-mouth frog-mouth fish-mouth.*

That head swivels suddenly, looks left. The creature comes closer, pushing past encroaching branches. Something strange about the way it moves.

I see its legs now: rag-tied, thick and powerful, bent like it's sitting on an invisible chair. The creature is leaning forward, so much so I don't understand why it doesn't fall flat on its strange face.

Both legs push down at the same time, softly springing the creature forward. Not a step, a *hop,* both long feet coming off the trail. It lands silently.

The three blue eyes flick down the trail, side to side. I think it heard Borjigin and is searching for the source of the sound.

The fire-builder turns, looks back the way it came, and I see why it doesn't fall—a *tail,* long and thick, balances out the forward lean.

It turns our way again, still searching, still wary. Strange, long hands adjust their grip on the club. *Two* fingers, not four, thicker than ours, as is the long thumb. Arms are wiry, corded with muscle.

That club bothers me, but I don't know why. Long and thin, like the handle of Farrar's shovel, but half wood, half metal. Nothing dangerous on the tip—no axe head, no spear blade. The club widens and flattens at the other end, the end held close to its body; maybe that part is for smashing things, just like Visca's sledgehammer.

A tap on my arm. Bishop, both hands on his red axe, nostrils flaring, staring at me. He gives his axe a single shake, asking me a silent question: *Should I kill it?*

Is this creature alone? If it spots one of us, will it sound an alarm? It doesn't seem to be wearing anything like the Grown-ups' bracelets, nothing that could hit us from a distance. Bishop can surprise it, kill it quick. This thing isn't like us—it is *other*—and we face so many threats already.

I don't know what to do.

Blue eyes scan the trail, the underbrush.

Two small hops bring the creature closer.

It wears a lattice on its chest, kind of like a necklace: it's made of bones. A bulging bag hangs from its hip.

Only a few steps away now—it wouldn't have time to react before Bishop buries his axe in that wide head.

I glance across the trail. From my angle, Borjigin is barely visible behind a covering of wide leaves. I can't see Coyotl at all. I have no idea where Visca is.

The fire-builder rises up slightly. The heavy tail rests on the ground, supporting its weight. It opens its wide mouth and barks out a single, harsh syllable.

More movement from farther down the trail. It wasn't alone. Three rag-tied creatures that look just like the first. No, their skin isn't as wrinkled, and they're a different color. Two are a purplish blue, the other is purplish red. The purplish-red one is the smallest of the four.

Then, two more creatures, less than half the size of the others—*children*. Their skin is a bright, deep red.

Bishop tenses. He's going to attack.

Kalle puts her little hand on his arm. Wide-eyed, she shakes her head.

That small gesture brings me back to our desperate situation—we need help. If we can eat what these creatures eat, it doesn't matter that they aren't human.

I look into Bishop's eyes, mouth the word *No*.

The six creatures suddenly spring down the trail. The adults move quietly and gracefully. The little ones have to make twice as many jumps to keep up. Those two are tiny, with big, blue eyes—I can't help but think of them as *cute*.

All of them continue down the trail, vanish into the jungle.

Everything has changed. Children. *Families*.

Their scent—burned toast—the same thing I smelled at the fire, at the hole in the wall . . . and at the Observatory. Creatures like these were watching us there. They didn't attack.

Bishop whispers in my ear: "What do we do now?"

I have no idea. I should have tried to talk to them, but I was too stunned, too afraid.

How long have those creatures been on Omeyocan?

They aren't like the spiders. The spider is an animal; these creatures wore clothes, jewelry, carried either a tool or a weapon. They acted together, as a unit, like we do. They protected their children.

I don't have to be Spingate to see that the creatures are well fed. And from what little we know, it seems we can eat what they eat.

The answer to our survival lies with something that isn't human.

I need to learn more.

"We'll follow them," I say. "Let's move."

We stay close together. Visca is in front. He sweats more than anyone I've ever seen; most of the dirt and plant juice have washed off his face. His pale skin looks reddened from the sun, although his black circle-star symbol still stands out clearly.

He keeps us on their trail. That's not easy, as we've crisscrossed at least a dozen intersecting paths. If the fire-makers made all of these paths, I wonder how many of them there are.

The building with the fire pit . . . one wall had been knocked in. We think a spider did that. Does that mean spiders attack the creatures just like they attack us? Could that possibly give us some common ground, a way to start communicating?

Every twenty or thirty steps, Visca stops, looks at the ground or an overhanging branch. I watch him carefully, see what he sees: a bit of overturned moss, a dangling wisp of colored thread clinging to a branch, a footprint in the dirt holding pooled-up water. This is how he tracks them. I wonder if I could do the same. I'm beginning to think that if I *really* paid attention, I could follow them using my nose alone.

That smell . . . *burned toast . . . my dad used to make breakfast. For me and Mom and . . . I had a little brother? Dad was great at dinner, especially pork, but breakfast was always a disaster . . . burned toast, runny eggs, and—*

Borjigin stumbles into me from behind—I stopped walking, lost in that unexpected memory.

"Sorry, Em," he says, too loud by far. "I was watching my feet."

"Be *quiet,*" I whisper.

He nods furiously. He's afraid of the creatures, of what else might wait for us in this never-ending jungle.

Kalle is scared, too. I can see it on her little face. We all are, even the circle-stars. We're just *kids,* reacting to an impossible situation. No help, no direction, no guidance.

I move down the trail again, catch up to Bishop.

That memory of breakfast. So *real*. But it's Matilda's memory, not mine. Why couldn't that have been my life? Why couldn't I have been born instead of hatched? A loving family, parents, a brother.

A new smell: roasting meat.

Visca raises a fist. We stop. He kneels, studies the ground, then we're moving again, down a steep, tree-thick slope littered with vine-covered rubble. At the bottom, a shallow pond that comes up to our knees. I look around, realize the uneven ground rises up on all sides and that the pond is roughly circular: we're in a crater, wider than the shuttle is long. A shiver runs through me—what kind of explosion could make a hole this big?

Visca keeps going. Soon we're climbing up the far side. The mostly hidden rubble makes for dangerous footing, *noisy* footing, broken blocks and bits of masonry clicking and clacking with our steps.

Near the top, Visca holds up a fist. Bishop kneels next to him, looks, waves me forward. The three of us crouch down in the underbrush, just our heads peeking out from behind the crater's lip.

We stare out at an uneven clearing. Vine-encrusted crumbling walls tower around the edge. Four walls, or at least parts of them, in that hex shape—I think the two missing walls were once where the crater is now. Beyond those ruined walls, the trees are thick, tall and old.

At the center of the clearing, a small, flickering fire. Above it, a little animal roasting on a spit. Juice bubbles out, hisses on the glowing coals below. I know I shouldn't be thinking of my stomach right now, but the meat smells *amazing*.

No sign of the creatures. They built a fire, started cooking that animal, then left?

I lean close to Bishop: "Where are they?"

His gaze flicks about the clearing. The way his eyes move reminds me of the rag-clad fire-builder back on the trail, looking for danger, not finding any.

"I don't like this," he whispers.

Neither do I, but that doesn't matter. I missed the first chance to talk to these creatures. I won't miss the second.

Creatures . . . that's no way to think of intelligent beings that might help us. I will call them *Springers,* at least until I understand what they call themselves.

"I'm going to the fire," I say.

Bishop shakes his head. "Let me. They could be dangerous."

Could be, that's true, but Bishop *is* dangerous. Back on the trail, he was ready to kill them all. Even the children, probably. If there's any chance for peace, for cooperation, I don't want him screwing it up.

"My decision," I say. "Stay here."

His face tightens. At the shuttle, he follows my orders without question. Out here, he expects I will follow his.

Not this time.

I step over the crater's lip. The clearing's footing is uneven, a once-hard surface shattered as if by an earthquake. Dirt, vines and leaves cover the ground, cling to broken bits of building. Anything exposed to the light is dotted with blue-green moss. The path we were on continues, a narrow line that winds through the larger bits of rubble.

I'm scared. I'm excited. I don't know what I'm doing. I realize I'm holding the spear tightly, sharp tip leading my way. Will they think I'm attacking? Maybe I should drop it. No, if they attack me, I have to be able to defend myself.

I move toward the fire, forcing my feet forward, one short step after another.

The fire pit is a ring of piled stones. Small bones are scattered about. The Springers have eaten here before, perhaps many times.

Over by one of the still-standing walls, I see a stack of round purple fruit, each as big as my fist. I walk to the pile. Some of the fruits are whole, some are smashed in a messy paste of purple skin and yellow flesh. The paste *stinks*—pungent, rotten, but with a hint of sweetness. I pick up a fruit: it's firm, bumpy. Yellowish lines run down its length.

Can we eat these? I'll have Kalle check. I slide the fruit into one of my coveralls' many pockets.

I turn to see Bishop circling the fire, looking at it closely. Visca and Coyotl crawl over the crater's lip, join him.

That makes me furious. Bishop disobeyed me, *again*. The circle-stars are so much bigger than I am, far more intimidating. What if they scare the Springers away?

Walking in a half-crouch, Visca joins me, looks down at the messy pile of fruit and paste. His sweaty, dirty face scrunches up. "Those smell awful. What are they?"

I shrug. "I don't know."

He uses the butt end of his sledgehammer to slide the paste aside. There is something smooth beneath, still smeared with thick globs of yellow. He kneels, picks it up with thumb and forefinger.

It is a small animal. Skinned.

"Same size as the one they're cooking," he says. "Why did they smear it with fruit? For flavor?" He holds it close to his face, sniffs, frowns, then smiles. "I'll tell Farrar this is their version of cookies and see if he eats it."

His laugh is cut short by a loud *bang* that makes me flinch, makes Matilda's memories say *fireworks*. In that same instant, something cracks against the old wall.

Visca drops the animal, stands, grips his hammer with both hands as the sound echoes away through the jungle.

A white spot on the wall that wasn't there before, surrounded by the blue-green moss, like someone chipped away a piece of stone.

Another *bang*—Visca's head snaps back.

He falls, limp.

Clumpy splatters of red goo on the wall's blue-green moss, wet chunks sliding down yellow vine leaves.

Visca doesn't move. He stares up. Eyes blank. Mouth open in surprise. A bloody hole above his right eye.

I hear Bishop shout something about running, but his voice is a distant dream, slow and meaningless.

That hole . . .

No . . . no-no-no . . .

I grab Visca, shake him. His head lolls to the side. The back of his skull is gone, blown apart. Chunks of bone dangle from his bloody, white-haired scalp. Brain smashed like fruit—red paste instead of yellow.

Bang: something hits the wall, showers me with bits of stone.

Bishop's hand on my arm, yanking me up.

We're sprinting for the crater. I clutch the spear, Bishop has his axe—it's red, the color of Visca's blood.

Motion on my right, past the clearing's broken wall. A Springer, pointing a wood-and-metal club at me.

That roaring *bang* again—a cloud of smoke billows out the end. Something whizzes past my head, moving so fast I hear it but don't see it.

We leap over the crater's edge. Legs kick empty air. Feet hit the downslope, I fall, the spear flies from my hands. The world spins. Something hard drives into my shoulder. Up, stumbling. My spear, *there,* I grab it and run. Bishop on my left. Up ahead, racing through the shallow pond, Borjigin and Kalle, Coyotl behind them.

My boots, splashing.

A *bang*, a split-second pause, then a small plume of water rises just in front of me.

Rushing up the far slope. Legs pounding, feet slipping on

hidden rubble, up and up and up. I don't want to die like Visca. I *don't want to die.*

Over the lip and into the jungle, plowing through vines and leaves. Branches and burrs tear at my skin, leaves slap at my face.

Another *bang*, then another, both from behind me. They sound farther away—we're escaping.

A Springer to my left, close, *so close,* maybe twenty steps away, half-hidden by wide leaves. Rags tied around arms and chest and legs and tail blend it into the jungle. The flat end of its club is on the ground. It's jamming a thin rod into the other end, over and over again.

Its fumbling hands toss the rod aside, a hurried motion—the end of the club snaps up, follows me as I run, *targets* me.

Bang: billowing smoke—my shoulder burns like I ran into a flaming branch.

It hurt me. It . . . it *shot* me.

(Attack, attack, always attack.)

I skid to a stop, boots sliding on muddy leaves.

I face my enemy.

The Springer takes a hop back, surprised.

Visca is dead. These creatures killed him. All we wanted to do was talk—these savages *murdered* my friend.

My face, so hot. My skin, prickling, poking, from my scalp down my arms, across my neck. My fear dies, drowned by that now-familiar rage. It blossoms up from an internal well of pure hate, threatens to engulf me, *control* me.

And this time, I let it.

The Springer plants the wide end of the club on the ground, fumbles with the bag on its hip. Shaking hands dig inside.

The club . . . it's not like the Grownups' bracelets that can be fired over and over. The club has to be reloaded every time.

"Em, come on!" Bishop, calling from the jungle up ahead.

I ignore him.

I lower my spear, and I charge.

The Springer pulls a wad of cloth from the bag, jams it into the club's metal end.

I tear through the jungle toward it, spearpoint leading the way.

Its trembling hands pull a small, round object out of the bag. Thick fingers fumble the ball, catch it, shove it into the end of the club.

My legs feel *perfect*, each sprinting step sure and firm. My feet find the soft places.

The enemy realizes the thin rod is on the ground. It bends, snatches it up along with a few twigs and dried leaves. Three wide eyes snap to me, lock in on my spear tip.

Ten steps.

A new scent, like wet charcoal, but so acrid it almost burns—the smell of its weapon.

My enemy slides the rod into the club's end, spastically jams it up and down.

Five steps, so close I see the color of its eyes: dark yellow. Almost like Bishop's.

Rod pulled out, tossed away.

The Springer lifts the club, holds the wide end tight against a narrow shoulder. Wrinkled purple fingers pull back some kind of metal catch, which clacks into place.

The narrow tip swings up, toward me—

My spearhead drives through the creature's belly with a squelching sound that's almost drowned out by my scream of revenge.

(Kill your enemy, and you are forever free.)

The toad-mouth opens. Purple skin, skin that seems young, healthy. Dark-yellow eyes stare out. The look on its face . . .

. . . Visca, lying on the ground, the back of his head ripped apart . . .

. . . Yong, surprised, confused, terrified, betrayed . . .

. . . the pig in the Garden, my knife slicing, blood spraying . . .

I yank the spear free. Something wet comes with it, squirts against my chest.

The Springer's club falls to the jungle floor.

A two-fingered hand grabs my shoulder, firm at first, then weaker until it can't hold on anymore.

The fish-mouth opens, lets out a deep-throated rasping sound no human mouth could ever make.

The three eyes blink. I have never seen a creature like this before, yet I know the look in those eyes, I understand the emotion on that face.

Fear.

The Springer sags back, rests on its tail for a moment, then slumps to its side.

Toad-mouth opening, closing. Opening, closing.

Thick blue fluid spreads across its stomach, staining the rags. Smells like licorice.

Open. Close.

Dark-yellow eyes blink once more, slowly, dreamily—I see the life in them fade, then vanish forever.

A big body skids to a stop next to me.

"Em, you're hit!"

My rage blinks out as if it was never there at all. An alien body lies dead on the jungle floor.

What have I done?

I shudder. My stomach convulses—I vomit bitter bile down the front of my black coveralls.

A low, droning howl from the direction of the clearing: *a horn,* echoing through the jungle. Another horn answers.

Bang!

To my left, chunks of bark scatter, exposing pale white splinters beneath. Four Springers leap over the crater's edge. Another is already standing still, reloading.

As one, Bishop and I turn and sprint down the narrow trail.

I hear bodies crashing through the jungle on our right. A glance—Springers, maybe six of them, moving fast through the underbrush, stopping, aiming . . .

Bang! Bang! Bang!

Balls whiz through the air, tear through leaves, smack against tree trunks.

My legs pump on their own, driving me forward, keeping me close to the moving, silent shadow that is Bishop.

He suddenly turns left, off the trail. I follow him, unthinking. Two shots from my right—I hear a ball crack against wood, see a branch fall. More Springers had cut off the trail: Bishop saw it just in time.

Another horn rings out from somewhere ahead of us.

I smell smoke. Not the kind that made me hungry, something else, something heavier, thicker.

Bishop skids to a halt behind a tree, yanks me in with him. Coyotl appears as if out of nowhere, pulling along a terrified Borjigin. Kalle is right behind them.

Bishop drops his axe, draws his knife. His hands grab my coveralls, slice and rip: my shoulder is exposed to the air.

A long gouge, oozing blood, like a single huge fingernail scraped away skin and muscle. My flesh smells cooked, like the meat over the fire.

"Didn't hit bone," Bishop says. He holds my face, makes me look at him. "No time to dress your wound. Be strong until I get you back to the shuttle. Strong and silent. Be the wind."

A frozen moment caught up in his stare. I see the real him, he sees the real me. I'm not his friend, his girlfriend, his leader or his follower—we are both soldiers, fighting to keep each other alive.

Bang! A chunk of tree trunk explodes right next to me, driving splinters into my cheek and neck. Bishop snatches up his axe, plunges deeper into the jungle. Borjigin, Kalle and I follow. Coyotl comes last.

The smoke smell grows stronger.

A flash of orange, a sudden heat—in front of us, a wall of fire that makes the jungle crackle and hiss in agony.

Bishop banks right, and so do we.

From all over the jungle, I hear the horns calling to each other.

I feel the heat before I smell the smoke or see the light: another wall of fire rages up in front of us.

The Springers are *herding* us, making us go where they want, but the fire will boil the flesh from our bones and we have no choice but to run from it.

We race through thick underbrush.

My legs scream at me to stop. My stomach heaves. I'm going to throw up again even though there's nothing left inside.

We burst into a wide clearing. A plaza of some kind. Building remnants and tall vine-draped trees rise on all sides. In the middle of the clearing is what looks like a fountain, long since run dry.

My boots thud on stone tiles, chipped and cracked by age . . . no vines, no moss, no mud.

At the plaza's edges, at least a dozen Springers.

They level their clubs at us.

Bishop stops. I stop. My stomach roils, my lungs burn, my legs shudder. Borjigin stumbles, falls hard. He rolls to his back, stomach and chest heaving—he can run no more. Coyotl stands next to me, bone club at the ready. Kalle points her little knife, defiant to the last.

The Springers that were giving chase tear out of the jungle behind us, cutting off any escape.

We are surrounded.

"Borjigin," Bishop barks, "get on your godsdamned feet or die on your back like a worm."

Borjigin finds some final bit of hidden strength. He stands, holds his knife in a trembling hand. The five of us huddle together, weapons ready as the creatures slowly tighten their circle.

I hear the fires they set to channel us to this place, the crackling of wood and the spitting of moisture. Thick smoke chokes the air.

Then, over the fire's roar, I hear another noise—the sound of something big ripping through the jungle.

And . . . the sound of *whining*.

The Springers' orderly approach disintegrates. They turn in place, aiming their clubs into the trees, looking for the source of that sound.

A giant spider rips out of the jungle and into the clearing.

Then a second spider. And a *third*.

The Springers squeal—a grinding, high-pitched, stuttering thing I've never heard before, but there is no mistaking those raw sounds for anything other than screams of horror.

The first spider scurries forward, kicking up sparks off the stone surface. A pointed foot raises high and plunges down, driving into a Springer's head, through the body, until the tip chinks into the plaza hard enough to kick up shards of tile.

Bang!

Bang!

Bang!

Cones of smoke belch forth. I flinch each time, waiting for the tiny rocks to punch holes in my body, but the Springers are shooting at the spiders, not us. My back presses into Coyotl, into Bishop, into Borjigin, into Kalle—we pack together, facing death on all sides.

Bishop screams out orders.

"When I say *now,* we run! Stay behind me, and *do not fall.* Coyotl, protect our rear."

A Springer leaps past us, fleeing for its life. The long hop is beautiful and impressive, but not enough to outrun a chasing spider. The flick of a yellow, three-foot-long foreleg bends the Springer in half like a wet twig, flings it against the long-dry fountain. I hear bones snap on impact. The Springer falls to the ground, twitching, three eyes glassy and unfocused.

Green eyes . . . like Spingate's.

Another Springer crashes down in front of me, head torn away. The ragged stump of its thick neck gushes blue blood onto the cracked stone.

Springers flee into the trees. The spiders give chase.

Bishop's voice, bellowing, all-powerful: *"Now!"*

I feel him go. I follow instantly, letting Kalle step in front of me so I can protect her. We sprint across the plaza toward the trees.

A spider erupts from the jungle directly in front of us, a ten-foot-tall explosion of spinning leaves and flying branches. Bishop tries to stop too fast; his feet slide out from under him—his head and back smack against the broken tiles.

The spider lurches forward, torn vines dangling from its legs and body, pointed feet driving down so hard I feel each step.

One of its five legs drags limply behind it. The spider towers above us, a specter of unstoppable death.

I rush forward, plant myself between Bishop and the oncoming spider. I raise my spear and I scream a challenge.

The spider stops.

Coyotl is there, his thighbone raised. He shakes with fear, yet he stands beside me. The spider will have to go through both of us to get Bishop.

The spider doesn't attack.

That fast-paced chinking sound again, but from behind. We turn: the other two spiders have closed in. We are trapped between all three of them.

Kalle and Borjigin struggle to help Bishop stand. Bishop tries to raise his axe, but he can barely hold on to it. The five of us huddle together.

The spiders are as motionless as the old stone fountain.

"Bishop," I say, "what do we do?"

I feel him shrug. "I was going to ask you."

Coyotl's thighbone clatters on the tiles. He seems dazed. He walks toward the limp-legged spider.

I grab his arm. "Coyotl, what are you doing?"

He effortlessly shrugs me off. He shuffles forward, toward the spider, moving like he's not even fully awake.

I want to rush in front of him, just like I did with Bishop, I want to attack the spider and save my friend, but suddenly my feet won't move—whatever bravery I held inside of me has turned tail and fled.

Coyotl steps between the spider's long, smooth, deadly yellow legs, legs that are bathed in streaks of blue blood. He sees something. He reaches up slowly—as if a sudden movement might spook the huge beast—and grabs a handful of torn vines dangling from the spider's body. He gently pulls the vines away, exposing a spot on the yellow shell.

I see what he saw—the same symbol that's on his head, that's on Bishop's head.

A circle-star.

TWENTY-FOUR

This close, I see details on the yellow shell. Dents, scratches . . . rivets . . . *rust stains.*

The spider is a machine.

The Springers killed Visca. They would have killed the rest of us if the spiders hadn't attacked. The spider outside the wall, the one that I thought bit me . . . it wasn't attacking us at all. The spiders don't want to hurt us—they want to *protect* us.

They are metal, yes, but there are no straight lines. The spider is all long curves. Maybe that's why they look so alive when they move, especially from a distance.

The yellow color, it's paint. Rust streaks where that paint is chipped and cracked. Irregular red-brown circles with misshapen globs of metal in the center—the balls fired from the Springer clubs, embedded in the spider's shell. *Dozens* of them, far more than were fired just now.

Around the clearing, I count five dead Springers, their bodies broken and mangled, blue blood soaking into the cracks between the tiles.

We lost one of ours. They lost five of theirs.

No . . . *six*.

The memory of my spear thrust comes rushing back. The sound of the blade entering the Springer's body. The feel of the metal glancing against bone before it punched out the other side. The look in the creature's intelligent eyes as life faded away.

Coyotl reaches up, runs his fingers over the circle-star painted on the spider's thick shell.

"Like mine," he says. "They belong to us."

One of its legs lies mostly limp. That's the leg that dragged behind, made the spider move with that funny gait. Coyotl runs his hands over the old, rusted, beat-up metal.

"The leg is broken," he says. "Not from a bullet, I don't think."

Bullet. That's the correct name for the metal balls, Matilda's memory tells me. And those aren't *clubs,* they are *guns*.

Bishop rubs the back of his head, unknowingly smears blood across his dirty hair.

"Coyotl, get up top and keep a lookout," he says. "Kalle, Borjigin, collect the dead Springers' weapons and their bags."

Coyotl scrambles up a spider leg with balance that surprises me. At the top joint, he stands, arms outstretched, then leaps gracefully onto the machine's back. Most of him is now hidden by ridges I didn't notice before—ridges that would protect him from bullets.

He runs his hands along the front ridge, stops at a triangular notch. Just behind that notch is a stubby metal tube with an opening as big as my head. I see the expression on Coyotl's face: he's having a flashfire, recalling something from his creator's past. He blinks, then wiggles the tube, pushes and pulls at it. It doesn't move. Finally, he lifts his black boot and gives it a solid kick.

The tube slides outward with a ringing metal sound and a light shower of dust. It's not stubby at all: it's long, longer than I am tall.

"Like the guns the Springers used to kill Visca," Coyotl says. "But bigger. This is called . . . a *cannon*. I think it's broken, though. Maybe it's too old."

If the Springers' clubs shot small bullets, what does that cannon shoot? I look at the other spiders: they have the same ridges, the same triangular notches, the same stubby tube.

I glance at the ruins surrounding this clearing, wonder what the buildings looked like when they stood tall, when the jungle was pushed back, under control. I imagine an army of shiny spiders. Other kinds of machines as well. Maybe some that fly like blurds. Machines rushing in, cannons firing, buildings burning and crashing, explosions tearing the streets to bits, Springers screaming and fleeing, burning and bleeding, *dying*.

"Em," Bishop says, "I need to dress your wound."

He doesn't wait for permission. He grabs my shoulder firmly, his thick fingers lying on either side of the deep gash. The stinging pain floods in all at once. I'd forgotten about it somehow.

"Does it hurt?" he asks.

"Feels great," I lie. "Do what you have to do."

One corner of his mouth turns up. I see pride in his eyes. The stubble on his face has grown thicker—not quite a beard but not far from it.

He uses his knife to cut my sleeve completely away. He takes a small bottle from one of his coverall pockets, sprays something on the wound that burns even worse than the bullet did. From another pocket, he takes a roll of the purple bandage and wraps it around my shoulder.

"How do you know how to do that?" I ask.

Bishop shrugs. "They taught us how to keep each other

alive. We need to get you back to Doctor Smith. I can't lose you, too."

Pain in his voice. Not from the cut on the back of his head, but from his soul. I feel it, too—we lost one of our own. It isn't the first time. Latu, Yong, the El-Saffani twins, Bello, Harris . . . and now Visca. Seven of us, gone forever. Of those seven, five were circle-stars. They are the first to fight, the first to die.

"We can't leave Visca," I say. "We have to go get his body."

Bishop shakes his head. "We don't know where we are, and the enemy is out there in the jungle."

"The pigs ate Latu," I say. "I won't leave Visca to be eaten by animals."

Bishop leans close to me.

"You're wounded and in no shape to fight. We're heavily outnumbered. Our enemy knows this terrain so well they herded us where they wanted us to go. We try and find that clearing again, we probably die. In the shuttle, you're the leader. Out here, from now on, you listen to me. Understand? I'm not going to lose anyone else today."

Maybe he's right. If I hadn't walked to the fire, would Visca be alive? Is this yet another death on my hands? Maybe. But my decision also led to finding the purple fruit.

Kalle and Borjigin return, burdened down with armfuls of guns and dangling bags. I take the fruit from my pocket. It's half-squashed, leaking amber-colored juice. I hold it out to her.

She snatches it, runs her bracer over it. We all watch. The jewels flash different colors, then gleam a shade of pink.

Kalle smiles.

"It's safe to eat," she says.

At least Visca didn't die for nothing.

"I saw that pile of fruit," Kalle says. "We should go back for it."

Bishop shakes his head. "With as many people as we have to feed, that little pile won't make any difference. We have a fruit for Spingate to study, but it doesn't matter if we don't get it back to her." He spreads his arms, indicating the jungle. "Besides, we don't even know where we are."

Everyone looks to the surrounding trees, as if one of them might suddenly tell us directions. We sprinted through the jungle for I don't know how long. Visca was our tracker, our guide.

Bishop glances up at Coyotl, who looks so gallant standing tall on that machine's back. Bishop walks to one of the other spiders, stands between two gore-splattered legs.

"Hello, I am Bishop. First name, Ramses."

He remembers his name? *Ramses*. What a beautiful word.

"We need to get back into the city," Bishop says to the spider. "Can you take us to the landing pad?"

The spider's body lowers until the metal belly clangs lightly against the broken tiles.

Bishop moves closer. On the side of the spider, I see three metal rungs . . . like a ladder. He steps onto them, swings a leg over the yellow and brown ridge, then stands tall atop the machine's back.

Parts of the *Xolotl* only worked for certain people. Parts of the shuttle only work for Gaston, for O'Malley, for Smith, for me. These machines . . . they answer to the circle-stars.

"We're going home," Bishop says. "Everybody, mount up."

TWENTY-FIVE

Three spiders stride through the jungle. Long legs keep them above the dense underbrush. Their yellow, brown and green coloring fades into our surroundings. They rattle, whine and vibrate in a way that doesn't seem right. If the machines were newer, not so beat up, I imagine they would be as silent as the circle-stars they were made for.

The ruins pass by. Blurds of all sizes buzz through the canopy. Some trees grow impossibly high, their wide, dark-yellow leaves drinking in the light. The same vines that cover the city's buildings dangle from tall branches. Late afternoon sun filters through, making leaves glow with a fuzzy warmth.

The beauty of Omeyocan takes my breath away.

The dense underbrush gives way: we find ourselves on the bank of a wide river. Tall trees rise up on either side, forming a deep, living, yellow chasm that borders angry water. Blurds skim the surface, dipping in to snatch up this planet's equivalent of tiny fish.

Ahead of us, the riderless spider doesn't slow. Long legs

plunge in and the machine turns downstream. The spider that Bishop and I ride follows, metal body half-submerging, leaving us just a bit above the roiling surface. It's almost like riding in Grampa's canoe during summer vacation.

Grampa's canoe.

A Matilda memory. I remember Grampa's laugh, his stubbly face. The canoe was red, and always smelled of old fish. It seems so real . . . like it isn't Matilda's experience at all, but *mine*. How can that be? I was created on a spaceship.

And yet . . . I remember how Grampa liked to tinker with old, useless antiques he called *watches*. He liked to show me the little bits and parts inside that fit together *just so*.

If Grampa were here, maybe he could fix these rattly machines.

I glance behind us, at the limp-legged, whining spider that carries Coyotl, Kalle and Borjigin. Like me, Kalle looks everywhere for any sign of the purple fruit. Does it grow on trees? Perhaps on a kind of smaller plant we haven't seen yet? Borjigin's eyes are closed, his head nestled against Coyotl's neck. Coyotl's arm is around Borjigin's shoulder, but he stares straight ahead, eyes scanning the riverbanks.

The way they sit together . . .

Like Spingate found Gaston, I think Borjigin and Coyotl have found each other.

I wish Bishop would put his arm around me like that, hold me tight. It would be nice to relax into him, not have to think about *all* the things, *all* the time.

"See any fruit?" he asks.

I shake my head.

"Neither have I. After Smith looks at you, we can take the spiders out and cover more area. But if we don't find the fruit, Em . . ."

He doesn't finish. He doesn't have to. If we don't find the fruit, we need to find the Springers again—and this time, *we* will be the ones attacking.

I wanted to talk to them, to make peace, but they ambushed us. Unprovoked. We did nothing wrong. They started this fight, not us. We're out of food and out of options.

If it's war they want, they messed with the wrong girl.

Ahead, the city's vine-covered walls rise above the trees, stretching in either direction from the river that cuts between two towers. White spray rages up from twisted bars and bent grates that perhaps once prevented anything other than water from passing through, but judging by the amount of rust, that was ages ago.

On top of the towers, I see long tubes that resemble the ones on the spiders' backs. Weapons. Once upon a time, I bet those protected the city. Now they are just rusted junk.

The spiders stick to the river, easily walk by the water-gate's remnants. Past the wall, Uchmal's four-sided buildings—abandoned, but not destroyed. The buildings are smaller here than they are around the landing pad, but they get bigger the farther in we go.

We hear the waterfall long before we see it. When we turn a bend, there it is before us. The river just drops away; beyond it, open air and an amazing view of the city. The Observatory soars higher than any other building, so obnoxiously large it makes the rest of Uchmal look small and weak.

We pass by the switchback steps that Spingate, Coyotl and Farrar climbed. Like the spider that chased us then—or we *thought* was chasing us then—our three spiders don't seem interested in tackling those steep steps. Off to my right, I see the pool where Bishop saved me from falling, where he held me, where he kissed me. If he remembers that moment, he gives no indication: he stares straight ahead.

I'm pretty sure the landing pad is southwest of us, but the spiders are heading due west.

"Bishop, where are we going?"

His brows knit with worry. "I don't know. I told them to go to the shuttle. Maybe they're heading to their nest."

We now know it's not a "nest," but the word still works.

"Should we get off?" I ask. "Find our own way back?"

He considers it, shakes his head.

"Your wound is worse than you think. The less you walk, the better. We're still getting closer to the shuttle, just not heading straight for it. Let's stick with the spiders for now."

Three spiders stride down the middle of a narrow, vine-choked road. On their backs ride five tired, hungry people.

Bishop guessed right—up ahead is the nest building. It is a strange construct, and *big*. Not as large as the Observatory, of course, but easily bigger than the food warehouse. Vine-covered, like all the rest, although it's not a ziggurat. If anything, it reminds me of a really, *really* big version of . . .

. . . no, that can't be right.

"Bishop, what does this place look like to you?"

He turns his head left, then right, taking it all in. "It's long and narrow. It's the only one I've seen with a curved top. I guess if it wasn't covered in vines, it might look a bit like . . ."

His eyes go wide. He stares at me, astonished. "It looks like our shuttle."

I nod. That's what I thought, too. It's a hundred times larger, so large I thought it was a building, but beneath a deep blanket of vines is the same streamlined shape as the ship that brought us down to Omeyocan.

We approach. I see lumpy piles of vines, some in the street, some closer to the nest. We pass one: it is an unmoving spider, blanketed by plants and moss. In places, little flowers jut from it, petals in shades of red and yellow. Tiny blurds buzz in and out.

How long has it been since this spider stopped moving?

Our mount walks past it toward a wide, open archway in the ship-shaped building. Blackened metal lines the archway's edges, like there was once a door here that was melted, ripped down and burned.

The unmanned spider enters first. We follow it in, Coyotl right behind us.

This building . . . it's cavernous. Huge girders soar above. Attached to them, machines that haven't moved in years. Here and there, holes overhead, rusted-out spots with dangling vines and sunlight cascading down.

Rust is everywhere. Rust and wreckage.

Unmoving, five-legged spiders are scattered all over. Some sit in an endless line of small, cozy stalls that seem to run the length of the building, nestled in like we were in our coffins. Some spiders on their sides, some on their backs, legs curled in as if they were real spiders, dead and dried up.

And in places, *pieces* of spiders. A rusted abdomen attached to a rack on the wall here, piles of ruined and useless legs there, stacks of metal tubes over there.

I think of Grampa's watches, all the little bits needed to make them run.

"Those are spare parts," I say, pointing to the pile of legs, the stacks of tubes. I gesture to the whole building. "This was some kind of factory, I think. A place to fix spiders that stopped working."

Our mount strides into an empty stall. On either side are metal racks packed with equipment that seems long since dormant. Moss grows on everything.

The spider lowers to its belly. Bishop steps down. He reaches his hand up to help me. I don't need his help . . . but maybe I *want* it.

I take his hand in mine. His skin is so warm.

Stepping over the ridge, I try my best to slide down gracefully, but as soon as my boots land on dirt and dead vines, my legs wobble; I'm weak from the long ride. I take one step, and they give out. I fall fast, but Bishop is faster—his big hands cinch around my waist. I hear my spear clatter to the ground.

Bishop holds me upright like I weigh nothing at all.

"Are you all right?"

I feel dizzy, and not just from blood loss. He's staring at me, concerned.

His dark-yellow eyes, locked onto mine . . .

"Yes," I say. "I think I'm all right now."

He sets me on my feet, but doesn't let go right away. He holds on a moment too long. He's *smiling*.

I smile back.

Then, as fast as the moment came, it's gone. Bishop blinks a few times, slowly releases me, takes a step back. He looks like he wants to say something—something I know I long to hear—but instead he calls out to the others, his powerful voice echoing off the rust-eaten walls and ceiling.

"We can't stay here long! Em needs to get back, so take a quick look and let's go."

He picks up the spear, hands it to me. I'm suddenly so tired. Bishop was right—my wound is worse than I thought.

We have to get back to the shuttle, I know this, but I can manage for a little bit more. This place . . . it's important. It is the answer to a question, I just don't know what that question is yet.

Kalle walks over, her little head tilted back. She turns slow circles, taking it all in.

"A factory," she says. "Amazing. It had to come from *Xolotl*, just like our shuttle."

"Hey! Come look at this!" It's Coyotl, his voice echoing from farther in the building. He's with Borjigin, who stares upward, mesmerized.

We walk to join them. Once again, my spear is less weapon, more cane.

Coyotl is gawking up at the curving wall, his head tilted so far he has to take a quick step backward to keep from falling on his butt.

He points. I crane my head, look. Nothing but more rust and vine-covered machinery. I start to ask him what he sees, then the image clarifies.

The thing I'm looking at, up high . . . it's the *top* of a machine that stands on the ground. A moss-speckled machine shaped roughly like a person, a *giant* person made of rusted blue metal. One arm ends in a wide, thick scoop, the other in a huge, three-pincered claw. In some places I can see right through the giant to the rusted-out wall behind it.

Borjigin is nodding, mumbling to himself. I've seen this enough times to know what is happening to him—a flashfire.

"A builder," he says. "It's . . . it's a Besatrix Terraformer. Model C-4. I . . ." He looks at me, confused. "I've seen these before. But I haven't. I couldn't. My creator . . . I think he helped design Uchmal. He knew how to operate these machines, how to maintain them. Maybe even repair them."

So the halves can do more than whisper in a leader's ear and count food. As organized and methodical as they are, I suppose it makes sense they would be the ones to design cities. I'm surprised they operated these machines themselves, though—but perhaps something so complicated couldn't be left to a simple empty.

Borjigin looks down the length of the building, nodding, eyes hovering on more giant machines. Each one he sees makes him mumble gibberish I don't really understand: what the machine is called, what it is supposed to do. It's nice that he remembers, but it doesn't matter—these machines are dead. Some are squat and look more like small buildings than people. Some have scoops. Some have great spikes. Some have saws so big they would neatly slice our shuttle in half. Some have wide, walled, empty areas that could hold a small mountain's worth of dirt and rock.

Borjigin laughs. His eyes dance with delight and with life, his fatigue forgotten for the moment.

"That's why we haven't seen anyone in this city, alive or dead," he says. "The Grownups didn't build Uchmal—these machines did."

Bishop shakes his head. "But the Grownups had to tell the machines what to do, didn't they? Where to go, what to build?"

"Yes, but they could do that from up there." Borjigin points a slim finger skyward.

His words overwhelm me. When the Observatory said we were the first people to set foot on Omeyocan, I thought it was wrong. It wasn't. We've searched hundreds of buildings and found nothing. No Grownups, no bones, no sign of anyone ever having been here before us.

The machines built Omeyocan. Matilda and her kind have *never* come down.

That means the Observatory was telling the truth. It is a

place—the only place—where we can get actual answers. Was it also telling the truth about Matilda? Was her rebellion made of murder, or did her actions actually *save* lives?

My knees give out: only the spear keeps me standing.

Bishop cups my elbow. "Em, are you all right?"

"I'm fine," I say. It's a lie. He knows it. My shoulder is killing me. If I don't get to the shuttle soon, Bishop will have to carry me yet again.

"We're leaving," I say. "We still have hours of walking before we reach the landing pad."

Borjigin shakes his head. "Give me a few minutes. I'm guessing the spiders are programmed to come back here after a fight."

"So *what*?" Bishop's words are a growl. "Em needs Doctor Smith. The sooner the better."

I would have expected Borjigin to shrink away from Bishop, but the boy stands tall.

"I think I can give the spiders new orders," he says. "I need a few minutes, and Coyotl's help. The spiders can get us to the shuttle faster than if we're on foot."

Borjigin is nothing like the stammering coward he was in the jungle. He's confident, believes in what he says.

"Make it quick," I say.

Coyotl and Borjigin run to their spider and get to work.

Bishop wants to disagree, but we're back in the city, and I hold the spear—it's my turn to give the orders again, and I'd much rather ride instead of walk.

TWENTY-SIX

Smith said I had a "flesh wound." Nothing serious, at least according to her. I was in her coffin only long enough to make sure the bleeding had stopped, long enough for Spingate and Gaston to take a quick look at what we brought back. There isn't time for anything more right now—decisions have to be made.

My people are once again packed in the coffin room on Deck One. I stand on the makeshift stage with Gaston and Spingate, who each have something important to say when I am finished. So many emotions on the faces that look back at me, a mixture of pride, disgust, respect and doubt, of love, fear and anguish. We are too many to all think the same way.

I tell my people what happened. The snake-wolf, the Springers, our run through the jungle, the spiders, the "nest" that must have come from the *Xolotl,* and—of course—Visca.

Many of the younger kids are crying. This is their first experience with death. Even if they weren't close to Visca, they knew who he was, and they know he is never coming back.

The young circle-stars don't cry, though. They now wear black coveralls and hold weapons of their own: axes, machetes, shovels, hammers . . . one girl even holds a pitchfork. While Bishop and I were gone, Farrar was getting them ready.

Good: when we fight the Springers again, we will need everyone.

After I finish, Gaston explains how the Springer guns work. He says they are *muskets,* primitive versions of the Grownups' bracelets. The fabric that goes into the barrel is an explosive material. When it ignites, the barrel channels the explosion, drives a metal ball out fast enough to kill. Maybe it is "primitive" in Gaston's opinion, but it makes our weapons look worthless in comparison.

"Em and the others brought back five muskets," he says. "Each one is handmade. The parts aren't really interchangeable, which is strange to me. Maybe they don't have factories that can mass-produce these. There is enough ammunition to fire each musket seven times. Beckett and I think we can use the shuttle to make more ammunition. Maybe even more muskets, but we're not sure yet."

Gaston steps back, his lecture finished. The people look terrified, and I don't blame them—there are monsters in the jungle that can kill us before we can even see them.

Spingate holds up the bashed purple fruit. She trembles with excitement.

"We tested it on the contaminated food," she says. "The juice of this fruit kills the red mold."

A roaring cheer rips the air. People grab at each other, unable to contain their joy. Gaston hugs Spingate, squeezes her and slaps her on the back so hard she winces and laughs.

If we can find enough fruit, we have an entire warehouse of

food—*years'* worth, enough to keep us alive while we learn to farm and hunt. Everyone is hungry, but now there is hope.

Aramovsky clasps his hands together and looks skyward.

"It is a miracle," he says. "We are delivered."

"Hardly," Spingate says quickly. "We only have this one fruit. We need many more so we can experiment, find the best way to use it. If this was really a *miracle,* we'd have all the food we wanted, wouldn't we?"

Aramovsky grins. "It's not a miracle that on the very day we run out of food, we discover fruit that will let us survive? It's not a miracle that we suddenly have guns and war machines? The gods provided tools of salvation—that doesn't mean they're going to do the work for us."

He steps onto the stage. I see O'Malley bristle: he doesn't like this. Well, that's too bad. Whispering in my ear isn't going to stop our enemy.

"The demons murdered brave Visca," Aramovsky says. "May the gods welcome him home."

In unison, half the crowd repeats his words: *"May the gods welcome him home."*

A chill runs through me. How did they all know to say that? So many, speaking at once . . . it calls back Matilda's vague memories of being in church. While I've been looking for food, how many people has Aramovsky talked to?

"They're not *demons,*" Spingate says. "They're intelligent beings."

"They attacked us, for no reason," Aramovsky says. He points to the fruit in her hand. "And they could have given us the secret to survival any time they liked. They did not because they are evil—they want us all to die."

Grumbles of agreement. Heads nodding.

Even though he's talking about demons and gods, is the core of what he says so wrong? We did nothing to the Springers.

"Now we have *weapons,*" he says. "We must take the spiders into the jungle and destroy the demons. The only way we can be safe is to wipe them out."

People murmur their approval. I usually disagree with Aramovsky, but this time he's right. The Springers attacked us once—they will attack us again. If I want to save lives, we need to kill our enemy, we need to be forever free.

Aramovsky puts his arm around my shoulders, keeps talking to the crowd.

"Em knows what must be done. She killed one of them. She will lead us into battle, we will win this war, and the gods will be—"

Splat—the purple fruit hits his face, spins down to the floor, where it lands in a wet pile.

He stares, stunned. Smelly juice drips from his skin.

In the following silence, Spingate growls her words at Aramovsky.

"Battle? *Kill them all?* You superstitious idiot." She casts her glare about the room. "And all of you, blindly agreeing with anything he says. Are you *stupid*? We can't go to war with the Springers—we need them."

Aramovsky's arm slides away from my shoulders. As it does, I can feel his hatred, an almost physical thing.

"I thought you knew math," he says to her. "There is only so much fruit. It's us or them."

Spingate rolls her eyes. "You want to wipe out an intelligent race that could show us how to survive? The red mold isn't the only threat here. What about poisons the purple fruit won't purify? What about the snake-wolves, or other predators we haven't seen? How many people in this room need to die before we understand what's safe and what isn't? The Springers know how to survive on Omeyocan—we don't."

Her words chisel away at the vengeful feeling in my chest. She's right. We've only been here a few days. There could be more dangers. Without someone to guide us, each lesson we learn might come from someone getting hurt. Or worse.

Coyotl bangs his thighbone against the shuttle wall. He's standing with Borjigin, both of them looking over the crowd of smaller kids in front of them.

"They killed Visca," Coyotl says. "We could have killed them first, but we didn't! First chance they got they attacked us. Aramovsky is right—they're demons!"

Spingate shakes her head. "They're not *demons*."

"You didn't see them," Borjigin says. "They're horrible to look at."

She screams her answer: "*We probably look horrible to them!* We have to find a way to communicate—we can't just march into the jungle and slaughter them!"

"We can," Aramovsky says. "We *must*. On the largest building in this city stands a statue of Em, of our own leader. It is a sign from the gods that she is destined to lead us to victory!"

Aramovsky smiles at me, eyes blazing with intensity. He wants me to embrace this "destiny." But it's not a statue of *me:* it's supposed to be Matilda. The way Aramovsky says it, though . . . it's hard not to wonder if he's right. Matilda isn't on Omeyocan, I am—can't old things take on new meanings?

"The Observatory has signs, too," Spingate says, staring at me. I'm suddenly the object of a battle between two powerful people, each trying to sway me to their way of thinking.

"Remember those *signs,* Em?" she says. "Should we make them all come true?"

The images of death, of torturing gears and halves. Murder of people like Spingate, Gaston, O'Malley, Zubiri, Borjigin.

"Of course not," I say. "But that's not the same thing—the Springers aren't like us."

Spingate shrugs. "How would we know? You said there were children. *Families.* Sooner than you think, we'll have families, too. Our children will inherit Omeyocan. What kind of a planet do you want them to have? One of war, or one of peace?"

Our children? That's crazy. We're not old enough for . . .

No, we *are.* Spin and I, Bawden, Smith, Johnson, Cabral, Opkick, D'souza . . . we all have the bodies of young women, not kids. And those of us that are kids won't stay that way for long.

A little girl hops on top of a coffin: Walezak, Zubiri's quiet friend.

"We should destroy the demons, before it's too late," she says. Her face contorts with rage. She pounds her fist into her palm as she talks. "Aramovsky is right—this planet was made for *us.* If we want it, we have to show that we're worthy! *Kill them all! Kill them all!*"

Half the room erupts in roars and cheers.

So much hate on Walezak's little features. It shocks me, disturbs me. She should be playing with dolls, not calling for slaughter. But she has a double-ring on her forehead. Like Aramovsky, she was made to preach religion.

Spingate waves her hands above her head, demanding the crowd's attention.

"War isn't a *game,*" she shouts. "If we try to solve this with violence, it won't just be Springers that die. We have a few guns—the Springers have more."

She points at the circle-star girl holding the pitchfork.

"What about you, Marija? Will you die from a bullet in the face?"

Spingate points at Borjigin. "Or you? Maybe a knife in the belly, a wound so bad even Smith's coffin can't fix it, so you die slow, screaming for help that no one can provide? Is that worth fighting our *ugly* enemy, Borjigin?"

Borjigin's eyes are wide. He doesn't answer.

"They were here first," Spingate says. "There could be thousands of them. *Hundreds* of thousands. If we attack them and fail, do you think five muskets and three spiders will stop them from pouring in here to wipe *us* out? What if they shot Visca because they thought *we* were attacking *them*?"

Aramovsky yells something at her, Gaston yells something back, but their arguments become background noise as her words bounce through my thoughts—*What if they thought we were attacking them*?

The city beyond the walls, utterly destroyed. Demolished buildings, deep craters . . . there was a war before we even arrived. The spiders, knocking down the wall of that building where we first found a campfire. Spiders, attacking and killing the Springers in the clearing.

Spiders, with the circle-star symbol . . .

Visca, his sweat washing the camouflage from his face, exposing that same symbol on his forehead . . .

The pieces click together.

So many people screaming—no one is listening. Those for war and those against it are arguing, even pushing each other.

I slam my spear butt hard on the stage.

"Enough! Everyone, *shut up!*"

Aramovsky smiles. He thinks I will take his side. He's wrong.

"The Springers attacked us, yes," I say. "They killed Visca, yes. But I don't think they're demons. If anything, to them, *we* are the monsters."

Aramovsky looks shocked, betrayed.

"That's ridiculous," he says. "We aren't monsters. We are the chosen people."

"Spiders kill Springers on sight," I say. "The spiders standing outside this shuttle have hundreds of little dents from Springer bullets. The ruins outside the walls are from a huge city—the spiders destroyed that city. They must have killed thousands of Springers. When you say we didn't do anything to the Springers, you're right. *We* didn't do anything, but our creators *did*."

I tap my forehead.

"We all have symbols. Visca's was the circle-star—the same symbol that's painted on the spiders. What if the Springers saw his symbol—a symbol they must fear, they must *hate*—and acted just like we would act if someone came to kill us?"

Spingate's eyes crinkle with a small smile. She's impressed: I found a possible connection that she missed.

"We don't know where the fruit grows," she says. "If we kill the Springers, we might not find it at all. That gnawing feeling in your bellies? It's going to get much, much worse. The fastest way to get rid of it is to find the Springers and *talk* to them, make them understand we are not our creators, that we mean no harm."

A few hands reactively go to stomachs. Aramovsky uses gods to get through to people—Spingate does the same with hunger.

Aramovsky shakes his head, his stare now burning with hatred.

"So one of us should just walk out past the wall and *ask* these killers for help? You already said how we would die horribly, Spingate, so who is going to go? *You?*"

She nods. "Yes. Me."

The crowd falls silent. They can't believe she just volunteered. Neither can I.

She points to her forehead. "I don't have a circle-star. If Em's right, maybe that will give me a chance. Em also said the Springers were about her size, which means they are about *my* size—maybe I won't be as intimidating as Visca was, maybe they won't shoot me right away."

She is so brave, and I am instantly proud of her all over again, *inspired* by her. This is my friend, my courageous friend.

Gaston grabs her arm.

"*Maybe* isn't good enough," he says. "It's too dangerous for you."

She pulls her arm away, holds it up, showing her golden bracer.

"If we do make contact, and they show us anything about the purple fruit, a gear needs to see it. Kalle did her part. Zubiri is *too* little. Now it's my turn."

In a panic, Gaston grabs for her bracer. "Then I'll go, I'm even smaller than you!"

She twists away from him. "What are you doing? Stop it!"

I raise a booted foot high, stomp down on the stage as hard as I can. The sound is almost as loud as a musket shot—it silences everyone, stops everything.

"Gaston, you're staying here," I say. "If the Springers do attack, you might have to fly the shuttle to get everyone away safely."

He snarls at me. "Beckett can fly the shuttle! Make someone else do this. You can't let Spingate go alone!"

"She won't be alone," I say. "I'm going with her."

Shouts of support, of disbelief. Aramovsky smiles, folds his arms and watches.

O'Malley steps toward the stage—he's coming in for a whisper. I hold up my hand to him, palm out. He stops in place.

"Don't bother," I say. "This is going to happen."

Bishop bangs his axe head against the coffin room wall, demanding everyone's attention.

"Send me instead," he says. "Just me. I move quieter than anybody, I can capture one and bring it back here."

O'Malley comes forward again. "He's right, Em, listen to Bishop."

"Taking a prisoner is an act of war," Spingate says. "Even if Bishop gets one, we have no idea if we can make it tell us what we need to know."

Too many voices. Too many opinions.

I raise the spear over my head.

"*Enough!* I've made my decision. Only two people are going—the leader, who has the authority to speak for all of us, and the scientist, who can understand what we see."

Spingate's eyes meet mine. We are bound together in this. We were the first of our people to awaken. We found each other before we found anyone else. If we are to die trying to stop a war, then we will die as we began: together.

"The Observatory," I say. "We'll go there."

She shakes her head. "I think this city is our territory, and the jungle is theirs. We need to go to them as a gesture of good faith. Can you take us to the clearing where Visca died?"

I remember the way Visca examined the trail, the surrounding plants, the footprints. I watched him carefully. Maybe I couldn't find my way from the old fountain to that clearing, but—just like he did—I can follow the path from the gate to the first fire pit, then to the clearing where he died.

I look at the boys who don't want us to go—Aramovsky, O'Malley, Bishop and Gaston—and I thump the spear butt lightly against the stage floor.

The decision is made, and it is final.

TWENTY-SEVEN

It's just me and Spingate.

The fire pit was once again empty. I managed to pick up the same trail Visca followed. I figure we're about an hour away from the clearing where he died.

We ripped a piece of white fabric out of a coffin and tied it to the end of my spear. O'Malley's idea. Maybe the Springers won't know it's a symbol of peace, but it will make us visible a long ways off—we want them to know we're coming.

The spiders are ours, and because of that, the city doesn't seem as dangerous. Spingate and I rode on a spider with Bishop and Coyotl to the now-familiar gate. Bishop again insisted he come with, and again I said no. The two boys will wait for us at the gate. If we find another way in, I'll send runners from the shuttle to bring them back.

Spingate seems so different now. This isn't the giggling, frightened girl I woke up with. Is she changing because her memory is returning? Is it her relationship with Gaston?

I don't know. And if she does, she's not very talkative.

We have no idea if this will work. I think I'm right about Visca's symbol, but can't be sure. Even if I am right, the Springers might kill us anyway. I killed one of theirs, after all. If they recognize me, what will they do?

I have to try, though. If we don't get food, I think Aramovsky will force a new vote—a vote I will lose. My people will want a new leader. I can't blame them for that; they want something good to happen. I tell them the truth. Aramovsky will tell them what they want to hear, and for that he will win.

If he does, there will be war.

The sun is high overhead. A strong wind drives dark clouds our way. Blurds whiz by, their split-second shadows sometimes passing over our faces.

Spingate finally speaks. She stares straight down the path when she does.

"I thought you were going to take us to war," she says. "I thought you were going to follow your violent nature."

Does she think so little of me? Can't she see what I actually did, not what she thought I would do?

"Violence is *not* my nature."

She stops suddenly, finally looks at me. There is fire in her eyes.

"It *is*." She points up. "We saw it on the *Xolotl*." She points back toward the city. "We saw it on the Observatory steps." She puts her fingertip on my chest. "And now we've seen it from *you,* when you killed that Springer."

I slap her hand away.

"The deaths on the *Xolotl* belong to Matilda, not me, and so does the Observatory. And as for the Springer, you weren't *there*. I had to kill to survive."

She huffs. "Did you? Because from what Bishop and Coyotl and Borjigin said, it takes the Springers a long time to load their weapons. Why didn't you just run away like Bishop did? Why did you go back to kill?"

(If you run, your enemy will hunt you . . . kill your enemy, and you are forever free.)

I went back because my father's words are always rattling in my head. When things overwhelm me, I listen to those words. They make me act like a puppet. Spingate is right—maybe I didn't realize it at the time, but I went back because I *wanted* to kill.

The sky darkens. Clouds close in.

I spot movement up high in the treetops. I stop, stare. Is there something behind the thick yellow leaves?

I point. "Did you see that?"

Spingate looks, concentrates, but shakes her head.

"No," she says. "It was probably just an animal."

The first drops of rain plunk against the jungle canopy. Then the skies open up—a light drizzle one second, a total downpour the next.

Spingate lowers her head and raises a hand to block the rain, but I ignore the splashing on my face—I keep looking.

Then it moves. Half my size, perhaps, the same yellow as vine leaves. Long, thin legs launch it from the treetop. Arms stretch out: something darker between the arms and the body, not *wings,* but *skin,* skin that catches the air and lets it glide. The small creature plunges through more vines and it is gone.

Spingate was right—it's just an animal.

We keep moving. The rain beats down.

"I'm glad you came," Spingate says. "But I wasn't sure if you should. I'm still not. I'll be honest—I'm afraid you'll do something bad, that you'll start the war you think you want to stop. And that's if you haven't started one already."

It hurts that she doesn't trust me, but in a way I'm glad she doesn't. One mistake on my part and people could die—that's more important than my feelings.

I take her hand. "I can't trust myself, either. But I can trust *us*. Help me get this right."

She squeezes my hand once, smiles at me, then lets go.

When I again look down the trail, I see something off to my left—the barrel of a musket, sliding out from behind a tree. A Springer, blue and wrinkled, aiming at me.

"Don't move," I say quietly. "They found us."

I slowly look to my right—and see a second Springer, purple-blue, less wrinkled, mostly hidden by a fallen log. It is also aiming a musket at me.

Up ahead of us, a third Springer steps onto the trail.

Bullets are going to rip through my body, blast my brains out like Visca. I'm going to die here. On the *Xolotl* I would have become dust, but here it's hot and wet. My body will rot away, drip into the mud.

"The spear," Spingate says.

"They can see the stupid white flag. They don't care."

"Not the *flag*," she says. "The *spear*. It's a weapon. We made a mistake, we shouldn't have used a weapon. Set it down, slowly, show them you mean no harm."

Set it down? Is she *crazy*? They could rush us, beat us to death with the flat part of their muskets and not even have to waste a bullet. If I strike first, if they miss like they did last time, I could quickly kill the one on the left.

(Attack, attack, when in doubt, always attack.)

My father's voice—again—but this time, my own voice seems to answer.

(Dad, shut the hell up.)

I tilt the spear forward, then let it go. It drops, wet white flag fluttering behind it until spear and flag both smack into the trail's mud.

From farther down the path, a fourth Springer steps out of the jungle, skin of pure purple. It stares at us with three green eyes, then hops our way. The other Springers start screaming, a nasty sound that calls up Matilda's memories of monkeys in a zoo. So *loud,* so *angry.*

My fingers flex. Without my spear, I feel naked.

Spingate takes my hand in hers.

"Be still," she says quietly.

The Springer comes closer. It holds a musket, hammer already cocked. The barrel points to the side, not aimed at anything. I see a knife with a white bone handle dangling from a belt sheath. A hatchet is stuffed through the belt as well, its surface black save for a sharp edge that glints in what little light peeks through the storm clouds.

I'm letting Spingate control this situation, but I shouldn't—she's never been shot, she's never *fought,* she's just a tooth-girl who hides behind a desk while the real work is done by circles, while the real danger is faced by circle-stars.

I yank my fingers free and reach for the spear.

Her hand latches down on my wrist, squeezing so tight the bones of my arm pinch together. The pain surprises me; she's far stronger than I thought. I look into her hard eyes. She mouths words: *Don't . . . you . . . dare*.

She slowly stands straight. Her grip on my wrist forces me to stand with her.

The Springer stops in front of us. Purple skin wrapped in jungle-colored rags. Angry green eyes.

The others of its kind are still shrieking. They have come out from their hiding places. Musket barrels waver, as if the Springers aren't sure where they should aim. It hits me—they wanted the purple one to stay clear. Now they can't fire for fear of hitting one of their own.

I realize that I can easily tell these four apart. Their strange faces . . . at first I thought they looked the same, but now . . . not even close. And none of them are the ones Bishop and I saw earlier.

The purple Springer's three green eyes bore into me, blinking slightly against the pounding rain. Purple doesn't even seem to notice Spingate. Wet skin gleams. That skin looks . . . *healthy*. I realize Purple is shorter than the others.

Shorter, because it's not fully grown.

When we first saw Springers on this path, two of them were children. Red skin. The bigger ones, the ones with wrinkles, they were blue. Do the Springers change color as they age? If so, the one in front of us isn't a child, but it isn't an adult, either. It's somewhere in the middle.

Like us.

The other three scream louder. Their tone has changed from alarm and aggression to something that sounds like pleading—I think they are begging Purple to get away from me.

It lets out a guttural bark, a single syllable that rings with aggressive command.

The Springers fall silent.

Rain pours down.

Purple leans close, examines me. It wears the same multicolored rags as the others, but also something they don't—a shiny copper chain around its neck that connects to corners of a copper rectangle hanging in front. The rectangle looks thick, heavy, with lines and swirls of a language I don't recognize.

The Springer leans back. Its gun butt comes up so fast I barely see movement before the wood cracks into my chin. I stumble, the world spins.

Spingate reaches for me. "Em, don't fight back!"

I hear a *thonk,* like a rock thrown against a hollow tree. Spingate falls face-first in the trail's thin mud. I get to my hands and knees, try to rise, to *fight,* but pain explodes in my back as the gun butt slams into me again. I fall to my belly.

I roll left twice, fast, creating space between me and the Springer. I pop up on my feet.

Purple stands between me and my spear. Before the Springer can even aim its musket, I rush forward, kick *up* and *out* as hard as I can—the toe of my boot catches the big, frowny jaw. Three eyes wince in pain. It hops backward, trying to aim the gun at me, but I rush forward, duck under the barrel.

I reach for the knife hanging from its belt.

A hammer blow to my left temple. I fall to my knees. Something cracks against my right cheek. The other Springers, they rushed in while I grabbed for the knife.

Blackness comes in waves. I taste blood. I tuck into a ball, knees to chest, hands over ears, elbows tight in front of me. Musket butts hammer down, striking my shoulders, my knees, my shins, my back, the top of my head. So many hits, so fast—I've never hurt so bad in my life.

Yes you have . . . yes you have . . . you can't remember because you don't WANT *to remember . . .*

I think of my Grampa. I think of the canoe.

The beating stops. The echoes of each blow radiate across my body, waves of pain overlapping. I hear myself crying.

A growl, a chirp.

I open one eye. Spingate is on the ground next to me, tucked into a muddy ball. Sobs rack her body. I look up. Purple is holding a piece of fabric toward me. I roll onto my back, coughing, blood bubbling from my nose. The Springer stands over me, green eyes glaring down.

"Ponalla," it says. The syllables don't sound all that different from ones we would make. What does this word mean?

"Ponalla," it says again, shaking the piece of fabric at me, insisting I take it.

I do. Rain soaks the cloth. It's a drawing of a Springer. An excellent drawing, full of detail. And it . . . wait. Something about that face. I recognize it—it's the Springer I ran through with the spear.

Purple stares at me. Those green eyes, so much like ours. I imagine I can read emotion in them. *Hate,* but also *anguish. Sadness. Loss.*

What have I done?

"Your friend," I say quietly. I hold up the wet fabric, offering it back. "Ponalla . . . your friend."

Ponalla was trying to kill me. Then it was just some evil *thing* that I had to destroy. Now, it has a name. It has a friend, heartbroken that it's gone. In that way, it was no different from us.

I killed it.

And I didn't have to. I could have run.

"I'm so sorry." I know Purple can't understand me, but the words come out anyway. "We were attacked, and it was confusing and I was mad, and . . . I'm *so sorry.*"

The green eyes watch me. Rage and loss recede briefly, replaced by confusion. Purple looks at the limp fabric in its two-fingered hand, then stuffs the drawing into its bag.

Spingate moans.

"Stay still," I say. "We're in trouble."

She slowly lifts her head. Blood and mud sheet her face like a dark mask.

Purple takes a single hop back, raises the musket, points it right between my eyes. I'm staring into a circle of blackness, knowing it will be the last thing I ever see.

The other three Springers hop over, raise their weapons. The four of them stand side by side. They are going to execute us.

Time slows. The smell of the wet jungle in my nose. The feel of damp air in my lungs. *Perfection.* The sky, red sun blocked by clouds. The rain on my face. The taste of my own blood—everything is so *wonderful.* How could I not have savored these things every second I lived? Even the Springers are beautiful in their own way. Sights, scents, sounds . . .

Wait . . . I only hear the rain.

The jungle makes no noise.

Behind the Springers, something silently rises up. Something dirty-yellow . . .

A snake-trunk snaps forward. Pincers drive deep into the far-left Springer. It screams, a wet sound of shock and surprise as bluish blood spurts from its mouth.

At the edge of the trail, the monster rises up. Much bigger than the one I saw before. The snake-trunk coils, lifting its victim high. The other Springers turn, their long guns awkward and hard to bring around. The snake-trunk whips down, smashing the already-dying Springer into another, crushing them both to the muddy ground.

Bang!

A Springer fires. If the bullet hits, it does nothing. The snake-trunk lifts—one Springer hangs limply from the pincers, another stays facedown in the mud, shattered and still. In the same instant, the dangling victim is again used as a weapon; the trunk slams it into the Springer that just fired. I hear bones snap on impact, see the shooter's upper leg bend where it should not.

Spingate pulls at my arm. "Come on, Em, *run*!"

The ground seems to hold me tight.

Purple stays calm despite the murderous beast standing only a few steps away. Purple takes aim—*bang!* Chips splinter from the bony chest plate. The monster stumbles. Pincers open—the broken and battered Springer drops onto the muddy path. It doesn't move; it will never move again.

The broken-legged Springer crawls down the trail, desperate to escape. A white bone juts from its thick thigh. Blue blood spills from that wound out into the mud.

Purple snatches up a fallen musket. He tries to aim, but the snake-trunk whips sideways, sending him tumbling into the wet underbrush.

Spingate pulls desperately at my arm.

"Get up! Please, *run*!"

I can't, but not because of fear. Purple is trying to save his friends. I killed Ponalla—I have to help Purple, I have to make things right.

The monster's pincers snatch up a Springer corpse, shove it into the wide mouth. Bite, *rip*—the body is torn in two. A leg falls free into the mud. *Chomp-chomp, swallow*.

It stops eating: it sees the crawling Springer. The monster drops the half-body and moves toward this live prey, clawed feet splashing against the trail.

My spear. I rush to it, snatch it up. The handle is slick with mud. I tear off the stupid white flag and toss it away.

The Springer with the broken leg crawls toward me. Just past it, the monster.

A flashfire memory, but not one of Matilda's . . . Bishop, in the hallways, hurling the spear at the fleeing pig. A vision of magnificence. I saw how he threw . . . I can do the same.

I heft the spear in my right hand, find the balance point. My fingers close on the shaft. Loose, not too tight.

My target: a crack in the beast's breastplate, leaking pink blood.

The monster's long-toothed mouth opens, roars, and on it comes, clawed paws splashing in the thin mud.

The wounded Springer crawls faster. Not nearly fast enough to escape.

I step back with my right leg and point my left arm forward, toward the charging nightmare. I push off my right foot, lunge forward, plant my left foot and I *throw*.

The spear hisses through the rain. The metal spearhead *thonk*s into the bone plate, in and *through*.

The monster staggers. Six black eyes blink. Spear sticking out of its chest, the monster changes its target—it starts toward me.

Purple rushes out of the jungle, short-handled axe in one hand, long-barreled musket in the other.

The monster sees him coming, swings a huge, mud-trailing paw at Purple, but the Springer ducks, slides across the wet ground, under the claws. Purple plants big feet, hops up and jams the musket barrel into the cracked, bleeding breastplate right next to my spear.

Boom!

Not much smoke this time—because most of it went inside the beast's big body.

The monster's legs wobble. Stagger-stepping right, it falls hard on its side. Big chest, heaving. Snake-trunk twitching, coiling absently. Legs stretching out as if the creature just woke from a nap.

It's still moving, but not for long: Purple attacks with the hatchet, hammering a spot between the two rows of black eyes. Swing, *thonk!* Swing, *thonk!* Swing, *thonk!*

I tear my eyes away from the brutal finish.

Spingate is kneeling next to the Springer with the broken leg. It trembles and twitches. From pain or terror, I'm not sure.

The rain washed away some mud from Spingate's face, exposing a huge cut on her forehead that gushes red. She puts her hands on the Springer's body, talks in a soothing voice.

"We won't hurt you. It's over. It's over."

She's trying to help, just like she did with Yong back on the *Xolotl*. That boy, that *terrified* boy, lying on the dust-thick floor between us, crying for his mother, bleeding to death because I stabbed him in the belly.

Was that only a few *days* ago? We were so young, so scared. It feels like a lifetime has passed since that moment.

Spingate pets, coos, keeps talking softly. It seems to be working. The Springer's shaking diminishes, even though I still see pure terror on that strange face—it is hurt so bad it can't flee, and it is at the mercy of what it must think of as two hideous aliens.

The jungle noises fade in. A few howls, an echoing hoot, and then the buzz of life joins the roar of the rain.

The monster is dead.

I turn.

Purple stands there, only a short hop away. In one hand, the hatchet, dripping pink, spotted with wet chunks of white. In the other hand, my spear, the blade coated in pink slime.

Purple glances down at the wounded Springer, at Spingate. She doesn't bother to look up, she keeps talking softly, keeps petting.

"We tried to help," I say. "We saved your friend."

Green eyes flick back to me. Still so full of hate, but there is something else there, something I can't read.

"I'm sorry I killed Ponalla," I say. "I truly am."

Seconds pass. The four of us—two humans, two Springers—do not move. I listen to the rain. I listen to the jungle.

Purple raises the spear. I close my eyes—I'm just too tired to fight anymore.

Something hits the ground in front of me.

I look—my spear lies flat at my feet.

Purple shoves the handle of the gore-splattered hatchet into its belt, then hops to its friend. Spingate scoots back, wanting desperately to help, knowing she can't.

Purple's thick hands grab the wounded Springer's leg, one on either side of the disgusting break. The wounded Springer says something soft and short, then Purple *yanks*. I see the bone slide back into flesh, hear a disgusting *crunch-snap*. The wounded Springer's toad-mouth opens in a silent scream.

Purple beckons me to join him. He pantomimes, points to the wounded Springer, points to his own narrow shoulders, points down the trail. I think he wants me to help carry his friend. I don't know if I'm strong enough, but I have to try.

"Spin, gather up the muskets," I say. "And take the bags of the two dead ones."

Booted feet splash through the mud as she runs to obey.

I look at Purple, nod.

It grunts something unintelligible. We both get under the wounded Springer's arms, and we lift.

Good *gods,* it is heavy.

Struggling to stay upright, I let Purple guide us down the trail.

The wounded Springer, it's *warm*. The Grownups were cold, disgusting. The Springer is neither: if I close my eyes, I could believe I was helping one of my own kind. It would feel much the same.

It is all I can do to focus on putting one foot in front of the other. The wounded Springer's weight is harder on Purple than it is on me. He can't hop, he has to put one foot in front of the other—a movement that turns him from graceful leaper to stumbling, awkward walker.

We struggle on for a long while until Purple finally stops. He points off to the left. Through the trees and the pouring rain, I see a six-sided ruin. Most of it is knocked down, vine-strangled like everything else on this planet, but part of it still stands. Matilda's memories call up something from our childhood—am I looking at a church steeple?

At the very tip, a copper sphere. Two rings surround it, the inner one with two opposing dots, the outer with four.

Spingate catches up, struggling under her load of muskets and bags.

"That doesn't make any sense," she says, staring up at the steeple. "That's the same symbol we saw on the Observatory. If we're the first people here, how can the Springers have that same symbol?"

I don't know. I don't care. I just want to help keep this wounded Springer alive. Maybe that will balance against all the killing I've done.

Maybe.

Purple adjusts his position under his injured friend. I do the same. Together we walk toward the steeple.

TWENTY-EIGHT

I use the tiny scissors to cut the last stitch, then put them back into the white case Spingate brought.

"All done," I say.

Spingate sighs. "How does it look?"

It looks awful. The bump on her head has a jagged red line across it marked with six ugly black stitches. It would have looked bad even if I didn't have two broken fingers, swollen and screaming each time I move.

"It looks fine," I say.

"Liar. Gaston will think it's hideous."

We're inside the steeple, the base of which is a decent-sized room with an uneven floor, part stone, part dirt. We sit on chunks of broken wall surrounding a small, crackling fire. The place smells of smoke, dampness and burned toast. Rain drips in through multiple cracks, creating several twitching mud puddles.

The wounded Springer lies near the fire, asleep. Spingate stitched his cuts first, then mine, explaining to me how to do it as she did. Five stitches on my cheek, three on my chin. The fire warms us some, but I'm still cold, wet and hungry. It's been a full day since my last meal, which I threw up after I killed that Springer.

I hurt all over. They beat me so bad. Except for my fingers, though, I don't think I have any broken bones. For that, at least, I am grateful.

Two dead Springers lie at the base of a wall, both covered in vines. One is only a partial body, a decapitated half-torso with one arm still attached. Purple brought his dead friends here, one at a time. After the second corpse, he pantomimed that Spingate and I needed to stay here, then left yet again. He's been gone for over an hour.

Strange, waist-high stone statues line the room's edges. The statues are chipped and cracked, streaked with dirt. Many limbs are broken off. Some statues lean against the old wall, as they are too damaged to stand on their own.

Most of the statues are Springers. The stone is carved to show they wear long coats, pants covering their strange legs, long sleeves for their tails. Ruffles, folds, pleats . . . the clothing seems formal. Were these Springers important? If so, how long ago did they live?

A few of the statues aren't Springers at all. I don't know what to make of them. Legs that bend the wrong way, like those of a praying mantis, but much thicker. Narrow body with a middle set of arms positioned just above the hips, arms that end in heavy, clumsy-looking hands. The trunk rises up to a misshapen head with one large eye and a vertical mouth below that eye. From the sides of that head, just under the eye, another set of arms, these thinner, more delicate. They end in dexterous-looking fingers.

"Those statues seem weird," I say. "What do you think they are?"

Spingate shrugs. "Maybe Springer gods. Or their demons. What I want to know about is that symbol on the steeple. This building must be older than the ones in our city, so how can we have the same symbol on the Observatory?"

She touches the bump on her head, winces. "I wonder if Smith's coffin will heal my cut so I don't have a scar."

I think of O'Malley, so concerned about fixing his face.

"That scar is yours and yours alone," I say. "Your creator didn't have one like it."

She thinks on that for a moment, then gives me a smile and a funny look.

"That's good," she says. "I hadn't thought of it that way."

I should be pleased, but I'm not. That funny look happens when I say something *smart*. Spingate is my friend, we work well together and she seems to accept me as leader, but deep down inside she doesn't consider me an equal.

Purple left some firewood. I put a fresh log on the fire, careful not to make the flames too big. Wouldn't want a spider to come crashing through the wall and kill us by mistake. I've had enough fighting for one day.

I see something in the dirt on the far side of the room. Is that a tiny *hand*?

I walk to it, brush away rubble and debris. It's a plastic toy, a chubby baby Springer wearing a tattered green outfit. Not scraps of fabric tied together for camouflage, but delicate, beautiful clothing.

It's a doll.

Like the dolls I had when I was a little girl.

How old is it? This ruined city that surrounds us, was it once full of children with toys? Parents, children, families?

How many living beings did our creators kill?

I hear movement outside. I grab my spear, wincing at the pain that comes from my broken fingers, and move to the old double doors that open to the jungle. Spingate picks up one of the muskets, grunts as she cocks back the hammer and locks it into place. She hasn't fired one yet, but she figured out how to reload it.

The doors swing open—it's Purple, his musket slung over his narrow shoulder, his knife and hatchet safely tucked away.

I lower my spear. Spingate carefully releases her musket's catch.

The clearly exhausted Springer waves us outside.

The rain has died down to a steady sprinkle. We follow Purple around the back of the ruined building. Tucked in behind a broken slab of wall is a narrow, wheeled cart. The cart is made of sticks and boards, bound together with dried vines. The wheels are mismatched. One is metal and reminds me of Spingate's symbol—it used to be a real gear in some large machine, perhaps. The other wheel is made of splintery wood. The wheels are close enough together that the cart would probably make it through the jungle's narrow trails. Two long handles, so someone could stand between them and pull the cart behind.

Atop the cart is a long pile of vines. Purple reaches out, lifts a handful so we can see beneath.

A human face—Visca.

Spingate hisses in air, covers her mouth.

Visca's dead eyes stare out. He was always the palest of all the Birthday Children. Now he is sheet-white. Dried blood crusts the bullet hole in his forehead. There are bite marks on his cheeks, and one of his ears has been chewed off—the jungle animals had started in on his corpse.

Purple looks at me. He wants me to understand. He brought

us the body of our fallen warrior. It is an apology, maybe, or perhaps an effort to show good faith. Whatever the motivation, this gesture moves me deeply.

"Thank you," I say. "This means a lot to us."

Dolls, families, love, revenge, honoring the dead . . . our two cultures are similar in so many ways.

Purple covers Visca's face.

We return to the steeple. Purple checks on his friend, who is finally awake.

"We need to talk to them now," Spingate says. "We have to find out about food."

"How? We don't speak their language, they don't speak ours."

"But they *have* a language," she says. "Maybe we can make each other's sounds."

Spingate steps toward them. She raises her hand to her chest, taps her sternum twice.

"Spin-gate," she says. She reaches across, taps my chest. *"Em."*

The Springer stares at us. It taps its own chest.

"Bar-kah," it says, the words half-growl, half-chirp. It points to its wounded friend. *"Lah-fah."*

A single, stunned laugh escapes me, makes Purple twitch in surprise and caution. *Barkah, Lahfah* . . . are those their names? Purple understood us?

Spingate points. "Barkah," she says, doing her best to imitate the sound. Then she points down: "Lahfah."

The wounded Springer's eyes widen and the toad-mouth opens, letting out a sound like shoes grinding on broken glass. It's as shocked that we can understand them as I was they can understand us. That sound—just like me, Lahfah is *laughing*.

Purple—I mean *Barkah*—points at Spingate.

"Singat," it says. Then it points at me. *"Hem."*

Lahfah's mouth opens wide again, filling the room with that grinding-glass laugh. For having a broken leg and two dead friends lying close by, this one seems full of good humor. I wonder what he's like in happier circumstances.

Are we making a connection here? Can we do this? Can we succeed where the Grownups just made war?

Barkah points at me again. *"Hem. Yalani."*

I look at Spingate. She shrugs. We have no idea what that means.

"Yalani," Spingate repeats, mimicking the sound as best she can.

Barkah stares at us, then unslings his bag and starts digging through it.

"Pellog jana chafe," Lahfah says. *"Rether page chinchi wag."*

He's babbling. He must think we understand all of his language, not just a couple of names.

"Yollo bis," he says, then roars with body-shaking laughter.

Barkah pulls out a piece of cloth and a black stick. When he does, another piece of cloth falls from the bag and lands, mostly flat, on the dirty floor. It is the picture of the Springer I killed.

"Ponalla," Lahfah says softly, mournfully.

Barkah stuffs the drawing back into his bag. He unfurls a blank piece of cloth, lies it flat on the floor, and sketches. Quick, purposeful lines. His hand is steady. He knows what he's doing—this alien is an artist.

The image takes shape before my eyes: the Observatory. And on it, tiny but clear, several layers up, a human figure.

Barkah points to it. *"Yalani."*

"He recognizes you," Spingate says. "From the statue of Matilda."

I don't know what to say, what to think. What do the

Springers know about our city and that massive building? Did he want to shoot me because I killed his friend, or because of something to do with that statue?

Wait . . . the statue of Matilda is tall, but insignificant compared to the size of the pyramid. Even if you're on the same street, the statue is too high up to make out any details. He couldn't possibly recognize me unless he had been close enough to see the statue's face.

I point to the base of the drawn Observatory.

"Did you go there? Did you watch us?"

Three green eyes blink at me.

I hold a hand over my eyes like I'm shielding them from the sun. I pantomime peering out, first this way, then that, my eyes squinting.

Barkah grunts, taps his chest, taps the bottom of the Observatory, points to me, then points to Spingate. He starts drawing madly.

"I don't believe it," Spingate says. "Is he saying he was there?"

We watch, amazed, as Barkah sketches. Bodies take form, as do faces. With just a few curves and shapes, he captures the essence of people I know: Bishop, Visca, Aramovsky, O'Malley, Spingate and me, all in the elevator, facing out.

"Godsdamn," Spingate says, breathless. "Barkah was down there with us. He watched us leave."

Lahfah thumps the end of his tail on the drawing, making charcoal dust jump. Barkah yells something at him. Lahfah yells back.

Barkah returns to the drawing with what I can only interpret as exasperation. Lines, curves, charcoal dust scattering. He stops, holds the drawing up for all of us to see.

He added Lahfah to the drawing.

"*Gromba, gromba, gromba,*" Lahfah says, clearly pleased.

Spingate laughs. "Looks like she was down there, too."

"*She?* I thought it was a *he*."

Spingate shrugs.

Lahfah points at her. "*Singat.*" He points at me. "*Hem.*"

Barkah pulls out more blank fabric. He draws quickly, efficiently, showing us the life of the Springers. Secret entrances in ruined buildings that lead to tunnels. Springers in those tunnels, families, entire underground villages.

He makes a few drawings of the surface: the jungle, quick sketches of plants, berries and animals that I hope are edible. He finishes every surface drawing with lurking, five-legged figures—spiders. The message is clear: the Springers *have* to live underground. If they stay on the surface too long, the spiders could get them.

"Like the boogeyman," I say.

Spingate nods. "Except their boogeyman is real."

Their entire culture, forced to live below the surface. Because our kind chased them there.

Barkah sketches a Springer. He spends a little more time on this drawing. He pulls three little tied-off pouches from his bag. They contain colored powders: red, blue, yellow. These he applies to his sketch with a master's touch. When he finishes, I am looking at a blue Springer, more wrinkled than any I have yet seen. This one looks very old.

I notice something hanging from the old Springer's thick neck. It looks like a metal rectangle, very detailed, as if the level of detail is itself important. I tap it, point to Barkah's necklace.

Barkah taps the necklace. I get the impression he's saying, *Yes, same as mine*.

I tap the drawing of the old Springer.

"Who is this?" I say to Barkah.

He—or she—can't understand my words, but I'm betting he can understand my meaning.

He makes a new drawing, a simpler one. A few strokes shows the old blue Springer, then two smaller, purple Springers next to him. He adds necklaces to these as well. He taps the second purple Springer, points to himself.

Then he makes a simple stick figure that clearly represents a Springer. The stick figure is on its knees, head low. Barkah quickly makes many more of these, filling the fabric. In seconds, there are hundreds of them.

"He's drawing them like they are kneeling," Spingate says. "Kneeling to the old blue one. That must be their leader."

More than a leader, I think—*royalty*.

"Maybe their king," I say. "Or queen."

Spingate looks at Barkah in a new light. "Then maybe we are very, very lucky—what if our new friend is a prince or a princess?"

A surge of hope courses through me. If Spingate is right, we could be talking to someone who can make decisions, or can at least speak directly to the Springer leader.

We could make peace.

Barkah reaches into his bag, pulls out a small wooden carving: a spider. He uses the toy's pointy foot to scratch out one of the two purple Springers with necklaces, dragging the tip back and forth until that young Springer is nothing but smears and torn fabric.

He sets the wooden spider right on top of that spot.

"A spider killed the royal child," Spingate says. "Barkah's sibling, maybe."

I'm shocked at how fast a story can be told with nothing but pictures. If spiders killed the king's child, and if the king thinks we're connected to the spiders, he would hate us.

Barkah pulls another small toy from his bag. It looks like a flat, wheeled cart with an angled framework on top, almost like thick tent poles without a tent. A long stick points out the back, as if the cart has a tail. He uses the toy to knock the spider on its side. He sets the cart down, looks at us.

"I don't get it," I say. "What does he mean?"

Spingate thinks for a moment. "Maybe he wants our help destroying the spiders?"

Barkah knows I was with Visca, knows the spiders saved me at the fountain, so he has to know the spiders are on my side. Is destroying the machines the price of peace between our two cultures? This could be the bargaining chip I need.

I pick up the little spider toy, hold it so everyone can see it.

"We can make these go away," I say slowly. "We can make it so they never hurt you again." I tap the drawings he made of the plants and animals. "But we need food." I point to my open mouth. "*Food*. Can you help us?"

Barkah stares at me, trying to work out my meaning.

"He doesn't understand," Spingate says, frustrated.

A short horn blast echoes through the jungle outside, the same sound from when the Springers set fires to herd us.

Barkah rushes to the doors, peeks out. He then hops between two of the strange statues and brushes dirt away from the warped wooden floor there. He slides his fingers into a small hole and lifts: a trapdoor, leading down.

He waves to us, wide-eyed and urgent.

"He wants to hide us," I say.

I grab my spear. Spingate and I run to the trapdoor, the floor squeaking beneath us with every step. Barkah is letting me keep my weapon, so if this is some kind of trick it's not a very good one.

The old stairs creak even more than the floor. Spingate is right behind me.

At the bottom, I step into standing water that comes up to my knees. This is a confined space, smelling of rot and mildew, dark save for a long, thin sliver of light—coming through a slot left by a missing board, just above ground level, that looks out on the jungle in front of the steeple's doors.

Noises from outside . . . I hear something coming.

The trapdoor quietly shuts behind us.

I can see through the tangled old vines outside the slot—Springer feet, legs, tails. Five Springers out there, maybe more. I see gun butts resting on the ground next to those feet.

The Springers talk. I recognize Barkah's voice. I squat down, changing my angle, and I can see his face. He's just in front of the steeple doors. He's talking to a blue, older and bigger . . . and then I see the blue's copper necklace.

"The king," Spingate whispers. Her breath is warm on my ear. "Is Barkah handing us over to him?"

Out in front of us, one of the Springers turns, looks around. Did it hear her talking?

Spingate and I stay motionless.

For a half-second, I swear the Springer's three eyes are staring right at us, but it looks away—it didn't see us through the thick vines.

I glare at Spingate, hold a finger to my lips.

The king's tail comes around quickly, slaps into Barkah's head. Barkah staggers, then straightens. He doesn't react, doesn't fight back. Some kind of discipline, parent to child? We don't even know if they *are* parent and child. We know almost nothing of these creatures.

I see Springers walking past Barkah and the king, coming from inside the steeple . . . they're carrying the dead. Then two more Springers, pulling a rolling cart with Lahfah on top. He's bundled up in a blanket.

Will they search the back of the church? If they do, they will surely find Visca's body.

The king's tail slaps Barkah's head once more, then the older Springer hops away toward the trail. His entourage follows, pulling the cart with Lahfah on top. They slide into the jungle. Just like that, they are gone.

Spingate's breath in my ear again: "Should we go up?"

She's getting on my nerves. How can she be so smart in her lab and so dumb about just staying quiet?

"Just *wait,*" I whisper.

That's exactly what we do. We stand in calf-deep water, our feet growing colder by the second. I try to imagine the king and his followers moving down the trail, try to project how far away they are.

The floor directly above us squeaks. When Barkah finally opens the trapdoor, we're shivering. He waves us up.

Save for his drawings and the statues, the room is empty.

Barkah seems shaken, upset.

Spingate steps close to him.

"Food," she says. She points to her mouth, her belly. "Food."

She's so single-minded she doesn't seem to understand how close we just came to getting caught. What would have happened to Barkah for hiding us?

"Maybe I can draw the purple fruit," she says, then moves to the fire. She flips over a sketch, picks up a piece of charcoal and starts to draw.

That catches Barkah's attention, makes him excited. He glances at the closed doors, then two hops take him to Spingate's side.

She sketches an oval. She starts to shade it in. The charcoal is messy. She's pressing too hard, sending dust everywhere.

She holds up the sketch for me to see. "Does this look like the purple fruit?"

"It looks more like a turd."

I hold back an embarrassed laugh. When Matilda was a little girl, saying the word *turd* would have gotten her punished. Badly. Our father didn't like nasty language of any kind.

Barkah squints at the drawing. He mumbles something I don't understand. I get the feeling he's not impressed with Spingate's artistic skills.

Spingate sighs. "Let me do it again."

She puts the fabric back on the ground, starts to draw, hesitates, wondering how to make it look better.

The air erupts with a *boom* so loud and hard that it shakes dirt down from what's left of the steeple's ruined ceiling. The sound echoes through the jungle even as another sound joins it, a steady roar that makes everything around me shudder.

"Oh no," Spingate says, then she's up and out the doors. Barkah and I rush out behind her.

High in the sky, a trail of white. Memories flashfire, more of Matilda's childhood floods in, and with a wash of heartbreak, fear and despair, I recognize what it is.

"A ship," Spingate says. "It just entered the atmosphere, it's coming down." She looks at me, dread in her eyes. "It has to be the Grownups."

Barkah hops into the steeple.

The twelve-year-old inside me cries out: *This isn't fair!* We were so close. We've worked so hard, lost so much. Brewer told us there was only one shuttle; he lied.

Barkah comes out with my spear in one hand and his musket

in the other. He tosses the spear at my feet. He waves his hand outward in a gesture that needs no translation: *Go away.*

Spingate shakes her head. "No, we have to learn from each other, we—"

Barkah opens his wide mouth and roars: a grinding, hideous noise. He holds the musket in both hands, shakes it at us. He's leaning forward, his tail out straight behind him. Open aggression looks the same on his kind as it does on ours.

Spingate takes a step back, surprised, maybe even hurt.

I grab her elbow, gently pull her away. "Let's go."

"But why is he mad? He must have also seen our shuttle come down."

"Look what happened after it did," I say. "Eight of his kind are dead because of us. We have to take Visca's body and get back to our people. *Now*. Look where that ship is going."

She looks to the sky. The white line descends toward the horizon. It's coming down fast.

Whatever it is, it will land inside the city walls.

"Maybe we should leave the body," she says. "It's going to slow us down."

"*He's* going to slow us down," I say. "Not *it*. We're taking him."

We run around to the back of the ruined church. We each take a pole of Visca's cart. It hurts so much to hold the pole, more to pull it, but pull it we do.

We head for the trail, Visca's tied-down body bouncing along behind us.

PART IV

HAUNTINGS AND HATREDS

TWENTY-NINE

By the time we reach the city gate, night has fallen. Spingate and I are drained. The cart is on wheels, but that didn't make the hike through the muddy trails any easier. Raw blisters cover our palms, our fingers. My hands feel like Visca's ghost hit them with his sledgehammer.

We call out. Coyotl slides through the tall doors, runs to us. I wait to see Bishop come out as well, but he doesn't. Of course not—as soon as that smoke trail arced overhead, he knew what it was and went back to protect the shuttle.

Coyotl carries Visca's body up onto the spider. Spingate and I join them. To think that this very machine might have been used to slaughter thousands of Springers, native beings who were guilty of nothing other than being where my kind wanted to live.

The spider is fast. The ride is smooth, *silent*—no more whine. And that rear leg . . . it's not dragging.

"Coyotl, is this the same spider you rode before?"

He beams with pride. "Borjigin fixed it. Gaston helped a little, so did Beckett, but mostly it was Borjigin."

It never occurred to me that we could repair the old machines. Can Borjigin fix any of the rusty ones in the nest?

The spider sprints down the nighttime street. If not for the rhythmic clack of metal feet on stone, I wouldn't hear anything save for the wind whipping across my face. In minutes, we're back at the landing pad.

A spider stands on either side of the shuttle ramp. Farrar is atop one, Bawden the other. Both of them have muskets slung over their shoulders. Borjigin is next to Bawden, doing something with the tube mounted there. Is he trying to fix the cannon?

In front of the ramp stand twenty young circle-stars, lined up in four rows of five. They wear black coveralls and boots. The shuttle's lights glint off the metallic thread of their Mictlan patches. Three of them hold muskets. The others hold tools, tools they will use as weapons.

Bishop is walking up and down the rows. I can't hear what he's saying. From the frightened and serious expressions on the faces of those kids, I assume he's preparing them to fight.

Twelve-year-old warriors. They were bred for this, yet they don't look like real soldiers. They look like dolls dressed up for war—only this time it wasn't the Grownups who chose the outfits, it was us.

Smith runs down the ramp, two little circle-crosses—one boy, one girl—right behind her. Spingate gets down off the spider first, then she and Smith help me descend. My hand doesn't seem to work anymore.

Smith takes my wrist, gently but firmly.

"This is bad," she says. "We need to get you in medical right away."

"No time," I say, even though all I want to do is crawl into that coffin and go to sleep, wake up feeling no pain. "Can you fix my fingers here?"

She looks at me like I'm stupid, then catches herself and again studies my hand.

"Pokano, go to medical," she says without looking up. "Find finger splints."

The little boy runs off. The girl circle-cross hovers nearby, waiting to be told what to do.

Smith turns to Spingate, sees the stitches on her forehead.

"You *fought*?"

"I didn't have a choice," Spingate says.

"Were you hurt? Did you get hit anywhere else?"

Smith reaches for Spingate's belly. Spingate brushes her hands away.

"I'm fine," Spingate says. She points up to the spider. "We have Visca's body."

Smith glances at me. Maybe a touch of respect in those eyes.

"Yilmaz, go to Deck Four," she says. "Prepare a coffin for corpse storage. That will arrest the decomposition process until we can arrange a proper burial."

"Yes, ma'am," the little girl says, then sprints for the shuttle. She already knows how to work the coffins? I've been away from the shuttle too much. I realize I didn't know her name—or the boy circle-cross's name, for that matter—until this moment.

Smith calls up to Coyotl. "Do you need help bringing Visca down?"

"He's heavy," Coyotl says. "Send some circles out to help me."

I leave them to take care of Visca. Spingate heads into the shuttle. I walk to Bishop. He suddenly stands stiff, at attention.

"Two spiders and twenty-one infantry ready to march," he says, barking out the words. "We need to find the invaders and kill them before they can mount an attack on the shuttle."

Some of the little circle-stars stare straight ahead, a few watch

Bishop, and the rest look at me. Some are ready to fight. Some are trying to hide their fear. If we march them out, I wonder how many of them will suffer the Grownups' bracelets, will be blasted into pieces like El-Saffani.

"Wait here," I tell Bishop. "Do not march until I get back."

He nods once.

I walk up the ramp, enter to confusion, to panic. O'Malley is in the coffin room, trying to calm hundreds of upset children. Aramovsky is doing the same. For once, the two of them are working together.

People see me and start shouting suggestions: everything from abandon the city and flee into the jungle to fly back to the *Xolotl* and beg the Grownups to forgive us.

I ignore these cowardly ideas and push through the crowd. O'Malley looks immensely relieved to see me. I pull him aside.

"Bishop wants to attack," I say.

O'Malley nods. "Of course he does. It's all he knows."

"You don't think we should?"

The words are out of my mouth before I realize why I'm asking him; for all of my issues with O'Malley, I instinctively seek his counsel.

O'Malley thinks for a moment. "Maybe we should attack, but not yet. We need to know exactly what came down. How many people? What do they want? Could be Grownup circle-stars come to wipe us out and recover the shuttle, or just Matilda, here to convince you to join her. What if it's Brewer? And what if the ship isn't even *from* the *Xolotl*?"

"Of course it is," I snap. "Where else could it be from?"

He shrugs. "I don't know. We don't know anything yet, and that's my point. To use Bishop's favorite word, we need to *reconnoiter* before we march our people into danger."

I look at the people packed into the coffin room. Many are

crying. Aramovsky is telling them to stay calm, that the gods will protect them.

O'Malley leans in close to do that thing I now despise, to *whisper*.

"Tell everyone you're going to find out what's going on," he says. "People are panicking. They need to know someone is doing *something*, even if you don't know what that something is yet."

His hot breath on my ear, on my neck. Shivers ripple across my skin. I'm surprised and disgusted with myself—how can my body react to him at a time like this?

"Go get Bishop," I say. "And his little circle-stars. Tell Bawden and Farrar to stay on their spiders as lookouts."

O'Malley slides through the crowd. Moments later, Bishop and his "soldiers" filter in, find places among the scared, crying, *noisy* kids.

My broken fingers scream at me. With my good hand, I whip my spear against a coffin three times, *bam-bam-bam*.

"Shut your godsdamned mouths!"

Silence. All eyes look to me.

There is no point in pretending we're not in trouble. As quickly as I can, I tell them about Barkah and the Springers, how there is real hope we can communicate and find a cure for the red mold, but right now we need to deal with the most dangerous problem first.

"A ship came down," I say. "We don't know how many people were in it. If we march out blindly, we leave the shuttle less protected. Bishop, myself and a few more will go find where the ship landed. *No one else* leaves the landing pad. While I'm gone"—I stare straight at Aramovsky—"O'Malley is in charge."

Aramovsky nods. "You're leaving Spingate here this time, aren't you?"

I scan the crowd, see her in back. She and Gaston are holding each other. She stares at Aramovsky, suspicious he mentioned her name.

There's no need to put her in danger again. I shouldn't even go myself, but I can't wait for people to report back to me—I need to know, and I need to know now.

"Correct," I say. "Spingate stays here."

Aramovsky smiles, spreads his arms, turns as he talks. "A wise choice," he says, to everyone rather than just to me. "Because now we're not just fighting for our *own* lives, we're fighting for those that come after us."

Spingate's eyes go wide. She shakes her head, silently imploring Aramovsky to stop talking.

He doesn't.

"We must congratulate Spingate, and Gaston as well"—Gaston rushes toward Aramovsky, pushing past people, stumbling over kids—"because she is *pregnant*."

A hush falls over the coffin room.

Gaston stops cold, just a few steps from Aramovsky.

All eyes turn to Spingate.

She sees Smith standing by the shuttle door, points at her. "I'll deal with *you* later."

Smith is clearly rattled. She glances from Spingate to Aramovsky, shaking her head at him as if to say, *How could you?*

Spingate gathers herself. She stands straight and tall. Despite her bruised face, the angry line of stitches on her forehead, her muddy, filthy hair, she is confident and proud—she has never looked more impressive.

"It's true," she says. "When Doctor Smith fixed my elbow, the med-chamber scanned me, found out I was a few days pregnant."

Smith must have told Aramovsky. In confidence, I'm sure, but he is so slimy, he was probably waiting for the right moment to use that information.

This news, it's overwhelming. And Spingate is my friend . . . why didn't she tell *me*?

The way she changed, became so serious, fighting to get her way when before she would go along with whatever I wanted to do. The things she said . . .

Our children will inherit Omeyocan. What kind of a planet do you want them to have? One of war, or one of peace?

I should say something to her, to everyone, but there are no words.

Aramovsky smiles wide, raises his hands, expertly commanding the room's attention.

"It has begun," he says. "Our children and our children's children are going to fill this planet. We are the chosen people. Omeyocan is our birthright. We will defend it from the Springers and anything else that tries to take it from us." He looks at me. "Go, Em. Go and find out what new threat we face."

Spingate is pregnant. And, somehow, Aramovsky managed to turn that into *him* ordering *me* to do what I just said I was going to do. That's why he chose this moment, he knew it would stun me, he knew he'd be able to make himself look like a leader.

My eyes seek out the one person who always makes everything easier.

"Bishop, let's go find that ship."

THIRTY

Gaston was so mad I thought he might attack Aramovsky. I had Farrar watch them while I sent Beckett to use the pilot-house map, see if he could figure out where the new ship landed.

It landed near the Observatory.

We ride Coyotl's spider. Five of us are aboard: me, Coyotl, Bishop, Bawden and a young, brown-haired circle-star named Muller. He's as tall as I am; I wonder how big he'll get in the next few years.

My fingers still hurt, although not as much. Smith put some bits of metal on them, which helped, and poked them with a needle, which helped even more. I glared at her the entire time—she refused to meet my eyes.

The clouds that block the stars are starting to break up. Twin moons cast enough light to see some detail of the vine-covered streets, the dark buildings that rise up all around us.

On foot, this trip took us half the day. Atop the sprinting spider, it doesn't even take half an hour.

As we drive, Bishop plans our strategy.

"Em, you and Muller will stay on the spider," he says. "Muller is a good shot. We'll stop a few blocks from where the ship went down. Bawden and I will continue on foot. I'll go left, she'll go right, we'll observe the ship from the flanks. Coyotl, once we get out, you wait one minute, then approach the ship straight on, but move *slow,* so the spider's feet don't make too much noise. Stay a block or so away, close enough so you can rush in if you hear gunfire."

All around me, heads nod.

"What if it's Grownups?" Bawden says. "Can we shoot them?"

Bishop shakes his head. "Don't fire unless fired upon. Stay low, stay out of sight. We only have three muskets—if there are four or more Grownups, and they're all armed, we're dead even if all three of us kill on our first shot."

The spider slows, stops. Coyotl steers the machine into the deep shadows of a smaller road.

"The ship is two blocks due east," he says.

Bishop and Bawden hop over the side, hit the ground and vanish into the shadows.

Coyotl moves the spider forward, but much slower. I can barely hear the pointed feet touching down. We travel one creeping, slow block, then I see it.

The ship looks . . . *lumpy*. Moonlight plays down on smoke rising up from a long path behind it. Vines smolder, some even flickering with tiny flames.

I don't know what to make of that ship. Our shuttle is streamlined, something born to slice through the air. This ship? It is a quarter the size and has no sleekness. Weird shapes stick out. I see rivets and bumps. Some parts look melted. Smoke—or maybe steam—rises up. A few spots are actually glowing, like metal heated in a fire. The machine *clink*s and *clonk*s, as if someone is tapping on it with tiny hammers.

Moonlight intensifies. The cloud cover is breaking. I see something moving near the ship. It's not a Grownup, not a Springer . . . it is a *person,* like us.

The wind picks up. I hear vine leaves start to rattle.

That person . . . it can't be . . .

I grab Coyotl's shoulder.

"Move in," I say. "Right now!"

"What? But Bishop said—"

"Now! *Go!*"

The spider lurches forward so fast Muller and I grab at the protective ridge to stop from falling backward. The silent machine streaks in with nothing more than a rapid *click-click-click* of pointed feet.

The person hears us coming, turns.

As the spider slows and stops, the last of the clouds blow clear. Moonlight streams down on a long-sleeved white shirt, a red and black plaid skirt, pale skin . . . and wispy blond hair.

The girl looks up at me.

"Hello, Em," Bello says. "I escaped."

THIRTY-ONE

It can't be. She's gone. Bello is *gone*.

Bishop rushes in from the left, slinging his musket. He engulfs Bello in a hug. She laughs and winces, hugs him back, her feet dangling.

"*Bishop,*" she says. "Oh my gods, it's good to see you!"

Bawden sprints in from the right, but she doesn't run to Bello. Musket butt tight against her shoulder, she scans the intersection, looking everywhere, ready to bring the barrel up on a moment's notice. Seeing nothing, she steps into the ship's open hatch.

Bishop has forgotten the danger—Bawden has not. Bishop is still hugging Bello, still laughing.

But *is* that Bello? Or is it Bello's creator, wearing my friend's body like a new suit?

Bishop sets her down. I haven't seen him smile like that since we landed.

"You're *safe,*" he says. "Was anyone with you?"

She shakes her head. "Only me."

Bawden steps out of the ship. "It's empty."

Coyotl hops over the spider's protective ridge, lands without a sound. He hugs Bello.

Bawden takes her eyes off the surrounding buildings long enough to squeeze Bello's arm and smile, then the circle-star with the shaved head is once again looking for threats.

Everyone is happy to see Bello—except me. Am I the only one who understands the danger?

"You escaped," I say. "*How* did you escape?"

She smiles up at me until she realizes I'm not smiling back. Her smile fades.

The others glance at me with odd expressions, like I should be down on the street with them, celebrating.

My mind is shouting at me to believe: *It's her! It's her! You left her and that was awful but she got away and now it's okay!* If I go down there, if I touch her, smell her, I know I will lose the ability to think about this logically. I'll stay on the spider until this is finished.

"It's me," she says, softly, "It's *me*."

It *is* Bello, I can see her, she's right in front of me.

It *isn't* Bello, can't be, she's been overwritten.

I reach out my good hand, take the musket from Muller. He's so surprised he doesn't even struggle to keep hold.

"Get out," I say to him.

There must be something in my voice, because the twelve-year-old kicks a leg over the protective ridge, scrambles down the rails and drops down to the vine-covered street.

I put the musket butt to my shoulder. My splinted fingers make it hard to hold the weapon, so I rest the barrel on the spider's protective ridge. I've never fired one of these, but I've seen it done, and it's not like it takes a Spingate or a Gaston to figure out how to pull a trigger.

I aim at Bello's chest.

Bishop looks at me, confused.

"Em, what are you doing?"

Everyone stands there like they don't know what to do. I certainly don't. I have no idea if this is my friend or an evil thing that is a thousand years old. I have to find out.

"Answer my question," I say to Bello. "How did you escape?"

I see tears in her wide hazel eyes—quick to cry, just like the Bello I knew.

Bishop shakes his head slightly. He can't process this. He and I were gutted that we had to leave her behind. The guilt has been with us every moment since, shaping us like strong hands forming wet clay. Now he is free of that guilt and the relief blinds him.

Bawden continues to scan the surrounding buildings, as if none of this matters to her.

Coyotl shifts from foot to foot, looking at Bello, looking at me.

Muller has no idea what to do. He looks from me, to Bello, to Bishop and back again.

I remember the black hand grabbing Bello's mouth, the black arm wrapping around her waist, yanking her backward into the greenery. I remember that look of terror in her eyes. I remember not being able to save her.

I remember *abandoning* her.

"How did you escape?"

"Brewer helped me," she says. The tears are coming fast now, wet trails glistening in the light of two moons. "The Grownups who grabbed me put me in a cell. There was a fight between the Grownups."

"About what?" I say. "What were they fighting about?

She slowly shakes her head.

"I don't know. I heard some explosions, some screams, then this Grownup opened my cell, said his name was Brewer. He took me to this ship."

It can't be that simple. It *can't*.

"They had you for days," I say. "Your brain would have been overwritten."

Her hands go to her shoulders . . . she's hugging herself, just like she did back on the *Xolotl* when she got upset.

"They tried," she says. "They put me in a coffin, put this thing on my head, but their machine didn't work." She closes her eyes, rubs hard at her temples. "I thought I was going to die. It hurt so bad, and it messed up my brain a little. I still recognize faces, but a lot of the stuff that happened since we came out of the coffins is gone. It's okay, though, because when the pain stopped, I was still myself. Did you hear what I said, Em? *Their overwriting machine failed.*"

"That doesn't explain how you escaped," I say. "You don't know how to fly, Bello. You're just a circle."

"I didn't fly the ship. Brewer told me to get in, that he'd handle the rest."

Brewer controlled so many things on the *Xolotl*. Is it possible he could have sent the ship down, guided it to this crash landing?

"Brewer told me there was only one shuttle left," I say. "How do you explain that?"

"Look at it." She gestures to the lumpy ship. "It's not a shuttle. It was used to repair the outside of the *Xolotl*. Something like that, I think . . . I don't remember his exact words, I was so scared."

Wouldn't Brewer have told me there was a second ship capable of reaching Omeyocan? But if he held back that bit of information, then Bello's story is believable. At the same time, if she really is a Grownup, I imagine she can lie without the slightest effort. I need Spingate and Gaston to take a look at her. And Smith—maybe there's a physical way to tell the difference between our Bello and whatever happens when we're overwritten.

Or . . . maybe I can remember something Bello and I talked about, something the Grownup Bello wouldn't know. We weren't together long, we didn't really talk about that much. Except for one thing . . .

"On the *Xolotl,* before we met Bishop's group," I say. "We all talked about our favorite desserts. What was Aramovsky's?"

Please say cupcakes, please say cupcakes . . .

Bello licks her lips. She's not looking at me, she's staring down the barrel of the gun.

"I . . . I told you, my memories are scrambled. Em, please . . . *it's me.*"

She doesn't know. Did the overwrite process damage her memories? Or is that the perfect lie—if she can't remember anything, there's nothing we can do to prove she is not who she says she is.

Bello clasps her hands together in front of her chest.

"Please," she says. "*Please* don't kill me."

Bishop steps in front of her.

"That's enough," he says. "Put down the weapon."

I stand there for a second, confused, until I realize my shaking hands could accidentally pull the trigger and shoot Bishop.

I lower the musket.

Dammit, Bishop . . .

Maybe I had the will to pull the trigger, but now I'll never know. That moment has passed—I can't bring myself to do it again.

"Let's get back to the shuttle," I say. "Bello, you come up here with Coyotl and me. The rest of you, run back on foot."

Coyotl guides her to the spider, helps her up. She finds a place to stand that is as far away from me as she can get.

Bawden finally slings her musket.

"Should someone stay with this ship?" she asks. "Muller and I can watch it."

Leave someone behind? Looking at Bello, that's the last thing I want to do now. Besides, we know Springers can get into the city. At least Barkah can. Spingate and I were making progress with him, but we didn't exactly part on good terms. He is an alien; as much as I'd like to think we could be friends, I realize I have no idea what he is really thinking, or what his kind is capable of doing.

"We're not splitting up," I say. "Everyone move out."

THIRTY-TWO

Bello stares up at me, crying silently.

"Close it," I say.

The medical coffin's lids rise up and shut tight.

I turn to face Smith, who is looking at some images floating above her white pedestal.

"I'll try," she says. "But even if the overwriting process changed her brain somehow, I'm not sure there's any physical way to tell. I've never examined Bello before, so there's nothing to compare her current state against. But I'll try, I really will."

Smith seems eager to help. She wants to get back into my good graces, perhaps—she knows I'm furious at her for betraying Spingate's confidence.

"Do your best," I say, wondering if she actually will without Aramovsky telling her to do so.

Outside the medical room, Bishop is waiting for me. He's anxious. The emotion doesn't suit him well.

"It's *Bello,*" he says quietly. "Don't you think we'd be able to tell if it wasn't our friend?"

I say nothing. We head for the pilothouse.

He wants to believe so badly when he should doubt her every word. I'm disappointed in him. When I thought I would do anything to keep him from thinking poorly of me, it never crossed my mind that the situation might someday be reversed.

In the pilothouse, Gaston, Spingate and O'Malley are waiting for us. The walls show images of people talking in the coffin room, the dark landing pad outside with three spiders standing watch, and Bello's closed coffin in the medical room.

"Smith doesn't know if she can detect overwriting," I say. "Spin, anything in your lab that would help us?"

She won't make eye contact. Right away, I'm sure she's holding something back. I'm so hungry, my fingers hurt, my shoulders ache and my head is pounding—I don't have patience for more secrets.

"Speak up," I snap. "Not telling me the truth is the same as lying to me."

She flinches. That hurt—I *wanted* it to hurt. I'm done with this girl hiding things from me.

Bishop crosses his arms. "Now you're starting in on *Spingate*? Who will you doubt next? Me?"

"If you keep acting like a gullible kid, yes. Bello could be playing you for a fool, so stop thinking we don't have to pay a price for leaving her behind, and *start* thinking about the safety of this shuttle and our people."

Bishop's lip curls. He's not used to anyone speaking to him that way.

Gaston puts his hand on Spingate's back, rubs a small circle. "Just tell her," he says.

She brushes back her thick red curls, struggles to force out the words.

"One of the things my progenitor studied was the overwriting process," she says. "I can only recall a little bit. Just snippets, really. I'll try to remember if there's a way to test Bello, but . . . Em, I . . . my progenitor . . . she *wanted* to learn how to erase people. She liked it."

Gaston glares at me like it's my fault I dragged that out of her, like all of a sudden Spingate is this fragile thing that needs protecting. Why, because she's pregnant? Spingate can take care of herself.

"I know how you feel," I say to her. "But we can't control the evil things our creators did. We can only control the choices we make. Do your best."

She nods. "I will. But I should be focusing on the red mold instead."

"Zubiri will do that," I say. "You focus on Bello."

O'Malley shakes his head. "So this is more important than food? The Grownups made receptacles so they could live on Omeyocan. If this Bello is a Grownup, then she got what she wanted. Anything she does to harm us also harms *her*. If our Bello is gone, I'm sorry about that, but we shouldn't be wasting our time with this. Besides, she's too small to be a threat."

What is he thinking? I'm small, and I've killed twice. But does he have a point? Bello is alone. What can she do—trick people to go back to her lumpy ship and return to the *Xolotl*? Only six of us would fit in there, seven at most.

No . . . there is a way for her to take *all* of us.

"Bello said she didn't fly the lumpy ship," I say. I look at Gaston. "If she's lying, if she *did* fly it here, does that mean she'd have the skills needed to fly the shuttle back to the *Xolotl*?"

I see realization hit home on my friends' faces. Bishop's arms uncross. O'Malley glances at the wall showing Bello's coffin.

Maybe now he understands that you don't have to be big to be dangerous.

"Maybe she could," Gaston says. "Different ships usually have different controls, though. I'd have to see that lumpy ship to know if she could fly the shuttle."

"Then go look," I say. "Right now."

"Coyotl will take you on his spider," Bishop says. "I'll send Muller as well, with a musket."

Bishop isn't volunteering to go, because he wants to stay in the shuttle—he finally understands the real threat might be here, with us, not somewhere out there.

"I won't go," Gaston says. "Bello could be one of *them*. I'm not leaving Spingate here alone."

"There's hundreds of us here," Spingate says. "I won't be alone."

"I'll watch out for her," I say. "I'll make sure Bishop watches her, too. Gaston, we need to know."

He shakes his head, squares his shoulders. "Send Beckett. He's studied hard, he knows how to fly."

Spingate rolls her eyes. "Gaston, I'll be fine. Go!"

He turns on her. "I said *no*. That baby is *ours*—you don't get to make all the decisions just because you're the one carrying it. *I'm* not going, *you're* not going, and if you had told me you were pregnant before you went out looking for the Springers, I would have said the same godsdamn thing then!"

Spingate's wide green eyes blink. She's shocked. So am I, so are all of us. We've never seen Gaston this angry.

She knew about the baby before she and I set out to find the Springers—but she hadn't told him. Maybe she didn't because she knows him better than I do, because she knew he would have fought against her going.

"We'll send Beckett," I say.

Gaston lets out a long breath. "Thank you for understanding. I . . . it's not that I don't want to do what you ask, it's just that . . . well, I have to keep Spingate safe."

That word, yet again. *Safe*—how can anyone still believe it exists?

THIRTY-THREE

I spent the rest of the night, the morning and most of the afternoon in a med-chamber, getting my broken fingers fixed. They still hurt, but nowhere near as bad. I can grip the spear properly again.

Bello got out of her med-chamber before I did, but I planned for that, telling Farrar to watch her closely.

I'd hoped to come out of medical to answers, but that didn't happen. Spingate found nothing to prove that Bello is a Grownup. Neither did Smith. Science and medicine have failed me, so I'm trying the only thing I can think of—having my friends see if they can spot anything weird.

Almost everyone is in the coffin room, listening to Bello tell of her escape. People want her story to be true. Of course they do—they want a future that is nice and neat. They want to believe that the Grownups' overwriting machine is a failure, and that we don't have to worry about evil creatures in orbit preparing to erase us.

The kids, especially, hang on Bello's every word. Not counting her, there are eighteen teenagers left in our group, people who were with Bello on the *Xolotl.* Beckett and Coyotl are at Bello's ship, leaving sixteen of us. At my subtle instruction, the teenagers don't just listen to Bello, they watch her, looking for any indication she is not who she says she is.

And besides—a good story is a welcome distraction from our growing hunger.

At least I know Bello won't try anything with all these people watching. Farrar will make sure she doesn't go farther into the ship, or go off by herself outside.

When Beckett, Coyotl and Muller return, I'll have more information. If Bello's ship could be flown by autopilot—that's what Gaston calls it when a ship flies itself—or if Brewer could have guided it down remotely, that means Bello *might* be telling the truth. I'll let her join us, but I'll make sure she's never alone.

If it turns out her ship can't be flown without a pilot? Then she's lying; she's a Grownup. I will lock her in one of the shuttle's storage rooms until we figure out what to do with her. We'll have to treat her like a prisoner. We'll have to question her.

A nagging voice in my head tells me, *Just lock her up now . . . or have her killed, immediately . . . it's the only way to be sure.*

It's not my father's voice this time, it's Matilda's. And to some degree, it's mine, too.

The only way to be sure . . .

I force myself to look away from Bello. If Matilda were in my shoes, she'd kill Bello, but I am *not* Matilda—I will find another solution.

Like the rest of us, I want Bello's story to be true. I want that desperately. Not just because I love her—the old her, anyway—but because if she's telling the truth, I can go look for Barkah.

My people are hungry. If that continues, I know Aramovsky will make a move. I think I have one day left before he does, maybe two.

I remember Barkah's anger at seeing Bello's ship. Did he react like that when our shuttle came down? Probably. His grandparents, or great-grandparents or even farther back than that, must have seen the first ships from the *Xolotl* release the war machines. To the Springers, perhaps ships mean death.

But Barkah had never seen actual humans before. None of his kind had. They'd only seen machines. Not that encountering people has been that much better for the Springers—my kind leaves a trail of death wherever we go.

Bello finishes her story by describing a daring run down a dark corridor, chased by horrifying Grownups. She reaches her lumpy ship just in time, is shot out of the *Xolotl* to safety. It's like something out of a storybook—it would be unbelievable if the same thing hadn't happened to us when we took the shuttle.

When she's done, people applaud. The kids scream with delight. They ask her to tell the story again. Blushing, Bello agrees.

Once is enough for me.

I walk outside. Night is falling. Bishop is at the base of the ramp, his axe in his hands. A spider stands on either side of him, guarding the shuttle.

For a few moments, I just watch him. He's dressed in his black coveralls. I take in his broad shoulders, the way his neck muscles flutter when he turns his head. He hasn't been to Smith's white coffin to have his numerous scratches repaired. Under that black fabric are scars that bear witness to our struggles.

I think of the way he looked in the Garden, when he stood under the bright lights with nothing on but tattered pants. I think of how he looked when he threw my spear at the pig. I wanted to touch Bishop's skin then. At the pool, I did. I'd like to touch him again, kiss him again . . .

I shut my eyes, give my head a hard shake. Now is most certainly *not* the time for such thoughts.

I walk down the ramp and stand next to him.

"Good evening, Bishop."

He's staring out toward the Observatory.

"They should be back," he says. "They should have been back an hour ago."

His voice is heavy with dread. The emotion is contagious. I was so busy watching Bello, trying to find the truth, that I forgot a trip to the Observatory is *much* faster on spiderback than on foot. Coyotl, Muller and Beckett should have already returned.

A cold feeling thrums in my belly and chest. I missed something, but what? My brain is trying to make a connection—not the muddy sensation of recalling Matilda's memories, this is something else. I missed something *new,* something that has nothing to do with my creator's life.

"Go after them," I say. "Take a spider, with Bawden and as many kids as you want."

He starts up the ramp. "And if they aren't at Bello's ship, how long should I spend searching for them?"

With Bishop and Bawden gone, Farrar will be the only older circle-star we have left—just Farrar and twelve-year-olds to defend the shuttle. That's not enough. I think of when we ran out of the Garden and abandoned Bello. It was a hard choice, and I hated myself for it, but it was the *right* choice.

"If they aren't there, then come back without them," I say. "As fast as you can."

He runs into the shuttle. I stand where he stood, looking out toward the Observatory. *Please,* let them be all right.

Moments later, Bishop runs down the ramp, Bawden and two young circle-stars behind him. Only Bawden carries a musket. Muller had one as well, which means Bishop is leaving three muskets here.

In seconds, the four of them are mounted and on their way. I watch the spider scurry over the vine ring, then sprint down the darkening streets. Out ahead of them, no sign of Coyotl and the others.

There's something about Bello's ship I missed, but what? I can't put my finger on it. She's a Grownup, I *know* it. It's time to lock her up. Just because I won't act like Matilda doesn't mean I can't do *something*—time to stop being so nice.

Pounding steps on the ramp behind me. O'Malley, in a panic.

"Em! Get in here! Aramovsky is calling for a new vote!"

I turn my back for one moment, and he does this? I'm almost glad, because he's moved too soon—many follow him, but not enough. He should have waited until hunger swayed more people his way.

I stride up the ramp and into the coffin room. Aramovsky is talking, turning, his arms outstretched, doing what he does so well. But he will lose this vote, then I will use that victory to block him from making another. He's *finally* made a mistake.

And then I see Bello—she's standing right next to him, whispering when he pauses. She notices me, stares at me, a cold hardness in her eyes. No tears this time. She smiles, sending a chill through me.

Aramovsky steps onto a closed coffin. He spreads his arms, and his voice booms.

"Someone has to speak out loud what all of us are thinking," he says. "Do we need new leadership? The majority of us—the people from Deck Four—never got a chance to vote at all. It's time to fix that."

He locks eyes with me.

"It's not that Em didn't do her best," he says. "But perhaps the job of leader is too much for a circle, too much for an *empty,* too much"—the corners of his mouth turn up in a grin of victory—"for a *slave.*"

The word hangs in the air, pressing down, pushing at locked memories. I see hundreds of faces go blank. I see eyes widen and heads nod. For everyone, even the kids, the mention of that word opens up flashfires—they know.

Gradually, all eyes turn to me.

The things I've done right, they suddenly don't matter. My leadership, keeping the group together, getting us off the *Xolotl,* learning the mysteries of Omeyocan, making contact with the Springers . . . *none* of it matters.

In an instant, with a single word, they see me as something different than I was. They see me as *less*.

I have to stop this, right now.

"I'm not a slave," I say. "None of us are. Just because the ring on my head says I'm *Service,* or the double-circle says Aramovsky is *Spirit* or the half-circle means O'Malley is *Structure* doesn't mean we have to be those things. We make our own choices!"

I look to O'Malley for support, hoping he will back me up, but he just stares at me, openmouthed, like I said something wrong—something *horribly* wrong.

"Spirit," Aramovsky says. "Structure . . . *Service.* I just now remembered what the symbols mean, but you . . . you already knew."

Bello's little grin. She told him. She knows the symbols' meanings because she's a Grownup. She told him what to say.

Nearly three hundred people are staring at me. A hundred different lies jump to my brain, but none of them make it to my tongue. There is a brief moment where I can say something, deny that I didn't keep information from my people, and then that moment is gone.

I am convicted by my own silence.

The eyes glare at me now. Even Spingate's, her expression somewhere between betrayal and outrage. *Not telling me the truth is the same as lying to me,* I said to her.

I'm guilty of the same thing.

And everyone here knows it.

THIRTY-FOUR

Things are falling apart.

Bishop and Bawden returned empty-handed—no sign of Beckett, Muller, Coyotl or the spider. Fear rages through the shuttle, fueled by Aramovsky instantly screaming to everyone that the Springers have taken our friends.

I feel lost. Did Barkah take our people? Bello's ship was near the Observatory, a place Barkah has been before. He was so angry when her ship came down—maybe he lay in wait, knowing that my people had been there once and might come back again. If not him, could other Springers have attacked?

Aramovsky said the disappearance of our people was further evidence of a lack of leadership, and that we need a vote, *immediately*. Bishop argued against it, so did Spingate, saying now wasn't the time, but they were shouted down.

I stand on the stage and tell people why they should vote for me, but my confidence is gone. Even though I hold the spear, our symbol of leadership, my words sound hollow. As I speak, I look to O'Malley, seeking some kind of guidance—the expression on his face tells me I have lost before the votes are cast.

I should have told everyone about the symbols. O'Malley talked me out of it. It's not just that people now remember circles were slaves—which is damaging enough by itself—there is also the fact that I knew something everyone wanted to know, deserved to know, and I didn't tell them.

They don't trust me.

I wouldn't trust me, either.

When I step off the stage, Aramovsky steps on.

I see Spingate talking in hushed tones with Gaston, Johnson and Ingolfsson. Is Spingate going to try for leader? I hope so. Anyone is better than Aramovsky.

But as soon as he begins his speech, I realize no one can beat him. Most of the kids gaze up at Aramovsky with wide-eyed adoration. Out of the nearly three hundred people in this room, only sixteen are teenagers.

Only now do I understand the significance of those numbers. While I was out searching for food, exploring, looking for Bello's ship, Aramovsky was quietly campaigning. The only reason he didn't call for a vote sooner was that he wasn't sure if he could win. I got us off the *Xolotl,* after all, and kept us alive all this time. I think those facts convinced many of the kids that I was best for the position.

Then Bello gave Aramovsky what he needed—a way to make some of my supporters change their minds. Bello is obviously a Grownup, but I have no proof, and right now no one in this shuttle is about to take me at my word.

Aramovsky finishes with a passionate statement that basically becomes an *I told you so*. He warned us about the "demons," and now three more of us are gone. He says we must not wait for the Springers to pick us off a few at a time, that if we want to be worthy of this great gift the gods have given us, we need to "be strong in the face of evil" and "drive the demons back to hell."

During the thunderous applause, I glance at Spingate. Her head droops: she knows there's no point in giving a speech of her own.

Opkick asks for other candidates. When no one volunteers, she calls for a vote. A simple show of hands, just like the vote on the *Xolotl* when I became leader.

She calls my name and she counts out loud. I don't know why she bothers; not even fifty hands go up.

She calls Aramovsky's name. Hands shoot up instantly. Even though over three-quarters of the kids are circles—like me—most of them vote for him.

He has won. He is our leader.

With that change comes a feeling of hopelessness. All the bad things that have happened so far are nothing compared to what will come next.

Opkick calls us both to the stage.

It takes every bit of will for me to meet Aramovsky's eyes. He's not smiling, which shocks me. He looks resigned to his new duty, as if it is a terrible burden thrust upon him rather than something he's worked for almost since we first woke up.

"Em, we wouldn't be here without you," he says. "I want to say—and I think everyone agrees—thank you for your leadership thus far. You got us off the *Xolotl,* got most of us down here safe. Everyone appreciates that, but now that we're on Omeyocan we face a different set of challenges. The people have spoken."

He holds out his hand toward me. I reach to shake it, then I realize what he wants.

My spear.

I feel my face flush red. I look like an idiot. My hand falls to my side.

My fingers tighten on the spear shaft. I don't want to give it up. I want to hit him. He will lead us to ruin.

Kill your enemy . . .

It would be so easy to stab him, just like I did the Springer in the jungle . . .

I glance to the shuttle doors. I see Bishop standing there, hands gripped on his axe. His eyes silently tell me that whatever I do, he will back me up.

Farrar wears the same expression. So does Bawden. All three are ready to fight for me.

I don't have to give up leadership. I can have Aramovsky and Bello locked up. If the circle-stars are behind me, I can stay in charge.

Attack, attack, always attack . . .

Aramovsky's hand is still out, empty and awkwardly hovering in midair. I see a flicker of fear in his eyes. He knows I could ignore the vote, imprison him, maybe even have him killed. I still have the power.

Matilda had power, too. She used it. Look what happened to her people.

I am not Matilda, and Matilda is not me.

I hand Aramovsky the spear.

He takes it. His fear vanishes. He's won. His mouth doesn't smile, but his eyes do.

Aramovsky gestures to the floor, asking Opkick and me to step off the stage. We do, leaving him alone to tower over us all.

"As your new leader, I must put first things first," he says. "The Springers have food. They had their chance to share it with us, but they chose the path of evil. They have what we need to live—so we will take it from them. Bishop, Farrar, you will drive the two spiders we have left. Take Borjigin to the spider nest. Schuster, Bemba and Zubiri, stand up."

Zubiri stands, as do a boy and another girl, both halves. Aramovsky is sending a combination of symbols: science and management.

"Borjigin, these three are your assistants," Aramovsky says. "Take them with you. I've talked to Bemba and Schuster, they think they remember working on machines. And Zubiri is our smartest young scientist—better to have her with you, solving problems that come up, rather than wasting her time in the lab. Why would we try to research a cure for red mold when we can just take food from the Springers? You will all work together to fix any machines that can be fixed. Bishop, choose three young circle-stars to go as well. Take all the remaining muskets. The rest of us will seal up in the shuttle for protection."

Borjigin walks to the stage, his hands together at his chest. He's almost in tears.

"What about Coyotl?" he says. "And Beckett, and Muller. Aren't you going to look for them first?"

Borjigin and Coyotl have grown close in such a short time. Aramovsky's expression of sympathy is so real I almost believe it. He bends slightly, leaning toward Borjigin.

"The gods decide our fates," Aramovsky says. "Don't worry—if Coyotl is worthy, the gods will return him safe and sound. Your duty is to give us an *army* of machines. And when they are ready"—he stands tall, raises the spear high, his eyes widen and his lip curls up—*"we will go to war!"*

The kids who voted for him jump and shout and cheer. They were afraid . . . Aramovsky gives them a way to attack what they fear. I wonder how many of these cheering faces will soon be dead.

I should have stabbed him when I had the chance.

Maybe I'm not the leader anymore, but I can't let this happen.

"Aramovsky!"

My voice echoes off the shuttle walls, loud enough to cut off the cheering. He looks at me, annoyed and impatient. I'm ruining his moment; I won't quietly go away.

"Yes, Em?"

"We can make peace with the Springers. No one has to die."

He looks to the ceiling and sighs. "We just had a vote. Everyone heard your speech, yet they voted for me."

"We don't know how many Springers there are," I say. "There could be thousands, all with guns. Even with the spiders, we won't come out unscathed." I look around the room, pointing at individuals. "You might die. And you. And *you*. And—"

The spear butt hammers down, rattling the stage.

"That will be *enough*!"

Aramovsky doesn't hide his rage.

"War is dangerous, but the God of Blood will protect the faithful," he says. "It is better for some of us to fall in battle than for *all* of us to starve."

People are staring at me now, annoyed that I won't shut up. It's truly over: Aramovsky has their hearts and minds. I need to get it through my head that he is the leader.

But maybe I can try one more thing.

"It will take some time to repair any broken machines," I say. "While that's happening, let a few of us go talk to the Springers. If we can get them to show us where the food is before your army is ready, then no one has to die, right?"

All eyes swing back to him.

Aramovsky's face twitches with hatred. It hits me—he *wants* war. If it isn't for food, he'll come up with some other reason. His upper lip twitches. He wants to kill me, right here and right now, but he can't; if he ignores what I'm saying, he's obviously passing up a chance to keep *everyone* alive.

And then how many votes would he win?

I pour on the pressure.

"The Springers might kill me," I say. "But if I can save the lives of any of our people, I will take that risk."

I'm leaving him no choice.

The smile slowly returns to his face. "Your bravery is a blessing to us all. Go, then—see if the gods will help you stop the bloodshed. Leave now, *right now,* because when we're ready to attack I will not hesitate. Every minute counts."

That was easier than I thought it would be. Could I have been wrong about him wanting war? Maybe there is a decent person in there after all.

"Thank you," I say, and I mean it. I look to Spingate. "Let's go."

She flashes a glance at Gaston that is as loud and clear as a gunshot: *Don't try to stop me.* She starts toward the shuttle door.

"No," Aramovsky says, the word a sharp command. "You stay, Grandmaster Spingate. We may need your brilliance to repair the spiders, and"—he lowers the spear tip so it points at her belly—"we can't risk the next generation."

Her fists go to her hips.

"You can't tell me what to do! I have the right to go where I want."

Aramovsky shakes his head. "You gave up that right when you became pregnant. Do as you're told, or I will have you escorted to your lab and confined there for your safety and the safety of the baby. Guards?"

Forty young circle-stars jump to their feet, stand at attention.

Black coveralls, weapons in hand—what they lack in size they make up for in numbers.

Spingate is furious, surprised, devastated. She looks around the room. No one stands to defend her. Even if Bishop, Bawden and Farrar wanted to protect her, they would be instantly overwhelmed.

Bishop was away from the shuttle almost as much as I was. All the while, Aramovsky was quietly whispering in little ears. I thought all the young circle-stars followed Bishop, but I was wrong.

For a leader you are wrong-wrong-wrong quite a lot, are you not?

Brewer's words. How right he was.

Little Kalle stands, steps forward from the crowd.

"I'll go with Em," she says. "I've been in the jungle already, I can help."

Aramovsky smiles down at her, benevolent, as if he's actually an adult with worldly experience and Kalle isn't just a few days younger than he is.

"My brave child, Em must go alone. She is the one who has spoken to the Springers. She knows she has no special knowledge that we need here, like you have. And she knows she's not a soldier, needed to defend us. This is the best way she can serve us all, and I salute her for it."

Now it is so obvious—he wants me to go alone because he wants me to die. The Springers can eliminate his main rival for leadership, and he doesn't have to lift a finger.

Still, I don't have a choice. If there is any chance I can pull this off and save my people, I have to take it.

Aramovsky tilts his head toward the shuttle door. "Gods be with you. Go now."

I am dismissed.

People step aside, opening a path to the shuttle door.

I step out onto the deck. The night is black, overcast, starless. A stiff breeze brings that smell of mint. Before I can walk down the ramp, Bishop rushes out to join me.

"Take a flashlight," he says, handing me his from a pocket in his coveralls. "And a med-kit." From another pocket, he hands me one of the white plastic cases.

He grabs me, pulls me in close for a hug.

"Stop halfway to the gate," he whispers. "I'll send help."

He turns and walks back into the shuttle.

There is nothing left but to face the path I have made for myself.

I walk down the ramp, across the landing pad, and head for the city gate.

THIRTY-FIVE

It is dark and drizzling. Blackness drapes the city in a shroud of hidden threats. I don't want to use the flashlight, because it will let anyone following know exactly where I am.

Just like Bishop told me to do, I stopped halfway to the gate. How long should I wait? I need to get out of the city, find Barkah's church. I still have no idea how to locate the Springers—my best chance is for Barkah to find me there.

The breeze makes leaves rustle, makes me see and hear things that I know aren't there. I feel so exposed. Maybe Aramovsky won't wait for the Springers to finish me off—what if he sends Bawden, or Farrar? Now that Aramovsky is the leader, would either of them obey his orders to kill me? Maybe, maybe not, but one of the little circle-stars certainly would.

My coveralls can't keep out all the weather. I'm wet. I'm cold. I'm hungry. I'm afraid.

I'm alone.

There is only one person you can always count on—yourself.

My father's voice. A new memory. Sitting on his knee, my

head against his chest. I'm crying. I was six years old . . . maybe seven. Something bad had just happened. Something that hurt me, terrified me. I'm looking at my father's face. A mustache, black. Kind eyes. Heavy, black hair, like mine. His forehead . . .

My father didn't have a symbol.

And . . . neither did I. At least not then.

He's crying, too. He's holding it back but I can see it, I can hear it in his voice even though he's trying to hide it.

Matilda, I have to send you away. I know you can't understand right now, but you will. The only way I can keep you safe is to hide you. There may come a time when the tooth-girls tell you to do something dangerous, or the double-rings try to hurt you because they know no one will punish them. If that happens, remember—do whatever it takes to survive.

I can smell soap on his skin. I can hear his rough hands petting my hair. This isn't a Matilda memory—it's not secondhand, as if I'm seeing and feeling what someone else experienced. It's like *I* was there, that my father spoke to *me*.

My *father*. His name was . . .

. . . his name was *David*.

He sent me away because of something my grandfather did. He sent me away to become one of the . . . the *Cherished*. That word has power. When I was at school, I did what my father told me—I did whatever it took to survive.

There is only one person you can count on . . .

I realize I'm standing in the middle of the street like a fool. What would my father think if he knew I was waiting for someone else to take care of me?

I watched Visca. I watched Bishop. I saw how the circle-stars blend in. I know how they track, I know how they move.

Maybe I'm not a circle-star, or a gear or a half—but I'm not an *empty*, either.

Not anymore.

I am the wind . . . I am death.

Someone is coming.

My back is pressed against a ziggurat's base layer. I'm wedged in behind the thick vines that cover the cold, wet stone. The breeze drives the drizzle sideways, makes the leaves surrounding me quiver.

Damn this overcast sky. I wish there was some moonlight, anything that would let me see who is out there.

I hold a jagged piece of masonry. In a city that is steadily deteriorating, this is one weapon that's not hard to find.

Who is coming? I hope it's Bishop. But if it isn't? If it's someone sent to kill me? Then I will kill them first.

A hissed whisper cuts through the darkness.

"Em?"

Is that Bishop? I can't tell. It's a boy, but the stiff breeze and rattling leaves make the voice impossible to recognize.

The clouds must break for a moment, allow a thin bit of moonlight to shine down. A boy, a *tall* boy, draped in shadow. Holding . . . is that a shovel?

Farrar. Did Bishop send him, or did Aramovsky?

The moonlight vanishes. The night is pitch-black.

I hear footsteps coming closer.

My fingers tighten on the rock. The rock is hard and jagged and final. It's not as elegant as my spear, but it will take life just the same.

He's coming my way. Not directly, he's searching, like he knows I should be in his area but doesn't know exactly where.

Closer. A few more steps, and I will crush his skull.

My hand shakes. My arm trembles. The wind and the leaves keep me hidden and silent.

Two steps away. Slowly, so slowly, I raise the rock.

"Em, are you there?"

This close, I instantly recognize the voice.

"O'Malley?"

He jumps away, surprised. His feet catch and he falls face-first.

I step out from the vines. O'Malley rolls to his butt, sees me, starts scrambling backward.

"No! Don't kill me!"

I stop, confused. He doesn't recognize me? No—of course he doesn't.

"It's me," I say. "It's Em."

His scrambling stops.

He slowly gets to his feet. He shakes his head, smiles in proud astonishment.

"You scared me," he says. "You certainly look different."

I do. Vines tied around my chest and waist and legs break up my outline. The skin of my face and hands is covered in plant juice and dirt. Twigs and leaves are woven into my hair.

"I saw Bishop talking to you when you left," he says. "I knew he was planning a way to get you help."

Of course O'Malley saw it—the master of whispers wouldn't miss such a thing.

"Why didn't Bishop come himself?"

"He couldn't. Aramovsky was watching him closely, rushing him out to the spider nest. I waited until Aramovsky wasn't looking, asked Bishop what I could do. He told me to get you any weapon I could find."

O'Malley picks up the shovel, offers it to me. I drop the rock and take it. The shovel is heavy and unbalanced.

"Be careful with it," he says. "Gaston helped me. He used a machine in the shuttle to sharpen it."

I drag my thumb across the edge, the way Coyotl showed me. It's *very* sharp. Probably sharper than the knife O'Malley wears on his belt, the one I used to kill Yong.

"What about you?" I ask. "Won't Aramovsky notice his right-hand man is gone? That's what you do, isn't it? You help the leader?"

"He'll notice eventually, but not right now. Opkick is his advisor—seems I'm not needed anymore."

Oddly, I feel bad for O'Malley. If Aramovsky had picked him, would he have still come after me? I don't know. Maybe it doesn't matter: I needed help, and O'Malley came.

He steps closer. He reaches out, slowly. His fingertips trace my hairline, as if he needs to touch me but doesn't want to mess up my camouflage. The drizzle wets his face, makes his cheeks gleam slightly from what little light penetrates the clouds.

"I didn't come just because Bishop couldn't," he says. "I came because . . . because I love you."

He has no idea that I almost killed him just now.

I've got one boy who won't tell me how he feels, and another who won't *stop* telling me how he feels.

"You should head back to the shuttle," I say.

He leans away, almost like I slapped him.

"But . . . but I'm going with you."

This wasn't just a delivery run. He's ready to head into the jungle with me. He knows how dangerous this will be. But he has no experience fighting, no survival training as far as I know. He's a *politician*—away from the safety of the group, he's useless.

Still, O'Malley is smart. He's strong. And just because he doesn't know how to fight doesn't mean he will back down from one. If I don't find the Springers, it's war; I'll take what help I can get.

"Keep up with me," I say. "And be *quiet*."

The jungle is alive with noise. Low hoots, squawks, yelps, growls and an occasional dying squeal. The stiff wind has carried away some of the cloud cover, giving us enough moonlight to walk by. I'm grateful for that, because the flashlight would make us easy targets for a musket shot. Barkah and Lahfah aren't the only Springers out here.

Our best chance is to find the church. Hopefully, Barkah is there, and—hopefully—he'll talk to me. If he's not there, then it will be time to use the flashlight and wander the jungle. If O'Malley and I are lucky, the first Springers we meet will want to talk, not shoot.

I found that first fire pit. I'm surprised I can follow the trail easily, even at night. I like to think that Visca would have been proud of me.

O'Malley is noisier than I would like, but I admit I'm impressed. He's quieter than Coyotl was, and *way* quieter than Borjigin. If we make it through the night alive, he might learn to be as silent as I am.

And when he talks, he whispers—for that part of creeping through the jungle, at least, he's a natural.

"You did a brave thing, coming out here," he says.

"You're out here, too."

He's behind me, so I can't see him, but I'm sure he's nodding. I hear a sharp slap as he smacks a bug that landed somewhere on his face or neck.

"It's been at least an hour," he says. "How much farther to this church?"

"You mean, if we don't get killed by a snake-wolf? Or shot by Springers? Or attacked by one of the other animals we hear?"

A pause.

"Yeah. If none of those things happen."

"I'll tell you when we get there. More walking, less talking."

It's almost funny to think about how confident he was back in the pilothouse, when he kissed me. In the safety of the shuttle, he swaggers. Out here, he's scared. I shouldn't tease him about that, though—I'm scared, too.

The animal noises fade, then go silent.

"What's happening?" O'Malley asks.

"Predator. Come on."

I lead him to the same kind of wide-leafed plant Borjigin hid beneath. We tuck under the leaves and wait.

Beneath my feet, a small tremble. A *regular* tremble, not the mad stampede of animals. O'Malley feels it, too—he looks at the ground quizzically.

"Uh, Em . . . just how big *is* this predator?"

Something's wrong. When the snake-wolf came, I didn't feel anything like this. The vibrations grow stronger, *thump-thump-thump-thump*.

Memories of our time on the *Xolotl* come rushing back. A rhythmic pounding, an organized stomping. Getting louder and louder. Shaking the ground.

O'Malley figures it out a split second before I do.

"Marching," he says. "But it would have to be so many. *Thousands*."

He looks at me, half in fear, half in disbelief.

"Springers," I say, and ice creeps across my heart.

I stand, scan the jungle. I need to get higher and see what's going on. There, a big tree, the trunk massive and gnarled, wider than most. If it's wider, maybe it's also taller.

I hand O'Malley the shovel.

"Stay here," I say.

Thick vines run up the big trunk, creepers that root in the ground and cling to the bark with hundreds of thin white tendrils. The vines—still wet from the drizzle—hold my weight, let me climb high enough to grasp a branch. I move quickly but carefully, mindful that everything I touch and step on is damp and slick.

Higher.

I draw even with the canopy, see the tops of trees all around me. I was right: this tree is taller than most.

Higher still.

The leaves rattle harshly just above my head—something yellow and small leaps from the tree. Arms spread, skin flaps catch air, and the animal is gone in an instant, banking to slide through vines and out of sight.

My heart hammers. That thing startled me . . . maybe I startled it. It was the same kind of animal I saw when Spingate and I were walking through the jungle. This close, though, I saw more of it. Seemed like it was holding something . . . maybe a stick?

I climb higher.

The trunk narrows, the branches thin. I reach the top—here the trunk is so slim the tree wobbles from my weight.

As if the gods are real and want to help me, the wind drops off and the last of the drizzle stops. One of the two moons escapes the clouds and turns the jungle into a maroon landscape.

I look out across the trees.

"Oh . . . oh no."

The canopy blocks most of my view, but through it I see so many Springers it looks like the entire jungle floor is moving.

A line of them march shoulder to shoulder, hopping in unison.

The line stretches off into the distance. I can't even see where it ends.

Some carry muskets. Most carry other weapons: axes, knives, swords and spears.

Behind the first line, a second.

And a third.

Thousands of them. My people are hopelessly outnumbered. The war machines will be our only hope of survival.

Closer the marchers come. I have to move soon or I won't be able to get down without being seen.

Wait . . . in the middle, straight out from me, behind the second line. Springers hacking at trees and vines, cutting away underbrush. Stretching out behind them, a maroon streak through the jungle—they are clearing an old road.

Something on that road. I squint, lean forward, as if those extra few inches can make a difference. I recognize the design. The toys Barkah showed me, the ones with the long, straight wooden tails, the carts that smashed spiders . . . they weren't toys at all. They were models of something real.

These are too big to call *carts*—I think *wagons* is a better word for them. The tent-poles-without-a-tent frameworks brush against overhanging branches. The thin, straight tails stretch out twice the length of the wagons themselves.

The wagons are big enough for several Springers to ride on top, although no one is riding. Instead, there are five Springers on each side, pushing the wagons over the broken, bumpy, just-cleared road.

Springers are marching on our city. They are prepared to take on the spiders and win.

My people will be slaughtered—I have to go back, I have to warn everyone.

The way the Springer lines angle away . . .

I turn and look back, see the city of Uchmal rising out of the jungle. Oh *no* . . . there is no way O'Malley and I could make it to the gates without the Springers seeing us. The only hope of escape we have is to continue along the trail as fast as we can go.

The Springer church . . . the cellar where Barkah hid Spingate and me . . .

Omeyocan's second moon slips from behind the clouds, adding pale blue light to the jungle. It's too bright—if even one of those thousands look up here, they'll see me.

I start down, dropping fast. My hands and feet slip on wet bark. I smash my knee, then my shin, but the pain doesn't slow me. I lose my footing a third time, fall into a branch that hammers my ribs. Can't stop—if I stop now we're dead.

Branches, vines, feet, hands . . . faster and faster.

When I reach the last branch, O'Malley is kneeling, half-hidden behind the wide trunk. I drop to the ground next to him, feel the rhythmic *stomp-stomp-stomp* of the marching army.

"Em, we have to get out of here!"

For once, I don't mind his whispers.

I peek around the trunk. Through the dense underbrush, I can see them coming—a line of alien soldiers hopping straight for us, weaving around trees, dipping down the far side of jungle-choked craters only to hop out the near side.

When I turn and run, O'Malley is right behind me. We stay low and sprint down the trail. Our booted feet eat up the distance, enough that I start to think we got away clean.

And then I hear the long, droning note of a horn.

They've spotted us.

THIRTY-SIX

We sprint through endless jungle ruins, doing our best to keep to the trail. Overhanging vines and encroaching leaves slap at us, splashing us with beaded drizzle that soaks our hair and runs down our faces into our coveralls.

A flash of lightning. Thunder follows two seconds later. As if the deafening noise ripped the bottom from the clouds themselves, the rain pours down again.

The horn echoes through the trees.

They are chasing us.

I think we're a little bit faster than the Springers, but hopping and landing on both feet makes them more stable on this rough, wet ground. I've fallen once, banged my chin on a tree root. O'Malley has fallen twice. He's bleeding from a cut on his temple. Each time we hit the ground, we're up before our momentum slows. We are wet and muddy and running for our lives.

I try to see where we are, but all the jungle looks the same. Are we near the church? Have we already passed it?

A double burst of lightning pulses across the night sky, and in that split-second glare I see it: the steeple, the rings with the six dots.

I turn off the trail, sprint headlong into the underbrush. I hear O'Malley crashing in behind me.

We enter the dark steeple. It's empty. O'Malley quietly shuts the double doors while I stumble to the wall, around the statues, until I find the trapdoor. I open it and urge O'Malley in.

From outside, I hear the horn again. Then, an answering call from the other direction—so close they must have been just ahead of us on the trail. Did they see us come in here?

O'Malley rushes down the rickety stairs, stands in water up to his knees. I descend a few steps, lower the trapdoor slowly, ease it into place, then join him.

Grunting and chirping outside: the Springers are close.

I look out the slot made by the missing board. Thin moonlight reveals two long blue feet tied up with strips of cloth. The feet are so close I could reach through and touch them.

We hear the Springers talking.

The floor above us creaks. There are at least three of them up there—if they find us, we're dead.

O'Malley's cold, wet hand takes mine. His strong fingers grip me tight. He is calm, resigned to this situation. I admit I didn't expect this from him. I would have thought he'd panic, or do something stupid to give us away. Instead, his steady presence gives me strength. His eyes tell me something deep and overwhelming: if he has to die, he is glad he gets to spend his final moments with me.

I loved this boy before he even woke up. I was the first thing he ever saw. Will I also be the last?

The floor above us creaks again, the sound of a Springer hopping from one spot to the next. Then the creaks move closer to the trapdoor.

The creaks stop.

We wait.

I peer out the slot, through the underbrush. No feet, just rain.

We stand there, still and motionless, for a long time. Any simple noise—a cough, a sneeze, a heavy breath—could mean our death. We listen to the rain come down. We wait.

I hear the horn blare. Distant, barely audible: the hunters have moved on.

When the floor creaks again, I start to shake.

Short hops, each producing a creak, the creaks coming closer to the trapdoor. A straggler? Or is it a squad of them, five or more, hoping to flush us out so they can shoot us dead? If it is only one or two, maybe we have a chance.

I grip my shovel with both hands. O'Malley draws his knife.

Maybe we will die, but we won't go easy.

The trapdoor slowly opens. Darkness beyond, hints of motion . . . a Springer. They have found us. If we can't see them, they can't see us. I wait, coiled and ready to strike. When the stairs creak, I will thrust the shovel point up at my enemy.

I can't breathe, I don't *dare* breathe.

"Hem?"

That single syllable makes me sag with relief.

Barkah has come for us.

THIRTY-SEVEN

Soaked and freezing, I climb the stairs.

Barkah hops back, giving me room.

He is not alone.

He stands with three Springers, all with lush, young, purple skin like his. I instantly recognize Lahfah, by both his face and the wooden splint on his leg. His face contorts in what I can only think of as an alien sneeze, and he lets out that broken-glass laughter.

"Hem!" he says.

The other two are wide-eyed, two-fingered hands fidgeting on their muskets. Are they afraid? Do I horrify them? When O'Malley climbs the stairs and stands next to me, the two guns snap up. Hammers lock, barrels point at us.

"Don't move," he says quietly.

"Wow, *Kevin,* thanks for that brilliant advice."

This isn't the time for sarcasm, but does he think he's the only person on this planet with common sense?

Lahfah hops between us and the guns, a fast movement that obviously causes pain in his broken leg. He yells at the new ones—that's the only word to describe the awful noise he makes. The two new ones yell back.

Barkah lets out a single, sharp shout. The yelling stops. The two new Springers lower their muskets. There is no question as to who is in charge here.

"I see it, but I can barely believe it," O'Malley says. "I mean, I know you told us about them, but . . . well, they aren't *human*."

I've never seen O'Malley in awe before. He stares at each Springer in turn. The two new ones stare at us in equal astonishment.

The rain beats down. The leaking roof creates the same quivering mud puddles I saw last time. The waist-high statues gleam wetly.

Barkah hops to me, reaches out slowly. I see the fingers of O'Malley's hand twitching, drifting toward the jeweled hilt of his knife.

"No," I say, calmly but firmly. "Pull that and we're dead."

O'Malley forces his hand still.

Barkah touches my sternum. He looks at his friends.

"*Hem,*" he says.

Then Barkah's finger slowly moves toward O'Malley. O'Malley stiffens, as if he's about to run back down the stairs.

"Don't you move," I say, forcing a smile. Then I wonder if smiles might be horrifying to them, with all those bare teeth and our squinty eyes.

O'Malley forces a smile of his own. "What if they have diseases?"

"Then you and I will be sick together. Stay still."

Barkah's fingertip touches O'Malley's sternum. Barkah looks at me, waits.

"Ohh, Malley," I say, sounding it out. "His name is *O'Malley*."

Barkah starts to talk, stops. His frog lips wiggle as he imagines how to make the sounds.

"Ohhh-malah," he says.

I laugh at the simple mispronunciation. I say the name slower, sounding it out, *"Oh . . . mal . . . eee."*

Barkah concentrates. *"Ohhh . . . mah . . . lah?"*

O'Malley looks at me, astonished. An alien just said his name—or at least tried to—and just like that, Barkah isn't quite as *alien* as he was a few moments ago.

"Oh-mah-lah," O'Malley says. He laughs with delight and relief. "Good enough for me."

A word pops into my head. I reach out and touch O'Malley's sternum.

"Kevin," I say.

Barkah thinks on it a moment, then says, *"Kevin."*

O'Malley's face lights up. "That's perfect!"

"Kevin," Lahfah says.

"Kevin," the other two Springers say in unison.

I shake my head in amazement. "Of course, your name is the one they can pronounce correctly."

Lahfah pokes one of the new Springers in the chest.

"Tohdohbak," Lahfah says.

I repeat the name as carefully as I can. So does O'Malley.

Lahfah points to the next one: its name is *Rekis*. Rekis seems pleased when O'Malley and I pronounce that name correctly. The delighted Springer hops from foot to foot.

The moment is surreal—we are introducing ourselves to aliens, who are probably teenagers just like us. We are laughing, together. This is simple, natural. Why was there ever a need for violence, war and death?

If these Springers are with Barkah and not with the army,

maybe they aren't soldiers. Are they too young to serve? I have no way of knowing. Whatever their role, I don't have time to worry about it—there is a war to stop.

How do I communicate that to Barkah?

I pantomime drawing on my open palm, point to Barkah's bag. He understands immediately, hands me a swatch of fabric and a stick of charcoal. I lay the fabric flat on a dry bit of floor. I point to Barkah, make a single mark. I point to Lahfah, make another. Then a mark each for the other two Springers.

I look up at Barkah, waiting to make sure he understands.

Lahfah does first. "*Kayat,*" he says, pointing to himself, then he points at Barkah—"*jeg*"—then at the other two Springers—"*nar, bodek.*"

"He's counting," O'Malley says. "Their words for one through four."

Simple math, simple drawings. They understand.

I need to tell him I saw the Springer army. I point in the general direction of Uchmal. I start making marks as fast as I can: parallel, short, leaving enough space so I can make ten, twenty, thirty, forty.

I point to the marks. I point to Barkah's musket. I point to my head.

"Bang," I say. I slump down and play dead.

The two new Springers jump away, babbling to each other. Barkah quickly silences them.

He pulls a roll from his bag, flips it open—it's a map of Uchmal. Rough, but I can spot the river, the waterfall, the big main roads, the mostly round city wall. The mountains to the west, the lake to the north, that crescent-shaped clearing to the northeast. It's everything I could see from the top of the Observatory—I wonder if that's where he was when he drew it.

Barkah lays the map on the floor, then chirps a command.

Rekis and Tohdohbak scramble to the dirt and rubble. Each of them brings back a handful of small rocks.

Barkah takes a rock, holds it between his finger and thumb. He moves it through the air, makes a strange noise with his mouth—like a little boy's impression of a rocket engine.

He sets that rock on the map, looks at us.

"The shuttle," O'Malley says. "That's where the landing pad is. They know exactly where we are."

Have they known all along? I think of Aramovsky saying how the Springers could come attack us whenever they like.

Barkah taps my cluster of marks, then he places three rocks outside the city walls, at the edge of the crescent-shaped clearing. He reaches into his bag again, pulls out three small, wooden spiders. He sets them on the other side of the clearing. He looks at me, waits.

"That must be where the Springers want to fight," I say.

O'Malley leans in. "*Three* spiders. But the Springers got Coyotl's spider, didn't they? Shouldn't there only be two?"

"Maybe Barkah doesn't know we don't have it anymore. He's not marching with that army, so maybe he's not part of it?"

The prince pushes the three rocks representing the Springer forces into the middle of the clearing. He pushes the three spiders out to meet them.

He pulls out more wooden toys, the ones with the wheels. He sets them on the map, in the jungle behind the clearing, on the Springer side of the battle lines. Then, he starts placing rocks with the carts. Dozens of rocks. He places more on the sides, and even more in the jungle *behind* the spiders.

"A trap," I say. "They're only going to show a few of their troops, lure the spiders out into the open. They'll have our people surrounded from all sides. They'll destroy us."

How long have the spiders been slaughtering Springers? How

long have the Springers cowered underground, waiting for a chance to fight? And along we come, mastering the spiders, getting them to march to our command. Maybe this is the moment Barkah's people have been waiting for, a chance to put all the spiders in one place so they can battle it out once and for all.

I don't know how they will lure Aramovsky to that clearing, but I don't think it will take much. Even if Bishop recognizes the trap, will anyone listen to him? Aramovsky has total control. He has already said he wants to march to the jungle and bring the war to the Springers—he's going to get my people slaughtered in the process.

Barkah makes one final drawing: a few lines, a half-circle, and it's done—a ziggurat with the sun rising behind it.

"Daybreak," O'Malley says. "They're going to spring the trap at dawn."

"How do we stop it?"

O'Malley doesn't answer.

I take Barkah's hand. He pulls back at first, surprised, but maybe the look on my face lets him know I mean no harm. His skin is warm, his grip strong.

"We have to stop this battle," I say. "You are royalty, or whatever—*you* have to get them to stop."

O'Malley's eyebrows rise. "Royalty?"

"Something like that," I say. "The one we think is the leader, he has the same necklace Barkah has. They are the only Springers we've seen with that kind of decoration."

That inexpressive, stone-faced look washes over O'Malley's face.

"To stop the battle, we need a unified front," he says. "You ask our people for peace, Barkah asks his."

"But Aramovsky won the vote. You were there, he's not going

to listen to me. And we don't know if Barkah's father—or mother, or whatever—will listen to him."

O'Malley reaches down to the map, moves the spiders back to the edge, then does the same with the rocks representing the Springers. The two sides are once again poised for battle. He walks to where the floor is dirt, looking for something particular.

"The Springers hate us because of what the Grownups did, what the spiders do," O'Malley says. He bends, picks something up. "Many of our people hate the Springers because of Visca's death and Aramovsky fanning the flames."

He picks up another bit I can't see. He walks back to the map.

"Those are key reasons, but mostly, I think the sides hate each other because we're so *different*," he says. "Different is scary. What we need is a gesture that shows we're not so different after all. A gesture that sends a clear message—no one has to die, we can talk to each other."

He has two bits in his palm: a ground-up piece of green glass, and what might have once been a small coin.

O'Malley gestures at Barkah with the coin. "This is you." He then gestures to me with the piece of glass. "And this is you."

He places coin and glass next to each other in the center of the clearing, right between the two opposing armies.

"The two of you, together," he says. "Show both armies it's possible for us to get along. If our people want to fight, they have to go through you, Em. If Barkah's people want to fight, they have to go through him."

I imagine the lines of Springers with their muskets and knives and axes. O'Malley is asking me to stand in the middle of that clearing, face them down as they rush forward, eager to kill us and take their planet back.

I look at Barkah. He's staring at the map. I wonder if he's imagining being next to me in that clearing, staring at mechanical monsters pounding toward him, the same machines that killed his sibling, that drove people underground.

Will he be brave enough to stand there?

Will I?

Do we even have a choice?

The sun will rise in a few hours. I could go back to the shuttle, but I already tried talking my people out of war—I failed. Aramovsky is just too powerful. And I get the strong feeling that if Barkah could have stopped this on his own, he already would have.

O'Malley slowly reaches for his belt. I see Rekis and Tohdohbak stiffen, but O'Malley doesn't draw the knife—he removes the entire sheath, blade still inside. He sets it in front of Barkah. O'Malley raises both hands, palms up, takes a step back.

"Peace," he says. "Peace."

It is an impossibly simple association: hands empty, a show of not having weapons. The knife is dangerous; O'Malley could have used it to attack, but he makes a point of giving it to the being that could be his enemy, that could use it against him.

O'Malley is unarmed. Defenseless.

Barkah stares at the sheathed knife. He pulls the hatchet from his belt, the one he used to hack the long-necked monster to bits. He offers it to O'Malley, handle-first.

The combined gestures of trust are unmistakable.

O'Malley takes the hatchet. He bows.

"Thank you," he says.

Barkah, the Springer that might be a prince, picks up O'Malley's sheathed knife and slides it into his belt. That's not what O'Malley intended, I don't think, but maybe an exchange of weapons means something to the Springers.

Barkah picks up the piece of glass and the coin. He makes a fist around them, turns his body to face me square. There is something ritualistic about the motion, like he wants to make sure I understand how serious he is.

"Peace," he says. *"Hem, peace."*

Lahfah lets out a singing sound that makes me jump. Barkah and the other two Springers join in. I look to O'Malley. Wide-eyed, he shrugs.

The singing stops. Each of the Springers reaches into its bag and comes out with different kinds of food: a long vegetable that looks like a white carrot; a handful of berries in a pocket of cloth; a chunk of dried meat; and something that makes me think back to the warehouse and Farrar's poisoning—alien culture or not, there's no mistaking the round, bumpy form of a homemade cookie.

I'd pushed my hunger down, forced it to hide away, somehow. Now it rears its head, undeniable and overwhelming.

The Springers tear their bits of food in half, offer the halves to us. I wind up with dried meat and half a cookie; O'Malley holds some berries and part of the carrot.

"This is ceremonial," he says. "Sharing food, and the singing. It must be part of whatever they think the weapon exchange means."

I sniff the cookie. The scent sends my hunger soaring.

"Not eating might insult them," O'Malley says. "But we don't know if this stuff is poisonous."

I sniff the cookie again, smell a trace of that purple fruit.

"Only one way to find out," I say.

I pop the cookie into my mouth. Why not start with dessert? Sure enough, it is sweet—crumbly and chewy at the same time. There is a funny taste to it, but overall it's delicious. Maybe *anything* would be delicious after two days without eating.

"Oh well," O'Malley says. "If they can't give us safe food, we're going to starve anyway."

He takes a big bite of the carrot. He chews once, twice, then his eyes close in pleasure.

"So good," he says. "Actual, real *food*."

I bite into the meat. It's so spicy it burns my tongue a little, but I don't care. I eat it all.

The Springers eat, too, big mouths taking surprisingly dainty bites. They are giving O'Malley and me funny looks. Maybe the way we eat is disgusting to them. I glance at O'Malley—he's smiling, chewing with his mouth open. Berry juice dribbles down his chin.

Well, *he's* disgusting, anyway.

I think about Farrar's horrible experience. If this food does to me what that food did to him, it won't take long. I close my eyes, wait for the choking to begin.

It doesn't.

The only bad thing that happens is my stomach grumbles even louder.

It *worked*. We can eat their food. If we can figure out where to get the purple fruit, how to use it, the whole reason for Aramovsky's war will vanish.

"O'Malley, can you draw?"

"Of course I can."

I point to the cloth I marked up with lines. "Draw the purple fruit I brought back to the shuttle. Quickly."

O'Malley starts right in. His lines are soft, delicate and perfect. The shape of the fruit is exactly right. He adds shading—it looks so real I could almost pick it up.

Barkah starts stamping his left foot. Hard to tell for sure, but I think he's delighted.

I tap my fingertip on the drawing, look at the Springer prince.

"This," I say. "Where do we find this?"

He gives me an odd look, and I'm pretty sure I understand what it means—he thinks I'm kidding.

I thump the drawing hard.

"*Please*. Where do we find this? Show us!"

Barkah glances at Lahfah. Lahfah hobbles to the double doors, motions for us to follow.

Outside, the rain has stopped. Twin moons shine down, lighting up the jungle with a spooky glow.

Lahfah hobbles to a tree, taps it. I look up, searching for the purple fruits. I don't see any.

"Where are they?" O'Malley asks. "Oh no, what if they aren't in season?"

Rekis and Tohdohbak both make that broken-glass noise: they are laughing at us.

The two Springers hop to the tree. Their hands grip a vine that clings tightly to the trunk. Together, they pull once, twice—on the third yank, the vine rips away from the trunk, chunks of bark coming with it. Rekis pulls a knife, slices the vine at eye-level. The severed end dangles there, held aloft by the rest of the vine that snakes through the branches above.

"Maybe they thought we meant something else," O'Malley says. "Should I go get the drawing?"

I would answer, but I'm holding my breath.

Rekis and Tohdohbak grip the part of the vine that's growing up from the ground. Together, they count—"*Kayat, jeg, nar*"—and they pull. The wet ground at the base of the vine breaks, lifts up a little.

"It can't be," I say. "All this time, it was that easy?"

O'Malley looks at me. "I don't understand."

"*Kayat, jeg, nar,*" and they pull again. The ground gives way. They stumble back, holding the vine. From the end dangles the purple fruit, thin strands of white fiber sticking off it, clods of dirt clinging to the purple surface and strands alike.

"We were looking in the wrong place," O'Malley says, astonished. "It's not fruit at all—it's a *root*."

The root of the vines that cover city streets, jungle trees, buildings, ruins . . . the secret to our survival has been all around us, all this time.

"Vines are everywhere," O'Malley says. "Aramovsky is taking us to war for something that's *everywhere* we look."

War.

I look at the night sky. Off to the east, the first hints of glowing red—maybe an hour until dawn.

"Barkah, we need to leave," I say. I reach out, tap his fist, the one holding the coin and the piece of glass. "We have to stop the battle."

He barks out orders. Rekis fast-hops into the building, comes out with the map and O'Malley's drawing of the fruit. Rekis keeps the map—Barkah takes the fruit drawing, rolls it up and carefully puts it in his bag.

The Springer prince pauses. He looks at the knife in his belt, traces the handle with his fingertips, admiring the weapon by both sight and touch.

Then he barks more orders.

Rekis and Tohdohbak plunge into the jungle, headed for the trail. Barkah follows, gesturing for us to walk with him. Lahfah unslings his musket and lumbers along behind, a hobbling rear guard.

Together, we're heading off to stop a war.

And, hopefully, not get killed in the process.

We move through the jungle. It's still dark, yet it's already getting hot. A thick mist glows with the light of two moons, blankets the endless, overgrown ruins.

Rekis and Tohdohbak are out front, making sure the trail is safe. O'Malley and I stay with Barkah. Lahfah is in the rear, struggling to keep up.

Our feet squish in thin mud. As we walk, I rub that mud on my face, tie new vines around me, smear juice in my hair and skin. If something goes wrong, I want to be able to fade away into the jungle.

O'Malley smiles at me.

"We're going to save everyone," he says. "I can feel it."

The moonlight seems to settle in his blue eyes, makes them sparkle. In all that's happened over the past few days, I'd forgotten how beautiful he is. He's not a warrior, yet he faced grave danger to be at my side. In a way, that's even braver than anything Bishop has done.

O'Malley—*Kevin*—sees me looking at him. He makes an awkward smile, then shakes his head and faces down the path.

"What?" I say. "What's so funny?"

"Nothing."

"No, come on, tell me."

When he looks at me again, the smile is gone.

"I told you I loved you," he says. "You didn't say how you feel about me."

I look down, watch my booted feet splashing along the trail. Why didn't I tell him how I feel? Because I didn't know for sure. I still don't. And besides, we have a war to stop.

"This isn't the right time to discuss it," I tell him.

A little bit of the light drains from his eyes. He's still smiling, but it's not quite as divine as before.

"I guess it's never the right time," he says. "After we stop this battle, what then? We have to gather food, learn to use the purple root, fix what machines we can, deal with Bello . . . there's always something, Em."

"A war isn't just a *something*. Can we focus on that for now?"

O'Malley's hands fidget with the hatchet Barkah gave him.

"It's all right," he says. "I get it. You want to be with Bishop."

Oh my *gods*—boys are exasperating.

"That's not what I want."

He raises an eyebrow. "It's not? You could have fooled me."

He speeds up, pulling ahead of me to walk side by side with Rekis.

"Hey there," O'Malley says with forced joviality. "And how is my favorite nonhuman today?"

Rekis laughs a broken-glass laugh, clearly delighted to be spoken to by an "alien."

O'Malley told me he loves me. Bishop didn't. Is that because Bishop can't . . . or because he doesn't?

"Hem?"

Barkah leans closer, blinking. I know, instantly, that the alien is asking if I'm okay. Our two races are drastically different, yet we can read each other somewhat, understand each other's intent. If we can do that, we can overcome any language barrier.

"I'm fine," I say. "Thank you."

Barkah points down the path. *"Kevin?"*

Is Barkah asking if O'Malley is all right, or if I'm upset because of him? Either way, the only answer I have is to shrug. I doubt Barkah knows what that gesture means, but if he's going to spend time with teenage humans, he'll figure it out soon enough.

When Matilda created me, why couldn't she have just

programmed away these stupid emotions? Life is hard enough without having to worry about who likes who.

Maybe I should go talk to O'Malley. When I said, *That's not what I want,* maybe what I meant was, *I don't know what I want.* O'Malley has his faults, sure, but he's been behind me every step of the way, almost from the moment he woke up. He supports me. He believes in me. And, unlike Bishop, O'Malley comes right out and says how he feels about me.

Things have been so desperate, so crazy, maybe I don't know what I want because I haven't had a moment to actually *think* about what I want. Now that I do . . . maybe I want the same thing O'Malley does.

And that scares me.

I see him up ahead, walking with Rekis and Tohdohbak. The hanging fog is a haze around them, blocking my view of anything farther down the path.

Rekis's long tail rises straight up, goes stiff. Barkah grabs me, stops me even as Rekis does the same thing with O'Malley. It's just like when Visca or Bishop put a fist in the air—a noiseless symbol for everyone to freeze.

Far up ahead in the mist, I see two figures approaching. Humans. I can't make them out.

O'Malley is farther ahead than I am. He must be able to see them better, because he calls out: "Coyotl, is that you?"

"Hey, O'Malley."

Coyotl's voice—he's *alive!*

O'Malley lets out a whoop of joy. I start to make the same noise, but Barkah squeezes my arm tighter, telling me to stay quiet.

"Hey," O'Malley says, his excitement audible, "is that Beckett with you?"

From the fog, another voice answers. "It is."

Beckett? They're *both* alive? Maybe Muller is as well. If I can take them to the battlefield with me, and with Barkah, *and* with the secret of the purple root—Aramovsky's power will evaporate like so much jungle mist.

I want to run to them, but Barkah won't let me go.

"We didn't expect you, O'Malley," Beckett calls. "You're not supposed to be here. Where's Em?"

Why would Beckett say *You're not supposed to be here*? Have they already been back to the shuttle? But if they have, why would Aramovsky send Beckett back out looking for me? Beckett is a gear . . . he's not suited for stumbling through a hostile jungle in the middle of the night.

"I have to be honest with you, O'Malley," Coyotl says. "I think your new friend is really, *really* ugly."

For an instant, the surrounding fog flashes like we're inside a cloud filled with lightning. Tohdohbak screams—his body is ripped apart, pieces of him scattering through the jungle.

THIRTY-EIGHT

Tohdohbak's death cry echoes through the trees. The blazing light blinks out as fast as it flared up, leaving me seeing spots. I think of El-Saffani.

Barkah slams into me, knocking me off the path to the right. We crash hard in the wet underbrush.

I scramble to my feet, crouching, hands tight on the shovel. We're under attack. Tohdohbak is dead. Coyotl or Beckett must have killed him. Back at the shuttle, Borjigin was working on the spider cannon. Did he fix it? Is that cannon like the Grownups' bracelets—the weapons that killed El-Saffani?

I can't see through this fog.

O'Malley, shouting for help, terrified.

I stay low, in the cover of the underbrush, and move toward the trail's edge. Barkah is on my right, doing the same thing, musket clutched in his odd hands.

A burst of red light blinds me as a *whump* rattles my ears, knocks me flat to my back. The world spins. I hear a Springer screaming in agony.

I roll to my hands and knees, ignore the pain as I slowly push myself up. My legs feel weak. I grab my shovel.

I see Barkah, his musket barrel leveled over a fallen log made fuzzy by blue moss that gleams with tiny spots of wetness. The hammer of his weapon is cocked back. He's trying to find a target through the fog. I run to him, kneel down.

I look over the log—something fist-sized and black, spinning through the air toward us. It hits the jungle floor, bounces once, then bursts with a *whump* and a flash of red light—an invisible punch slams me backward through the underbrush. I hit the ground hard, skid, roll into a thick bush.

Every part of me hurts. My ears ring. The ground seems to lurch and buck beneath me, even though I'm lying flat. What is happening? Where is O'Malley?

A groan: Barkah, maybe twenty steps away, crumpled and unmoving, on his side at the base of a tree, his musket next to him. He's hurt. Together, he and I can stop a war—I have to help him, protect him.

Somehow, I held on to my shovel. I lean on it, fight to regain my balance as I struggle to stand.

I hear footsteps. I drop down, let the underbrush cover me.

Through the thick fog, someone is approaching Barkah. Black coveralls. Coyotl? Beckett? Moonlight gleams blue and maroon off the person's arms and legs. No . . . those reflections are from a metallic frame worn on his body . . .

. . . a *pitch-black,* gnarled body . . .

The bottom falls out of my world . . . those aren't coveralls.

I'm looking at a Grownup.

It's big, not quite Bishop's size, and wears some kind of suit. A mask covers its face, clear bubbles of glass showing the red eyes beneath. Lines of reflective metal run down its thick arms and legs. On its right arm, just below the elbow, is a silver bracelet, white stone glowing softly, long point ending behind the wrist.

A spider cannon didn't kill Tohdohbak—a bracelet did. Just like the bracelets that killed El-Saffani.

In that horrid instant, everything becomes clear. That thing I couldn't place, that feeling that I had missed something: Bello wasn't the only one in the lumpy ship.

Brewer said the Grownups couldn't survive on Omeyocan, couldn't breathe the planet's air—it never occurred to me that they could bring their own air with them.

Overwritten Bello was nothing more than a decoy. We focused on her when the *real* threat had left the lumpy ship before we even arrived. When I sent Coyotl, Beckett and Muller out, the Grownups must have grabbed them.

Someone joins the Grownup—it's Beckett, dressed in black coveralls, wearing a bracelet on his right arm.

Beckett has been overwritten.

Coyotl, too. He must be. And, if he's still alive, Muller.

Beckett and the Grownup cautiously move toward Barkah. They don't see me. I am a camouflaged black blob crouching in the black shadows, hidden by leaves and vines.

I could slink away into the jungle. If they catch me, I will be overwritten. Everything that I am will be erased.

Barkah moves weakly, one of his three eyes a wet, ruined wreck.

The Grownup takes a step closer to him.

That tingling feeling, spreading down my scalp. Rage detonates inside me like a crater-making bomb. Our creators . . . they bring death everywhere they go.

Yes, I could run, but the time for running is over.

I am the wind . . .

My pain forgotten, I lean forward in a careful jog that grows to a silent sprint.

Barkah struggles to rise, looks up, sees the Grownup.

"Ugly bastards," the Grownup says, and points his bracelet right at Barkah's face.

. . . I am death.

My foot cracks a branch. The Grownup turns, sees me coming, swings the bracelet-arm in my direction, but the wrinkled abomination is too old and too slow.

I thrust the shovel forward, putting all my strength, weight and speed behind the blow. The point punches into the black throat, *through* it. I feel metal on bone, the impact shuddering down the wooden handle, and then no resistance at all.

A head tumbles through the air, trailing a curving arc of red-gray blood. The mask flies away. The body, lifeless and limp, sags to the ground. The head lands, rolls, stops.

Beckett stares at the severed head, his face contorted with horror. I start toward him, but stop instantly when his arm snaps up, bracelet point aimed at my chest.

He's five steps away. Too far—I'm as good as dead.

Beckett lowers his arm slightly, seems confused. Why doesn't he shoot me?

"Matilda? Is that *you* under all that gunk?"

Red-gray drips from my shovel blade.

I take one step closer—his arm snaps up again. I freeze.

"Ah, of course, you're *Em,*" he says. "So strange. I haven't seen your face in a thousand years. You look so young. But then again, I guess I look young, too."

It's him, and it's not. There's just enough moonlight for me to make out his red hair, his tan skin, the gear symbol on his forehead. This is the shell of a boy I knew, yet his familiar eyes burn with a hate far beyond the years of his body.

"Go away," I say. "Leave us. Get in that ship and return to the *Xolotl*. No one else has to die."

He shakes his head. "I'm supposed to take you to her. But you know what? If her shell dies, then the old hag has no future. No one will listen to someone who is just going to wither and crumble." He grins. "If I kill you, that creates a power vacuum. And nature *abhors* a vacuum."

His bracelet's white stone glows brighter.

A thunderous *bang* from right behind me.

Beckett blinks, confused.

Blood spurts from a neat hole in his throat. Red and rich, not grayish and sickly, it sprays onto the jungle floor. He tries to say something, but no sound comes out. He takes a single, weak step forward, then falls flat on his face.

He doesn't move.

Barkah's musket is across his lap, smoke still curling from the barrel. He's trying to reload it, his every movement clearly an exercise in agony.

I pull the bracelet off Beckett's limp arm, slide my own hand through the opening. When the ring is almost to my elbow, something contracts, squeezes. The bracelet clings firmly on my arm. Its lethal point is just behind my wrist.

If only I knew how to make the damn thing fire.

I kneel by Barkah's side. "Can you move?"

His middle eye is a mangled, horrible sight. The other two green eyes blink, look at me, show recognition.

He tries to put the rod into the barrel, winces. I set my shovel down, take the musket and do it for him. He hands me a bullet. I pack that down as well, slide the rod into its holding slot, then hand the musket back.

I hold my left hand in front of him, palm up. I point to him, then place my right pointer and middle finger on the upturned palm. I bounce them, doing my best impression of a Springer's hop.

"Move," I say. "Can you *move*?"

"Move," he answers. He understands. *"Hem, move."*

Shovel in one hand, I reach under Barkah with the other and struggle to lift his weight. The alien makes sharp grunts of pain. The blast threw him hard into that tree, maybe broke things inside him.

I have to get the prince to safety—but I also have to find O'Malley.

From behind us, another flash of white lights up the fog. How many Grownups are out here? The enemy seems to be everywhere; the jungle is made of them.

We stay in the underbrush, move parallel to the path. Dragging the heavy Springer along with me, I am not the wind anymore. I am *noise* . . . I am a *target* . . .

Then in front of us, a dead Springer, stomach sliced open, splashes of blue blood and yellowish innards strewn about the wet vines and dead leaves. I recognize the curve of the mouth: *Rekis*.

Barkah lets out a mournful groan. The sound is heartbreaking.

He points just past the body, at Rekis's musket. The hammer in the middle, it's cocked back. It's loaded.

Noise from behind us: human shouts and calls, bodies moving through the mist. I recognize one of the voices—Coyotl.

Barkah gently pushes me away. He stands on his own two legs, points to me, points to Rekis's musket.

I have the bracelet, but I don't know how to use it. I drop the shovel and pick up the gun.

Barkah takes one experimental hop forward. His body shudders in pain, but he pushes past it, takes a second hop.

"Hem, move."

He wants to run. He wants to hide. That's the smart thing to do. Just as I need him to end this war before it starts, he needs me to make it out of here alive. The two of us fleeing into the jungle is the smart thing.

But I will not leave O'Malley.

I wave a hand in the direction of the trail.

"Go," I say. "Move. Escape."

His two remaining eyes show despair. He doesn't want to leave me, but he is in no shape to fight.

A rustling to our right. Our muskets rise up instantly, aim at a shaking bush—Lahfah hops out from behind the dark leaves.

I point at him, then at Barkah.

"Get him out of here," I say quietly to Lahfah. "Move."

Maybe he understands me, or maybe he just wants to get his prince clear. Lahfah pulls at Barkah, urging him down the trail.

I turn and run into the mist, toward the danger, toward O'Malley. My body feels electric, on edge.

I hear voices. I slide to my right, into the underbrush, crouch between two wide, curving leaves that cover me completely. A small gap between them lets me see down the trail. Moonlit mist surrounds me. This is the perfect spot. The shadows are my friends.

"She killed Beckett!" A Grownup man's voice. I hear him, but can't quite see him. "And Visca! She cut off Visca's damn *head*! I'm going to kill that little bitch!"

Something about that voice is familiar, but I can't place it. Another voice answers, one I know by heart, one that makes every inch of me crawl with fear.

"Farrar, don't you dare."

That voice . . . *Matilda*.

She was on the lumpy ship with Bello. She's *here*. She's come for me, to erase me.

"Hurt her, and you *die,*" she says. Her voice is coming closer. "Or I'll make sure your shell dies. I'll watch you wither away to nothing. Find out if there are any more hopping vermin around here, kill them, then catch her."

I hear footsteps squish in mud, hear small branches crack and snap—they are coming closer.

Even if they're old and slow, they're still faster than the wounded Barkah and Lahfah—if I let Matilda and Farrar pass by, they will quickly catch up to the Springers.

Coming down the trail, through the mist, I see a Grownup. A little shorter than I am, moving with painful, jerky motions: it is Matilda.

And with her, taller, *thicker,* old and wrinkled but made of solid muscle—that has to be Farrar.

They both wear masks and the suits of thin, shiny metal. Like the one I just killed. *Visca* . . . I killed Grownup Visca.

Farrar comes first, a few steps ahead of Matilda. He wears a bracelet on his extended arm, sweeps it left, then right, then straight down the trail. He doesn't see me. In seconds he will pass by me.

I can end this, *all* of it, right now. I can shoot him with the musket at close range, drop him.

And then I must kill Matilda.

The musket will be empty. I can use the wide, flat end . . . I can swing it hard, smash it into her face, knock her down . . . then I will cave in her skull.

For El-Saffani. For Beckett. For Coyotl. For Muller. For Latu. For Visca. For Harris. For Bello. For Yong.

Matilda is my enemy . . . kill her, and I will be forever free.

She *deserves* to die, deserves it for the thousands of humans she has murdered, for her slaughter of *millions* of Springers, for the culture she tried to destroy, for the ship she transformed into a nightmare, and for the enormous city she turned into cinders.

Farrar and Matilda creep closer.

I stay so very still.

I am the wind . . . I am death . . .

Five steps away.

My musket's hammer is already cocked. I silently raise the barrel, aim it to my left. I won't even have to extend it past the leaf: Farrar will move right past me.

Three steps.

I put my finger on the trigger.

One step.

On my right, the big leaf rustles, splashing me with beaded rainwater as it is pushed aside.

The red-eyed, masked face of a Grownup is only inches away. How could I have not heard it coming? It is the biggest Grownup I have ever seen, with wide shoulders and huge muscles stretching out the gnarled black skin.

Then I realize how it snuck up on me.

It's *Bishop*.

A flash of black smashes into my face.

As I fall, I see the two moons high above—one blue, one maroon—and then nothing.

PART V

DESTINY AND DOOM

THIRTY-NINE

I wake.

My head pounds and throbs. Feels like it's full of jagged rocks, grinding against each other.

I'm on my back. Lights above blind me. I blink madly. I try to raise a hand to block the lights, but I can't move.

"She's coming to."

That voice . . . the hiss of a Grownup, a woman, but so familiar. I almost recognize it.

"Thank you," says a second voice, one that is unmistakable and full of the promise of death—*Matilda*.

She has me. Panic bites deep. I struggle to push it back, to stay in control.

I can see a little now. The lights above are embedded in a carved ceiling. I'm indoors. I try to sit up, but something cool, solid and curved pins my wrists, my waist, my ankles.

White fabric to my left, to my right.

I'm in a coffin.

I yank and twist and lurch. I've broken bars like these before, and I'm much stronger than I was then. I pull until the coffin shakes with my effort, until my bones feel like they are going to break . . .

Something is different.

These bars, they're smooth, not rough against my skin. They aren't rusted . . . they're *new*.

My arms give out in mid-pull, as if my muscles, bones and skin realized escape is impossible before my brain does.

I lie there, chest heaving, not knowing what comes next.

A head leans in, silhouetted by the bright light. A Grownup. Wrinkled, charcoal skin covered by a mask. Through that mask, I see one bulging red eye, and a white patch where the other eye used to be.

"Hello, pretty girl," Matilda says.

I can't move. Death stares down at me.

She turns, looks somewhere to her left. "Lower the sides of the husk. I want to get a good look at her."

A buzz, then a soft clacking sound. All four sides of the coffin slide down and away. On my left, Matilda, and just past her, a closed golden coffin—it's been polished until the carvings gleam with a lifelike vibrance. On my right, a waist-high, curved, red metal wall with that strange symbol engraved on it in black.

I'm in the Observatory.

Farther down on my right, two wrinkled Grownups—wearing the same metal-and-mask array as Matilda—are standing on the pedestal platform. One is tall and thin. The other is the shortest I have seen yet; by height alone, I know it is the Grownup version of Gaston.

I look past my bound feet, knowing what I will see—the big, black X, shackles and crown dangling. Behind the X, the mural of an old man, a younger man driving a knife through his chest.

Everything is clean. All the dust is gone.

Where is O'Malley? Did he escape? I hope Barkah and Lahfah got away.

Somewhere behind me, I hear a voice I know all too well.

"You have what you wanted," Aramovsky says. "Now give me what I need."

My body surges, thrums with sudden, blind hope.

"Aramovsky, kill her! Get me out of here!"

I thrash at my restraints with newfound strength. He has to strike fast . . . how many circle-stars did he bring with him? He . . .

Wait . . . what did he say?

Matilda continues to stare down at me. I hear footsteps, then I see him, Aramovsky, standing beside her, my spear in his hand.

He is wearing red robes, just like those of the torturers carved into the Observatory walls.

My body starts to shake. I struggle to breathe. Why is he standing with her? Why isn't he *fighting* her?

Matilda reaches up a wrinkled, old arm and rests her hand on Aramovsky's red-robed shoulder.

"You're lucky, boy," she says. "You lured my shell away from the others, but she was almost killed by that disgusting vermin army."

I can't believe what I'm hearing. Bello didn't just give Aramovsky the secret of the symbols so he could take over as leader—she told him where to send me.

He gave me up to Matilda.

"We didn't know there were so many of them," he says. "If you had grabbed her at the gate, like you were supposed to, she wouldn't have been at risk." He tilts his head toward me. "Besides—she looks fine."

Matilda adjusts her mask, as if the fit bothers her.

"She looks *filthy*. But we did run late. Sometimes old bodies do not react as quickly as one would like. At any rate, a deal is a deal." She looks off to her left. "Bring them."

I hear heavy footsteps approaching. I crane my head up to see—it's Coyotl, young and strong and smiling, carrying a large, carved box.

I feel heavier, like I'm sinking into this coffin, like I'm drowning in darkness. Coyotl has been overwritten—same as Bello, same as Beckett. Coyotl walks and talks and looks like my friend, the one who taught me how to sharpen the spear, but my friend is gone forever.

He sets the box down on my thighs.

"See, Matilda?" he says. "I told you she was in good shape."

A whining tone to his voice. He is desperate to please her, but Matilda is far from pleased.

"*Your* body has far less damage, Uriah," she says to him. "Look at her. She hasn't fixed anything. Some of those scars are never going to come out."

Coyotl shrugs. "You might have to hose her down first. All that camouflage on her face . . . somehow she fooled herself into thinking she's a knight."

A *knight*? Is that what the circle-stars are really called?

"The folly of youth," Matilda says. "Such beauty, yet she doesn't care. I was like that once. I won't make that same mistake again. I'll treasure my youth. This time, I'll savor every last moment of it."

Coyotl reaches into the box, pulls something out, holds it up for Aramovsky to see—it's a silver bracelet. The ceiling lights play off the white stone, gleam against the long metal point.

"Twenty of them," Coyotl says.

Aramovsky slowly reaches out a trembling hand, takes the bracelet.

"*Twenty,*" he says. "With these and our war machines, we'll slaughter the Springers. How do I use it?"

Matilda pulls Aramovsky closer to her. I see his lip curl slightly, involuntarily.

"Remember our deal," she says, her words syrupy sweet. "When you attack, you will *not* use people on the list I gave you. Their creators are waiting—those shells must not be risked."

He hasn't attacked yet. There's still time.

Aramovsky nods. "I understand. And should I still send you Bishop, Gaston and Borjigin?"

"Yes," she says. "And make sure you do it before the battle. We need to take out the strongest first, a few at a time, so there are no more accidents. Make sure they come alone, and through the entrance I showed you. We'll gas them there so they don't put up a struggle—these children are dangerous." Matilda looks down at me. "You cut off Visca's head with a shovel? Really, my dear, that's so . . . well, so *savage*."

An insane cackle bubbles out from behind her mask.

Aramovsky lifts the box off my thighs. He starts to turn away, then stops, turns back, leans close.

"Don't be afraid," he says. "The gods want this for you."

He means it. He believes every word.

I spit in his face.

He stands, shocked and angry, spit clinging to one closed eye. He wipes it away with the sleeve of his red robe.

"You've always thought you were smarter than me," he says.

"Not smarter," I say. "*Deadlier*. Tell your gods I'll send you to meet them very soon."

Coyotl guides Aramovsky away, somewhere behind me. They must be walking to the racks with the empty plastic bins.

"Leave her be," Coyotl says. "I'll walk you out and show you how to use the bracelets."

My brave words ring hollow. The reality of my situation pushes down on me. I have failed in every way. Barkah's people outnumber mine a hundred to one, maybe more, but those bracelets will even the odds. Aramovsky is only going to use people that don't have a living Grownup ready to take over their body. Many of those that fight will die, sacrifices to the God of Blood. Those that do not fight will be rounded up a few at a time, then their minds will be wiped, their young bodies used as a vessel for ancient evil.

Just as I will be used.

Matilda delicately reaches for my face. I thrash my head away, lurch at my restraints, but there is no escape. When her hand comes close enough, I bite at it.

She pauses, her fingertips just out of reach.

"Biting, *again*?"

Matilda walks to the platform, grabs something there, brings it back. She's holding a thin red cane. She shows it to me.

"Remember when Grampa used one of these on us if we cursed? You know what he always said—*Spare the rod, spoil the child*."

A flick of her wrist raises it, another flick brings it down on my stomach.

Agony engulfs me. My body convulses: my muscles tighten so suddenly and completely that wrists and ankles and hips smash against the bars holding them down. I *burn,* I'm burning up I'm going to die *I don't want to die I—*

She lifts the rod and the pain stops.

My breath comes rushing back. I taste blood.

"Silly girl," Matilda says. "You bit through your lip. I suppose that serves you right, but don't damage yourself any further."

The withered hand reaches for my face. I don't want that pain again, so I close my eyes and stay still.

Rough, dry fingers on my forehead, sliding across my skin.

"Look what you've done to my pretty hair," she says. "I can't wait to feel a brush slide through it once again. It's been so long."

This dead thing is *petting* me. I'm terrified and disgusted. I'm hateful and alone.

She makes a *tsk-tsk* sound. I feel her pull something out of my hair.

I force myself to open my eyes and look at my killer. If I am to die, I will die facing my enemy.

She's holding a bit of twig.

"As soon as the transfer is done, I'm going to take a long bath," she says. "I'm going to clean up this filth you've caked on yourself. This is no way for an empress to look."

"Brewer said he was on our side," I say. "Why did he lie about the shuttle being the only way down here?"

"He didn't lie. There used to be five shuttles. During the rebellion, Brewer's people destroyed all but one—then he locked us out of the hangar. When you made me take you to the hangar, I didn't think it would be open, but Brewer unlocked it for you. That was the first time I'd laid eyes on a shuttle in two centuries."

"Then what about Bello's ship?"

"We built it," Matilda says. "We thought we might need a way down to Omeyocan someday, and two hundred years is a lot of time to make contingency plans. Brewer ruined the shuttle fleet, but there is so much of the *Xolotl* he doesn't control, where he can't see what's happening. The ship we made isn't as elegant as the one you stole, but it was good enough to get thirteen of us safely down to the surface. While you dealt with Bello, the rest of us came here and prepared."

I look her up and down, take in her old, ruined body. How could she have reached the top of the Observatory in order to get down here?

She keeps petting me. I have to clench my teeth together to resist biting her again.

"I'm sure you're wondering about all those steps," she says. "Sometimes it's hard to remember how unimaginative I was at your age. There are other entrances to this place, pretty girl. Do you think I wanted to spend my next life trudging up and down *three thousand steps*? If you and your Bishop had walked around the temple and looked *carefully,* you would have found a normal entrance that leads right to this very spot. No symbol required, no steps involved."

She called it a *temple*. Just like Aramovsky did.

My head hurts so bad . . . it feels like my brain has been crushed and smashed, and this sense of failure is making it worse.

"Coyotl and Beckett were overwritten," I say. "Is Muller still alive?"

"You sending those three out was a wonderful break for us. And with a functioning pentapod, no less. Little Victor Muller is locked up in an Observatory prison cell, where he'll stay until we retake the shuttle. We will take the shuttle up to the *Xolotl* instead of the awful ship we came down in. Aramovsky said you didn't take any joy rides, fortunately, so there should be enough fuel for the return trip."

The taller of the two Grownups on the pedestal platform calls out: "We are ready."

That's the woman. Her voice, so old, yet so familiar . . .

Please, don't let it be her . . . please don't let it be her . . .

"Is that Spingate?"

Matilda laughs. "Spingate was on Brewer's side. I had Bishop cave in her skull with one of those silly tools she liked so much. Don't worry, pretty girl—Aramovsky will make sure your Spingate is armed and in the first wave he sends against the vermin."

"No! You can't make her fight—she's pregnant!"

"Amazing," Matilda says. "You hormone-engorged little brats didn't waste any time, did you? Rutting around like animals. How about you, *Em*?" She spits my name like it's a curse word. "Were you a sinful slut like Theresa? Did you steal my virginity from me?"

"I didn't do anything. I don't know about anyone else, just Spingate and Gaston."

"*What?*"

The word is a shout—commanding, insistent—that comes from the pedestal platform. The little Grownup steps onto the floor and walks toward us. He stops next to Matilda.

"Captain," she says. I'm surprised to hear respect in her voice . . . does this tiny man intimidate her?

He stares down at me through his mask, two red eyes thrumming with excitement and intensity.

"The Spingate shell is pregnant with my child?"

I don't know what to say. Will they want to kill her and the baby, or will the truth keep her off the battlefield? This creature is a thousand years old, but there has to be *some* bit of the Gaston I know still in there.

I nod.

He turns to Matilda. "I will tell Aramovsky to bring her to me." Without waiting for an answer, he walks off into the shadows.

One-eyed Matilda seems rattled. She gestures to the platform, to the lone Grownup standing there.

"Obviously, that is not Theresa Spingate," Matilda says. "But I'm sure you know this one's shell. May I present the lovely and talented Doctor Kenzie Smith?"

The Grownup on the platform bows stiffly. She starts to stand, then freezes, a gnarled hand going to her back.

"Oh," she says. "Dammit, that *hurts*." She slowly straightens, holds on to a pedestal for balance. "Let's get this started. I need to sit down soon."

Matilda rubs her nasty hands together. The skin is so rough I can *hear* it.

"Finally, we're ready," she says.

"Not *you,* Matilda," Smith says. "I'm afraid Bishop hit your shell on the head a little too hard. There could be a concussion. We have to wait so that I can make sure there isn't any damage I need to fix first."

Matilda's one eye swirls madly. She's furious. She glares at someone in the corner. I crane my head up to see: the hulking form of Old Bishop. He's been standing there the entire time, silent, unmoving.

"You stupid oaf," she says to him. "I told you to be careful."

I hear concern in her hiss of a voice, perhaps even fear. Brewer said the longer we were alive, forming our own memories and connections, the less chance the process had of working. But it worked on Bello, Coyotl and Beckett, so it will likely work on me—unless my grinding headache causes problems, somehow.

"I've waited so long," Matilda says. "A few hours more won't matter."

She gives my hair a final pat.

"Since you've been so difficult, my dear, let's watch something together while we wait. Kenzie, open it."

The golden coffin to my left makes the same sound mine

made. The sides lower. My heart shatters. I want to wake up, I want all of this to be a horrible dream.

It's O'Malley.

He's lying on white linen, held down by the same kind of bars that hold me. He's blinking, just coming awake.

"O'Malley! It's Em! Look at me!"

He turns his head, terror wrinkling his face. He sees me, recognizes me, then starts looking everywhere—up, left, right, down toward his feet. He cranes his head back, trying to see behind him.

"Em . . . are we in the Observatory?"

On the platform, one of the pedestals starts to glow.

"Pre-imprinting preparations complete," Smith says. "We're ready. Bring in Kevin."

I'm confused for a moment—Kevin O'Malley is right next to me—then with a chest-ripping blast of horror I understand.

And so does he.

"No," he says. "Don't do this!"

Past our feet, I see Coyotl helping a masked Grownup walk toward the black X, a Grownup so old and withered he can barely move.

"Is it time?" the old one says. "Is it finally my time?"

The voice sounds ancient, like it's made of dust and worm-eaten wood. And yet, I recognize it, instantly.

It is the voice of Kevin O'Malley.

In the coffin next to me, my friend starts to scream.

FORTY

Behind the clear mask, Old O'Malley's red eyes appear cloudy, unfocused.

Matilda pets my hair.

"Just watch, little one," she says. "Your turn is coming soon."

I shake my head, over and over. "Please, don't kill him."

O'Malley pulls at his restraints. His eyes blaze with animal panic. He grunts desperately, throws himself left and right.

Matilda is standing between my coffin and his. She turns, raises the red cane, snaps it down on his stomach. His back arches so suddenly and severely I wonder if his spine might snap. His throat grinds out a *guh-guh-guh-guh* sound that makes me scream in helpless rage.

She lifts the rod.

"You will not hurt your body, not now," she says to him. "Struggle again, you get the rod again."

Coyotl mostly drags Old O'Malley to the black X. Old Bishop comes over to help. Together, they raise the shriveled Grownup's arms, lock the shackles around his wrists, then restrain his ankles.

Bishop removes Old O'Malley's mask. Those disgusting folds of wet flesh—they either cover the Grownup's mouth, or they *are* the mouth. Sickening to look at.

Coyotl slides the black crown onto the withered creature's head. Rheumy red eyes stare out with a combination of confusion and excitement. The old monster starts to cough.

"Hard to breathe . . . I need my mask."

Coyotl gives him a hard pat on the cheek. "Don't worry, Kev . . . in a few minutes, the mask won't matter."

The old one's red eyes seem to go clear for a moment. He stares at my O'Malley.

"By the gods," the old thing says. "It's . . . it's *me*."

The young and the ancient lock eyes.

A low growl starts in my O'Malley's throat, builds to a scream as he starts to thrash against his restraints.

Matilda lowers the rod.

My O'Malley again goes rigid. He shudders and bucks, tries to beg her to stop but his mouth won't form words.

"*You horrible* BITCH*,*" I roar. "Stop it or I'll *kill you*!"

Matilda turns to me, smacks the rod down on my thigh. The charge sets my body ablaze. I try not to scream—I fail.

She lifts the rod.

"No cursing," she says. "Children should know the rules."

Old O'Malley is half giggling, half coughing.

"My shell is so *strong,*" he says. "So much vigor!"

Everything grows blurry as tears fill my eyes.

"*Please,* Matilda!" I'll beg, I'll plead, I'll sacrifice myself, whatever it takes. "Let him go and I swear I'll let you do it to me."

My O'Malley's head turns fast to face me, his features

contorted with both fear and anger. "Em, no! Don't promise them anything!"

Even now, with blood on his lips from where he bit through them, his cheeks streaked with tears, he is beautiful. How could I not have told this boy that I loved him? I am desperate for him to live, even if that means my own death.

I tear my eyes away from him, force myself to look at her.

"Matilda, *please*." My voice is weak, subservient. "I swear, I'll do whatever you want. I won't fight."

She pats my head, makes that *tsk-tsk* sound with her unseen mouth.

"Oh, my dear, you can fight all you like—it won't make any difference."

"Preparations complete," Old Smith calls out. "Ometeotl?"

"Ready for instructions, Doctor," the room answers.

"Perform transference power-up and preflight checks."

The entire room hums, a long droning sound that makes my hair stand on end.

Coyotl walks over to my O'Malley. The overwritten circle-star leans close, the expression of gleeful hate something I would have never thought could exist on his face.

"This is going to hurt," Coyotl says. His words ring with a sick joy. "*So* much."

My O'Malley can't fight anymore. He has nothing left. All he can do is cry.

"Em, please," he says in a whisper. "Help me."

Sobs rack my body. I can't do anything—I am powerless. Leader, empress, monster, friend, enemy . . . when it matters most, I am none of those things.

I am nothing.

I am just a circle.

I am *empty*.

Old O'Malley coughs, harder than before, struggles to draw breath.

"I hope . . . my old self hasn't changed *too* much," he says. "I was never a crybaby like that."

Matilda laughs. It sounds like my laugh.

"Kevin, you've been a lying, manipulating, backstabbing *crybaby* for a thousand years," she says. "Some things don't change."

The room darkens. Old Smith raises her arms, and they are bathed in color. The same lights that made Spingate glow like an angel soak into Old Smith's cratered skin, make her look like a moving statue that has disintegrated and blackened with age.

"Ometeotl, commence final bio-scan of receptacle."

"Scanning, Doctor Smith."

The humming increases, almost drowns out my O'Malley's sobs and Old O'Malley's cough.

What little rage that still burns inside me is extinguished by a wave of hopelessness. My friend is going to die. He's an arm's length away, if only I could reach out to him. Right here, right now, Kevin O'Malley will cease to exist. And I can't stop it.

"Bio-scan complete, Doctor Smith," the room says. *"Zero risk factors. Ready to commence upon your order."*

Old Smith lowers her glowing hands. "Commence transference."

The humming grows louder, fills the room, bounces off the ceiling and walls.

My O'Malley thrashes, but not of his own will—his body is reacting: twitching and trembling, quivering and lurching.

They're killing him.

The hum goes on forever. It fills my head, rattles my ears and teeth. It blocks out everything. I want my hands loose, not so I can escape but so I can drive my fingers into my ears, try to block that sound of death.

And then, the volume lowers, lowers, lowers . . . the humming stops.

I look at my friend. He's on his back, staring straight up at the ceiling. His chest heaves. He blinks rapidly, shakes his head. He wiggles his nose, curls his lips, clicks his teeth as if he's trying out his face for the first time.

Please-please-please let it have failed . . .

O'Malley's head turns toward me. He smiles—but it isn't *his* smile.

"Hello, young lady."

In that instant I know my friend is no more. I'm numb. I feel nothing. I am as cold as a corpse.

The monsters have won. And I'm next.

Matilda walks to his coffin. She presses a small green jewel set just behind his head. O'Malley's restraints clack open. He sits up, stretches out his arms, rubs his legs, looks at his fingers like they are made of magic and wind. His eyes shine with wonder and awe.

"I can't believe it," he says. "There's no . . . I feel no pain. I knew my old body hurt, but until this very moment I hadn't realized I spent every minute of every day in pain, and now . . . nothing. It's *gone*."

He swings his legs over the side, lets his feet dangle.

The tears in my eyes make him shimmer and wave.

Matilda puts a hand on his shoulder.

"Slowly at first," she says. "Your body is fine, but your mind must get used to moving it again."

O'Malley brushes the hand aside, all but pushes Matilda out of the way. He slides off his coffin-table and stands.

"Praise be," this new person says. "Praise be to all the gods, it *worked*."

A desperate, haunting moan of anguish makes my hair stand on end. At the X, the gnarled, restrained Grownup O'Malley lifts his head. His frail lungs try to draw in air, air that is killing him. He looks around the room, disoriented.

"It didn't work," he says. "We . . . we must try again. I'm still trapped in this hideous body. Oh, I hurt *so bad,* even worse than before."

I don't understand. It *did* work, I can see the young O'Malley and I know he is not mine.

Young O'Malley starts to laugh.

Old O'Malley's head snaps up. For the first time, the red eyes clear all the way, blink rapidly.

"No," he says. "This can't be."

Young O'Malley walks closer to his old self, does a little stumbling dance.

"Come on, now, *Chancellor*! You knew this would happen."

The wrinkled monster looks around the room madly. I realize that he is looking for someone to help him.

"Wait," he says. "I didn't think it would be like this."

Young O'Malley reaches toward Bishop, palm up. The hulking monster hands over a sheathed knife. O'Malley takes it by the hilt, then grips the sheath and pulls the blade free.

The knife—ornate, golden, bejeweled—looks exactly like the knife in the painting behind the X, the one with the young man driving the blade into the old man's chest.

Young O'Malley smiles wide, points the tip at his former self.

"If it makes you feel better, old man, this is *exactly* how *I* thought it would turn out. Which means it's exactly how *you* thought it would turn out, too. My, how interesting to talk to one's self!"

The old monster pulls at the restraints, but he was weak even before this ordeal began.

"Please," he says. "I'm not ready. It's not *fair*. I want to live! Why did I spend a thousand years in agony if I don't get to live?"

So much pain in that voice, so much betrayal—I almost feel sorry for him. The overwrite, it doesn't *move* the consciousness of the old person, it *copies* it, leaving two versions. The old version remains trapped in its fragile, failing body.

Young O'Malley flips the knife in the air, catches it by the hilt. He walks closer to the X.

"Don't be sad, Old Me. You got to live for a thousand years—I'll get to live for a thousand more."

From behind the fleshy folds hiding its mouth, the old monster screams nonsensical words, babbles and begs, but it does no good. Young O'Malley places the point of the knife on his old self's chest, then leans in. The gnarled skin punctures. Red-gray blood leaks down. There is a moment of hesitation, then a *crack* as the knife punches through bone and sinks deep.

The old monster twitches.

"No," it says in a faint hiss. "I was supposed to . . . to live . . . *forever*."

The head droops.

The old man moves no more.

Young O'Malley—now the *only* O'Malley—pulls the knife free. He wipes the flat of the blade against his dead former self, scraping free the red-gray blood. He slips the knife back into the sheath, then slides the sheath into the belt of his black coveralls.

The lump in my throat changes, becomes a fist—I turn my head to the side just before I vomit bits of spicy meat all over my coffin's white linen and onto the stone floor.

"Kenzie, she vomited," Matilda says. "Is her brain all right? Does she have a concussion?"

Old Smith shuffles off the pedestal platform. Her gnarled fingers grip my face, turn my head left, then right.

"Hard to tell," she says to Matilda. To me, she says, "How is your head?"

"It *hurts,*" I say. "So bad."

Matilda huffs. "Like she's going to tell you the truth, Kenzie. Don't be gullible."

"So your former self can lie," Smith says. "Well, isn't that a surprise?"

"Get her ready." Matilda's voice rings with eagerness. "I'm done waiting. We're going to do it *now,* concussion or not."

The diseased, rotten stink of Smith's fingers combines with the acrid smell of my vomit; my stomach threatens another round. There's no food left to throw up, but my body doesn't care.

"Wait a little longer," Smith says. "Matilda, you only get one chance at this, and Bishop *did* knock her unconscious."

Smith releases me. I can still smell her fingers.

Matilda glares at Bishop. "Thank you so much for that, lover."

Lover? The old me and the old Bishop . . . *lovers*?

"You wanted her here," he says. "And here she is."

It's the first time I've heard the huge old monster speak. The sound tears at my heart. It is *his* voice, the voice of the boy who kissed me at the waterfall, the voice of the boy who—when all was lost and I was sent off on my own to die—whispered to me that he would send help. It is his voice, matter-of-fact and to the point, but it is also *not:* it is breathier, shorter . . . it is *tired*.

Matilda huffs in disgust. "Maybe you did it on purpose. Maybe you *tried* to hurt her so I couldn't transition!"

Bishop says nothing.

Matilda sighs. "Fine, we will wait." The old creature looks down at me. The mask hides the fleshy folds that in turn hid her mouth, but I know she is smiling—I can tell by her one remaining, red eye.

"Soon, my pet. Soon we will be one."

FORTY-ONE

The nightmare gets worse. It envelops me, makes me want to give up, to shut down forever.

My Bishop lies in the coffin to my left, where O'Malley died.

In the coffin past him, my Gaston, and in the fourth and final one, my Borjigin.

Old Bishop, Coyotl, O'Malley and a few other Grownups I don't know dragged them in, unconscious, locked them down. They are all awake now, the sides of their coffins lowered. Borjigin sobs, seems unable to accept that Coyotl is doing this to him. My Gaston cursed at everyone until Matilda went to work on him with the rod.

He's not cursing anymore.

We are all about to be overwritten. We will be *erased*.

Spingate is here as well. She's shackled to a heavy ring mounted in the wall. She's crying. She knows she can't do anything for anyone. None of us can. We are all helpless.

The new O'Malley struts around the room, laughing and joking. Same body, different soul—he is an abomination.

The hulking, ancient form of Old Bishop stands to my left, at the head of my Bishop's coffin. Most of the other Grownups seem shriveled, all used up, but not Old Bishop—he has their gnarled skin, red eyes, mask and metallic life-support frame, but a thousand years of life haven't made him any less lethal.

My Bishop stares up at him.

"I'm going to kill you," he says to his progenitor.

Old Bishop nods. "I know you would try, but the restraints are far too strong. It is best if you make your peace with the gods." The ancient monster reaches down, places a hand on my Bishop's shoulder. "I am sorry it has to be this way."

My Bishop sneers. "Maybe it's better that I die now than live and become *you*. You are no warrior—you are a *coward*."

Old Bishop stares for a moment, then hangs his masked head.

My Bishop senses his words have hit home. He tries to rise up, but of course, he can't.

"At least let me *fight* for my life," he says. "Don't you want to know if you could beat me?"

Old Bishop's red eyes swirl. He looks at my Bishop's face, then above his head—I see a green jewel there, the same one Matilda pressed to release O'Malley.

The massive Grownup gently reaches for it. I hold my breath. His wrinkled, black finger rests lightly on the jewel.

"Don't be stupid, lover," Matilda calls out. She's on the pedestal platform with Smith. "Do you really want to prove what a big man you are by damaging the body you're about to inhabit? Leave him be—it's your turn to transfer."

Old Bishop's hand drops to his side.

"I want to live," he says to my Bishop. "I am sorry." He lumbers to the black X. "Uriah, Kevin, prepare me."

Coyotl scurries over, as does O'Malley. It is devastating to see their young faces so eager to help, so *excited* about killing off another of my friends.

My Bishop sniffles once. Then twice. No, not sniffling . . . he's *smelling* the air. I don't smell anything.

Old Bishop removes his bracelet weapon. He hands it to O'Malley, who slides it onto his own arm. Coyotl shackles one of Old Bishop's wrists, O'Malley the other. They lock down his ankles.

Old Bishop looks at each restraint as he tests it, giving it a short pull. His head suddenly snaps up, eyes darting about the room.

"Release me," he says.

O'Malley throws back his head and laughs. "No cold feet now, Ramses old chap. I know you're afraid you'll be stabbed in the heart—because you *will* be—but the you that does the stabbing will enjoy it, I promise."

Old Bishop pulls hard on his shackles; the metal rattles so loud that O'Malley takes a surprised step back.

"Release me *now,* I smell something."

And then I smell it, too—burned toast.

The Springers are here.

Coyotl's nose wrinkles: his eyes widen.

"Oh, *shit,*" he says.

A flash and a deafening roar from somewhere past my head.

Coyotl spins in place, falls.

Borjigin cries out, as if he still doesn't understand that the Coyotl he knew was already gone.

O'Malley dives away from the X, hits the ground and rolls into a crouch at the foot of my coffin.

Old Bishop rattles the X even harder.

"Kevin, *come back,*" he screams. "Let me out of here!"

Another gun roars. My ears ring. The overpowering scent of wet charcoal fills the room, singes my nose.

I still can't move. Spingate screams in fear. Gaston is cursing for someone to let him go. Borjigin is crying, the sound somehow heartbreaking despite the insanity and death that surrounds me.

Springers screech a grinding war cry that sets my teeth on edge.

Another gun roars, then another.

O'Malley pops up. He levels his arm on me, using the bars across my ankles to steady his bracelet, and fires off a blast of white light.

I try to kick my feet to throw off his aim, but I can barely move my legs. He drops back down behind the coffin. He's using me for cover. If the Springers chance a shot at him . . .

I look left: my Bishop's arms trembling, every huge muscle popping out, his face scrunched in quiet effort. Past my feet, Old Bishop is doing the same, pulling at the metal restraints that hold him to the X.

Through the chaos, I hear a voice that is not human.

"*Hem! Hem!*"

Barkah has come for me.

"I'm here! Can't move!"

The sharp shriek of metal breaking, metal *dying*—two curved pieces sail through the air as my Bishop's right hand flies up.

Then a sound almost exactly like it, but this one comes from the black X—Old Bishop's left leg kicks free. Pieces of broken ankle restraint clatter across the floor.

My Bishop fights with the thicker bar around his waist. He slides his fingers under it, lifts, grunts, but he can't get leverage.

I remember how Matilda let O'Malley out.

"Bishop, the jewel above your head! Push it!"

He reaches up, fingers frantically searching the fabric above him.

Another Springer gunshot.

Coyotl is somewhere on the floor, screaming in agony.

Old Bishop grunts and jerks, making the entire X-frame rattle. His right foot comes free. He plants his feet on the stone floor and twists his body, pulling hard on his right wrist. I see red-gray blood trickling down from where the shackle cuts into his withered flesh just before that shackle gives way.

My Bishop finds the jewel-button: his restraints pop open. His face sheened with sweat, he leaps off his coffin-table and slaps the jewel above my head, releasing me.

"Free the others," he says, then launches himself toward his progenitor.

Old Bishop braces and *heaves*—the entire X-frame rips free from the stone floor. He bends at the waist and twists sharply: the heavy X slams into the oncoming younger boy, sending him tumbling.

I slide off the table and squat down at the foot of my coffin. O'Malley is gone, I don't see him. The room is filling up with swirling musket smoke.

As my Bishop gets to his feet, his progenitor tears off the last. The two men rush at each other, slam together at full speed, punching and kicking.

A Springer is at my side, pulling me away from the fight. Its skin is a lush purple, but it is not Barkah. I don't recognize this one. Three yellow eyes plead with me to move.

By the curved red wall, a Grownup I don't recognize blasts a Springer with white light; even as that one cries out and is torn to pieces, two more Springers leap high and kick out, knocking the Grownup to the hard stone floor. I recognize one of them:

Lahfah. Ceiling lights flash off his hatchet as he brings it up and whips it down, again and again, arcs of red-gray blood splashing across the floor and walls.

Musket smoke swirls, stings my eyes, burns my throat.

Three Springer guns roar almost at the same time, *bangbangbang*—on the platform two pedestals shatter, erupting in flames that wash over Dr. Smith. Her withered body ignites like a bonfire, flames shooting up to the curved ceiling.

Matilda isn't on the platform. . . . *where is she?*

The ceiling sparks . . . the fire catches, it *spreads*—the ceiling is not stone, but something else. This entire room is about to become a furnace.

The battle rages around me, Grownups fighting for their lives, Springers taking revenge for generations of slaughter.

I stumble to Gaston's coffin-table. He's still trapped, and coughing so violently he's splattering spit on his mouth and chin. I press the jewel above his head—he's off in an instant, dashing to the wall where Spingate is chained.

I free Borjigin. He rolls off his coffin-table, hits the ground hard. He pushes himself up, starts toward the sound of Coyotl's screams.

I grab Borjigin, stop him, shout in his face.

"That's *not* Coyotl. Your Coyotl is dead! Help me with Spingate!"

Wet-eyed Borjigin stares back at me for only a second. In that brief moment, I see despair in his soul. He wipes his eyes with his sleeve hard enough to turn the skin instantly red, then he nods.

"Stay low," I say, and push him toward Gaston and Spingate.

The smoke was annoying before—now it's dangerous, a thin cloud that roils across the ceiling in noxious curls. The Springer next to me coughs hard, wide cheeks puffing out.

Gaston and Spingate are pulling hard on the ring that holds her shackles to the wall, but the ring is anchored in stone and does not budge. Borjigin and I join them—even with all four of us, it makes no difference.

The Springer pulls his hatchet from his belt. He uses the butt end of the blade like a hammer, attacking the stone around the ring.

"Harder," Gaston screams at him. "*Hit* that godsdamned bastard!"

The stone behind the ring splits. Gaston re-grips the ring, plants one foot against the wall, screams and leans away, using every muscle he has.

The ring rips free. Spingate grabs it, holds it—her wrists are still bound by the shackles attached to it, but now she can run. Gaston's eyes dart everywhere, looking for a way out.

The pedestal platform is fully ablaze, tall flames angling off the ceiling. Sweat pours from my skin.

Through the smoke, I see a Springer by the bin racks, waving madly at me—it's Barkah.

I push Gaston and Spingate toward him. "Go to that Springer, *now.* He will help you."

Gaston makes no heroic comment about how he'll stay and fight, because this fight doesn't matter to him—all he cares about is getting Spingate out, getting their baby out. Coughing hard, he wraps his arm around her waist, guides her toward the racks.

I shove Borjigin after them. He's not a fighter—all he can do is get in the way.

Smoke is everywhere. I can't see friend or foe. Where is Bishop? And where is Matilda? I'm going to kill her, I'm going to end this.

I crouch down low. My new Springer friend crouches next to me, its eyes narrowed against the burning smoke. Blinking madly, it rises up slightly to look around—and is engulfed by white light.

Heat so intense I feel it cook my skin before my body reacts on its own, throwing me away from it—the Springer is ripped apart, a living being one second, splattering piles of sizzling meat the next. Blue blood splashes out, all over the floor, all over me.

I sit there, unthinking, staring at my fingers. They are spotted with beads of blue, each drop reflecting the raging fire above, like a thousand tiny jewels all dancing in perfect time.

That could have been me . . . what do I do, what do I do . . .

Hands grab me, yank me to my knees. It's Borjigin, coughing so hard that spit flies from his open mouth. He drags me away from the mess and the sickening smell of scorched Springer.

"Come on," he grunts. "I'm not leaving you here."

I'm almost to my feet when he cries out, falls down next to me, holding the back of his head. I turn to face the danger—a fist drives into my nose. I stumble back, slump to the floor.

"You two aren't going anywhere."

It's O'Malley.

I'm dizzy, can't focus. I taste blood on my lips. I roll to my hands and knees, try to keep from falling to my side as the world spins.

O'Malley stands in front of me, aiming his bracelet-point somewhere into the room. This close, I see him work it, see how he flicks his fingers straight out, flat as a board, and a split second later the bracelet flashes with white light.

I hear another Springer scream.

O'Malley laughs. He's enjoying the slaughter. On my hands and knees, my eyes are at his waist level. There, in his belt, the ornate knife he used to murder his creator.

The boy I love is dead.

Now I must kill him a second time.

I reach out, feel the knife handle against my palm an instant before my fingers curl tight around it. One pull—fast, firm—and the blade slides free from the sheath.

O'Malley felt the tug. He looks down, sees the knife in my hand. He opens his mouth—to say *no,* maybe—but he doesn't have time to say even that.

I stab. The knifepoint slides through his coveralls into his belly, angles up inside his chest. The blade sinks deep, doesn't stop until the hilt thumps against his body.

He makes a noise—half-sigh, half-cough.

"You killed him," I say.

I pull the blade out. Blood spills instantly, spraying on my hand, my sleeve.

Red blood.

"I loved him, and you *erased* him."

I stab him a second time, again driving the blade *up* and *in*.

O'Malley stares down with an expression of disbelief. Wide eyes. Open mouth. He shakes his head, just a little, as if to say, *This can't be happening*.

His expression changes, melts into something else. The eyes look at me with warmth, with love.

It's the real O'Malley . . . *my* O'Malley . . . and he *smiles*.

"Thank you," he says.

He collapses. I catch him as he falls. His back on my thighs, my arm under his head. He's shivering. His blood . . . it's everywhere. The knife is still sticking out of him.

"Kevin! Hold on! I'll get you out of here."

He grabs my shoulders with what little strength he has. His fingers dig into my coveralls.

"Too late," he says. He tries to take a breath, but a spasm cuts it short. A shudder courses over him, *through* him, and his face shifts from love to pure hate. The same eyes glare at me, but it is not the same person. From deep in his throat, he growls out words.

"You always were a *bitch,* Savage."

His neck relaxes, his head tilts to the side.

Dead eyes stare out.

He was still in there.

Borjigin hauls me up, tries to drag me to the racks, to whatever way out is hidden in the shadows.

I knock his hands away. I grab O'Malley's silver bracelet, slide it clear from his hand.

"Hem!" It's Barkah, screaming to be heard over the roaring flames. *"Hem, move!"*

I stand, crouching against the blistering heat that blazes down from a fire-engulfed ceiling. My lungs burn and rebel—I cough so hard I can't draw a breath.

The only Grownups I see lie motionless on the blood-splattered floor. None of them are Matilda. Or Gaston.

Four Springers stand victorious. Coughing, bloody, wounded, exhausted—at least three of their kind are dead, but they *won.*

Through the smoke and flames, I see a final battle still under way.

By the ruins of the X, the old Bishop straddles the young one, raining down blow after blow, smashing gnarled, black fists into ravaged pink flesh. Any one of those punches would shatter me completely.

I slide the bracelet onto my right wrist. I feel it squeeze down on my forearm.

My lungs burn, my eyes water, the heat is cooking me alive, but I am not finished here.

Old Bishop stands on wobbly legs. His hands are a mangled mix of torn flesh and blood.

On the stone floor in front of him, my Bishop struggles to move.

The worm of rage writhes inside my chest.

I stride toward them. Borjigin and Barkah fall in at my sides.

Old Bishop stares at me, mask cracked and askew, chest heaving, red eyes blazing with pride.

"I *won,*" he says. "I beat him."

I point my right arm at him. "And you still lose."

He looks down again, then to the pedestal platform, where the corpse of Smith is lost in the raging column of fire. He looks at the broken X, then back at me, and I understand—even if I didn't have him dead to rights, he has no way to overwrite his defeated, younger self.

The big, broad shoulders sag. The shine of victory leaves his eyes. He is old, sad, exhausted.

"I am so tired," he says. "I *hurt.* All my life, I tried to do the right thing. I followed orders. But those orders . . . they were for the *wrong* things. I followed them anyway."

He grabs his mask, tears it off, tosses it aside. He points down at my Bishop, at what was supposed to be his new body.

"Help him choose the *right* thing," the ancient man says.

My scorched throat and sizzling lungs won't let me answer him, so I nod once.

He puts his shoulders back and stands rigid.

"I am Ramses Bishop, and I am ready to finally rest."

I flick my fingers forward. My arm tingles with deep pinpricks, then the white light flashes out and tears the black monster to pieces.

I am the wind . . . I am death.

I stumble, have to grab a coffin-table to stay upright. Borjigin and Barkah help my Bishop up. His face is a swollen, bloody ruin. I can't believe he's still alive. He coughs up globs of blood.

The other Springers swarm around us, push me stumbling through the thick smoke. I can't see anything, so I let them guide me. I have to focus just to stay on my feet.

The sound of the flames recedes slightly, then a door creaks shut and the blaze's roar drops to a dull crackling.

A torch flares to life. We are in a narrow hallway carved out of the Observatory's rock. The Springers gently urge us on.

Only now do I get a good look at Barkah: leg bleeding, a blood-spotted patch over his middle eye, the other two eyes half-lidded from pain and exhaustion, his every move a source of agony. He didn't run and hide—as badly as he was hurt, he found more of his kind and came to rescue me.

I glance at the Springer faces, and see one other that I recognize.

"*Hem,*" Lahfah says.

He isn't laughing anymore. How could he, after what we've been through?

I gently check my nose—even the lightest touch fills my face with pain. I think it's broken.

Bishop gently pushes Barkah and Borjigin away from him.

"I can stand on my own," he says.

He leans a hand against the wall, takes a rattling breath, then starts walking.

We all move down the hall. I try to understand what just happened, parse out the madness of the last few minutes. O'Malley is gone *(he was still in there and I killed him I KILLED HIM)*. I didn't see Matilda's body, or Gaston's—I'm positive they're both still alive. I tried to send Borjigin away, assuming he was weak, but he came back for me.

Borjigin saved my life, true, but without Barkah and his

friends we would *all* be dead. The Springer prince is brave beyond words. Although he unleashed violence just now, he did so because he wants peace.

Together, we can deliver on that promise.

The corridor is long and straight—like the ones we walked on the *Xolotl*—but at least this one is flat.

"Matilda," Bishop says, his voice a croaking, broken thing. "Is she dead? You're not safe until she is."

"She's alive," I say. "I'm sure of it."

Matilda won't stop until she gets me. And we have no idea what this city holds—she built it, maybe there are places other than the Observatory where she could wipe out my mind.

I assume Matilda got away . . . so where would she go?

No, that's the wrong way to think about it—where would *I* go? If I was defeated, if my friends were killed, what would I do?

"Bello's ship," I say. "Matilda is too old to run far. She'll try and use Bello's ship to get back to the *Xolotl*. I don't know what time it is—are we sure Aramovsky is still going to attack? If he isn't, we can go after her."

"He is," Bishop says. "Aramovsky sent some of the young circle-stars out scouting on spiders. They had just come back when he ordered me here. They reported hundreds of Springers near a clearing west of the city. He said he was going to attack at dawn."

I quickly explain what Barkah showed me about how the Springer king is luring Aramovsky in.

"Our people will be outnumbered a hundred to one," I say. "Aramovsky is leading them into a trap."

Borjigin shakes his head. "I don't think so." He's still wiping at his eyes with his sleeve. The skin there is rubbed raw. "Before he ordered me here, I'd repaired four more spiders, so he marched with six of them. Zubiri and the others were working on other machines, but I wasn't paying attention to them and don't know what they might have fixed. The thing is, I fixed the cannons. All of them. The bracelets are *nothing* compared to what the spiders have now. Em, Aramovsky will slaughter Springers by the thousands."

I wince and glance at Barkah, forgetting for an instant that he doesn't speak our language. He has no idea that the Springer king's trap is going to turn into a massacre.

We reach the end of the tunnel. We push through thick vines, find ourselves on the street—it's still dark. We still have a little time, at least.

Coyotl's spider stands there, motionless. Gaston and Spingate are beneath it. Five musket-armed Springers are on top of it. Their skin is reddish purple. More red than purple, really, and they are significantly smaller than Barkah, Lahfah and the others, so small their muskets look bigger than they are. These Springers are still children—the equivalent, perhaps, of our twelve-year-olds. Maybe Matilda came for Coyotl's spider, but saw these armed youngsters and chose to slip away rather than engage in a shootout.

Borjigin walks to the spider. He puts a hand on one of the five legs, hangs his bloody head and starts to cry.

Far off on the horizon, I see the glow of morning. The sun isn't up quite yet, but we don't have long.

If I try to stop the battle, Matilda will reach her ship. She might escape. I want her *dead*. I don't want to have to choose between those things, but that's what a leader does: make choices.

"Barkah and I have to get to the clearing," I say. "Before the sun rises. He and I can stop this."

Bishop's swollen face shows doubt that I can accomplish that, but he doesn't argue.

"We're in the middle of the city," he says. "The clearing is way past the wall. Even with the spider, you won't make it before sunrise."

The moonlight shines down on his face: one eye swollen shut, cuts dripping blood, his lower lip puffed out and badly split.

For the first time since we left the fire behind, Gaston speaks.

"If we take the spider, we're only ten or fifteen minutes from the landing pad—then the shuttle could reach the clearing in less than ten minutes, including the time I need to fire up the engines."

The words hang in the air.

My friends are watching me, waiting. Bishop, Borjigin, Gaston, Spingate . . . even Barkah and Lahfah. There was no vote this time, and I don't care—I know what must be done, and I will lead the way.

If we do as Gaston suggests, then we can never go back to the *Xolotl.* I swore I would die on Omeyocan before returning to that ship of horrors. But believing you won't use an option and removing that option completely are two different things. If something else goes wrong down here, if there is another kind of mold, if the Springers decide they want war no matter what, if there is a disaster, *anything,* the shuttle won't have enough fuel to let us run away.

Another decision, and all mine to make.

I make it.

FORTY-TWO

A thin arc of sun breaches the horizon. Long rafts of clouds blaze crimson, underlit against the dark-blue sky. Omeyocan's twin moons are starting to fade, ready to sleep the day away until the nightfall comes again.

We had to leave most of the Springers behind—there wasn't enough room for everyone. With me, Bishop, Spingate, Gaston, Borjigin, Barkah and Lahfah, it's a tight fit, but we manage to hold on even as Borjigin guides the spider up and over the landing pad's thick ring of vines.

The shuttle awaits us.

Farrar and a dozen young circle-stars crouch near the ramp. Three of the young ones aim muskets at us. The others hold knives or various tools: picks, shovels, axes, more.

The spider's five hard feet *clack-clack-clack* against the landing pad's metal surface. The machine slows; I'm off and down before it even comes to a complete stop.

The circle-stars see the Springers, shuffle backward, agitated and afraid.

"Hold your positions," Farrar barks to his charges.

The young circle-stars hold their places, but they don't take their eyes off Barkah and Lahfah. Farrar can't look away from them, either, not even when he talks to me.

"Em, what's going on? Did you see Aramovsky?"

"Get everyone inside," I say as I start past him toward the ramp. "We're taking the shuttle."

He grabs my arm, spins me around.

"Aramovsky is the leader now," he says. "We're not going anywhere without his orders, and those *things* aren't coming aboard no matter what."

Bishop leaps over the spider's protective ridge, grunts in pain when he hits the ground. Fists curled, he limps toward us.

I hold up a hand, telling him to stop. He does, just a step away. Bishop is ready to fight, but in his condition, it's a fight he won't win.

"Aramovsky betrayed us," I say to Farrar and the circle-stars. "The Grownups are on Omeyocan, and he's working with them. Do you know why he didn't take you to the battle?"

Farrar looks at me doubtfully. "We're here to protect the shuttle against Springer attack."

"You're here because there is a Grownup waiting to put you in a box, to invade your body and wipe you out, forever," I say. "They don't want you getting hurt or killed in the battle. They've already murdered Coyotl, Beckett and O'Malley. You were all supposed to be next."

I see the conflict on Farrar's face, on the faces of the kids. They are afraid that I am right, but I am not the leader and I broke their trust when I didn't tell them about the symbols. I also came here with Springers, the creatures they've been told are evil demons who want them all dead.

Gaston and Spingate climb down from the spider.

"Hurry up, you boneheads," Gaston says as he heads up the ramp. "We don't have time for this."

Spingate follows him, as does the still-sobbing Borjigin. Farrar watches them go by—he has no idea what to do.

I reach out, take his hand, make him focus on me.

"Farrar, I'm telling you the truth."

He shakes his head. "Even if you are, I have to follow orders. I have—"

Bishop's huge fist crashes into Farrar's jaw. Farrar's hand slides from mine. He drops, unconscious.

Bishop draws himself up to his full height, shouts commands at the shocked young circle-stars.

"All of you, get in the shuttle, right now, or I will *throw* you in it. And take Farrar to medical so Smith can look at him. *Move!*"

The kids rush to Farrar, their previous instructions forgotten in the face of Bishop's commanding presence. It takes five of them to lift the unconscious man and carry him up the ramp.

I shake my head at Bishop. "I was handling that."

Bishop shrugs. "Enough talk. We don't have time for it."

He limps into the shuttle, leaving me with Barkah and Lahfah.

I gesture to the open door.

"Move," I say. "Peace."

Lahfah's eyes scan the gleaming metal shuttle. Has he been told about these flying machines since he was little? Did his culture fill him with stories about the carnage that machines like this wreaked on his people? Asking him to go inside must be like asking him to walk into a monster's mouth.

If Barkah thinks the same thing, he doesn't show it. My brave new friend hops up the ramp.

Lahfah looks to the sky and taps his throat. For some reason, the gesture makes me think of a human sighing heavily in exasperation. He follows his prince up the ramp.

I run into the shuttle, gesture to Lahfah and Barkah to stay in the entryway.

In the coffin room, I see dozens of kids. All the symbols are represented. Of the people my age, I see Okereke, Cabral and Opkick. I don't see Bawden, Johnson, Ingolfsson or D'souza—they are with Aramovsky's army, cannon fodder to be used against the Springers.

I look for Zubiri—she's not here.

And then I see Bello.

My frustration and anger draw down to a single point: *her*.

"Your fault," I say. "It's your fault O'Malley is dead."

Her eyes go wide—not with fear, but with annoyance.

"The transfer didn't work on Kevin? That's too bad, but how in the hell is that *my* fault?"

On Kevin . . .

She thinks I'm talking about that wrinkled old monster . . . Bello thinks I'm *Matilda*.

Rage engulfs me without warning, hot and tingling and all-powerful. She isn't really just Bello anymore, she is *all* the Grownups, she is the reason we have suffered endlessly, the reason my friends are dead.

I rush her, hurdling coffins and kids alike.

Bello shakes her head—a confused *What are you doing?*—then I am on her. I slam her into the red wall. The back of her head hits hard enough to make the metal thrum. She cries out in pain and surprise. I bend my right arm, whip my elbow at her face—O'Malley's silver bracelet slams into her mouth.

She falls, spitting blood and teeth.

"You *used* us," I say.

I viciously kick her ribs with the toe of my heavy black boot.

She lets out a sound that is more hiccup than groan, rolls to her back. Her hands rise up, trying to surrender or ward off the attack—I don't know which, and I don't care.

"You were supposed to *protect* us."

I drop my knee into her stomach as hard as I can. The wind shoots out of her all at once. Her eyes widen in shock and fear—the fear of not knowing if she will ever draw another breath.

"You wanted to make us *just like you*."

I'm vaguely aware of kids screaming, of my fellow circles shouting at me to stop, yet none of them lay a hand on me.

I straddle Bello, pinning her hips to the floor. I punch her in the eye, feel the skin of my knuckles split.

"You are all *monsters*!"

I rear back, hit her again. Her head bounces off the floor. I hit her a third time, smashing her nose.

Blood covers her face. Her eyes are open, but they don't really see anything.

"You couldn't just let us be," I say. "It didn't have to be like this."

I aim the point of my bracelet right between her tear-filled eyes.

"Crying doesn't fix anything," I say. "You cry because you are *weak*."

She trembles. She's beaten, she's helpless, and I don't care.

All I have to do is straighten my fingers, then she will be no more.

The shuttle shudders. I hear and feel a rumble.

The engines—Gaston has started them up.

It's enough to distract me, to make me look at what I have done.

A deep cut above Bello's eye pulses with red blood. Her nose lies at an angle, bone or maybe cartilage sticking out of a jagged rip that leaks blood down her cheek. Her upper lip is split, bleeding badly. Her front two teeth are gone, and the left incisor is broken in half, a splintered tip jutting from bloody gums.

A strong hand, gentle on my shoulder.

"That's enough," Bishop says. "Come to the pilothouse."

The kids are staring at me, wide-eyed, openmouthed, as are Okereke, Cabral, Borjigin and Opkick. A handful of Aramovsky's young circle-stars stand there, their faces alive and drinking in the violence. They look at me with newfound respect. I have spoken a language they were programmed to understand.

Bishop lifts me, sets me on my feet.

"Put Bello in an empty storage room," he says. "Lock her in. Don't hurt her further."

People rush to gather her up, just as the kids outside rushed to gather up Farrar after Bishop knocked him out.

At the coffin room entryway, Barkah and Lahfah stare at me. How much of Bello's beating did they see?

The shuttle shudders again. The unseen engines scream so loud I almost cover my ears, then the noise drops down to a mere roar.

I sprint to the pilothouse, gesturing for the two Springers to follow me.

Inside, both Gaston and Spingate are bathed in color.

"Preflight checks complete," Gaston says. "Shuttle, give us handholds."

Spots on the black floor rise up, seem to flow right out of the solid surface. Gaston and Spingate each grab one. Barkah and Lahfah do the same.

"The floor of the pilothouse accommodates for sudden banks or thrust, but it's not a perfect system," Gaston says. "That means hold on tight. Shuttle, open internal comm."

"Internal comm open, Captain."

When Gaston speaks again, I hear his words echo throughout the shuttle. "Everyone, get into a coffin and stay there. This ride will be short but the landing might be bumpy."

He waves his hand. I hear something click. He looks at me, and when he talks his voice is normal.

"We're ready," he says. "Is this still what you want?"

Behind Gaston, one of the walls shows the rising sun. The blazing red orb has just lifted free of the horizon.

"Take us to the clearing," I say. "As fast as you can."

Gaston nods. "Shuttle, initiate flight plan."

We lift off. I feel us banking slightly this way and that, but as Gaston told us, the floor shifts instantly at each movement, tilting to counter the effects. Despite that, I grip the handhold far harder than I ever held the spear.

We rise quickly. Images on the walls change, showing us the spreading grandeur of Omeyocan. In seconds we are up high, much higher than the Observatory. We can see mountains off in the distance, great rivers, vast plains and the ever-present yellow jungle.

Barkah and Lahfah look terrified, but they hold on tight and make no noise. They have suffered much. A broken leg, a ruined eye, burned and blistered skin. Some of their cuts have crusted over, others still leak blue blood.

"Five minutes," Gaston says.

The sun is up—has the battle already begun?

I look at Bishop. Cuts and welts dot his swollen face. His knuckles drip blood to the pilothouse floor. The beating his creator gave him . . . I don't know how any human being could keep going after that, yet here he stands, at my side and ready to go even further.

"You look terrible," I say.

He smiles. "And you look like a warrior."

I keep one hand locked on the handhold while the other feels my face. My broken nose. O'Malley, hitting me so hard. His knife. The way it slid into him . . . the shock on his face, his horror at knowing he'd gotten what he'd sought for a thousand years and I had just taken that away from him.

"You had to do it," Bishop says softly. "But what you killed, that wasn't O'Malley."

He knows my thoughts.

I want to believe he's right, but I can't. Kevin was still in there, at least some small part. If I had captured him rather than killing him, maybe I could have found a way to bring him back. Instead, I stabbed him to death.

In my head, I know I did the only thing I could. There was too much going on, blood and death and fire all around—there was no other option.

In my heart, though, I will always know I could have found a better way.

Bishop reaches out, touches my cheek. So gentle. It is almost enough to make me forget the horrors, forget the things I've done.

"And my progenitor," he says. "Don't feel bad about killing him, either, because doing so saved my life."

I nod again, but I know that is a lie, too. Bishop's creator was done fighting. Maybe forever. I could see it in his strange, red eyes. He'd won his battle, somehow proving to himself that the man he'd become after a thousand years of experience and wisdom was superior to the raw talent and energy he was as a youth. But that victory cost him—he could no longer see my Bishop as an empty shell waiting to be filled. Even after a thousand years, there was a good man in there. A man who finally remembered right from wrong.

And when he did, I ripped him into pieces.

Yong . . . the pig . . . Ponalla the Springer . . . Old Bishop . . . O'Malley . . . Old Visca . . .

All dead by my hand.

And Bello, beaten to a pulp, alive only because the shuttle's engines distracted me.

Why am I like this?

What's *wrong* with me?

How many more will I kill?

"I am the wind," I say quietly. "I am death."

Bishop nods in solemn understanding. "Someone has to be, Em." He glances at Barkah, at Lahfah, taking in their wounds. "In every civilization, someone has to be."

"We're in visual range," Gaston says. "Three minutes from landing."

The front-wall view changes from a crystal-clear picture of endless yellow jungle flowing by to a slightly shaking image of the crescent-shaped clearing. It curves away from us, as if we are approaching the bottom point of a quarter moon that is surrounded by tall trees.

On that clearing, I see lines of tiny, moving things, morning sunlight glinting off of metal. A long line of Springers, marching forward, muskets in hand.

Then, from the trees on the opposite side of the wide clearing, four yellow machines scurry out.

Spiders.

We are too late. The battle is about to begin.

FORTY-THREE

"Gaston, get us there, *now,*" I say. "Go faster!"

He nods. "Give me maximum thrust."

The shuttle lurches forward so violently that the floor beneath me can't accommodate fast enough; I almost lose my grip on the handhold.

Lahfah is chittering and chirping. I'm not sure if he's scared of the ride, or dreading what he sees on the battlefield.

Images on the pilothouse wall gain detail as we close in. I see my people at the edge of the jungle, hiding behind trees and cowering in shallow ditches. Most of them hold tools that should be used for farming, and most of them are circles—fodder for Aramovsky's war.

The Springer lines stop. A staccato flash of glinting metal as hundreds of muskets take aim. As one, they fire, and are obscured by a long grayish cloud of smoke.

One of the advancing spiders slows to a stop.

From the other three, beams of white light shoot out, sweeping across the Springers. Clouds of dirt and grass fly into the air, clouds that I know also contain meat and bone, blood and brains.

Barkah cries out, a howl that rends my heart.

The remaining Springers flee. What came forward as an organized line runs away as scattered individuals.

But the spiders don't stop. On they march, to the middle of the clearing, beams blazing new holes, turning living beings into explosions of fluid and char and vapor.

I feel so helpless.

"Dammit, Gaston, get us there!"

"The poles you're holding aren't designed for aggressive flight," he says. "There's too much inertia to—"

"*Do it!* We'll hold on! Put us down between the Springers and the spiders. We have to push our people back."

Spingate looks away from the little images of light floating around her, locks eyes with me.

"We're in range for the shuttle's missiles," she says. "We can destroy the spiders."

The missiles . . . I'd forgotten that Gaston told me the shuttle has weapons.

But if we destroy the spiders, will we kill whoever is riding them? If we had left a few minutes earlier, we might have stopped this. And now the only way to end it is if I order the death of my own people?

The image before us now shows the battlefield in perfect detail. Torn earth. Burning vines. Smoldering corpses. Severed limbs. Springers, trying to crawl despite missing legs, or hopping around holding bloody stumps that used to be arms. In the motionless spider, I see two young circle-stars and a tooth-girl, unmoving behind the protective ridge, a pool of blood filling the deck beneath them.

"Thirty seconds to landing," Gaston says. "We're coming in fast, so this is going to be rough—hold on tight."

"Em, I have missile-lock," Spingate says. "Do you want me to fire on the spiders?"

I open my mouth to say yes, but nothing comes out.

Something rolls forth from the Springers' side of the clearing—dozens of those strange wooden wagons Barkah showed me. Springers push them along at a fast clip, wheels bounding over uneven ground. The wagons aren't empty anymore: each one carries a boulder bigger than the biggest Springer, a boulder wrapped in ropes. The long wooden tails no longer trail behind, but stick up at an angle like some kind of off-center teeter-totter.

A spider-beam lashes out, catches one of the wagons dead-center. Springer bodies pop and burn; the wagon flames bright, becomes an instant inferno of wood and rope.

The wagons halt. The wooden tails swing straight up, snapping tight the ropes around the boulders; the boulders swing backward, then up, then over—they streak through the air toward their targets.

The heavy rocks hit the ground, bounce and roll at terrible speed. The first two whiz past the lead oncoming spider.

The next one hits.

Stone smashes into metal. The full-speed spider not only stops, it's thrown backward, metal shell now wrapped around the embedded boulder. A human body flies free, spinning limply. The spider flips and skids to a stop. Broken and twisted yellow legs stick up in the air. Two more riders stumble to their feet, disoriented, probably injured.

Another boulder grazes the second spider, shearing off two legs as it rolls past. The spider crashes, spins wildly. Bodies fly, moving so fast and so violently that if the riders aren't already dead, they will be when they hit the ground.

The other boulders sail past, all misses. They tumble across the clearing, losing speed—except for one. It must have hit a hard patch, because it sails higher like a ball bouncing off a floor. The boulder smashes into our side of the clearing, pulverizing human bodies.

In a span of seconds, the "outmatched" Springers have destroyed two spiders and killed the crew of a third. Now I understand why the Springers wanted the spiders in one place—with that many wagons, at least some of the two-dozen-odd boulders were bound to connect.

The last attacking spider's legs flash in a mad chopping motion as it slows, stops and retreats.

From the edge of the clearing, a fresh wave of Springers pours forth. I can't hear them, but I can see their open mouths and I know they're bellowing a war cry.

"Twenty seconds to landing," Gaston says.

The Springer line closes in on the two spider riders stranded in the middle of the clearing. The riders take cover behind their ruined machine. I silently urge them to *run,* but the smaller of the two clutches her arm to her chest, and the bigger one won't leave. There is just enough detail for me to make out who they are—it's Bawden and . . . *Zubiri.*

The shuttle lurches left.

"Fifteen seconds," Gaston calls out.

I look to our side of the clearing, to see what Aramovsky does next, and when I do, the trees themselves seem to move forward.

It's a *giant*—a walking giant covered in vines, leaves, even whole trees jammed into gaps and spaces. One arm ends in a huge scoop shovel, the other in a pincer. It's the construction machine we saw in the spider nest. We're flying, but I swear I can feel the ground shake with each step of the huge metal feet.

Lahfah points at it, jabbers something fast and panicked, then re-grips his handhold as the shuttle shifts right.

"The Springers can't stop that thing," Bishop says. "Muskets and rocks aren't going to do anything to that."

"Missiles will take it out," Spingate says. "Em, what do we do?"

The giant's long strides eat up the distance. The Springers fire muskets at it, which doesn't slow it in the least. Everything is happening too fast. We can destroy it, but just like the spiders, I'll be killing my own people. Unless . . .

"Spin, hit the ground in front of the big machine, and also in front of the Springers, but try not to kill anyone. Do it *now*!"

Her hands grab symbols made of light.

"Launching," she says, her voice calm and level.

The shuttle vibrates. Our view is temporarily blinded by spots of moving fire, then by streaks of smoke snaking out and away from us—some toward the Springers, some toward the giant machine.

The smoke lines touch the ground.

Expanding half-spheres of dirt and grass rise up, driven by churning fireballs. The Springers are knocked away—hard—many of them lifted off their feet and thrown backward.

A fireball rises up in front of the giant machine, splashing it with debris. Its lumbering ceases as the people inside it duck for cover.

Rubble rains down onto the battlefield.

Bawden covers Zubiri with her own body.

I point to them. "Gaston, put us down there! By that ruined spider!"

The shuttle banks to the right, throwing me hard against the handhold. The shuttle banks left, then *up*. Bishop loses his grip and tumbles away. He hits the door, bounces off it just as the shuttle levels out, trembles once, then stops.

"We're down," Gaston says.

Bishop is on his stomach, moving weakly.

"Gaston," I say, "tell Smith there are wounded on the field. Spingate, stay in the pilothouse and be ready with the missiles. If I raise my left fist, you take out the giant, understand?"

"Understood." Her gaze is steel. "You know that will kill whoever is inside it, right?"

I nod. If I have to kill again to stop this, if I have to carry yet another haunting face around with me wherever I go, so be it.

"Lahfah, Barkah, *move,*" I say. "Bishop, get up."

He looks hurt, more damage on an already brutalized body. Later I will feel sympathy for him. I'm not giving him the choice of staying down.

He's struggling to his hands and knees. "I'm coming, just get out there and stop this!"

I run from the pilothouse to find the shuttle doors already opening. I step onto the platform and am assaulted by the odors of battle—metal, scorched wood, wet charcoal, burning mint and a sickening stench of cooking meat.

I slide my silver bracelet off my arm. I don't want to get blasted to bits if one of the kids mistakenly thinks I'm going to shoot Aramovsky. I hold the bracelet by the long point, raise it up high so all my people can see it. Then, I throw it, as hard as I can. It spins through the air, gleaming in the morning sun. The point plunges into a bloody patch of fresh dirt. There it stands, open circle sticking up, almost like a gravestone marking the deaths of today's fallen.

This is my chance—my one chance—to stop the slaughter. I push away my pain, my heartbreak, my fear. I square my shoulders, and I stride down the ramp like I own this world.

Like an *empress*.

War's crumbs dot the clearing's ravaged ground. Twists of burned vines and clumps of soil. A torn Springer head and shoulder, smoke drifting up from the half-open toad-mouth. A severed human hand—dark-skinned.

Lahfah limps down the ramp behind me. Barkah hops out, confident and regal despite his wounds and ravaged eye. Like me, he has pushed his pain down below, prepared himself for this one moment that will make all the difference. At the bottom of the ramp, the pair turn and hop toward the Springer lines, screaming as loud as they can—I can only hope they are telling their kind to stay back, to give me time to do what must be done.

Three spiders stand not ten strides away. They are battered and rusted, even more than the ones we first saw in the jungle. Their cannons, though, gleam and shine.

The spiders on the left and right are each crewed by three kids—a gear, who must be the driver, and two black-clad circle-stars armed with silver bracelets pointed directly at me. I know that if I make any sudden movement, they will fire.

Standing on the middle spider: Aramovsky, the man who makes children go to war. He holds the spear.

My spear.

His red robes blaze in the morning sun. A long-pointed bracelet adorns his right arm. Standing atop the spider's back, staring down with fury and excitement, he looks like an angry god of war.

"You told me to wipe out the vermin," he says. "Now you've brought two of them with you? If you want to help me finish this, use those rockets to destroy their trebuchets!"

Like Bello, he thinks I'm Matilda. Of course he does. When he left the Observatory, I was locked in a coffin. It could not possibly be a worse time to do it, but I can't stop myself—I start laughing.

"You know something, Aramovsky? You always thought you were smarter than me."

It takes him a second to understand. His eyes flick to the Springers. He snarls at me.

"Where is Matilda?"

As if in answer, the sky fills with a broken sound that quickly grows to a roar. I've heard that sound before, when Bello's ship came down. But this time, the ship is going *up*.

I point to a line of smoke streaking into the sky. "Matilda is there. Probably with Old Gaston. They *left* you, Aramovsky. And don't bother looking for Coyotl, O'Malley or Beckett, because they're all dead."

His eyes narrow. So much *hate* in them. His hand squeezes on my spear, so tight the blade trembles.

"Knights," he says, "kill this traitor!"

From the shuttle platform behind me, Bishop's voice booms out, echoing across the clearing.

"Hold your fire!"

No one moves. Aramovsky thinks he speaks for the gods, but Bishop truly has the voice of one.

"The Grownups are gone, Aramovsky," Bishop says. "And your time as leader is over."

Aramovsky's mouth opens. He looks rattled, but recovers quickly. He raises the spear over his head and shouts his answer.

"The vermin want to murder you in your sleep, take away what the gods have given you! If Em and Bishop aren't with us, then they are *against* us. Do not listen to their blasphemous lies. The time has come to take this planet for ourselves."

He points the spear to his right, up at the towering metal monster covered in vines and trees.

"Lead the assault! Crush the Springers!"

Please don't move . . . please don't listen to him . . .

The massive machine lifts a foot, extends it, sets it down with a thump that shakes the entire clearing.

Barkah must have stopped the Springers from attacking, but if the giant presses forward, then they will fight back.

I have no choice.

"Aramovsky, who is driving that thing?"

The monstrosity takes another thundering step. I hear the Springer horns sound all through the jungle.

"Abrantes and Aeschelman," he says, "both young halves, and two brave young knights—Cody and Cadotte. You wouldn't know them, because you never *talked* to them like I did."

Kids. Would it be any better if it was people my age? No, not really.

"Why, Em?" Aramovsky spreads his hands, turning in place and speaking to everyone, like he always does when he's trying to make me look bad. "Do you think you're going to talk them out of it? Maybe shout to the sky and the stars and the sun, hope that they hear you?"

I shake my head. "No. I just want to know who I killed."

The monster machine takes another step.

I raise my left fist.

Spingate does not fail me.

A *hiss,* a roar of flame—two smoke trails shoot out from the top of the shuttle, covering the distance almost instantly. The missiles hit at the same time, one near the head, the other sliding into the chest. Fireballs erupt, billowing up to the sky and down to the machine's knees. A cloud of angry orange rises, driven higher by the column of flame beneath it. The vines catch fire, as do the full-size trees jammed into the nooks and crannies. Every inch of the machine bubbles and burns. The fireball dissipates, replaced by a column of greasy black smoke.

The machine moves no more.

From inside it, I hear screams.

The Springer horns fade out.

On either side of the clearing, no one moves.

With one gesture, I have demonstrated not only the ultimate power on this battlefield, but the willingness to use it. The Springers have no choice but to understand—if I'm willing to kill my own kind, I'm willing to kill them, too.

I am the wind . . . I am death.

We all stand there, motionless. We listen to the screams fade, then die out.

The fire roars on. The machine that was made to build cities, then converted to kill, is now a colossus of flame and smoke.

Aramovsky stares at it blankly. He prepared well for this battle, far better than I expected. He had his people salvage spiders. He acquired weapons that gave him the advantage. He had children repair a machine that looked like it was rusted and long since worthless. He was led into a trap, but in the end, he might have won anyway.

Three of the six spiders at his disposal are out of the fight. The Springers have probably reloaded their carts by now, and will assuredly take out at least one more spider if not all three. Aramovsky is vastly outnumbered. And his weapon of awe—the one thing the Springers could not possibly bring down with flying boulders—burns like the biggest bonfire ever created, the crew of four people inside it turning into ash.

People that I killed. What have I done? I make choices, and people die.

Bishop brushes past me. He's trying hard to hide a limp. Bleeding, his face swollen and cut, his coveralls ripped and torn, he squares his shoulders and stands in front of Aramovsky's spider.

"Knights, *hear me,*" he shouts. "You voted for Aramovsky, but he is false. Everyone he left behind was to be sacrificed to the Grownups, so they could be overwritten. You are here only because there is no Grownup waiting to erase your mind. You are *expendable.*"

He spits that last word with a power I didn't know he possessed, with so much venom it makes my hair stand on end. But he's not done talking.

"No one else has to die. The Springers showed Em how to kill the red mold. We will have food, all we can eat. *Em* did that, not Aramovsky. She killed my creator. She saved my life. I have fought beside Em. I have *bled* with Em. She is honorable. She is brave. She is willing to sacrifice for the greater good. She is not a knight, but she is everything we knights aspire to be. If you want to fight the Springers, you'll have to go through her. And to get to her, you'll have to go through *me.*"

Bishop can barely stand, yet his words carry thunder. Where is the spoiled boy who bullied anyone who disagreed with him? That person was a child in a grown man's body, but—like me—that child is gone.

And more than that . . . he's bluffing. His legs tremble. He couldn't fight one young circle-star, let alone all of them. This time, though, it isn't about Bishop's physical presence. The person who doesn't like to talk is ending this with his words.

The spider on the left: a circle-star lowers her bracelet. Next to her, a circle-star boy takes his hands off the cannon's controls and steps back. The spider crew on the right does the same. The little gear girl driving Aramovsky's spider swings a leg over the rail and descends, abandoning him.

Aramovsky watches them all, eyes cold and consumed with rage.

He's lost. He knows it.

A tap on my arm. It's Barkah.

"Hem." He gestures toward Aramovsky. *"Move."*

We do. Barkah and I walk to Aramovsky's spider. I climb the rungs. I stand before the red-robed "leader" of our people. Barkah climbs up as well, then stands next to me, shoulder to shoulder. Human and Springer together, facing down a common enemy.

Aramovsky sneers at me. "The food doesn't matter, you gullible idiot. Don't you understand? *They . . . aren't . . . human.* This war will happen now, or it will happen later. Someday they will come for us. They will kill us because *we . . . aren't . . . them.* And if you're still alive, you'll know you sold out your own people to these monsters."

"The only monster here is *you,*" I say. "No more fighting. No more death."

Aramovsky's chest heaves. There is a scream inside him, a scream that has no voice, no home. I know he is thinking the same thing I thought when he took the spear from me, that he can run me through, fight to keep what he believes is his and his alone.

Slowly, gently, Barkah draws the knife given to him by O'Malley. The knife with the double-ring made of red stones. The knife with the blade as long as my forearm. The Springer prince keeps the knife at his side. The tip points down, not at Aramovsky, but the message is clear.

Aramovsky stares at it, eyes wide. Threatening an unarmed person is one thing—facing an armed opponent is another.

"Barkah and I are in this together," I say. "You attack one of us, you attack *both* of us. You wanted to kill Springers, Aramovsky? Well, here's your chance. If you're going to fight, then do something with that spear besides just pose with it."

The fingers of his bracelet hand twitch. Maybe he's wondering if he can fire twice before one of us gets to him. But I don't think he'll try. For him, the bracelet and the spear are little more than props. He is a leader, yes, but he is no warrior. When the time for speeches is past, when he must kill or be killed, Aramovsky's conviction turns to cowardice.

He doesn't move. I wait, let everyone see he's afraid to back up his words with actions.

I hold out my hand.

"If you won't do yourself what you ask others to do for you, then *give me back my godsdamned spear,* you murdering bastard."

We stare at each other. The universe fades away: there is only the two of us.

Infinite moments pass by.

Aramovsky breaks. He looks away. Without another word, he tilts the spear toward me.

I take it. The cool wood feels nice in my hand.

"Remove that bracelet, Aramovsky—and get off my spider. I'll deal with you later."

He slides the bracelet from his arm, lets it clatter to the spider's metal deck.

As I watch him descend the rungs, I hear sounds of surprise and alarm from my people.

While Aramovsky and I faced off, the Springers—*thousands* of them—quietly closed in. Their line runs under the shuttle, winding around the landing gear, spreading out wide on either side. Some of them stare at the shuttle in open amazement, gawking at something their kind hasn't seen in generations. Far more stare at us, muskets leveled, enough that one volley would probably kill everyone.

My people reply in kind, leveling bracelets, climbing to spiderback and manning cannons or crouching low with hoes and picks and axes and shovels. Even if all of us die in that first salvo, Spingate and Gaston remain safe inside the shuttle. If the Springers attack, I know she will unleash the shuttle's weapons, try to wipe out this violent species so that her unborn child may someday live safe and free.

If I don't do something now, I haven't stopped the slaughter, I've only delayed it.

"Lower your weapons," I shout at my people. "This fight is over!"

Some comply, some don't.

Barkah yells at his kind, loud and commanding. I don't know what he's saying, but the result is immediate: most of the Springers lower their musket barrels. They haven't put their guns down, but they aren't aiming them at us, either.

We're doing it. Barkah and I, together, we're going to stop this.

Then, a bark of command from behind the Springer lines. The muskets snap up again, each one dead-level, aimed at me, at Bishop, at the spider riders, at the children holding tools. My people do the same: we're one trigger twitch shy of a bloodbath.

Another bark from behind the lines, somewhere under the shuttle. Straight out from my spider, the Springer line splits.

Four of the biggest Springers I've seen yet hop forward, their muskets aimed at me. Bluish-red skin marked with scars, weapons strapped to their bodies: axes, knives, swords. Any one of them looks like a match for Bishop when Bishop is at his best.

Two of them move slightly to the right, two slightly to the left.

From between them hops forward an old Springer, one whose blue skin is turning ashen and gray. Hanging from his neck is an ornate copper plate.

Barkah's parent: the Springer king.

I angle my spear toward the Springer prince.

Barkah looks at it. After watching Aramovsky give it to me, I think he understands the weapon's significance.

"Your turn," I say. "I'm afraid I can't do the talking here." I give the spear a little shake. "Together. We do this *together*."

His two good eyes—two alert, pain-filled eyes—look at me.

"Hem . . . peace."

I nod. "Peace."

His right hand reaches out, grips the spear. As one, we raise my people's symbol of leadership.

Barkah talks. I don't understand a word he says. I see Springers' guns waver, see the aliens looking at each other, looking at their ruler. Perhaps some emotions are constant in any intelligent species—these Springers are confused, they are being told two things and don't know which is true.

The Springer king's entire body contorts. His eyes widen, his lips angrily curl back, show teeth. He screams at Barkah. He turns and screams at his people, first to the left, then repeating the same thing to the right.

And then I hear something soft, something nearly silent. If I wasn't standing right next to Barkah, our arms together raising the spear, I wouldn't have heard it at all. The sound sends a chill up my spine, tells me that something is horribly wrong.

It is the sound of broken glass.

Quietly, to himself, Barkah is *laughing*—laughing like a person who is watching a plan unfold, like someone who knew exactly what was going to happen.

The Springer king turns to face us. He says something, and the bodyguard on his right hands over his musket. The Springer king puts the butt to his thin shoulder: he aims it at us.

He says something else, something angry, definitive and commanding.

I again hear Barkah's tiny broken-glass laugh. The prince raises his left arm.

He's wearing Aramovsky's bracelet.

I freeze. I didn't even see him pick it up.

I stare. So does the king. That sense of command, of absolute authority, it leaves his eyes. For a horrible moment, I can read his emotions: shock, disbelief . . . betrayal.

Barkah flicks his two fingers forward.

The beam lashes out. White fire engulfs the king. The alien scream—a sound I will *never* be able to forget—lasts only a split second, then ends forever as his body rips into a hundred pieces. Blue blood and meat chunks splatter on the Springers behind him, splash his bodyguards with charred gore.

The spear is yanked from my hand.

Barkah raises his arms, the spear held in one hand, the other hand outstretched, letting the morning sun glisten off his bracelet.

He talks for a few seconds. Again, I don't know what he says, but I don't have to understand the words to see their effect: the long, seemingly endless line of Springer guns hovers, flutters, lowers. One or two at first, then in a wave, until all the muskets point down at the ground.

One by one, the Springers lower their heads. They drop.

They *kneel.*

There must be a hundred bodies scattered across the battlefield. Humans and Springers alike, shredded by weapons both primitive and advanced. And I suddenly wonder if it didn't have to be this way, if Barkah could have stopped all of it—but he didn't *want* to.

Maybe what he really wanted was to become the leader of his people.

As with many things, maybe our two races are more alike than we are different. Barkah wanted *power*.

The Springer prince—no, the new *king*—turns to me. He thonks the spear butt on the deck, leans the tip toward me, offering me the weapon.

"Hem . . . peace."

Yes, peace. At what cost? And for how long?

I take the spear.

While I don't know what the future holds, this battle, at least, is finished.

EPILOGUE

It is a beautiful day on Omeyocan. The reddish sun beats down. Blurd wings sparkle in the light. I smell fresh-baked bread and roasting meat. We will eat well tonight.

A short distance from the Observatory, Muller slows my spider. He's done this enough times now that he doesn't need to be told what to do. The child soldier stops us in front of the black X, lowers the machine's belly. Metal clangs against stone; no more vines on this street, as we cleared them away.

Muller—or *Victor*, as he prefers to be called—missed the battle entirely. Matilda locked him in an Observatory cell. Once things calmed down, we found him and let him out. He's a circle-star, so he's still somewhat bitter he didn't get a chance to fight. Like most kids with his symbol, he's constantly eager to prove himself. If I have my way, he'll never get that chance, because we'll never fight again.

I hand him my spear.

"Hold this for a moment?"

He takes it, holds it as if it's a magical talisman. Maybe he'll hold it permanently one day; if so, he'll find out it's far more burden than blessing.

I climb out.

The black X is bent and twisted from the fire's heat. We moved it out here into the open, where it serves as a monument to the people and Springers who died in that fire.

"Hello, Kevin," I say. "I'm sorry I didn't make it yesterday. Or the day before. Kalle and Walezak got into a fight. Kalle is working to see if there's a way to get our Bello back. She might be in there, somehow—just like you were. Walezak says it's a sin, and that Grownup Bello's wisdom and experience are too valuable to lose. Something like that. Anyway, they got into a fistfight, if you can believe it. Oh, and I had to check on the first crops. I told you they found corn seeds in the food warehouse, right?"

Kevin doesn't answer, of course. He never does. His bones are buried here along with his progenitor's, Coyotl's, Old Bishop's and those of the other Grownups who died in the Observatory battle. I wonder if they, too, listen to me when I talk.

"I can't stay long today," I say. "Spingate sent for me, said she found something really important. She wanted Borjigin and Barkah, too. I'll come back and tell you what it is as soon as I can, okay?"

Kevin doesn't answer.

"Spin is really close to having the baby," I say. "Smith says it could be any day now. Hard to believe how much time has passed since Gaston told everyone she was pregnant. He said if it's a boy, they will name it after you. Isn't that nice?"

Kevin doesn't answer.

I reach out, lay one hand on the twisted black metal. It's hot from baking in the sun. The first few times I did this, it made me cry, but I don't cry anymore.

Not every time, anyway.

"I miss you," I whisper. "I miss you so much."

Muller softly clears his throat, reminding me I'm already late.

I turn away from the X, scale the spider and stand next to the young circle-star. He hands me my spear, then urges the spider on without saying a word.

Since the standoff in the clearing, Muller has become my driver and assistant, of sorts. Bishop calls him my "bodyguard." Muller is taller than me now. He's our best marksman, and I've seen him training with knife, hatchet and fists. His lanky frame belies his ability as a gifted, deadly fighter. I hate to think I actually need a bodyguard, but I know I do—as the leader of my people, I'm a target for the Springers that want to drive us out. We still can't fully trust them. Perhaps we'll never be able to.

And then there is the constant fear that Matilda and the Grownups will return. For all we know, they're here already. Gaston thinks they could fly a ship to the far side of Omeyocan and land without us knowing. The thought is terrifying, but also galvanizing: Barkah and the Springers understand the Grownups are the ones that savaged their race for generations—not us. If Grownups attack, they will be met with unified resistance. While our problems with the Springers are many, having a common enemy outweighs them all.

Muller drives the spider to the Observatory. Once again, he lowers the war machine's belly to the ground.

"Shall I escort you in, Em?"

I'm sure he wants to protect me, but there is another reason he'd like to come inside.

"I can make it on my own, thank you. You don't mind staying out here, do you?"

He looks crestfallen. Like most of the circle-stars, Muller can't hide his emotions. It's so easy to tease him.

"Oh, wait," I say. "I'm seeing Spingate, and Zubiri might be with her. Zubiri isn't the *real* reason you want to go with me, is it?"

He shakes his head. "No! I'm supposed to stay with you is all, honest! Bishop told me to—"

I can't help but laugh at him. "It's all right, you can come."

It's funny when I think about it, but in a way, Aramovsky got his wish. Part of it, anyway. He wanted us all to live in the Observatory. Turns out, that was an excellent idea.

In the days following the battle, we were unsure of Barkah's intentions as the new Springer leader. We couldn't stay in the shuttle anymore, as it was too crowded, but we also needed a place that was defendable. We're still outnumbered at least a thousand to one, something I can't ignore. Barkah can't possibly control all of his kind. The Observatory gives us the space we need, and has only a few entrances, which we can seal up tight.

Borjigin's progenitor was trained to manage buildings, guide construction and repair, do all the things needed to make a city operate. Our Borjigin discovered the Observatory has lights, clean running water, temperature control—everything we need.

The telescope part doesn't work, though. Apparently it needs a different kind of power. Zubiri figured out that the power source was in the room where O'Malley died, at the bottom of the shaft surrounded by that red metal wall. The fire destroyed the power cable, and also dropped some debris on top of the power source, breaking it. Zubiri, Spingate and the other gears have been working for a long time to fix it.

The Observatory has *thousands* of rooms, more than enough for everyone to have their own space. Aramovsky's wish came true for him, especially: he's locked in a stone cell in the building's lower levels—the same cell Muller was locked in, actually. Bello is locked in another cell. If she and Aramovsky shout loud enough, they can sort of hear each other. They'll stay in those cells until I'm damn good and ready to figure out how to put them on trial for their crimes.

There is even space for the hundred red-skinned Springers that live with us. Some train with Spingate and the scientists, some with Bishop and the circle-stars, some with Smith for medicine, some with the halves for civil engineering and management. It's part of Barkah's and my effort to bridge the gaps between our species, to create cooperation and harmony.

And some of the young reds work with our "plain-old circles." Just like with humans, not every Springer is cut out for math, science, planning or war.

It breaks my heart, but Okereke, Johnson, Cabral and Ingolfsson still don't seem interested in learning a particular skill. I've asked them. If someone tells them what to do, they're happy to do it. And most of the twelve-year-old circles—who are now closer to thirteen—feel the same way. Out of all the circles, only a handful of kids and D'souza seem interested in becoming something other than what they were designed to be.

Some of those ambitious circles are out in the jungle, living with the Springers. Just as we have much to teach them, they have much to teach us. D'souza leads the effort of learning how to farm and prepare food, how the Springers gather, hunt and trap.

I talk to D'souza—her first name is Maria—at least twice a day. She's learning the Springer language, learning to be a Springer in much the same way that Bishop teaches Muller how to be a knight. Maria gives me hope that I'm not the only one capable of being something more than the Grownups designed us to be, that any of us can create our own destiny.

If it sounds like our two races are getting along well, they aren't. If we could have ended the battle before it began, then—maybe—we could have all been friends. But 213 Springers died that day. Another hundred or so bear permanent injuries. We lost fourteen people, and have permanent injuries of our own. No matter how many times Barkah and I tell everyone that we're all working together now, each race distrusts the other. We are just too *different*.

There have been fights between our races. Mostly with fists, some with weapons. We've had people beaten and cut—our kids are told to never go out alone, especially at night. If it wasn't for our circle-crosses and the Observatory's medical facilities, our death toll would have climbed higher still. Springers, too, have been hurt as some of our youth have sought to repay violence with violence.

But we're trying. And as devious as Barkah turned out to be, he's trying, too.

I invited the entire Springer population to move into Uchmal, so the city walls could keep out those predators lurking in the jungle. A few accepted, most declined. The sins of our creators won't fade overnight. Not to mention the fact that we use spiders constantly—for any Springer, the sight of those metal monstrosities still fills them with terror.

Instead of moving into our city, the Springers are rebuilding their own. They finally have the opportunity to live aboveground. They're starting small, working with a few of the hexagonal buildings that had the least damage. Finally free from the constant threat of spiders, they are even trying to build their first factories so they can mass-produce goods for farming, hunting, construction and more. Making each item by hand takes too long. I even have two of the kids who were stored in the shuttle—Bariso and Nevins—helping them design a rifle to replace their muskets.

As for Bishop and me, I want to spend more time with him and he wants to spend more time with me, but the things we have done haunt us both. Being around each other reminds us of those things. I know he's working just as hard as I am to build our new way of life—for now, that is enough.

I gaze up at the massive Observatory. We've lived here for 271 days now—Opkick has kept a close count—yet the size still staggers my imagination. Borjigin estimates this building alone took the machines twenty or thirty years to make. The whole city? Probably along the lines of a half-century.

We haven't cut the Observatory's vines, because they mostly cover up horrible images that none of us need to see. We'll get rid of those images someday, but for now there are more important things to do.

We've found a total of three ground-level entrances into the Observatory. We think there is at least one more, though, a secret exit from the main room that Matilda and Old Gaston must have used to escape. She helped design the city, after all—the secrets she knows will hurt us if she ever comes back.

Our main entrance is the one Barkah used to rescue us, the same entrance young Springers used for years to explore the Observatory and steal food stored there. Seems our wrapped packages were more than just a trophy for young Springers who proved their bravery by entering the city and risking spider attack—our food is something of a delicacy to them. Right now, it is a central unit of trade between races. They get CRACKERS and PROTEIN BARS and COOKIES, we get fruit and vegetables, meat, grains, and a certain kind of tree bark. Turns out, bark is absolutely delicious.

"Come on," I say to Muller. "Let's go see your girlfriend."

His face flushes, but he doesn't deny it. I should really stop teasing him so much.

At the Observatory entrance, Barkah, Lahfah, D'souza and Borjigin are waiting for me.

Barkah still has Kevin's knife in his belt. Every time I meet the Springer leader, I can't help but notice that.

D'souza no longer wears black coveralls. Strips of colored cloth are tied around her arms, legs, stomach, and strategically around her waist and chest. Her beautiful brown skin is even darker now, as she spends every day in the jungle. She carries a Springer bag, a hatchet tucked into her belt, and a musket slung over her shoulder.

Barkah wears a patch over his ruined middle eye, but the two remaining green eyes are bright, full of excitement for life. He loves his role as the leader of his people.

"Hem," he says. *"Feel well . . . today?"*

I can't help but smile. Barkah is picking up our language. I only wish I was as good at picking up theirs.

"Yawap," I say. "Tallik . . . tallik cree?"

Lahfah's frog-mouth trembles like she's trying to hold something back, then it opens wide with grinding-glass laughter. We now know "he" is a "she." Her leg is fully healed, thanks in no small part to young Pokano, the circle-cross who has chosen to focus specifically on Springer physiology.

I look to D'souza. "What is she laughing at? I tried to say, *I feel fine.*"

"Close," she says. "You said, *I feel poop on my face.*"

I laugh, embarrassed. Lahfah laughs harder. Barkah growls at her. She stops, but her body continues to shake with held-back amusement. The two of them go everywhere together. Lahfah has an unstoppable sense of humor, which is good, because Barkah doesn't seem to have one at all.

Borjigin is impatient. He looks at the thin rectangle in his hands, which he calls a "messageboard." He and Opkick found several of them in an Observatory storeroom. They use them to get information when they are out in the city or the jungle, far away from pedestals.

"We're *late,*" he says. "Can we please stop joking about feces and get inside?"

I'm the leader of the people, but Borjigin is in charge of extending the reach of power and clean water, the continuous searching of unexplored buildings, a thousand other things necessary to make this city livable. He works even harder than I do, and—like Barkah—has little time for jokes.

We're about to enter when Okereke, Johnson and a young circle named Mehmet walk out. They are covered in mud and greasy char. They stink of dirt and some kind of mineral scent I can't place. They are laughing and excited.

"You're filthy," I say to Okereke. "What have you three been up to in there?"

"Helping Spingate," he says. "And Zubiri."

"Helping with what?"

He shakes his head, all smiles. "She made us promise not to say anything until she talked to you first. But it's really amazing."

Borjigin's fingers drum impatiently on the messageboard.

"Fine," I say. "Borjigin, lead the way."

The hallway we used to flee the fire is now illuminated by a glowing ceiling rather than torchlight. The floor is swept clean, the stone walls are spotless.

The long walk brings us to the room where Coyotl's mind was erased, where Old Dr. Smith burned to death, where Springers died, where I shot Old Bishop and stabbed O'Malley. I wish we could center things elsewhere, but Spingate and Gaston both insist this room was designed to be the hub of all the Observatory's abilities.

While I will never recover from those memories, the room looks completely different. The golden coffins have been moved elsewhere in the building, and modified by Smith and Pokano to become sources of health and healing rather than destruction. The burned ceiling was scraped away, painted white, all the lights repaired. We covered up that horrible mural. We found a storeroom with replacement pedestals; a half-dozen of them adorn a rebuilt platform, and a dozen more are set up in the space the coffins once occupied.

Despite all the cleaning and painting, this place still smells faintly of smoke and scorched flesh. Every time I come in, I look at the spot where O'Malley died.

Springers and kids alike study at the floor pedestals. Some are learning math and science, some are helping develop Borjigin's plan for the city.

Spingate, Gaston and Zubiri are standing on the platform. Spingate's belly is curved with the life growing inside of her. She walks funny now, has to in order to balance the weight—Smith says the baby is overdue.

Gaston has grown something, too: a beard. It is thick and black, and it annoys Bishop. As big as Bishop is, all he can manage is a thin blond scraggle. Gaston is fond of saying that facial hair defines being "manly," and will continue to say so until it stops enraging Bishop.

And then there is Zubiri.

Most of her face has been repaired. Smith is still working on replacing her missing teeth. Five of them are in and set, three more to go. I'm told that after the next operation, Zubiri should have her smile back. The one thing she can never have back, though, is her left arm.

She lost it in the battle. It was torn off in the spider crash, severed just above her elbow. Smith could do nothing for that.

Coffins can do miracles on skin and bone, fixing up that which is damaged, but regrowing body parts is beyond the technology's abilities.

Spingate looks up from her work. She sees Muller, smiles.

"Grandmaster Zubiri," she says, "can you go to the shuttle and bring me back the bracer from storage? And Em, I need Zubiri back here sooner rather than later—would you mind if Victor gives her a ride?"

Zubiri and Muller—I correct myself, *Victor*—stare at each other. I'm not sure they even remember I'm here.

"I don't mind at all," I say. "Just don't be gone all day."

"We won't," the two of them say in unison, and they rush out of the room before we can change our minds.

We've learned that Zubiri is brilliant. *Genius* is the word Spingate uses to describe her. Perhaps someday soon Zubiri will lead these research efforts instead of Spingate, but the girl's mind isn't always on her work. Maybe if she hadn't had her arm ripped off and her face smashed so hard she needed eleven reconstructive surgeries, maybe if she didn't wake up every night screaming in horror as she relives that moment, then she could concentrate more.

And, of course, maybe if she wasn't in love with a boy.

Gaston is staring at an image of stars hovering above a pedestal. He waves us to join him.

I step onto the platform. It's wide enough that Barkah and Lahfah can come up with me. Borjigin stays on the floor, looking at his messageboard and talking to D'souza.

"So, I'm here," I say to Spingate. "What's so important that Barkah and I both had to come?"

She looks at the Springer, as if wondering if she made a mistake to ask for him. She shakes her head, chasing away that thought. Whatever this is, it must affect both species equally.

"Zubiri fixed the power supply in the hole," she says.

I look to the red wall in the room's center, realize that a heavy black cable is running up from the hole, over the wall and under the pedestal platform. A cable just like it burned up in the fire.

"Spin, that's *great*! Does that mean the telescope is working?"

"Sort of," she says. "First I have to tell you what we found in the hole. Only Zubiri, myself and a few other young gears have been down there—until today. Today we needed Okereke to take the heavy cable down and connect it. He saw things in the walls that the rest of us hadn't noticed."

She picks up a box that is sitting on the platform. It's filled with dirty objects.

"Borjigin, I need your expertise," she says, and pulls out a piece of masonry from the box. "Can you tell me what this is?"

He and D'souza join us on the platform. The bit of masonry is flat on two sides, broken on the other. It looks like a small chunk of a corner of a building, but the angle is wider than ninety degrees.

"A piece of Springer building," Borjigin says. "One-hundred-twenty-degree angle. Their specific type of concrete. You can tell because they like to mix in wood mulch." He points to several small air spaces in the concrete. They look like slots where wood splinters would fit in perfectly.

Spingate nods. "That's what I thought, too. It was found in the dirt walls of the hole, the layer just below the floor of this room."

Borjigin nods. "Of course. The Grownups leveled the Springer city and built on top of it. There's going to be all kinds of debris buried beneath Uchmal."

Spingate seems nervous. She takes another piece from the box, offers it to him.

"This was below that layer," she says. "What is it?"

It's flat on one side, melted and torn on the other. It's not masonry. I've never seen anything like it.

Borjigin stares at it. He turns it over.

"I don't know what it is," he says. "Some kind of composite. A support beam, maybe. I haven't seen this material in any Springer architecture, and it isn't in anything built by the Grown-ups. You said it was *below* the Springer layer?"

Spingate nods, reaches into the box.

"The whole layer is full of it. Okereke found this as well."

She hands him what looks like a plastic doll, or perhaps a small statue. This I recognize: the body is the same reverse-legged shape as the statues in Barkah's church. Two back-folded legs, two lower arms, two arms coming out the sides of the one-eyed head.

Borjigin shrugs. "I don't know what that is."

Barkah gently takes it from Borjigin.

"Bu, Vellen," the Springer says, examining it. *"Kollo regatta jumain."*

Words I don't know. I glance at D'souza.

"He's talking about the *Vellen,*" she says. "The Albonden won't tell me much about them."

Albonden. It's still hard for me to get used to that word. That's the name of Barkah's tribe. D'souza insists we all use it instead of *Springers,* but most of my people ignore her.

"Is Vellen another tribe?" I ask.

D'souza shakes her head. "I think *Vellen* is the name of their gods, because the rest of what he said roughly means *those who came before us*."

Barkah sets the plastic doll back in Spingate's box.

Borjigin shakes his head. "Spingate, are you saying that not only did we destroy the Springer city to build Uchmal, but the Springers destroyed an *earlier* city, populated by *another* race, to build theirs?"

But . . . that can't be. The Springers were here first. My race wanted their land, slaughtered them, nearly wiped them out. Does this discovery mean that the Springers weren't just part of the natural balance of Omeyocan, that they, too, demolished what came before them to take over this land?

Spingate shrugs. "I'm just saying that these layers are in the hole. Okereke said the hole goes much deeper and it looks like there are even more layers. He didn't descend past the power source, though—he said it felt *too creepy*."

This is making my head fuzzy. Our creators destroyed the Springers, who maybe destroyed these Vellen. . . . did the Vellen destroy another race before them? And if so, why are so many races building a city in exactly the same place?

"We'll have to go down there," I say. "You were right to bring Barkah and me both in for this."

Spingate shakes her head. She seems nervous, maybe upset.

"That's not the main reason I asked you here," she says. "I said we *sort of* fixed the telescope. What I mean is there are two kinds." She points a finger up. "The Goffspear telescope, the big optical one in this building, still isn't working. Without Okadigbo, we just don't know what's wrong with it, let alone how to fix it. But it turns out there are other telescopes in the city and in the jungle—*radio telescopes*. We got those working. They've been feeding us information for a few hours now, and we found something. Gaston, show her."

Gaston waves his hands over a pedestal. Above it, a green, blue and brown sphere appears: Omeyocan, spinning slightly. Above that is a red point of light. Farther out and in a different direction, a blue point.

He points to the red one. "That represents the *Xolotl.*"

Just the name of that ship calls up so many awful memories. But if that red dot is the *Xolotl,* what's the blue dot?

I point to it. "I'm guessing this is what you really brought us here to see?"

"You guessed right," Gaston says. "Do you know what a *radio wave* is?"

I shake my head.

"Think of when you're out in the city," he says. "Sometimes when you yell very loud, it sounds like your words bounce back to you?"

I nod. "Especially with big buildings around."

"Radio waves are like that, only on a larger scale," he says. "They go out into space. The Observatory sends out this radio signal. Think of a ball that keeps getting bigger and bigger at the speed of light. When the radio waves hit something, they bounce back to Omeyocan, where the radio telescopes detect them." He points to the red light again. "This is from the radio waves hitting the *Xolotl* and bouncing back."

It takes me a second to understand what that means. The red light is the *Xolotl,* a ship in orbit . . . so the blue light is . . .

This can't be. It *can't.*

"You're telling me there is another ship out there?"

Spingate nods. She's staring at the dot, gently pulling at her lower lip with her thumb and forefinger. In a way, she didn't look this afraid even when the Springers were beating the hell out of us.

Gaston notices, puts his arm around her shoulders, gives her a light squeeze.

"Definitely another ship," he says. "Almost as big as the *Xolotl.* And it's coming our way."

Since I woke up, I think I've spent every day in fear. Afraid for my life, for the lives of others, but this fills me with a new sense of foreboding.

"More Grownups," I say. "They're coming for us."

Gaston huffs. "I *wish*. At least we'd know what we're dealing with. We haven't been able to fully recover the Observatory's memory, but I did get some information on the path the *Xolotl* took to get here. This new ship is on a completely different trajectory."

I stare at him instead of the blue dot. "Maybe you could say that in words I could understand?"

"It's not more Grownups." He lets go of Spingate, taps the red dot. A line extends from it, arcing away to my left, away from Omeyocan.

"That's the path the *Xolotl* took to get here," he says. He taps the blue dot. Another line appears, curving away and to my right. "*That* is the path the new ship took."

The ships came from completely different areas of space. It took the *Xolotl* a thousand years to reach this planet. That new ship could have been traveling equally long, but from another direction.

"If it's not Grownups," I say, "then who?"

When Gaston speaks, his voice is quiet and steady, free of any trace of the mockery or bravado that usually define him.

"When the Grownups got here, they destroyed the Springer civilization. Based on what Okereke found in the hole, we think the Springers destroyed another race that was here before them—meaning the Springers are probably from somewhere else, just like we are. Three races have occupied this same area. So who is in that new ship? My guess is it's a *fourth* race. And based on what the Grownups did when they arrived, and what the Springers probably did when *they* arrived, we have to assume this fourth race isn't coming here for milk and cookies."

No one speaks. The blue dot blinks softly.

I couldn't have possibly anticipated this. No one could have. We *earned* peace. An uneasy peace, certainly, but humans and Springers are working together, trying to build bridges that will lead to us sharing this planet. Not as one people, perhaps, but as cooperative neighbors. We've fought for that, and now a tiny point of blue light tells me it might all be for nothing.

"How long?" I say. "How long until it arrives?"

Gaston scratches his beard. "About two hundred days."

We don't know what it is. We don't know what's in it. We don't know if it is friend or enemy.

Spingate clears her throat. "It's likely they detected our radio wave, so they know that we know they're coming. We're trying to figure out how to send a communication, but we're not sure how to do that, or if they would even understand. Should we—"

The room speaks, cutting her off.

"*Grandmaster Spingate,*" Ometeotl says. "*Contact Gamma-One detected.*"

Farther out from Omeyocan, past the blue dot and in yet another direction, a yellow dot appears.

Spingate and Gaston say nothing.

"Is that the sun?" I ask. "One of the two moons?"

Spingate slowly shakes her head. "The *Xolotl* is labeled Alpha-One. That was the first thing the radio wave detected. Then it detected the blue dot, which we labeled Beta-One. The wave keeps expanding, continues to detect things that are farther out." Her hands rub absently at her swollen belly.

Gaston turns quickly to another pedestal. He calls up glowing symbols, grabs them, moves them, turns them.

The yellow dot grows a line: it points out into yet another area of space.

"A third ship," he says, his voice flat, stunned. "Estimated time to orbit, two hundred eighty-one days. Maybe it's a ghost image or something, or an asteroid, or—"

"Grandmaster Spingate, contact Delta-One detected."

A green dot appears. This time I don't have to ask what it is—it's all too clear.

Gaston works the controls.

"Getting the estimated time to orbit," he says. "Roughly . . . three hundred thirty-two days."

Three ships, out there in the blackness of space. They are all coming from different directions.

They are all coming *here*.

Our fight for Omeyocan is long from over.

ACKNOWLEDGMENTS

Scott would like to thank the following people for their research expertise:

Dr. Joseph A. Albietz III, M.D.
Maria D'souza
Dr. Nicole Gugliucci, Ph.D.
A Kovacs
Dr. Phil Plait, Ph.D.
Chris Grall, MSG, U.S. Army Special Forces (Ret.)
John Vizcarra

And these lovely people for story feedback:

Abby Parrill-Baker, Ph.D.
Daniel Baker, Ph.D.
Lindsey Baker
Jody Sigler

READ ON FOR AN EXCERPT FROM THE FINAL INSTALLMENT

IN THE GENERATIONS TRILOGY

ALONE

by Scott Sigler

PUBLISHED BY DEL REY BOOKS

A stabbing pain jolts me awake.

My neck . . . the needle, the *snake* . . .

No, not a stab. A poke . . . a poke of cold metal. I lift my head, look around. My silver bracelet. I wear it over the sleeve of my black coveralls, its wide ring circling my right forearm just below the elbow—I must have rolled over in my sleep, laid my neck on the long point that extends from the flat ring down to just behind the back of my wrist.

I'm cold. I'm wet. It's raining again. Correction: it's raining *still*. I was sleeping on the tiny metal deck of a spider cockpit, other people crammed in around me. My thigh is numb—I rolled over onto the combat knife I always have strapped to my thigh.

So tired. As uncomfortable as I am, I just want to go back to sleep.

A boy's voice: "Em, wake up."

Victor Muller, part of my spider's three-person crew.

"D'souza spotted them," he says. "She's coming."

That wakes me up for real. If Maria is coming, maybe it's time to fight.

Finally.

I sit up. Muscles, cramped and stiff. My cold skin feels like it's made of half-dry clay. Our black coveralls are good at keeping us warm, but in the jungle the dampness always finds a way in.

Ten days of this. Ten days of hiding, without fire or heat, without a hot meal, eating prepackaged food and jungle plants. Ten days since I bathed—I want a shower almost as much as I want to catch the Belligerents. I want to lie on my couch, Bishop's arms around me, as I watch the jungle from afar, not from within.

I miss him. I miss his eyes, his hair and his smile. I miss the very smell of him. If we're able to force our enemy to battle—and that is a very big *if*—I might be hurt in the fighting. Possibly even killed. Before I left, he told me he loves me.

Did I tell him the same thing?

I think I did. Yes, I must have.

You would have told O'Malley, and you know it.

Well, hello, Annoying Little Voice. How nice of you to show up now.

Annoying Little Voice always wants me to second-guess myself, to doubt my decisions. It tells me things would be better *now* if they'd gone a different way *then.* If I'd made better choices. If I'd had stronger self-control. I hate that damn voice.

Wiping the last of the sleep from my eyes, I reach up and grab the armored ridge that surrounds the cockpit. I stand, slowly, careful not to jostle the branches that hide our position.

The twin moons of Omeyocan—one bluish, one green—shine through sparse cloud cover. In the daytime, this jungle is bright with yellow leaves, brown tree trunks and long blue vine stems.

At night, everything is a blue-green shade of gray. The plants gleam with wetness.

Spingate still insists on calling our machines "pentapods," but no one listens to her about that. To us, they are *spiders*. Five-legged, yes, but spiders all the same. The machines are meant for a two-person crew: driver and cannon operator. We use them with crews of three, adding one person who can fire with whatever weapon they have at hand. Three makes for close quarters. The cockpit is open-air. No glowing holograms here—all the controls are manual, built to last a thousand years, to take a real beating and keep on working. A waist-high, horseshoe-shaped armored ridge surrounds the cockpit, protects us from bullets and musket balls. The ends of the horseshoe blend into the cockpit's rear wall, which comes up to my sternum. If I stand straight, I can rest my arms on the spider's sloping back and fire my bracelet at whatever is behind us.

We've repainted the spiders to cover up centuries of superficial damage. Each one has black numbers on the sides (ours is 05), while most the shell is dark yellow with jagged stripes of brown and blue—the colors of the jungle. When the machines work correctly, they blend in well. Of course, they're all a couple of centuries old, so they don't work correctly all that much. Parts often clatter and gears frequently grind, making unmistakable noise. We do our best to fix those problems when they come up.

There are two legs in front, two on the sides—one each below where the armored ridge blends into the back wall—and one leg in the rear. The three-jointed legs all end in hard, sharp points, which can slice right through any enemy unfortunate enough to be in our way.

I ride in the cockpit's right side. Yoshiko Bawden, the driver, is on my left, in the middle. She's a tall, muscular circle-star who thinks it's funny to make fake burp sounds. When she's not being crude, though, she is a fierce warrior. She's always kept her black hair shaved down. Before we began this campaign, she had some of her fellow circle-stars tattoo the word KILLER on the right side of her head. She has a pitchfork strapped across her back and a bracelet on her right arm, over her coveralls. She used to use an axe, like Bishop does, but she prefers the pitchfork for jungle fighting. I have known her almost since I first woke up, and am so grateful to have her steady presence as part of my crew.

"Little" Victor Muller is on Bawden's left, where he mans the beam-cannon. He's not little anymore, though. When the circle-star came out of his coffin, I was a bit taller than he was. Now my eyes come up to his chin. He's added muscle as well. He's not at thick as Bishop, probably never will be. Victor has the same wiry frame my friend Coyotl had—long, lean, athletic. Victor wears a bracelet on his right arm. In his hands, he holds a spear. Not *my* spear, of course, but one that looks close to it. A repeating rifle is slung over his back. He's become one of our best warriors, almost as skilled as Farrar, Bishop and Bawden, who are all fully grown.

I am brave enough to fight, but I'm not stupid—I want people in my crew who can protect me. I'd rather have Bishop instead of Victor, of course, but right now it's more important to our people that Bishop remain back in Uchmal.

The lower half of our spider is buried in the jungle floor, the upper half covered in branches and vines. Sometimes you hunt your enemies—but only if you can find them. When you can't, your best bet is to set a trap and hope your enemies fall into it.

It looks like they finally have.

Nearby, a light rustling from the jungle. I see what looks like a thick, yellowish snake rise from the underbrush and move toward us. The furry snake ends in wicked, hooked pincers that can snap together so hard they'll damn near cut a person in two. A few meters away, the animal rises up in full from the underbrush. A year ago, the sight of this predator would have scared me half to death. Now? It only scares me a quarter of the way.

When I first saw these creatures, I didn't have the memories or words to describe them. It's still hard. Different people have remembered different things at different times, filling my head with images of animals that Matilda only read about in books. The heavy body of a bear. The thick trunk of an elephant. Below where the trunk connects to the head is a piranha's dagger-toothed mouth. Claws of a tiger. Body covered in brown-striped yellow fur. Heavy plates of mottled yellow bone on its chest. Three beady black eyes in a line on each side of the head, which is also plated in yellow bone.

On the back of this beast, on a saddle made of tough leather, sits Maria D'souza, a fellow "empty."

She took to calling the big predators *hurukans*. We're not sure where that word comes from, but as soon as any of us heard it, we agreed it was the perfect name.

"Hail, Em," Maria says. "*Guthana, Yalani.*"

Maria greets me first in English, then in the Springer language. She always wants the Springer fighters in her squad to know I am in charge—*yalani* means "leader."

"Hail, Maria," I say. "You've found them?"

She nods. "The Belligerents are coming from the east, closing in on the cornfield. I have the Creepers circling behind them to cut off any escape. Barkah and his infantry battalion are positioned to the north as a reserve, per your orders."

We have them.

"How many Belligerents?" I ask.

"Maybe a hundred," Maria says. "All on foot. No cavalry of any kind."

"Excellent. Where do you want us?"

Maria points north.

"Straight ahead, *Yalani*. My squad will attack from the southwest. When you strike, we'll be on your left flank."

Atop the 650-kilo hurukan she calls Fenrir, Maria is a striking figure. She wears cloth strips of yellow, green, and blue, just like the Springer warriors. Vine juice and dirt cover her brown skin, helping her blend into the jungle. She has half a dozen knives strapped to her body and a repeating rifle slung across her back. When the violence began months ago, I offered her one of our precious bracelets. She declined. She chooses to use the same weapon as the Springers in her cavalry squads.

The snake-wolves are the top predators of this world. As far as we can tell, they kill and eat everything they see. That used to include the Springers. Then came Maria, who somehow learned how to not only capture the beasts but *tame* them as well. She's trained others to do the same.

Mounted atop her monster, Maria D'souza has become a death-goddess of the jungle. She has killed more enemy soldiers than anyone. Except for Farrar, of course, but that's why we used him as bait.

We used to think Barkah controlled all the Springers on Omeyocan. We were wrong. There are four main tribes that we know of. Barkah's tribe, the Malbinti, claims the areas around Uchmal. The Khochin are far to the south of our city. The Podakra are just a day's ride to the west. The largest tribe of all, the Galanak, fill the jungle to the northeast.

"Belligerents" is what we've come to call the Springers that attack us at every turn. We haven't taken any alive yet, but based on the clothing of those we killed in battle they have members from all four known tribes, *including* the Malbinti. Barkah doesn't know why some of his people joined them.

The Belligerents don't have uniforms, but they do have one unifying element. In addition to the jungle rags of blue, yellow and green, they all wear at least one bit of red.

Red—the same color as the robes Aramovsky wore, as the robes in the carvings on the Observatory.

In the past few months, the Belligerents have been burning our crops, attacking us when we go outside the walls. Whatever their reasons, the Belligerents are aggressive and trying to kill my people.

I can't allow that to continue.

"Get into position," I say to Maria. "We attack immediately."

Maria and Fenrir vanish into the jungle with barely a sound. How something that big can move so quietly, I have no idea.

"Finally," Bawden says. "Those bug-eyed bastards can't escape this time."

I give her a short glance. Bawden was close with J. York, a circle boy who was one of three people killed by Belligerents a few months ago. Bawden wants revenge. Too many of my people want revenge.

"Our allies are also *bug-eyed bastards,*" I say. "Do you forget that? Or do you want to cuss at the people who are fighting on our side?"

Bawden answers with only a belch, which makes Victor laugh.

I'll never understand circle-stars.

"Clear away the brush," I say. "We go now."

Victor and Bawden toss aside our cover of branches. My spear is held by a bracket mounted on the cockpit's rear wall. I yank the spear free, then raise it high and circle it in the air—the signal for my unit to move out. Branches rustle around us as two other spider crews clear them away and prepare to leave. A dozen young circle-stars silently rise up from hidden places in the underbrush. They wear black coveralls, like me, but are wrapped in vines, their faces and hair smeared with dark mud. They make ready to march, make ready to fight.

Including me, my unit has twenty-one humans: nine on spiderback, twelve on foot. Maria's squad—"D'souza's Demons"—has three snake-wolves and their riders, along with eighteen Springers on foot. Squad Two—called "the Creepers" and led by Lahfah, Barkah's mate—has the same numbers as D'souza's Demons. That means we'll attack with a combination of sixty-three troops, three spiders and six snake-wolves. We're slightly outnumbered, but technology is on our side. And in reserve, we have two hundred Springers led by Barkah himself. I almost feel sorry for the Belligerents we're about to attack.

Almost.

"Bawden, lead us out."

She does. Our spider rises up, the cockpit now four meters above the jungle floor. Mud drips down from the dented yellow shell and the black *05* painted on either side.

We march to battle.

PHOTO: © JOAN ALLEN

New York Times bestselling author SCOTT SIGLER is the author of sixteen novels, six novellas, and dozens of short stories. He is also the co-founder of Empty Set Entertainment, which publishes his YA Galactic Football League series. He lives in San Diego.

@scottsigler

scottsigler.com

Facebook.com/scottsigler